Praise for Ruth Ware's instant *New York Times* bestseller

THE DEATH OF MRS. WESTAWAY

Starred reviews from *Kirkus Reviews, Library Journal,* and *Booklist* * Named one of the best books of the year by *CrimeReads* and the New York Public Library * Included in summer reading lists by *USA Today, People,* the *New York Post, PopSugar, Good Housekeeping, AARP The Magazine, Bustle, CrimeReads, Harper's Bazaar,* Goodreads, BookBub, *Literary Hub, Insider,* Today.com, *DC Refined,* and *BuzzFeed* * Among "the ten best thrillers and mysteries of 2018" according to *The Washington Post* * One of *BuzzFeed*'s "20 Thrillers That Will Mess with Your Sleep Schedule"

"Fans of *The Woman in Cabin 10,* rejoice. Ruth Ware is bringing you another page-turning tale of suspense. . . . Thrilling and clever, *The Death of Mrs. Westaway* will be hard to put down."

—*PopSugar*

"A delightfully chilly mystery."

—*People*

"This British writer knows how to hook crime novel/psychological suspense fans."

—*USA Today*

"[A] captivating and eerie page-turner."

—*The Wall Street Journal*

"Ruth Ware returns with another chilling page-turner."

—*Us Weekly*

"A classic never goes out of style. Consider the confident simplicity of the dry martini, the Edison lightbulb, and Meghan Markle's wedding dress. Now, add to that list Ruth Ware's new novel, *The Death of Mrs. Westaway* . . . a perfectly executed suspense tale very much in the mode of Daphne du Maurier's *Rebecca*."

—*The Washington Post*

"Nobody writes psychological thrillers like Ruth Ware. Nobody. And her latest atmospheric novel, about a woman who is the accidental recipient of a mysterious letter offering her a large sum of money, is no exception. You'll thoroughly enjoy playing detective along the way."

—*HelloGiggles*

"Ware's fourth novel is her best yet, with steadily increasing tension, a complicated twisty mystery, and a sharp, sympathetic heroine who's up to the challenge of solving it . . . well-crafted, gothic-tinged suspense."

—*Library Journal* (starred review)

"Ware's novels continue to evoke comparison to Agatha Christie; they certainly have that classic flavor despite the contemporary settings. Expertly paced, expertly crafted."

—*Kirkus Reviews* (starred review)

"Ware, who, with a run of acclaimed thrillers, including *The Lying Game* (2017), has established herself as one of today's most popular suspense writers, twists the knife quite expertly here. . . . The labyrinth Ware has devised here is much more winding than expected, with reveals even on the final pages . . . a clever heroine and an atmospheric setting, accented by wisps of meaning that drift from the tarot cards."

—*Booklist* (starred review)

"Evocative prose, artfully shaded characters, and a creepy, claustrophobic atmosphere keep the pages of this explosive family drama turning."

—*Publishers Weekly*

"I've adored Ruth Ware's work for some time, ever since I picked up her first playful puzzler of a mystery, *In a Dark, Dark Wood*. She's been making her way through classic mystery settings, making each her own, and her new volume promises to continue the trend, in a tale of a con artist headed to a family funeral that promises to be the most entertaining fictional British burial since the film *Death at a Funeral* first graced our screens."

—*Literary Hub*

"The bestselling writer of psychological thrillers (*In a Dark, Dark Wood* and *The Woman in Cabin 10*) has a new winner . . . the situation grows increasingly complicated and creepy, Agatha Christie–style."

—*AARP The Magazine*

"Ruth Ware's master storytelling again sets readers on edge."

—RT Book Reviews

"If you've been pining away for a first-rate gothic murder mystery for the past forty-odd years since Agatha Christie's passing, hie yourself to your local (or online) book vendor for Ruth Ware's *The Death of Mrs. Westaway*. It has everything you're looking for. . . . Atmospheric and twisting in a very Christie-like manner (manor?), *The Death of Mrs. Westaway* is guaranteed to keep you flipping pages well past your bedtime."

—BookPage

"Ruth Ware continues to revitalize the traditional mystery for millennial audiences in *The Death of Mrs. Westaway*, for another mystery that functions both as tribute to the genre's tropes and a playful revisioning of the drawing-room mystery."

—CrimeReads

"Ruth Ware has written another gripping thriller. . . . Creepy and atmospheric, *The Death of Mrs. Westaway* will keep readers on the edge of their seats. Ware spins a convincing web of intrigue and tension."

—Shelf Awareness

"If you, like me, have a weakness for British haunted-house novels, this one, by the author of *The Woman in Cabin 10* and *The Lying Game*, might keep you flipping pages late on a summer's night."

—The Seattle Times

"Just as the cards disclose meanings deeper and more complicated than their superficial ones, the novel hints at haunting emotional truths under its playful tribute to traditional crime novels."

—The Columbus Dispatch

"[Ruth Ware's] newest novel, *The Death of Mrs. Westaway*, may be her best novel yet, and it's most definitely my favorite Ware novel thus far."

—The Nerd Daily

"With lots of clever twists and surprises, this creepy and entertaining thriller will keep you in suspense right up until the last few pages. If you're a fan of Ware's *The Woman in Cabin 10*, you'll also enjoy this chilling and gripping thriller."

—TripSavvy

"*The Death of Mrs. Westaway* is a tautly atmospheric novel that is perfect to curl up with on a stormy night. . . . There are a lot of psychological thrillers being published these days, but *The Death of Mrs. Westaway* is one of the best I've read this year."

—*All About Romance*

"Though set in the present day, the novel feels timeless—further cementing Ware's reputation as a skilled mystery author writing in a classic vein."

—Bookreporter.com

"Ruth Ware, with her modern melding of traditional mystery and domestic suspense, never fails to impress, and her latest, *The Death of Mrs. Westaway*, continues her winning streak in the mystery department."

—*CrimeReads*

"*The Death of Mrs. Westaway* by Ruth Ware is the standard by which other suspense novels must be judged, and frankly it's doubtful any forthcoming books can approach, much less exceed, that standard."

—*New York Journal of Books*

"This is the mystery I've been raving about to everyone, but particularly to fans of Daphne du Maurier's masterpiece, *Rebecca*. . . . A gloomy ancestral mansion, never-ending rainstorms, a maniacal killer, and plot twists aplenty grace this standout suspense novel."

—Maureen Corrigan, book critic, *Fresh Air*

"Ruth Ware is a magician. Her novels—suspenseful, sophisticated, relentlessly compelling—blow the dust off half a dozen crime genres, from Golden Age whodunits to psychological suspense. And *The Death of Mrs. Westaway*, her latest, is also her best: a dark and dramatic thriller, part murder mystery, part family drama, altogether riveting. More, please, and soon."

—A. J. Finn, #1 *New York Times* bestselling author of *The Woman in the Window*

The Death of Mrs. Westaway

RUTH WARE

SCOUT PRESS
New York London Toronto Sydney New Delhi

Scout Press
An Imprint of Simon & Schuster, Inc.
1230 Avenue of the Americas
New York, NY 10020

Originally published in Great Britain in 2018 by Vintage. Vintage is one of the Penguin Random House group companies.

First Scout Press trade paperback edition April 2019

SCOUT PRESS and colophon are registered trademarks of Simon & Schuster, Inc.

For information about special discounts for bulk purchases, please contact Simon & Schuster Special Sales at 1-866-506-1949 or business@simonandschuster.com.

The Simon & Schuster Speakers Bureau can bring authors to your live event. For more information or to book an event, contact the Simon & Schuster Speakers Bureau at 1-866-248-3049 or visit our website at www.simonspeakers.com.

Interior design by Jaime Putorti

Manufactured in China

10 9 8 7 6 5

The Library of Congress has cataloged the hardcover edition as follows:

Names: Ware, Ruth, author.
Title: The death of Mrs. Westaway / Ruth Ware.
Description: First Scout Press hardcover edition. | New York : Gallery/Scout Press, 2018.
Identifiers: LCCN 2018004355| ISBN 9781501156212 (hardcover) | ISBN 9781501156250 (softcover)
Subjects: LCSH: Inheritance and succession—Fiction. | BISAC: FICTION / Suspense. | FICTION / Thrillers. | GSAFD: Suspense fiction. | Mystery fiction.
Classification: LCC PR6123.A745 D43 2018 | DDC 823/.92—dc23
LC record available at https://lccn.loc.gov/2018004355

ISBN 978-1-5011-5621-2
ISBN 978-1-5011-5625-0 (pbk)
ISBN 978-1-5011-5622-9 (ebook)

For my mum. Always.

One for sorrow
Two for joy
Three for a girl
Four for a boy
Five for silver
Six for gold
Seven for a secret
Never to be told

29th November, 1994

The magpies are back. It's strange to think how much I used to hate them, when I first came to the house. I remember coming up the drive in the taxi from the station, seeing them lined up along the garden wall like that, preening their feathers.

Today there was one perched on the frost-rimed branch of yew right outside my window, and I remembered what my mother used to say when I was little and whispered "Hello, Mr. Magpie" under my breath, to turn away the bad luck.

I counted them as I dressed, shivering next to the window. One on the yew tree. A second on the weathervane of the folly. A third on the wall of the kitchen garden. Three for a girl.

It seemed like an omen, and for a moment I shivered. Wishing, wondering, waiting . . .

But no, there were more on the frozen lawn. Four, five . . . six . . . and one hopping across the flags of the terrace, pecking at the ice on the covers over the table and chairs.

Seven. Seven for a secret, never to be told. Well, the secret part may be right, but the rest is wide of the mark. I'll have to tell, soon enough. There'll be no choice.

I had almost finished dressing when there was a rustle in the leaves of the rhododendrons in the shrubbery. For a minute I could not see the cause, but then the branches parted, and a fox slunk quietly across the leaf-strewn lawn, its red-gold fur startlingly bright against the frost-muted winter colours.

At my parents' house they were quite common, but it's rare to see one in daylight around here, let alone one bold enough to cross the huge exposed stretch of lawns in front of the house. I've seen slaughtered rabbits, and split bags of rubbish left from their scavenging, but they are almost never this bold. This one must have been very brave, or very desperate, to stalk in full sight in front of the house. Looking more closely, I thought perhaps it was the latter, for he was young, and terribly thin.

At first the magpies didn't notice, but then the one on the terrace, more observant than the others, registered the shape of the predator easing its way towards them, and it flew up from the icy flags like a rocket, chak-chakking its alarm, the warning loud and clear in the morning quiet. The fox had no hope after that. The other birds took to the sky, one by one, until at last only one was left, sitting on the yew, safely out of the fox's reach, and like a stream of molten gold, it slunk back over the grass, low to the ground, leaving the solitary magpie on the branch, crowing out its triumph.

One. One for sorrow. But that's impossible. I will never feel sad again, in spite of everything, in spite of the storm that I know is coming. As I sit here in the drawing room, writing this, I can feel it—my secret—burning me up from the inside with a joy so fierce that I think it must sometimes be visible through my skin.

I'll change that rhyme. One for joy. One for love. One for the future.

CHAPTER 1

The girl leaned, rather than walked, into the wind, clutching the damp package of fish and chips grimly under one arm even as the gale plucked at the paper, trying to unravel the parcel and send the contents skittering away down the seafront for the seagulls to claim.

As she crossed the road her hand closed over the crumpled note in her pocket, and she glanced over her shoulder, checking the long dark stretch of pavement behind her for a shadowy figure, but there was no one there. No one she could see, anyway.

It was rare for the seafront to be completely deserted. The bars and clubs were open long into the night, spilling drunk locals and tourists onto the pebbled beach right through until dawn. But tonight, even the most hardened partygoers had decided against venturing out, and now, at 9:55 p.m. on a wet Tuesday, Hal had the promenade to herself, the flashing lights of the pier the only sign of life, apart from the gulls wheeling and crying over the dark restless waters of the channel.

Hal's short black hair blew in her eyes, her glasses were misted, and her lips were chapped with salt from the sea wind. But she hitched the parcel tighter under her arm and turned off the seafront into one of the narrow residential streets of tall white houses, where the wind dropped with a suddenness that made her stagger and almost trip. The rain didn't let up. In fact, away from the wind it seemed to drizzle more steadily, if anything, as she turned again into Marine View Villas.

The name was a lie. There were no villas, only a slightly shabby little row of terraced houses, their paint peeling from constant exposure to the salty air. And there was no view—not of the sea or anywhere else. Maybe there had been once, when the houses were built. But since then taller, grander buildings had gone up, closer to the sea, and any view the windows of Marine View Villas might once have had was reduced to brick walls and slate roofs, even from Hal's attic flat. Now the only benefit to living up three flights of narrow, rickety stairs was not having to listen to neighbors stomping about above your head.

Tonight, though, the neighbors seemed to be out—and had been for some time, judging by the way the door stuck on the clump of junk mail in the hall. Hal had to shove hard, until it gave and she stumbled into the chilly darkness, groping for the automatic timer switch that governed the lights. Nothing happened. Either a fuse had blown, or the bulb had burned out.

She scooped up the junk mail, doing her best in the dim light filtering in from the street to pick out the letters for the other tenants, and then began the climb up to her own attic flat.

There were no windows on the stairwell, and once she was past the first flight, it was almost pitch-black. But Hal knew the steps by heart, from the broken board on the landing to the loose piece of carpet that had come untacked on the last flight, and she plodded wearily upwards, thinking about supper and bed. She wasn't even sure if she was hungry anymore, but the fish and chips had cost £5.50, and judging by the number of bills she was carrying, that was £5.50 she couldn't afford to waste.

On the top landing she ducked her head to avoid the drip from the skylight, opened the door, and then at last, she was home.

The flat was small, just a bedroom opening off a kind of wide hallway that did duty as both kitchen and living room, and everything else. It was also shabby, with peeling paint and worn carpet, and wooden windows that groaned and rattled when the wind came off the sea. But it had been Hal's home for all of her twenty-one years, and no matter how cold and tired she was, her heart never failed to lift, just a little bit, when she walked through the door.

In the doorway, she paused to wipe the salt spray off her glasses, polishing them on the ragged knee of her jeans, before dropping the paper of fish and chips on the coffee table.

It was very cold, and she shivered as she knelt in front of the gas fire, clicking the knob until it flared, and the warmth began to come back into her raw red hands. Then she unrolled the damp, rain-spattered paper packet, inhaling as the sharp smell of salt and vinegar filled the little room.

Spearing a limp, warm chip with the wooden fork, she began to sort through the mail, sifting out takeout fliers for recycling and putting the bills into a pile. The chips were salty and sharp and the battered fish still hot, but Hal found a slightly sick feeling was growing in the pit of her stomach as the stack of bills grew higher. It wasn't so much the size of the pile but the number marked *FINAL DEMAND* that worried her, and she pushed the fish aside, feeling suddenly nauseated.

She *had* to pay the rent—that was nonnegotiable. And the electricity was high on the list too. Without a fridge or lights, the little flat was barely habitable. The gas . . . well it was November. Life without heating would be uncomfortable, but she'd survive.

But the one that really made her stomach turn over was different from the official bills. It was a cheap envelope, obviously hand-delivered, and all it said on the front, in ballpoint letters, was "Harriet Westerway, top flat."

There was no sender's address, but Hal didn't need one. She had a horrible feeling that she knew who it was from.

Hal swallowed a chip that seemed to be stuck in her throat, and she pushed the envelope to the bottom of the pile of bills, giving way to the overwhelming impulse to bury her head in the sand. She wished passionately that she could hand the whole problem over to someone older and wiser and stronger to deal with.

But there was no one. Not anymore. And besides, there was a tough, stubborn core of courage in Hal. Small, skinny, pale, and young she might be—but she was not the child people routinely assumed. She had not been that child for more than three years.

It was that core that made her pick the envelope back up and, biting her lip, tear through the flap.

Inside there was just one sheet of paper, with only a couple of sentences typed on it.

Sorry to have missed you. We would like to discuss you're financal situation. We will call again.

Hal's stomach flipped and she felt in her pocket for the piece of paper that had turned up at her work this afternoon. They were identical, save for the crumples and a splash of tea that she had spilled over the first one when she opened it.

The message on them was not news to Hal. She had been ignoring calls and texts to that effect for months.

It was the message *behind* the notes that made her hands shake as she placed them carefully on the coffee table, side by side.

Hal was used to reading between the lines, deciphering the importance of what people *didn't* say, as much as what they did. It was her job, in a way. But the unspoken words here required no decoding at all.

They said, *We know where you work.*

We know where you live.

And we will come back.

• • •

THE REST OF THE MAIL was just junk and Hal dumped it into the recycling before sitting wearily on the sofa. For a moment she let her head rest in her hands—trying not to think about her precarious bank balance, hearing her mother's voice in her ear as if she were standing behind her, lecturing her about her A-level revision. *Hal, I know you're stressed, but you've got to eat something! You're too skinny!*

I know, she answered, inside her head. It was always that way when she was worried or anxious—her appetite was the first thing to go. But she couldn't afford to get ill. If she couldn't work, she wouldn't get paid. And more to the point, she could not afford to waste a meal, even one that was damp around the edges, and getting cold.

Ignoring the ache in her throat, she forced herself to pick up another chip. But it was only halfway to her mouth when something in the recycling bin caught her eye. Something that should not have been there. A letter in a stiff white envelope, addressed by hand, and stuffed into the bin along with the takeout menus.

Hal put the chip in her mouth, licked the salt off her fingers, and then leaned across to the bin to pick it out of the mess of old papers and soup tins.

Miss Harriet Westaway, it said. *Flat 3c, Marine View Villas, Brighton.* The address was only slightly stained with the grease from Hal's fingers and the mess from the bin.

She must have shoved it in there by mistake with the empty envelopes. Well, at least this one couldn't be a bill. It looked more like a wedding invitation—though that seemed unlikely. Hal couldn't think of anyone who would be getting married.

She shoved her thumb in the gap at the side of the envelope and ripped it open.

The piece of paper she pulled out wasn't an invitation. It was a letter, written on heavy, expensive paper, with the name of a solicitor's firm at the top. For a minute Hal's stomach seemed to fall away, as a landscape of terrifying possibilities opened up before her. Was someone suing her for something she'd said in a reading? Or—oh

God—the tenancy on the flat. Mr. Khan, the landlord, was in his seventies and had sold all of the other flats in the house, one by one. He had held on to Hal's mainly out of pity for her and affection for her mother, she was fairly sure, but that stay of execution could not last forever. One day he would need the money for a care home, or his diabetes would get the better of him and his children would have to sell. It didn't matter that the walls were peeling with damp, and the electrics shorted if you ran a hair dryer at the same time as the toaster. It was home—the only home she'd ever known. And if he kicked her out, the chances of finding another place at this rate were not just slim, they were nil.

Or was it . . . but no. There was no way *he* would have gone to a solicitor.

Her fingers were trembling as she unfolded the page, but when her eyes flicked to the contact details beneath the signature, she realized, with a surge of relief, that it wasn't a Brighton firm. The address was in Penzance, in Cornwall.

Nothing to do with the flat—thank God. And vanishingly unlikely to be a disgruntled client, so far from home. In fact, she didn't know anyone in Penzance at all.

Swallowing another chip, she spread the letter out on the coffee table, pushed her glasses up her nose, and began to read.

Dear Miss Westaway,

I am writing at the instruction of my client, your grandmother, Hester Mary Westaway of Trepassen House, St Piran.

Mrs Westaway passed away on 22nd November, at her home. I appreciate that this news may well come as a shock to you; please accept my sincere condolences on your loss.

As Mrs Westaway's solicitor and executor, it is my duty to contact beneficiaries under her will. Because of the substantial size of the estate, probate will need to be applied for and the estate assessed for inheritance tax liabilities, and the process of disbursement cannot begin until this has taken place. However if, in the meantime, you could provide me with copies of two documents confirming your identity and address (a list of acceptable forms of ID is attached), that will enable me to begin the necessary paperwork.

In accordance with the wishes of your late grandmother, I am also instructed to inform beneficiaries of the details of her funeral. This is being held at 4 p.m. on 1st December at St Piran's Church, St Piran. As local accommodation is very limited, family members are invited to stay at Trepassen House, where a wake will also be held.

Please write to your late grandmother's housekeeper Mrs Ada Warren if you would like to avail yourself of the offer of accommodation, and she will ensure a room is opened up for you.

Please accept once again my condolences, and the assurance of my very best attentions in this matter.

Yours truly,
Robert Treswick
Treswick, Nantes and Dean
Penzance

A chip fell from Hal's fingers onto her lap, but she did not stir. She only sat, reading and rereading the short letter, and then turning to the accepted-forms-of-identification document, as if that would elucidate matters.

Substantial estate . . . beneficiaries of the will . . . Hal's stomach rumbled, and she picked up the chip and ate it almost absently, trying to make sense of the words in front of her.

Because it *didn't* make sense. Not one bit. Hal's grandparents had been dead for more than twenty years.

CHAPTER 2

Hal wasn't sure how long she sat there, puzzling over the letter, her eyes flicking between the folded white sheet and the search page of her phone. But when she looked up, the clock on the microwave said five to midnight, and she stretched, realizing with a pang of anxiety that the gas fire had been burning the whole time. She stood and turned it off, listening to the cooling click of the elements, mentally adding on another fifty pence to the gas bill already lying there, and as she did, her gaze fell on the photograph on the mantelpiece.

It had been there almost as long as Hal could remember—ten years at least—but now she picked it up, looking at it afresh. It showed a girl, maybe nine or ten years of age, and a woman, standing on Brighton beach. They were laughing, with their eyes screwed up against a gusting wind that blew their long dark hair into identical comic upsweeps. The woman had her arm around the girl, and there was a look of such freedom, such trust between them that Hal felt her heart clench with a pain that she had almost grown used to over the last three years, but which never seemed to fade.

The girl was Hal—and yet she wasn't. She wasn't the girl who stood in front of the fire now, her hair cropped short as a boy's, her ears pierced, the tattoos on her back just peeping out from the neck of her threadbare T-shirt.

The girl in the photograph had no need to mark her skin with remembrances because everything she wanted to remember was right beside her. She didn't dress in black, because she had nothing to mourn. She didn't keep her head down and her collar up when she walked home, because she had nothing to hide from. She was warm, and well-fed, and most of all she was loved.

The fish and chips had grown cold, and Hal bundled them up in the paper and pushed them into the bin in the corner of the room. Her mouth was dry with salt, and her throat ached with grief, and the thought of a hot mug of tea before bed was suddenly comforting. She would make the tea, and fill a hot-water bottle with the rest of the kettle, something to take the chill off the sheets, help her to sleep.

As the kettle began to hum, Hal rummaged in the cupboard above it for the box of tea bags. But almost as if it were what she had really been looking for, her hand found something else. Not the lightweight cardboard box, but a glass bottle, half-full. She didn't need to get it out to know what it was, but she took it down anyway, weighing it in her hand, feeling the liquid slosh greasily inside. Vodka.

She only rarely drank these days—she didn't really like the person she became with a glass in her hand—but then her eye caught on the two notes lying across the coffee table, and with a quick movement she twisted off the cap and poured a generous measure into the cup she had been intending for the tea.

The kettle bubbled as she lifted the cup to her lips, smelling the acrid, slightly petrolly smell, watching the meniscus tremble in the dim light coming in from the streetlamp. For a moment the imagined taste was sharp in her mouth—the fiery burn, followed by that little addictive buzz. But then something inside her stomach seemed to turn, and she poured it down the sink, swilled out the cup, and made the tea instead.

As she carried it through to the bedroom, she realized with a kind of weariness that she had forgotten the hot-water bottle. But it didn't matter. She was too tired to care, and the tea was hot and good. Hal curled up in bed, fully clothed, sipping the tea and staring at the bright screen of her phone.

On the screen was Google images, and it showed a hand-tinted postcard, from perhaps 1930, featuring a country house. It had a long frontage of cream-colored stone with Georgian-style windows, covered in ivy. Chimneys poked up from a slate-tiled roof, a dozen or more, all in different styles. To the rear was more of the house, which seemed to be redbrick and built in a different style. A lawn spread out in front of the building, falling away, and a scrawled inscription across the picture read, *We had a very good tea at Trepassen House before driving on to Penzance.*

That was Trepassen House. *That* was Trepassen House. Not a modest little bungalow, or a Victorian terrace with a pretentious name. But a bona fide country seat.

A share, however small, of a place like that could do more than pay off her bills. It could give her back the security she had lost when her mother died. Even a few hundred pounds would give her more breathing room than she could remember for months.

The clock at the top of the screen showed half past midnight, and Hal knew she should sleep, but she did not close down her phone.

Instead she sat there in bed, with the steam from the tea misting her glasses, searching, scrolling, and feeling a strange mix of emotions spreading through her, warming her more than the tea.

Excitement? Yes.

Trepidation too, a good deal of it.

But most of all something she hadn't dared to feel in many years. Hope.

CHAPTER 3

Hal woke late the next morning. The sun was already up, slanting through the bedroom curtains, and she lay still, feeling the mingled excitement and dread in the pit of her stomach, and trying to remember the source.

Recollection came like a twin punch to the gut.

The dread was the pile of bills on the coffee table—and, worse than bills, those two typed notes, hand-delivered. . . .

But the excitement . . .

She had spent all last night trying to talk herself out of it. Just because it was where Hester Westaway had lived, there was no guarantee that she had actually owned that huge rambling place on the postcard. People just didn't have houses that size these days. The fact that she'd died there didn't mean she owned it. In all likelihood, it was a retirement home now.

But the housekeeper, whispered a voice in the back of her head. *And that line about opening up a room for you. They wouldn't say that about a retirement home, would they?*

"It doesn't matter," Hal said aloud, startling herself with the sound of her own voice in the silent flat.

She stood, smoothing down her rumpled clothes, and picked up her glasses. Settling them on her nose, she gave herself a stern look in the mirror.

It didn't matter whether Hester Westaway owned a room, or a wing, or a cottage in the grounds, or the whole damn place. There had clearly been some sort of mistake. She was not Hal's grandmother. The money belonged to someone else, and that was all there was to it.

Tomorrow she would write back and tell Mr. Treswick that.

But today . . . Hal looked at her watch, and shook her head. Today she had barely time for a shower. It was 11:20 and she was very nearly late for work.

SHE WAS IN THE SHOWER, the hot water drumming on her skull, driving out all other thoughts, when the voice whispered again, beneath the roar of the water.

But what if it's true? They wrote to you, didn't they? They have your name and address.

It wasn't true, though, that was the long and the short of it. Hal's only grandparents had died years ago, long before she was born. And her grandmother hadn't been called Hester, she had been called . . . Marion?

Maybe Marion was a middle name. People do that, right? They use one name for everyday, and have a different one on their papers. What if—

Shut up, Hal said inwardly. Just shut up. You know it's not true. You're persuading yourself because you want it to be true.

Still, the voice niggled away in the back of her head, and at last, more in an effort to convince herself than anything else, Hal turned off the shower, wrapped a towel around her shoulders, and made her way back into the bedroom. Beneath the bed was a heavy wooden box, and she dragged it out, wincing at the screech of castors on the wooden floor, and hoping that the downstairs neighbors weren't treating themselves to a lie-in.

Inside was a rat's nest of important papers—insurance documents, the rental contract on the flat, bills, her passport. . . . Hal sifted through the layers, feeling like an archaeologist of her own history. Past the insurance schedule, past the bill for the time a pipe had burst in the attic, and then down to a stratum that was nothing but pain—her mother's death certificate, the copy of her will, the police report, her faded driver's license, never used again. Beneath them all was a veil, folded into a neat square—fine black gauze, edged with droplets of jet.

There was a lump in Hal's throat as she put it aside, hurrying past the bitter memories to the older stuff underneath—papers her mother had chosen to keep, more neatly filed than Hal's haphazard shoving. There was an envelope with her own exam certificates, a program for a school play she had been in, a photograph of herself looking sheepish with a long-gone boyfriend.

And then at last a plastic folder marked *Important—birth certs* in her mother's neat hand, and inside, two red-and-cream certificates, handwritten, and topped with the extravagantly ornate crown emblem. *Certified copy of an entry,* read the top of the page. First Hal's: *Harriet Margarida Westaway, born 15th May 1995. Mother: Margarida Westaway, occupation: student.*

The space for "father" was left blank, a line drawn firmly through the box, as though to stop anyone from adding their own theories.

And then, beneath it, another certificate, older and more creased—*Margarida Westaway*. Her mother. Hal's eyes skipped to the "parents" column—*Father: William Howard Rainer Westaway, occupation: accountant* and beneath that *Mother: Marion Elizabeth Westaway, maiden name: Brown.* No occupation was given for her grandmother.

Well, that was that then.

She didn't realize how much she had been hoping against hope until the sense of deflation set in, tentative thoughts of debt repayment and security collapsing like a pricked balloon.

Substantial estate . . . whispered the voice in her ear, seductively. *Beneficiaries of the will . . . family members . . .*

There's always your father, whispered the voice again, as she dressed. *You have another grandmother, you know.* Hal shook her head bitterly at that. If your subconscious could betray you, Hal's just had.

For years she had fantasized about her father, spinning increasingly elaborate tales to the girls at school to cover her own ignorance and her anger at her mother for telling her so little. He was a pilot who had gone down in a crash in the sea. He was an undercover policeman who had been forced to return to his real life by his superiors. He was a celebrity, whose name couldn't be revealed, or they would be hounded by the tabloids, and her father's life would be ruined.

At last, when the rumors had reached the ears of the teachers, someone had had a quiet word and Hal's mother had taken her aside and gently told her the truth.

Hal's father had been a one-night stand—a student her mother had met in a nightclub in Brighton and had slept with for the first and last time on the night they met. He had a Spanish accent, and that was all Hal's mother knew.

"You didn't even find out his *name*?" Hal had asked incredulously, and her mother had bitten her lip and shaken her head. Her cheeks were scarlet, and she looked more uncomfortable than Hal could ever remember.

She was very sorry, she said. She hadn't wanted Hal to find out this way, but Hal *had* to stop spinning these . . . Her mother had stopped there, too kind to say the word she had been thinking; but even at seven, Hal was good at reading people, and perceptive enough to understand what it was her mother hadn't said.

These lies.

The truth was, her father was no one special. Who he was, where he lived now, she had no idea, and would probably never know. He had likely gone back to Spain or Mexico or wherever he had come from in the first place. But one thing she did know for sure—he was most certainly not a Westaway.

Wherever the mistake had come from, it wasn't there. But a mistake it was. Somewhere, wires had been crossed. Maybe there was some other Harriet Westaway in another city, rightfully entitled to this money. Or maybe it was like one of those heir-hunter programs, where someone had died without legitimate heirs, and the money would go to waste if the executors didn't track down some relative, however distant, to scoop the pot.

Whatever the truth was, the money wasn't hers, and she couldn't claim it. And the voice inside her head had no answer to that.

Hurrying now, Hal shoved the papers back underneath the bed and dressed. Her hairbrush seemed to have gone missing, but she combed her hair as well as she could with her fingers, and checked herself in the mirror by the front door. Her face looked even paler and more pinched than usual, the forlorn wet spikes of black hair making her look like an extra from *Oliver Twist*. Makeup would have helped, but it wasn't really Hal's style.

But as she pulled on her coat, still damp from the night before, the voice piped up with one last remark. *You could claim this money, you know. Not many people could, but if anyone can pull this off, it's you.*

Shut up, Hal said inwardly, gritting her teeth. Shut. Up.

But she didn't say it because she didn't believe it.

She said it because it was true.

1st December, 1994

Today is the first day of Advent and the air should have been full of new beginnings and the countdown to a momentous event, but instead I woke up heavy with a kind of nameless dread.

I have not read the cards for over a week. I haven't felt the need, but today, as I sat at the desk at the window, the eiderdown around my shoulders, I felt my fingers itch, and I thought that perhaps it would comfort me to shuffle them. But it was only when I had spent some time sorting and shuffling and dealing different spreads, none feeling right, that I realised what I needed to do.

There were no candles in my room, so I took one from the big brass candlesticks on the mantelpiece in the dining room, and a box of matches from the fireplace. I slipped the matches into my pocket, but the candle was too long to fit, so I slid it inside the sleeve of my cardigan in case someone met me on the stairs, and asked what I was doing.

Up in my room I set everything out on the table—cards, candle, matches, and an empty teacup. I melted the candle a little at the wrong end and stuck it into the cup to make a firm base, and then I lit it, and I passed the tarot cards through the flame three times.

When I had finished, I blew out the flame and then simply sat, looking out of the window at the snowy lawn, weighing the cards in my hand. They felt . . . different. Lighter. As if all the doubts and bad feelings had burned away. And I knew what to do.

Spreading the major arcana facedown on the desk, I picked three cards and then placed them in front of me in a spread. Past. Present.

Future. The questions crowded in my mind, but I tried to clear my head—to focus on just one thing, not a question, but the answer unfurling inside my body.

Then I turned the cards.

The first card, the one that represented the past, was the Lovers upright—which made me smile. It's often a mistake in tarot to take the most obvious reading of a card, but somehow here it felt right. In my deck, the card shows a naked man and woman entwined, surrounded by flowers, his hand on her breast, and a glowing light from above bathing them both. It's a card I love—both to look at, and to draw—but the words that come with it aren't always positive: lust, temptation, vulnerability. Here, though, cleansed by fire, I saw only the simplest meaning—a man and a woman in love.

The next card I turned over was the Fool—but upside down. It was not what I was expecting. New beginnings, new life, change—all that, yes. But reversed? Naïveté. Folly. Lack of forethought. I felt the smile fade on my lips and I pushed the card away, and hurried on to the third and most important—the future.

It was another card reversed, and I felt my stomach drop away a little, for the first time almost wishing that I had not begun this reading, or at least not done it now, today. I know my deck too well to need to turn the picture upright, but even so I studied it with fresh eyes, seeing the picture as if anew, from upside down. Justice. The woman on her throne was grave-faced, as if conscious of her responsibilities, and the impossibility of finding truth in a world like ours. In her left hand she held the scales, and in the other a sword, ready to mete out punishment or mercy.

I spent a long time looking at the woman on her throne, trying to understand what she was telling me, and still, as I'm writing this, I don't know. I hoped that writing in my diary would clarify what the cards were trying to say, but instead all I feel is confusion. Dishonesty? Can that really be true? Or am I reading it wrong? As I sit here I am sifting back through all the other, deeper, subtler meanings, the willingness to be deceived, the traps of black-and-white thinking, the mistaken assumptions—and none of them reassure.

I have been thinking all day about that last card—about the future. And still I do not understand. I wish there were someone I could talk to, discuss it with. But I already know what Maud thinks of tarot. "Load of wafty BS," was what she said when I offered to do her reading. And when she succumbed, finally, it was with a snort and a cynical look. I could see her thoughts running across her face as I turned over the cards she had chosen and asked her what question she was seeking answers to.

"If you're so bloody psychic, shouldn't you be telling me?" she said, flicking the card with her fingertip, and I shook my head, trying to hide my annoyance, and told her that tarot isn't a party trick, the kind of mentalism that cheap magicians practise on Saturday night TV—telling people their middle names or the inscription on their pocket watch. It's something bigger, deeper, more real than that.

I cleansed the deck after that reading, upset not just because she touched the cards, but because she touched them with contempt in her soul. But now, thinking back to that day, I realise something. When Maud turned over the future card, I told her something else, something that I should have reminded myself today, and something that gives me comfort. And it's this: the cards do not predict the future. All they can do is show us how a given situation may turn out, based on the energies we bring to the reading. Another day, another mood, a different set of energies, and the same question could have a completely different answer.

We have free will. The answer the cards give can turn us in our path. All I have to do is understand what they are saying.

CHAPTER 4

It was almost midday as Hal hurried along the seafront, clutching her jacket against the biting wind. It cut like a knife, chapping at her face and fingers and nipping at the skin of her knees, where her jeans had ripped through.

As she pressed the button for the pedestrian crossing she felt that flutter again, in the pit of her stomach. Excitement. Trepidation. Hope. . . .

No. Not hope. There was no point in hoping. The papers in her mother's box had put an end to that. There was no way this could possibly be true. For her to claim that money would be . . . well, there was no point in trying to evade the reality of what she was considering. It would be fraud. Plain and simple. A criminal offense.

If anyone can pull this off, it's you.

The thought flitted treacherously through the back of her mind as she crossed to the opposite pavement, and she shook her head, trying to ignore it. But it was hard. Because if anyone had the skills to turn up at a strange house and claim a woman she'd never met as her grandmother, it was Hal.

Hal was a cold reader, one of the best. From her little booth on Brighton's West Pier, she told fortunes, read tarot cards, and made psychic predictions. It was the tarot she was best at, though, and people came from as far away as Hastings and London to get her readings, many of them coming back again and again—returning home to tell their friends about the secrets Hal had divined, the unknowable facts she had produced, the predictions she had made.

She tried not to think of them as fools—but they were. Not the tourists so much, the hen parties who came in for a giggle and just wanted to ask questions about the size of the groom's dick, and the prospects of him coming up to scratch for the wedding night. They shrieked and oohed when Hal trotted out her well-worn phrases—the Fool for a new beginning, the Empress for femininity and fertility, the Devil for sexuality, the Lovers for passion and commitment. Occasionally she palmed the cards she needed for a satisfying message, pushing them forwards to the querent to avoid an off-putting spread, full of minor cards, or trumps like Death or the Hierophant. But at the end of the day, it didn't really matter what they turned up—Hal made the images fit with what the women wanted to hear, with just enough of a frown and a shake of her head to make them gasp impressively, and a reassuring pat to the hen's hand when she reached her final conclusion (always that there would be love and happiness, though tough times might come—even with the most unpromising match).

Those, Hal didn't mind fooling. It was the others. The regulars. The ones who believed, who scratched together fifteen, twenty pounds, and came again and again, wanting answers that Hal could not give, not because she could not see what they wanted—but because she couldn't find it in herself to lie to them.

They were the easiest of all. The ones who made appointments—giving a real name and phone number, so that she could google and Facebook them. Even the customers who walked in off the street gave so much away—Hal could guess their age, their status; she noticed the smart but worn shoes that showed a downward change in fortune, or the recently bought designer handbag that indicated the reverse. In the dim light of her booth, she could still see the white line of a recently removed wedding ring, or the shaky hands of someone missing their morning drink.

Sometimes Hal didn't even know *how* she knew until after—and then it was almost as if the cards really were speaking to her.

"I see you've had a disappointment," she would say. "Was there . . . a child involved?" and the woman's eyes would well, and she would nod, and before she could stop herself a story would spill out, of miscarriage, stillbirth, infertility. And only afterwards Hal would think, *How did I know that?* And then she would remember the way the woman had looked out of the window of the waiting room as Hal came to find her, at the woman walking with a baby in a sling and a toddler with candy floss stains around her mouth, and the stricken look on her client's face, and Hal would realize.

Then she felt bad, and sometimes she would even give back the money, telling the customer that the cards had told her it would be unlucky to take payment, even though that only seemed to increase their fervor and make them more certain to return, banknotes in hand.

Mostly, though, Hal liked her job. She liked the raucous, drunken hen parties. She even liked the stags who came in bellowing and skeptical and full of suggestive cracks about feeling their crystal balls. And she felt that in some small way she helped some of her more vulnerable clients—she wasn't base enough to tell them only what they wanted to hear, she told them what they needed to know as well. That truth wasn't found at the bottom of a bottle. That drugs weren't the answer. That it was okay to leave the man who was responsible for the bruises that peeped from behind the neckline of that blouse.

She was cheaper than a therapist, and more ethical than many of the psychics who posted cards through people's doors, claiming to heal incurable disease with crystals, or offering contact with dead lovers and children—for a price, of course. . . .

Hal never made those promises. She shook her head when the clients asked her if she could contact David or Fabien or baby Cora. She was not in the business of séances, profiting off grief that was all too nakedly visible.

"The cards don't predict the future," she said again and again, insuring herself against the inevitability of things turning out differently, but also telling them what they needed to know—that there were no firm answers. "All they show is how things *could* come out, based on the energies you brought with you to the reading today. They're a guide for you to shape your actions, not a prison cell."

The truth was, however much she tried to tell them otherwise, people liked tarot because it gave them an illusion of control, of forces guiding their lives, a buffer against the senseless randomness of fate. But they liked Hal because she was good at what she did. She was good at weaving a story out of the images the clients turned up in front of her, good at listening to their pain and their questions and their hopes; and, most of all, she was good at *reading* others.

She had always been shy, tongue-tied in front of strangers, a fish out of water at her raucous secondary school; but what she hadn't realized was that during all those years spent coolly standing back and watching others, she had been honing her detachment and learning the skills that would someday become her trade. She had been watching the versions people gave of themselves, the tells that showed when they were nervous or hopeful or trying to evade the truth. She had discovered that the most important truths often lay in what people *didn't* say, and learned to read the secrets that they hid in plain sight, in their faces, and in their clothes, and in the expressions that flitted across their faces when they thought no one was watching.

Unlike most of her clients, Hal did not believe the cards in her pocket held any mystical power, beyond her own ability to reveal what people had not admitted even to themselves.

But now, as she hurried past the Palace Pier, the smell of fish and chips carried on the sea wind making her empty stomach rumble, Hal found herself wondering. If she believed . . . *if* she believed . . . what would the cards say about Trepassen House . . . about the woman who was not her grandmother . . . about the choice that lay ahead of her? She had no idea.

CHAPTER 5

"Morning, treacle!"

"Morning, Reg," Hal said. She pushed a fifty-pence piece across the counter of Reg's booth. "Cup of tea, please."

"I should say. It's cold enough for brass monkeys today, ain't it? Right. Let's see. Cuppa Rosie . . ." he muttered to himself as he dropped a tea bag into a cracked white mug. "Cup . . . of . . . Rosie for my favorite twist."

Twist and twirl. Girl.

Reg was not from Brighton, but London, and he sprinkled his conversation with a liberal amount of Cockney rhyming slang in a way that Hal was never quite sure was genuine. Reg definitely qualified as Cockney—at least, he did on his own account, having been born within the sound of Bow Bells and grown up running the streets of the East End. But there was something a touch pantomime about his persona, and Hal suspected that it was all part of the patter that the tourists liked. Diamond Cockney geezer, with his treacle tarts and cups of Rosie Lee.

Now he was looking at the hot water urn and frowning.

"Bloody urn's playing up again. I think the connection's loose. You got ten minutes, Hal?"

"Not really. . . ." Hal looked at her watch. "I was supposed to be opening up at twelve."

"Ah, don't you worry about that. There's no one down your side, I'd-a seen them go past. And Chalky's not here yet, so you won't have no bother with him. Come inside and have a sit-down."

He opened the booth door and beckoned Hal in. Hal wavered, and then stepped over the threshold.

Chalky was Mr. White, the pier manager. Hal was self-employed and to some extent set her hours, but Mr. White liked the booths to be open in good time of a morning. Nothing more depressing, he always said, than a shuttered-up pier. The West Pier already had to work harder than its twin sister, the Palace, to lure the punters down the prom, and when takings dropped, as they always did in the winter months, Mr. White was prone to start reassessing the leases of the underperforming booths. If there was one thing Hal could not afford at the moment, it was to lose her booth.

Inside Reg's kiosk it was warm, and smelled strongly of bacon from the grill at the back. Reg's stock-in-trade was bacon sandwiches and cups of tea in the winter months, and Mr. Whippy ice cream and cans of Coke in the summer.

"Won't be a minute," Reg said. "How are you anyway, my dear old mucker?"

"I'm all right," Hal said, though it was not really the truth. Those two typewritten sheets of paper on the coffee table at home were giving her a sick feeling in the pit of her stomach, and she was half afraid of finding another envelope when she opened up the booth this morning. If only. If *only* Mr. Treswick's letter had been really meant for her.

The urn was up to temperature now, and she watched Reg as he expertly manipulated the spigot and mug with one hand, while flipping the bacon with the other. Somehow talking to the back of his head felt easier than addressing his face. She did not have to see the concern in his eyes.

"Actually . . ." she said, and then swallowed, and forced herself on. But the words, when they came, were not the ones she had been intending to say. "Actually, I might be better than all right. I got a letter last night, telling me I might be heir to a secret fortune."

"You what?" Reg turned, mug in his hand, open astonishment in his face. "What did you say?"

"I got a letter last night. From a solicitor. Saying I might be due a substantial bequest."

"You winding me up?" Reg said, his eyebrows almost up to his nonexistent hairline. Hal shook her head, and seeing that she was serious, Reg echoed her shake of the head, and handed the tea across.

"You be careful, love. There's a lot of these scammers about. My trouble got one the other day, telling her she won the Venezuelan lottery or some nonsense. Don't you be handing over no money. Not that I need to tell you that." He gave her a wink. "No flies on you."

"I don't think it's a scam," Hal said honestly. "More like a mistake, if anything. I think they might have got me mixed up with someone else."

"You think it's one of these heir-hunter things, where someone's died and they're trying to track down the long-lost rellies?" He was frowning again, but it was not with worry now, more as if considering a conundrum.

"Maybe," Hal said. She gave a shrug and sipped cautiously at the scalding tea. It was hot and bitter, but good. The cold, clammy thought of the notes on the coffee table was starting to recede, and she felt a flicker of some old memory stir inside her—the sensation of what it had been like to wake in the morning and not worry about every bill, not think about where the next rent payment would come from, not worry about the knock on the door. God, what she wouldn't give to get that security back again. . . .

She felt something harden inside her—a kind of steely resolve.

"Well," Reg said at last, "if anyone deserves a break, it's you, my darlin'. You take any money they offer you and run, that's my advice. Take the money and run."

CHAPTER 6

"Good-bye," Hal said, as the three tipsy girls rolled out the door, shrieking and laughing down the pier towards the bars and clubs. "May fortune favor you," she added, as she always did, but they were already gone out of earshot. Glancing at her watch, she realized it was 9 p.m., and the pier would be closing soon.

She was tired—exhausted, in fact—and earlier that evening, as the time stretched on, and the pier had stayed empty of visitors, she had thought about giving up, switching the sign off, and going home, but she was glad she had stayed. After almost no clients all day, there had been a mini-rush at seven o'clock—two coworkers came in to ask what they should do about a bullying boss, and then the three drunk girls looking for a laugh around eight. She hadn't made a lot, but with luck she would cover the rent on the kiosk this week, which was more than she could guarantee in the off season.

With a sigh, she turned off the small space heater at her feet and stood, ready to switch off the little illuminated sign outside her kiosk.

MADAME MARGARIDA it read in flowing, ornate letters, and though the description didn't really suit Hal, conjuring as it did some kind of Gypsy Rose Lee figure, she had not had the heart to change it.

SPECIALIST IN TAROT, PSYCHIC READINGS, AND PALMISTRY said the smaller letters below, although in truth Hal didn't really enjoy reading palms. Perhaps it was the physical contact, the warm dampness of the sweaty palm in hers. Or perhaps it was the lack of props—because in spite of her skepticism, she loved the tarot cards as physical objects, the finely drawn images, their soft fragility.

Now, though, as she flicked the switch in her booth and the light clicked off outside, there was a rap at the glass. Her stomach flipped, and for a moment she froze, even her breathing stilled.

"I've been waiting," said a hectoring female voice. "Don't you want customers?"

Hal sighed, feeling her tension drain away, and she opened the door.

"I'm sorry." She used the calm, professional voice that somehow became part of her persona the moment she picked up the cards. It was halfway between serene and serious, and a tone deeper than her own, though it was harder to conjure than usual, with her heart still thumping with the aftermath of the sudden rush of fear. "You should have knocked earlier."

"If you was a real psychic, you would've known," said the woman with a sour triumph, and Hal suppressed another sigh. She was going to be one of those.

It always baffled Hal why skeptics were so drawn to her booth. It wasn't like she was forcing anyone to come. She wasn't making any claims for her services—she didn't pretend to cure anything, or advise dangerous courses of action—she didn't even say that her readings were anything other than a bit of fun. Weren't there better people to debunk? And yet they came, and folded their arms and pursed their lips, and refused to be led, and looked grimly delighted at every failure, even while they wanted, desperately, to believe.

But she couldn't afford to turn a customer away.

"Please come in and sit down, it's a cold night," Hal said. The woman drew up a chair, but didn't speak. She only sat, her herringbone coat drawn firmly around herself, chapped lips clamped together, eyes narrowed.

Hal settled herself at the table, drew the box of tarot cards towards her, and began to run through the practiced introduction she always used when new clients walked in off the street: a few generalized guesses designed to impress the listener with her insight, a sprinkling of braggadocio, all mixed in with a potted history of tarot, aimed at people who knew little about it and needed a context to understand what she was about to do.

She had only run through a few of the phrases when the woman interrupted.

"You don't look like much of a psychic."

She looked Hal up and down, taking in the frayed jeans, the thick-gauge earring, shaped like a thorn, through her right ear, the tattoos peeping out from beneath her T-shirt.

"I thought you'd have a costume, and a veil with dangly bits. Like a proper one. *Madame Margarida* it says on the sign—you don't look like much of a madame. More like a twelve-year-old boy."

Hal only smiled and shook her head, but the words had broken her rhythm, and as she resumed her little speech she found herself thinking of the veil at home in the drawer under the bed, the fine black gauze with the jet drops sewn around the edge. She stumbled over the well-worn phrases and was glad when at last she reached the end of the spiel.

She added, as she always did, "Please, tell me what brings you to consult the cards today."

"Shouldn't you know that?" the woman snapped.

"I sense many questions in you," Hal said, trying not to sound impatient. "But time is short."

And I want to go home, she thought, but did not say. There was a silence. The wind howled through the struts of the pier, and in the distance Hal could hear the crash of the breakers.

"I got a choice," the woman said eventually, her voice grudging, as if the words were wrung out of her. She shifted in her seat, making the candle flame gutter.

"Yes," Hal said carefully, not quite a question. "I sense that you have two roads ahead of you, but they twist and turn, and you can't see far. You want to know which you should take."

In other words, a choice. It was pretty pitiful stuff, as well it might be, given how little she had to work with, but the woman gave a grudging nod.

"I will shuffle the cards," Hal said. She opened the lacquered box where she kept her work cards and shuffled them briefly, then spread them out on the table in a long arc. "Now, hold the question you came to consult me about in your mind, and indicate a card to me. Don't touch, just point with your finger to the card that calls to you."

The woman's jaw was clamped, and Hal sensed a turmoil in her out of all proportion. Whatever had driven her here tonight was no ordinary question; she had come against her will, turning to something she believed in spite of herself. When she leaned forwards, a cross glinted out from behind her buttoned-up cardigan, and she gestured jerkily at a card, almost as if she suspected a trap.

"This one?" Hal said, pushing it out from the deck, and the woman nodded.

Hal placed it facedown in the center of the table and glanced discreetly at the clock positioned behind the woman's back. Usually she did the Celtic Cross, but she was damned if she'd spend half an hour with this woman when she was tired and cold and her stomach was rumbling. A three-card spread was the very most she was going to do.

"This card"—Hal touched the card the woman had chosen—"represents the current situation, the problem you have come to consult me about. Now choose another."

The woman flicked her finger towards a second card, and Hal placed it alongside the first, facedown again.

"This card represents the obstacle you face. Now choose one final card."

The woman hesitated, and then pointed at the first card in the deck, to the far left of the spread. It was one people rarely chose—most people picked towards the middle in a fairly even spread, choosing the cards closest to them, while a very few, the most suggestible types, picked up on the implicit instruction in *final* and chose a card towards the right of the spread, at the bottom of the original pack.

To pick the first card was unusual, and Hal was surprised. She should have known, she thought. This was someone perverse and contrary, someone who would do the opposite of what they thought you wanted.

"This final card represents the advice the cards are giving you," Hal said.

She turned the first card, and from the other side of the table she heard a choking sound, as the woman's hand went to her face, to cover her mouth and smother a name. Looking up, Hal saw that the woman's eyes were wide and harrowed, and full of tears, and suddenly she knew. She knew why the woman was here, and she knew what the image on the card meant to the woman sitting opposite.

The young man setting out with his pack into the sunshine was handsome and smiling, turning his dark face to the sun, and only the cliff edge at his feet gave a clue to the deeper, darker meanings of the card—impetuosity, naïveté, impulsiveness.

"This card is called the Fool," Hal said softly, and when the woman gave a little broken sob and a nod, almost in spite of herself, she went on, "but tarot isn't about simple meanings. The Fool, though he can symbolize foolishness, doesn't always mean that. Sometimes this card means new beginnings, sometimes it means doing things without thinking about the path ahead, without considering the future."

The woman gave another dry, choking sob, and said something that sounded like "His future!" in a tone of such bitter disbelief that Hal could not help herself—she put out her hand.

"I . . . forgive me, but . . . is your question about your son?"

The woman began to cry at that, broken and in earnest, and as she wept she nodded, and Hal heard words tumbling out—names of drugs, of treatment centers she recognized in Brighton, needle exchanges, of money stolen from handbags, of treasured heirlooms sold and pawned, of sleepless nights waiting for a call that didn't come. The story between the racking sobs was plain enough—a desperate struggle to save a son who did not want to be saved.

A choice, the woman had said, and Hal knew what that choice was, and she wished now that she had not opened the door.

With a feeling of foreboding, Hal turned the second card. It was the Wheel, reversed.

"The second card you chose represents the obstacle you and your son face together. This is the Wheel of Fortune, or the Wheel of Life. It symbolizes fortune and renewal and the cycle of life, and shows that you and your son have come to a turning point"—a little, reluctant nod, as the woman swiped fiercely at her eyes—"but here it's reversed—that's what we call it when the card is upside down like this. The Wheel reversed represents bad luck. This is the obstacle that has come into your life. There are negative forces here that are out of your control, but they are not always completely external—they come about as the result of choices we've made in the past, your choices and your son's, of course."

"*His* choices," the woman said bitterly. "His choices, not mine. He was a good boy, until he took up with those boys at his school and started dealing. What was I supposed to do—stand by and watch him sink into depravity?"

Her eyes were bleak holes in her skull, and as she waited for Hal's response she bit at the chapped skin of her lips, pulling at it with her teeth until a bead of blood appeared. Hal shook her head. Suddenly she wanted this to be over very much indeed.

"The last card represents a possible course of action, but"—the hunger in the woman's eyes made her add hastily—"it's important to know that it is not a prescription. The cards don't predict the future—they don't give a fail-safe course. They simply tell you what could, on a given day, be one outcome to your problem. Some situations have no simple resolution; all we can do is steer the course that causes the least harm."

She turned the card, and the High Priestess turned her serene face up to the dim, flickering light. From outside there was a gust of wind, and in the distance Hal heard a seagull's scream.

"What does it mean?" the woman demanded, all her skepticism gone, subsumed by desperation for answers. She stared down at the figure on the card, seated on her throne, her hands spread like a benediction. "Who is she—some kind of heathen goddess?"

"In a way," Hal said slowly. "Some call her Persephone, some say she is Artemis, goddess of the hunt. Some call her even older names. In French she's called la Papesse."

"But what does she *mean*?" the woman said again, more urgently. Her fingers closed like claws on Hal's wrist, painfully tight, and Hal had to fight the urge to pull away.

"She means intuition," Hal said shortly. She disengaged herself from the woman's grip under pretense of rearranging the cards into a single pile, the Priestess on top. "She symbolizes the unknown—both the unknown within ourselves, and the future. She means that life is changing, that the future is always uncertain, no matter how much information we can gather."

"So what should I do?" the woman cried. "I can't go through this over and over, but if I throw him out, what kind of mother does that make me?"

"I believe . . ." Hal stopped, and swallowed. She hated this part. Hated the way they came to her asking for answers she couldn't give. She thought carefully, and then began again. "Look, this is a very unusual spread." She turned the rest of the pack over and spread them out, showing the woman the ratio of major to minor cards, the fact that the vast majority of the pack were numbered pip cards. "These cards—these numbered ones, with the suits on them—these are what we call minor cards. They have their own meanings, of course, but they are more . . . mutable, perhaps. More open to interpretation. But these others"—she touched the cards the woman had chosen, and the rest of the trumps, dotted through the spread—"these symbolic cards are called the major arcana, or trumps. To have a spread that's completely composed of trump cards, as you had, that's statistically very unusual. There just aren't that many of these cards in the deck. And the point is that in tarot, these cards represent the strong winds of fate—the turning points in our lives—and when you get a large number of them in a reading, it can mean that the situation is largely out of your hands, that it will play out as the fates intend."

The woman said nothing; she only looked at Hal, her eyes so hungry they made Hal almost afraid. Her face in the candlelight was shadowed, the eye sockets sunken.

"Ultimately," Hal said softly, "you have to decide for yourself what the cards are telling you, but my feeling is that the Priestess is telling you to listen to your intuition. You know the answer already. It's there in your heart."

The woman drew back from Hal, and then she nodded, very slowly, and bit her white, chapped lips.

Then she stood, threw down a crumple of banknotes on the table, and turned on her heel. The kiosk door banged behind her, letting in a gust of wind, and Hal snatched for the notes, spreading them out, and then shook her head when she saw how much had been left.

"Wait," she called. She ran to the door, forcing it open against the thrust of the wind. It caught from her fingers and slammed back against the side of the kiosk, making her wince for the fragile Victorian glass, but she could not spare more than a glance back to check it was okay. The woman was already disappearing.

She began to run, her feet slipping on the wet planks.

"*Wait!*"

The wind had picked up, and a mix of rain and salt spray stung her eyes as she reached the entrance to the pier, the illuminated sign above the entrance casting long, flickering shadows.

"Wait, come back!" she called into the wet night, straining through the drizzle for a shadowy figure. "This is far too much!"

She was panting, but now she tried to still her breath, listening for the sound of footsteps hurrying through the darkness; she could hear nothing above the roar of the sea and the patter of the rain.

The promenade was empty, and the woman had disappeared into the darkness as if made from rain herself.

HAL WAS WET AND SHIVERING by the time she gave up, the notes still crumpled in her hand, fast softening in the rain that dripped from the canopy. Sixty pounds the woman had left. A ridiculous sum—more than four times Hal's usual charge for a fifteen-minute reading. And for what—for making a few simple guesses, and telling her to listen to what she already knew?

Shaking her head, she pushed the notes into her pocket with a shiver and turned around, ready to go back to her booth, close up for the night. As she passed beneath the covered entrance, she put her hand down automatically to pat the plastic guide dog with the slot in his head for charitable donations, as hundreds of children did every time they passed him. Hal had always patted him as a little girl, every time she visited her mother, and sometimes, if they had had a bit of money to spare, her mother had let her put a pound in the slot at the top. It was a custom she tried to keep up—though lately, the pounds had dwindled to fifty-pence pieces, and sometimes to pennies.

Tonight, with those anonymous letters fresh in her mind, she hadn't been intending to give anything at all, but now, as she passed through the high, arched gates, she hesitated, and turned back.

The dog sat patiently beneath the inadequate shelter of the canopy, along with two other donation boxes, though the others were less popular with children. One was a ship in a frame, for the Royal

National Lifeboat Institution, and the other was a giant ice cream cone with a sign saying SUPPORT THE WEST PIER'S CHOSEN CHARITY! THIS MONTH WE ARE DONATING TO:——and a space to advertise the current good cause.

Now Hal bent to look at the wet paper slip that had been inserted. It was hard to read the letters, for rain or seawater had got in behind the plastic and made the ink run, but Hal could just make out the words. THE LIGHTHOUSE PROJECT—DRUG REHABILITATION IN BRIGHTON AND HOVE. Hal felt in her pocket for the fistful of wet notes the woman had left, and she thought of the pile of red demands on the living room table, and the typed note slid beneath her kiosk door.

Her hand shook as she counted out the banknotes, and then one by one, she shoved them into the slot of the ice cream cone, trying not to think of the shoes they could have bought, the bills she could have paid, and the hot dinners she could have eaten with the money.

At last the final note fluttered through the slot, and as she turned for her kiosk, the cone lit up, its bright pastel glow throwing a long shadow into the rainy night as she walked away.

CHAPTER 7

Hal shivered as she made her way back to her kiosk. She wished she had brought her coat in the headlong rush to catch up with the woman. Now she was wet through, and she would have to walk home in cold, wet clothes, and waste more money on gas to try to warm up before bed.

She picked her way carefully, avoiding the broken planks, feeling the rain-wet wood slippery beneath her feet, the puddles glittering in the few lights still showing. It wasn't yet ten o'clock, but the pier was almost closed—the ballroom was locked, Reg's tea kiosk was shuttered, and the candy floss stand had the blinds pulled down inside. NO CASH LEFT ON THESE PREMESIS, read the sign, though if Hal hadn't seen it a hundred times before she would have had a hard time making out the words, with the strings of lights swinging in the gusting wind and casting crazy lurching shadows over everything. The pier didn't shut for the winter—it had once, but now it was a year-round operation, like its twin sister farther up the beach—but there was a definite air of winding down at the end of the season, and Hal sighed as she thought of the long winter days that lay ahead. Now, though, she wondered—could she afford to keep going? But if she didn't, what was the alternative?

When she got back to the kiosk, the door was closed, though she had no memory of shutting it. She put her hand to the salt-rusted knob and turned the door handle, and slipped inside the dark booth, feeling relief as the wind dropped and the vestigial warmth from the space heater enveloped her.

"Hello, sunshine," said a voice, and the red-shaded lamp on the table clicked on.

Hal felt the blood drain from her face, and her heart started beating in her ears with a sound like the crash of waves on a beach.

The man standing in the pool of lamplight was very tall, and very broad, and very bald, and he was smiling, but not in a pleasant way. He was smiling like someone who enjoyed scaring people—and Hal was scared.

"Wh . . ." she tried, but her voice didn't seem to be working. "What are you doing here?"

"Maybe I've come for a reading," the man said pleasantly, but he had his hand in his coat pocket, caressing something in there in a way Hal didn't like. He spoke with a slight lisp, his speech whistling through a gap in his two front teeth.

"I'm closed," she managed to say, trying to keep her voice steady.

"Ah, don't be like that," the man said reproachfully. "You could manage a reading for an old friend of your ma's, now, couldn't you?"

Hal felt something inside her grow cold and still.

"What do you know about my mother?"

"I've been asking around about you. Friendly curiosity like."

"I'd like you to leave," Hal said. There was a panic button in her booth, but it was on the far side, where the man himself was standing, and in any case, it would all depend on whether the pier security guard was in his office.

The man shook his head, and she felt the panic rise up, choking her.

"I said, get out!"

"Tut-tut," said the man, shaking his head, the smile slipping for a moment, though it was still there in his eyes, a kind of amusement at the terror he saw in her, and at the way she was trying to hide it. The lamplight glinted off his bald head. "What would your ma say to her little girl, treating an old friend of hers like that?"

"I'm not a little girl," Hal said through gritted teeth. She wrapped her arms around herself, trying to stop her hands shaking. "And I don't believe for a second you knew my mother. What do you want?"

"I think you know what we want. You can't say we didn't try to do this the nice way. Mr. Smith wrote you that note himself, he did. He wouldn't do that for all his clients."

"What do you *want*," Hal repeated stonily, but it wasn't really a question. She knew. Just as she knew what the note meant. The man shook his head again.

"Come on, now, Miss Westaway. Let's not play games. It's not like you didn't know the terms when you signed up."

"I've paid off that money three, four times over," Hal said. She heard an edge of desperation creeping into her voice. "For God's sake, please. You know I have. I must have given you more than two thousand pounds. I only borrowed five hundred in the first place."

"Terms is terms. You agreed to the interest. If you didn't like it, you shouldn't have agreed to it."

"I had no other choice!"

But the man only smiled again, and shook his head.

"Naughty, naughty. We always have choices, Miss Westaway. You chose to borrow money off Mr. Smith, and he wants it back. Now, he's not an unreasonable man. Your debt is currently at . . ." He pretended to consult a piece of paper he held in his hand, though Hal was pretty sure it was all for show. "Three thousand eight hundred and twenty-five pounds. But Mr. Smith has kindly offered to take three thousand cash as a final payment and we'll call it settled."

"I haven't got three thousand pounds!" Hal said. She felt her voice rising and swallowed, forcing herself to lower it from a shout to a more reasonable level.

Slow down.

It was her mother's voice in her head, soft and calming. Hal remembered her telling her about how to deal with difficult clients. *Make them realize you're in control, not them. Don't let them make all the demands—remember you're in charge of this reading. You ask the questions. You set the pace.*

If only this *was* a reading. If only she had this man across a table with the cards in between them . . . but she didn't. She would just have to work with the situation she was in.

She could do this.

"Look," she said more reasonably. She drew a shaky breath, made herself unfold her arms from their defensive posture, spread her hands to show honesty. She even forced herself to smile, though it felt like a rictus grin. "Look, I want this settled as much as you do—more, actually. But I haven't got three thousand or any way of getting it. You might as well ask for the moon. So let's try to work out what I can offer that your boss will find acceptable. Fifty pounds a week?"

She didn't stop to think about how she would come up with the money. Fifty pounds a week was money she just didn't have at this time of year. But maybe Mr. Khan would let her defer the rent by a month, and Christmas often meant a small surge in business, with work Christmas parties and late-night shopping. Regardless, she would find the money.

"Here—" She went to the table, picked up the latched box that she kept on the side with the day's takings. Her hands were shaking almost too much to work the lock, but at last she got it open, and when she held out the notes, she made herself look up at him through her lashes and smile, a little girl's smile, shy and pleading, appealing to his better nature—if he had one. "Look, there's . . . twenty . . . thirty . . . nearly forty pounds here. Take that to be going on with."

Never mind that she still needed to pay Chalky White for the lease on the kiosk. Never mind the bills, and the rent, and the fact that she had no food in the house. Anything to get him out of her kiosk and buy her some time.

But the man was shaking his head.

"Look, you've gotta understand, if it was up to me, I'd love to. There's nothing I'd like better than to help out a young girl like you, all alone in the world." His eye swept appraisingly round the little kiosk. "But it isn't up to me. And Mr. Smith, he feels like he's been very generous, and you've taken advantage of that generosity. Mr. Smith wants his money. End of."

"Or what?" Hal said, suddenly weary of it all. She shoved the notes in her pocket, and deep within her, in the core of her, she felt a flicker of anger ignite, its determined warmth beginning to replace her chilly fear. "What's he going to do? Seize my goods? I've got nothing to offer you. You could sell everything I own and it wouldn't raise three grand. Take me to court? I didn't sign anything—you've got nothing except your word against mine. Or maybe he'll go to the police? You know—" She paused, as if the idea had only just struck her. "Yes, that's an idea. Maybe we *should* do that. I think they'd be interested in his loan collection methods."

That wiped the smile off the man's face, and he leaned forwards, so close to Hal's face that she could feel his saliva flecking her forehead as he spat the words. She forced herself not to flinch away.

"Now, that, Miss Westaway, is a very, *very* stupid suggestion. Mr. Smith has a lot of friends in the police, and I think they'd be upset to hear you talking like that about one of their mates. You say you didn't sign anything? Well, guess what that means, Miss Clever-clogs? No bloody evidence. You've got nothing to take to the police except for your word against mine. I'm going to give you one week to raise that money, and I don't want to hear any fucking nonsense about not having any way of getting it. You sell something, you rob someone, you stand on a street corner and give randy businessmen blow jobs in the backseat of their cars for twenty quid a pop, *I don't fucking care.* I want that money by this time next week. You reckon you've got nothing now? You can have a lot less than this, sweetheart. A *lot* less."

With that he turned and, very casually, swept everything off the shelf behind the table. Hal flinched as the contents went crashing down: the crystal ball on its wooden stand, the carved painted ornaments, the clay pot she had made her mother for some long-ago Christmas present, the books and cups, and the china vase of Kau Chim sticks . . . Down they came, smashing one by one across the desk and floor below.

"Oops," the man deadpanned, the lisp of the *s* somehow making the word sound even more sarcastic. He turned and gave her a wide, gap-toothed smile. "Sorry about that. I'm a bit clumsy, me. Broken bones too. *Lots* of bones. Knocked out three teeth the other day. Accidentally. But accidents happen, don't they?"

Hal found she was trembling. She wanted to run away from the booth, hammer on the door of the security guard's office, crouch under the dripping boardwalk of the pier until he went, but she could not—would not—give way. She would not show him her fear.

"I'll be off now," he said. He pushed past her to the door, and as he did, he put out one hand and casually tipped the table, sending the tarot cards flying into the air and Hal's cup of tea, left over from the morning, smashing to the floor. The cold tea spattered Hal's face, making her flinch.

In the doorway he paused, turned up his collar against the rain.

"Good-bye, Miss Westaway." That sibilant, whistling *ssss*. "See you next week."

And then he was gone, slamming the door behind him.

AFTER, HAL STOOD FOR A long moment, frozen, listening to his steps receding up the pier. And then something inside her seemed to release, and with shaking hands she pulled the latch of the kiosk door shut and then stood, her back to the door, trembling with relief and fear.

It had been almost a year ago that she had taken out the loan, and now she couldn't believe she had been so stupid. But at the time she had felt backed into an impossible corner—it had been winter, and takings from the pier had fallen, and fallen, until one awful week she had made only seventy pounds. The other stallholders had shrugged, and told her some weeks were just like that—inexplicably bad. But for Hal, it had been a disaster. She had no savings to fall back on, no second job. She was behind on the rent, behind on the bills, she had no way of covering the lease on the kiosk, even. She had tried everything—she'd advertised for a roommate, but no one wanted a flat where the landlady slept on a sofa in the one room. She'd attempted to find bar work, but it clashed with the times she was supposed to be at the pier, and in any case, one look at her empty CV and most of the places she'd tried had simply shaken their heads. Even the people at the job center had sucked their teeth when she told them she'd never even finished her A levels. The fact that her mother had died two weeks before she had been supposed to take the exams didn't really matter.

Touch up a relative, one of the guys on the pier had said, *call in a favor from a mate,* and Hal had not known how to reply, not known how to explain quite how alone in the world she was. Yes, she had grown up in Brighton, had even had friends here before her mother's death, but it was hard to explain how frighteningly fast their lives had diverged after the accident. She remembered turning up to school the day after the funeral, listening to them laughing about mobile phone bills, boyfriends, being grounded for some minor misdemeanor—and feeling like she was in a separate world. The image that had kept coming to her at the time was of a railway track, with the route stretching out ahead, already planned: A levels, university, internships, careers . . . and then a switch had been thrown, and she had been hurtled down a completely different route, simply trying to survive, to pay the bills, to get by from day to day, while her friends continued on down the old familiar track that Hal herself should have taken, if not for that speeding car.

There had been no time for A levels. She had dropped out of school, taken over the kiosk, and coped in any way that she could—one moment trying to forget, cropping her hair so that she didn't see her mother's face in the mirror quite so painfully every day, drinking herself into oblivion when she could afford the alcohol; the next moment holding on to her memories with painful intensity, inking them into her skin.

The person she was now was not the girl she would have been. The girl who had given her pocket money to the homeless, frittered away pennies on the pier, whiled away Sundays eating popcorn in front of bad films—she was gone. In her place was someone hardened, someone who had had to *become* hardened in order to survive. The laughing confidence of that girl on the beach had been stripped away, but inside, Hal had found a very different kind of strength that she had barely even known was there—a cold, hard core of determination that made her get up on frosty mornings to walk to the pier, even when her nose streamed with cold and her eyes were red with weeping, a kind of steel that made her carry on, putting one foot in front of the other, even when she was too tired to keep going.

She had become a different person.

The person she was now walked past beggars and turned her face away. The TV had been sold, and she never had Sundays off anyway. She was always tired from working, and always hungry, and most of all . . . most of all she was lonely.

A few months after the funeral she had seen a group of her old friends in Brighton town center—and they had not even recognized Hal. They had walked straight past her, talking and laughing. She had turned and opened her mouth, ready to call after them—then stopped. A chasm had opened between them, and it was too wide for any of them to bridge. They would not have understood anything about the person she had become.

So she had watched them walk away without saying a word; and then, just weeks later, they had scattered, to universities all around the country, to jobs and careers and gap years, and now she didn't see them anymore, even from afar.

But she did not know how to explain all that to the pier worker. *No*, was all she had said, her throat tight with loss and anger at his casual belief that everyone must have *someone* to fall back on. *No I can't do that.*

She couldn't quite remember how the suggestion had come about, but at last she had become aware of someone who did loans, no collateral needed. The interest was high, but the lender would accept small repayments, even let you skip a week if you couldn't keep up. It was all unofficial—no office premises, meetings in odd places, envelopes of cash. But it seemed like the answer to a prayer, and Hal jumped at it.

It wasn't until a few months in that she had the wit to ask how far she was getting in paying back her debt.

The answer had rocked her back on her heels. Five hundred pounds, she had borrowed—she'd actually only asked for three hundred, but the man had been nice enough to suggest that she up it a little, to see her through any rough patches.

She'd been paying it back at the rate of a few pounds a week for about four months. And now the debt was over a thousand.

Hal had panicked. She had immediately paid back the unspent portion of the original loan, and upped the repayments to the maximum she could afford. But she'd been too optimistic. She couldn't keep up with the new schedule, and after one particularly bad week at the pier, she missed a payment, and then a month later, she missed another. As the repayments spiraled and the calls from Mr. Smith's collectors got more and more aggressive, Hal realized the truth. She had no way out.

Eventually, she did the only thing she could do. She simply stopped paying. She stopped answering calls from unregistered numbers. She stopped answering the door. And she started looking behind her when she walked home alone at night. The one saving grace, she had kept telling herself, was that they didn't know where she worked. On the pier, she was safe. And—up until now—she had at least felt secure in the knowledge that there was a limit to what they could do. She had no goods for them to seize, and she was fairly sure that the arrangement itself was on the shady side of legal. They were highly unlikely to take her to court.

But now it seemed that they had tracked her down, and their patience had run out.

As Hal's shivering subsided, the words the man had uttered seemed to echo inside her head. *Broken bones. Broken teeth.*

Hal had never thought of herself as cowardly—or vain—but at the thought of that steel-toe-capped boot casually swinging towards her face, the crunch as it met her nose and teeth, she couldn't help flinching.

So what could she do? Borrowing money was out of the question. There was no one she could ask—no one who had that kind of funds at their disposal, anyway. And as for turning tricks on the street corner as the man had suggested . . . Hal felt her mouth twist in grim revulsion. Brighton had a thriving sex trade, but she wasn't that desperate. Not yet.

Which left . . . stealing.

You have two roads ahead of you, but they twist and turn. . . . You want to know which you should take. . . .

BACK AT THE FLAT, HAL let herself in the front door and stood silently in the hallway, listening. No sound came from above, and when she reached the topmost landing, the door to her flat was closed, no light showing beneath it.

As she peered at the door lock in the dimness, though, she thought there was something different about the scratches on the plate, as if someone had been at work with a picklock. Or was that just her own paranoia? Surely all lock plates had chips and scrapes on them, from keys carelessly shoved in, clattering against the metal.

Her heart was beating fast as she inserted her key, unsure of what she might find on the other side, but as the door swung wide and she groped for the light, her first thought was that everything was miraculously untouched. There was the post where she had left it on the table. There was her laptop. Nothing broken, nothing stolen for part payment.

Hal's heart slowed, and she let out a sigh, not quite of relief but of something close to it, as she shut the door behind her and double-locked it, then shrugged off her jacket. It was only when she went across to the kitchen counter to turn on the kettle that she noticed two things.

The first was a pile of ashes in the sink—ashes that had definitely not been there when she left. It looked as if a sheet of paper had been burned . . . perhaps two. Peering closer, Hal made out letters on one of the scraps that had not yet crumbled to fragments, silvery against the black background. . . . *u're fina* . . . she made out, and beneath it . . . *ll again*. . . .

Hal knew what it was, even without glancing behind herself at the coffee table, where she had left the letters from Mr. Smith, neatly stacked beside the bills. She knew they would be gone, even before she looked around. But still she could not stop herself from checking, from moving the pile of final demands aside, searching desperately in case they had gusted off the table when she opened the door.

It was no use. The letters were gone—and with them any evidence she could have shown to the police.

And something else was missing too, she realized with a lurch. The photograph on the mantelpiece, the picture of Hal and her mother, arm in arm on Brighton beach, their hair gusting in the sea wind.

As she stepped towards the shelf where it should have been, something crunched beneath her boots, and when she looked down, there it was—the frame faceup on the hearth, the glass smashed to smithereens by a stamped foot, the picture scratched and torn by the grinding of a heel into the broken frame.

Her hands shaking, eyes swimming, Hal forced herself to pick it up, cradling it like some small, broken animal, picking out the shards of glass from the paper. But it was no good. The picture was ripped and ruined, and the laughing faces of that girl and her mother were gone for good.

She would not cry. She refused to. But she felt something huge and bitter and wild with grief rise up inside her. It was the injustice of it that stung so, like acid in her throat. She wanted to cry out with it, scream with the unfairness of it all.

I want a break, she wanted to sob. *Just once, I want something to go my way.*

She found herself sinking to her knees, bowed down beneath the weight of it all, and for a moment she crouched over the broken shards of glass, her head bent, hugging her knees to her rib cage as if to make herself as small and safe as possible. But there was no safety anymore, no one to hug her and clean up the mess and make her a hot cup of tea. She was going to have to deal with this herself.

As she began to pick up the glass, sweeping the splinters carefully with the sleeve of her coat, Reg's voice sounded in her head, his comforting Cockney croak. *If anyone deserves a break, it's you, my darlin'. You take any money they offer you and run, that's my advice. Take the money and run.*

If only she could. She slipped the glass into the bin, the torn scraps of photograph fluttering after.

You have two roads ahead of you, but they twist and turn. . . . You want to know which you should take. . . .

Hal's phone was in her pocket, and, almost without being aware of what she was doing, she pulled it out and opened up the Trainline website.

December 1.

7 a.m.

Brighton to Penzance, return.

She clicked.

If anyone can pull this off, it's you. . . .

When the ticket prices came up on-screen, she couldn't suppress a wince. The money in her pocket wasn't enough to cover the fare. Not even a single. And her overdraft was already maxed out. But maybe . . . *maybe* if the website didn't check in with her bank . . . She pulled out her bank card, tapped in the number, and held her breath. . . .

Miraculously, the payment went through.

Even so, Hal didn't quite believe it until her phone vibrated with an e-mail. *Here's everything you need for your Penzance trip,* it read, and below that, a ticket collection number confirming her purchase.

Her stomach clenched and turned, as if she were riding a ship in rough seas and a wave had dropped away beneath the hull. Was she really going to do this? But what was the alternative? Wait here for Mr. Smith's minions to pay her a return visit?

I might be heir to a secret fortune.

The words she had spoken to Reg echoed in her ear, half taunt, half promise. Hal stood, feeling the stiffness in her limbs, the tiredness of her muscles now that the adrenalized fear had abated.

It might be true. And if it wasn't, perhaps she could *make* it true. All she had to do was make herself believe it.

WHEN SHE HEADED TO HER bedroom, she told herself it was to go straight to bed. But instead, she pulled her mother's battered suitcase from the top of the wardrobe, and began to pack. Shampoo, deodorant. That was straightforward. What to wear was more difficult. Black was not a problem—more than half Hal's wardrobe was black or gray. But she couldn't turn up to a stranger's funeral in ripped jeans and a T-shirt; people would expect a dress, and she had only one.

She pulled it out of the bottom drawer where she had shoved it after her mother's funeral three years ago, held on a blazing May day. It was respectable, but far too summery for December, made of cheap, flimsy cotton, with short sleeves. She could wear it with tights, though her only pair of tights was laddered at the top of the thigh. Hal unrolled them, examining the damage. She had carefully stopped the run with a blob of nail varnish, and now she would just have to hope that the fix held.

Next, a couple of T-shirts, a hoodie, and her least-threadbare jeans. A spare bra. A handful of knickers. And finally her precious laptop, and a couple of paperbacks.

The last thing was the most difficult. ID. They would expect ID, and the letter had asked her to bring it. The problem was, Hal had no idea what information they already had. Her full birth certificate was out of the question, but she could take her passport, or her short-form birth certificate, neither of which made any mention of parents. Those simply confirmed something they already knew—Hal's name. The problem was, both documents also gave her date of birth.

If they were expecting someone aged thirty-five, it would all be over as soon as they saw her—they wouldn't even need to get to the passport. But Hal thought she could pass for anything from fifteen to twenty-five, maybe even thirty at a pinch. Unless Hester Westaway had married and had children very young, there was a good chance that the woman they were looking for was within that range; but if the solicitor's documents showed a baby born in December 1991 and Hal produced a passport showing she was born in May 1995 . . .

Hal pulled out the letter again, scanning for acceptable forms. The second column, proving her address, was no problem. *A utility bill,* said the letter. Well, she had plenty of those. And the utility company couldn't possibly tell the solicitors anything they didn't already know, apart from the state of her overdraft.

But the first column was more of a problem. Passport, driving license, or birth certificate. She didn't have a driving license, and a passport would be too hard to alter without access to serious cash. Which left . . . the birth certificate.

Hal rummaged in the box under the bed again, looking for the envelope she had cast aside earlier. When she found it, she flipped past her mother's certificate to her own, beneath. There was the full one . . . and yes, there beneath it was the short form. *Name: Harriet Margarida Westaway,* it read. *Born: 15th May 1995. Sex: Female. District: Brighton, East Sussex.*

If they didn't have a date of birth already, it would be easy—a simple question of handing over her real papers.

If they did . . . Hal peered at it, holding it up to the light, looking at the paper. It was not a very sophisticated document—the paper was watermarked, but that wasn't obvious from the surface, and the ink looked nothing special. With a bit of time and a scanner, she could probably use the real document to forge something fairly convincing.

The crease lines were old and soft, and Hal folded it up carefully and put it in an inside pocket of the case, along with the utility bill.

She was zipping up the case when she stopped . . . and reached into her bedside drawer where a small tin box rested, battered and losing its paint. It had once held Golden Virginia, though it had long since lost the scent of tobacco.

Opening it up, Hal let her fingers rest on the cards inside, feeling their frayed edges, the soft pliability of the aging cardboard, watching the familiar images flicker past as she riffled through them, their faces watching her, judging her.

On an impulse, she tipped the pack into her palm and, without shuffling, made a single cut, her eyes closed, only one question in her mind.

She opened her eyes.

The card in her palm was a young man standing in a storm-swept landscape, at his back a sky full of scudding clouds, at his feet a tumultuous sea. In his hands was a sword, upraised, as if about to strike. The page of swords. Action. Intellect. Decision.

In that instant Hal knew, if she were reading for a client, what she would have said: *The swords are the suit of the mind, of thought and analysis, and the page is a card full of energy and decision. There are stormy waters all around—but he is striding out with his sword upraised. Whatever the challenge he faces, the page is ready to meet it, and he is someone to be reckoned with.*

There is no such thing as a clear green light in tarot, she would have said. *But this card—this might be the closest thing to it.*

But beneath the practiced spiel she could hear her mother's voice, words she had told Hal again and again. *Never believe it, Hal. Never believe your own patter. The actor who loses his grip on reality, the writer who believes her own lies—they're lost. This is a fantasy—never lose sight of that, however much you want to believe.*

And there was the slippery truth of it—the confirmation bias known so well to scientists and skeptics. She *wanted* to believe the page's message. She wanted to believe in his green light, even as she clapped the two halves of the deck together, and slid them back into the tin, and closed the lid.

As she brushed her teeth in the tiny bathroom, gazing at her own reflection, soft-focus and unfamiliar without her glasses, Hal told herself, *I don't have to decide. I can sleep on it. Nothing is final.* But she took her toothbrush with her when she went back into the bedroom. She stood uncertainly by her bed for a moment, shivering in the cold breeze from the drafty window, and then, almost defiantly, she shoved the toothbrush inside the open case and, with a rasping scratch, zipped it up, and climbed into bed.

It was a long time before she put her book down and turned out the light, and longer still before she slept. And when she slept, she dreamed—of a young man standing over her, his sword upraised.

CHAPTER 8

Hal's mother had taught her tarot, and she'd been familiar with the images on the cards almost before she could walk—the smiling High Priestess, the stern Hierophant, the scary Tower with the lost souls falling away. And she had accompanied her mother to the booth on West Pier often enough as a little girl, when school was off and her mother couldn't find anyone to babysit. She'd sat quietly behind the curtain in the corner reading a book, listening to her mother's skillful back-and-forth, and she grew to understand the tactics almost without realizing—the leading questions, the graceful forks: "A brother . . ."—a slight frown from the client—"no, wait, someone *like* a brother. A friend? A male relative?"

Hal learned how far to generalize and when to backtrack when you had hit a rut. She watched how her mother stopped trying to apply a statement when the client was stubbornly shaking his or her head, and how she changed tack with an unruffled, "Ah, well, I will leave that image with you to decipher. Perhaps its meaning will come to you later, or it may be a warning for the future."

So much she had picked up without even trying. But to conduct a reading herself . . . that was another matter.

In the end, though, she had no choice. A couple of days before Hal's eighteenth birthday, her mother was killed in a hit-and-run on a hot summery day, right outside their flat, by a speeding driver who was never found. Hal was left reeling, grieving—and broke.

When the pier manager, Mr. White, came to her a few weeks later, his ultimatum was not unkind—he wanted to give Hal first refusal, he said. But the kiosk could not remain empty in the height of the season. If she wanted her mother's booth it was hers, no question. But she would have to start soon. It was June, the pier was full every day and every evening, and shuttered kiosks were bad for everyone.

And so Hal had picked up her mother's cards, turned on the neon sign outside the booth, and become Madame Margarida in her turn.

The regular clients were easy. She had watched her mother read time and again for these people, had listened to them spill the details of wayward husbands, tetchy bosses, unhappy children. And the drunken walk-ins were not too bad—she could bluff her way through those, and besides, they tended to be tourists who would never be back.

No, it was the bookings that worried her. The people who paid for a full hour's consultation, who rang up beforehand to make sure she would be in.

For those, Hal did something her mother had never resorted to. She cheated.

It was scary how much you could find out online. Hal had never used Facebook before her mother's death, but in those early, uncertain days she created a fake profile, with an unthreatening picture of a blond girl taken from Google images, and christened her "Lil Smith."

Lil was a conscious choice—a name that could be short for Lily, Lila, Lillian, Elizabeth, or a hundred other names. Smith was obvious, as was the unassuming prettiness of the girl.

It was amazing how readily people accepted a friend request from someone they had never met, but much of the time she didn't even need to do that, for their privacy settings were wide open, and she could find out details of their family, their employer, their education and hometown, all without ever leaving her room.

Now, as the train sped west, she opened up her laptop and turned her attention to the Westaways, a nervous fluttering in the pit of her stomach.

The first Google hit was a death notice in the *Penzance Courier* for Hester Mary Westaway, born September 19, 1930, died November 22, 2016, at Clowe's Court, St. Piran. The brief obituary stated that she was the widow of Erasmus Harding Westaway, by whom she had had three sons and a daughter. *She is survived by her sons, Harding, Abel, and Ezra Westaway, and her grandchildren,* read the notice.

Was she supposed to be the daughter of one of these men?

Neither Abel nor Harding was a big Facebook user, but nor were they hard to find. Only one hit came up for each name, and Harding had helpfully listed his hometown as St. Piran, and tagged Abel as his brother. As Hal scrolled down through his profile, looking at photographs of weddings and christenings, family parties and first days at school, she felt a lump in her throat. There was a wife, Mitzi Westaway (née Parker), and three children, Richard, Katherine, and Freddie, ranging from early to mid teens.

Abel was younger by a good few years, a kind-looking man with a neat brown beard and hair the color of dark honey. His relationship status wasn't visible, but scrolling through his profile pictures Hal picked out a handsome blue-eyed man called Edward in many of the photos. There was a tagged photograph of the two of them together in Paris on Valentine's Day 2015, and another of them hand in hand at some kind of formal event. *Black and White Ball for the Orphans of the Philippines,* read the caption. Both men were wearing black tie, and Abel was smiling up at his companion with a kind of anxious pride.

Both profiles exuded an air of comfortable wealth that made Hal's heart hurt with a kind of longing envy. There was nothing ostentatious, no yachts or Caribbean cruises. But there was casual mention of holidays in Venice, skiing in Chamonix, private schools, and tax planning. The evolving slide show of profile pictures showed children on ponies, four-wheel-drive cars, and polo equipment, and their Facebook memories were of restaurant meals and family get-togethers.

Of Ezra there was no sign.

Judging by Facebook, both Abel and Harding were old enough to have a child in her twenties, but it was the daughter who kept drawing Hal's attention. *She is survived by her sons.* What had happened to the daughter?

Without a name, there was no way of finding out, and there was no mention of a sister on either Harding's or Abel's Facebook profile. After a moment's thought, Hal—or rather, Lil Smith—put in a friend request to Harding's eldest son, Richard Westaway. She deliberately did not ask Abel. He had only 93 friends, and didn't look the type to accept unsolicited friend requests from mystery girls. Harding was an even worse choice—he had only 19 friends and didn't seem to have checked his account for almost four months. Richard, on the other hand, had 576 friends and had already posted an update checking in at a service station outside Exeter.

Hal was just opening up another tab, when a notification flashed up—Richard had accepted her request. She clicked through to his profile and liked the first photograph that came up—Richard's muddy face brandishing some kind of cup. *Thrashed St Barnabus at rugger AGAIN. Pretty sure their fly half was a girl with facial hair* 🤔, read the caption. Hal rolled her eyes, and returned to Google search.

There was nothing for Trepassen House on the land registry, and there were no businesses registered there. It wasn't listed under care homes, or inspected as a food premises. There seemed to be no indication that it was anything other than a private home. Google maps brought it up, though, and Hal switched the view first to satellite and then to street view. Street view was unhelpful, showing nothing but a country lane flanked by a long brick wall with yews and rhododendrons shrouding anything behind it. Hal clicked along the road for a few miles in either direction, until finally she came to a wrought-iron gate across a driveway, but the photo was taken from the wrong angle to provide any view of the house, and she switched back to satellite.

The blurry image was too small to show anything apart from a gabled roof and a gated expanse of green punctuated by trees, but if nothing else, Hal could see that the place was big. Very big. This looked like a stately home, almost. These people had money. *Serious* money.

"Tickets, please," said a voice over her shoulder, breaking into her thoughts, and Hal looked up to see a uniformed conductor standing in the aisle next to her. She rummaged in her wallet for a moment and held out the ticket. "Home for the weekend, are we?" he said as he punched a hole in it, and Hal was just about to shake her head, when something stopped her.

She had to step into this part sometime, after all.

"No, I . . . I'm going back for a funeral."

"Oh, I'm sorry." The conductor handed her back her ticket. "Anyone close?"

Hal swallowed. She felt the cliff yawning beneath her feet. *It's just a role,* she told herself. *No different from what you do every day.*

The words seemed to stick in her throat, but she forced herself on.

"My grandmother."

For a moment the statement felt like what it was—a lie. But then she rearranged her face into an expression . . . not of grief, for that would be too much, for this woman she could not possibly be close to. But a kind of solemn regret. And she felt a shiver of something run through her—the same shiver she felt when she switched on the light outside her booth and stepped into her role.

"Very sorry for your loss," the conductor said, and he nodded gravely, and passed on up the corridor and into the next carriage.

Hal was putting the ticket back into her near-empty wallet when the train dipped into a tunnel, causing the lights to flicker out, so that for a second the only illumination was the glow of her laptop, and the sparks of the wheels on the track, like lightning flashes against the blackened brick of the tunnel.

The screen of her laptop glowed emerald bright, the huge expanse of grass, the narrow snaking road, and suddenly Hal felt a kind of anger wash over her.

How could one family, one *person,* have so much? The grounds of Trepassen House could fit not just Hal's apartment block, but her entire road and most of the next one. Just the cost of mowing those lawns was probably more than she made in a month. But it wasn't just that—it was everything. The ponies. The holidays. The casual acceptance of it all.

How could it be right that some people had so much, while others had so little?

The lights came back on with a strobing flicker, and another Facebook notification popped up. Another update from Richard. Hal clicked on it, and a picture filled the screen—Richard and his family against a backdrop of paneled wood, all of them beaming proudly. Harding had his arm clasped so hard around his son that the boy was staggering slightly.

Richard has shared a Facebook memory, said the caption, and peering closer Hal read, *Prize-giving day at St A's. Ma doing the ol maternal pride thing so hard i thought she might rupture something. Just gotta make sure Dad makes good on our deal—500 squids for not flunking maths—and then HELLOOOO Ibiza!*

As the train swooped out of the tunnel into daylight, Hal felt again that fluttering sickness in the pit of her stomach—but she knew in that instant that she would not turn back.

For the flutter wasn't only nerves. It wasn't even just envy. It was also a kind of excitement.

CHAPTER 9

It was almost three when the train drew up at Penzance. Hal paused for a moment beneath the big clock hanging above the platform, the sounds of the station echoing around her, trying to decide what to do.

TAXIS, read a sign above her head, and she shouldered her bag and followed the direction arrow to a rank at the front of the station. But a few feet away from the QUEUE HERE sign, she paused, and checked in her wallet.

After a sandwich on the train—egg and cress, the cheapest on offer at £1.37—she had £37.54 left. But would that be enough to get her as far as St. Piran? And if it was, how would she get back?

"You waiting, sonny?" said a voice from behind her, making her jump. Hal turned, but there was no one in sight. It was only when a face leaned out of the taxicab window that she realized it was a taxi driver who had spoken.

"Oh, sorry." She shoved her wallet back in her bag and walked across to the taxi. "Yes, I am."

"Sorry, my love." The man's face was red as she approached. "I didn't realize—it was the short hair, see."

"It's fine," Hal said honestly. It happened too often for it to bother her anymore. "Listen, can you tell me how much to get to St. Piran's Church? I've not got very much cash on me."

Or off me, she thought, but didn't say. The taxi driver looked away, and began tapping something into a screen on the dashboard—a sat-nav, or a phone, Hal thought, though she wasn't sure.

"'Bout twenty-five quid, my darlin'," he said at last. Hal drew a breath. This was it, then. If she got in this cab, she was stranded—no way back without relying on the goodwill of whoever she found at the other end. Was she really going to do this?

"The train now departing from platform three is the delayed 14:49 to London Paddington," said the tinny voice of the station announcer—breaking into her thoughts like the universe reminding her once again that she didn't have to follow this through, that she could simply turn around and catch the train straight back home.

Where Mr. Smith would be waiting for her in six days' time . . .

If anyone can pull this off, it's you.

"D'you 'ear me?" the taxi driver asked. His Cornish burr made the words sound less abrupt than they would have coming from a Brighton cabbie. "Twenty-five pound, I said, is that all right?"

Hal took another deep breath, and looked back at the train station. The pictures from Facebook and Google rose up in front of her eyes—the sprawling expanse of land, the holidays, the cars, the clothes, like stills from a Jack Wills brochure. . . .

She thought of the heel grinding into her mother's photograph. Of the smashed ornaments in her kiosk, and the fear she had felt when that lamp clicked on. She thought of what she would give for just a couple of thousand pounds of that money—not even enough to buy one of those cars, a tenth of it maybe.

They have everything already. They don't need more money.

She felt again that sensation of something sharp and hard crystallizing inside her, a kind of hot pain cooling into brittle resolve.

If she failed, she would be stranded. So she would just have to ensure that she didn't fail.

"All right."

The driver reached back and the rear door of the taxi swung open, and with a feeling like she was about to step off a cliff, Hal pushed her mother's suitcase inside, and climbed in after.

"LOOKS LIKE A FUNERAL," SAID the voice from the front seat of the car, and Hal jumped and looked up.

"Sorry, what did you say?"

"I says, it looks like a funeral," the driver repeated. "At the church. Is that what you're here for? Relative, is it?"

Hal peered out of the window, through the lashing rain that had started as they left Penzance. It was hard to see much through the gale, but she could make out a small stone church perched on a headland with gray clouds swirling behind, and a little gaggle of black-coated mourners making their way from the entrance to the graveyard towards the church.

"Yes," she said, almost under her breath, and then more loudly, as the driver cupped his hand to his ear, "Yes, that's what I'm here for. It's . . ." She hesitated, but it was easier the second time around. "It's my grandmother."

"Well, I'm very sorry for your loss, my darlin'," the driver said, and he took off his flat cap and placed it on the seat beside him.

"How much do I owe you?" Hal asked.

"Twenty be fine, my love."

Hal nodded, and she counted out one ten-pound note and two fives onto the little tray between them, and then paused. Could she afford a tip? She looked at the coins left in her purse, counting them under her breath, wondering how she was going to get from the church to the house. But from here she could see the digital display in the cab, and it read £22.50. Damn. He had undercharged her. Feeling guilty, she put another pound on the tray.

"Thank you kindly," the driver said, scooping up the change. "Take care in that rain now, my darlin', catch your death on a day like today."

The words made Hal shiver for some reason, but she only nodded, opened the door, and slid out into the driving rain.

As the car drew away, its tires splashing in the wet road, Hal stood for a second, trying to get her bearings. The rain spattered the lenses of her glasses, and at last she took them off to peer through the downpour at the lych-gate in front of her, and the little gray church hunched against the cliff top. A low stone wall encircled the graveyard, and beyond it Hal could see a dark rift in the ground—it was too blurry to be certain, but from the shape, she felt fairly sure it must be the open grave, awaiting the coffin of the woman she was about to defraud.

For a moment, Hal had an almost overwhelming urge to turn and run—no matter that it was thirty miles to the nearest train station, no matter that she had no money, and her cheap black coat and shoes were no match for the driving rain.

But as she stood, hesitating in the downpour, a hand tapped her shoulder and she swung violently round to find a little man with a neat gray beard peering at her from behind rain-misted glasses.

"Hello," he said, his voice a strange mix of diffidence and assertion. "Might I be of assistance? My name is Mr. Treswick. Are you here for the funeral?"

Hal hastily put her own glasses back on, but they did nothing to make the face in front of her more familiar. The name Treswick rang a bell, though, and Hal searched frantically through her mental file of names, trying to match the figure in front of her with a family member. And then, suddenly, with a rush of mingled relief and trepidation, she found it.

"Mr. Treswick—you wrote to me!" she said. She put out a hand. "I'm Hal—I mean, Harriet Westaway." At least, put like this, it was not a lie. Not exactly, anyway.

There was a pause. Hal felt her stomach clench with nerves. This was the moment of truth—or one of them. If the real Harriet Westaway was thirty-five, or blond, or six feet tall, it was all over before it had begun. She could kiss good-bye to even entering the church, let alone a legacy. It would be back to Brighton on the same train, with her wallet dented, and her pride considerably bruised.

Mr. Treswick didn't say anything at first, he only shook his head, and Hal felt her stomach drop away. Oh God, it was over. It was all over.

But then, before she could think what to say, he took her hand, pressing it between two warm leather gloves.

"Well, well, well . . ." He was still shaking his head, in disbelief, Hal realized. "Well, I never. How very, very glad I am that you could make it. I wasn't certain you would receive the letter in time—it was not an easy task tracking you down, I must say. Your mother—" He seemed suddenly to think better of the direction the conversation was taking, and stopped, covering his confusion by removing his glasses and wiping the rain from them. "Well," he said as he resettled them on his nose, "never mind that now. Let's just say, it was touch-and-go that we found you in time. But I am so glad you were able to attend."

Your mother. In the sea of uncertainty, the words felt like something firm for Hal to hang on to—one fact she could begin to build upon. So it was as she'd thought—Mrs. Westaway's dead daughter was her link to all this.

Hal had a sudden picture of herself wading through shifting, clutching mud—and finding something solid to rest on for a moment.

"Of course," she said, and managed to smile, in spite of the way her teeth were clenched against the cold. "I'm g-glad too."

"Oh, but you're shivering," Mr. Treswick said solicitously. "Let me show you inside the church. It's an absolutely filthy day, and I'm afraid St. Piran's has no heating at all, so it's not much better inside. But at least you'll be dry. Have you—"

He paused as they reached the lych-gate, opening it up and standing aside for Hal to pass through.

"Have I . . . ?" she prompted as they stood in the shelter of the gate's arch for a moment. Mr. Treswick polished his glasses again—futilely, Hal realized, looking at the stretch of graveyard they still had to cover.

"Have you met your uncles?" he asked diffidently, and Hal felt a sudden flood of warmth around her heart, in spite of the chilly day. Uncles. *Uncles.* She had uncles.

You do not, she told herself sternly, trying to dampen down the sensation. *They are not your relatives.* But she could not think like that. If she was going to pull this off, she had not only to pretend, she had to believe.

But what should she say? How could she answer his question? She stood for a long moment, trying to think, before suddenly realizing that she was gaping at Mr. Treswick, and that the little man was looking at her, puzzled.

"No," she said at last. That at least was a no-brainer. There was no point in pretending she knew people who were standing right over there, and who could give her story the lie the instant they saw Mr. Treswick. "No, I never have. To be honest . . ." She bit her lip, wondering if this was the right path to take, but surely it was better to tell the truth where she could? "To be honest," she finished in a rush, "I didn't know I *had* any uncles until you wrote. My mother never mentioned them."

Mr. Treswick said nothing, only shook his head again, though whether in resigned understanding or baffled denial, Hal wasn't sure.

"Shall we?" he asked, glancing up at the iron-gray sky above. "I don't think the rain is going to lighten at all, so we might as well make a dash for it."

Hal nodded, and together they scurried the short distance from the lych-gate to the church.

On the porch, Mr. Treswick wiped his glasses yet again and tightened the belt of his mackintosh as he ushered Hal ahead of him, but as he was about to follow, his head cocked like a spaniel's at the sound of an engine, and he turned back.

"Ah, if you will excuse me, Harriet, I believe that is the funeral cortège. May I leave you to seat yourself?"

"Of course," Hal said, and he disappeared into the rain, leaving her to enter the church alone.

The door was just ajar, as some protection from the driving wind and rain, but as she slipped inside, the first thing that struck her was not the cold, but the lack of people. There could not have been more than four or five people dotted about the pews. She had assumed that the group of mourners she had seen from the taxi were latecomers, joining those already in the church, but now she realized that she must have seen the arrival of almost everyone here.

There were three very elderly women in the second pew from the front, a man in his forties who looked like an accountant seated towards the back, and a woman in a district nurse's uniform perched by the entrance, as if poised to make a quick getaway, should the service drag on.

Hal looked around, trying to assess where she should sit. Was there a rule with funerals? She tried to remember her mother's service at Brighton Crematorium, but all she could recall was the little chapel overflowing with pier folk and neighbors, grateful clients, old friends, and people she didn't even recognize but whose lives her mother had touched. At the back they had been standing, crushing against the wall to make room for more mourners, and she'd seen Sam from the fish-and-chip kiosk giving up his seat to let an elderly neighbor at Marine View Villas sit down. Someone had kept a place for Hal at the front, but for the rest, she was not sure how they had decided who sat where, or what hierarchy of mourning might apply.

Whatever the rules were, though, surely anyone who had never met the deceased ranked pretty low.

In the end, she took a seat towards the back, but not so conspicuously as the accountant and the district nurse—three or four rows in from them, on the right-hand side. Her glasses were still streaked with drying raindrops, and she took them off to clean them, listening, as she did so, to the rustle of feet, and the drumming of the rain on the roof, and the occasional cough from the women at the front. She tried not to shiver.

Hal had only two coats—the battered leather jacket she wore every day, and a dark trench coat mackintosh that had been her mother's and was too big for her. The leather jacket was black, at least, but it hadn't seemed right for a funeral, so she had worn the trench coat. It had felt warm enough on the train, but at some point in its long storage, its waterproofing had worn off, and the fabric had soaked right through in the brief run from the taxi. Now she sat in the cold church and felt the rain leaching through to her skin. Her hands, when she looked down at them in her lap, were bluish, and she had to shove them into the pockets of the flimsy coat to stop her fingers shaking with cold. At the bottom of one of the pockets she felt something round and rough chafe against her numb skin, and when she pulled it out, she smiled. Gloves. Something warm, at least. It felt like a present from her mother.

She was just pulling them on when there was a blast of sound from an unseen organist, and the doors of the chapel were flung open, letting in a gust of wind that sent the thin paper orders of service scurrying down the aisle.

The priest—or vicar, Hal was not sure which—entered first, and behind him came four men in black suits, holding between them a narrow, dark-wood coffin.

The rear left-hand bearer Hal recognized straightaway as Mr. Treswick, his mackintosh shed to reveal a black suit and tie beneath. He was struggling a little with his position, for he was shorter than the other three men, and kept having to raise his corner higher than was comfortable to compensate.

At the front right was a balding man in his fifties who Hal thought must be Harding Westaway. She looked hard at his round, jowly face and pale, wispy hair, trying to imprint it on her memory. He had the air of a man who had eaten a good meal, but would always want more, nibbling at nuts and cheese and fruit, and then complaining of the subsequent indigestion. There was something both self-satisfied and yet self-doubting about him. It was a strange combination. As Hal watched, he brushed at his hair a little self-consciously, as though feeling her appraising eyes.

To his left was a bearded man with dark blond hair fading to gray at the temples, who looked close enough to the images she'd seen of Abel Westaway for Hal to guess that the final bearer, on the rear right, must be the third son, Ezra.

He was by far the youngest man in the group, and where his brothers were fair, Ezra was dark, and deeply tanned. He was also the only person in the whole church who was not wearing an expression of careful sorrow—in fact, as he drew level with Hal, he flashed her a curving Cheshire cat smile, and she felt a jolt of shock—it was so very inappropriate for the time and place.

In confusion, she turned away, pretending she hadn't seen, and faced the front of the church, feeling her cheeks burn.

It wasn't just the smile—though that was bad enough. It was that there had been something . . . something *flirtatious* in his grin, in the twinkling eye, close to a wink. *He doesn't know he's your uncle,* she told herself. *He has no idea who you are.*

That's because he's not your uncle, replied her conscience, snippily.

It was like two voices warring in her head. Hal pressed her gloved hands to her forehead, feeling the coldness of the rain still soaked into the wool, and she knew if she didn't get it together she wouldn't even make it as far as the wake, she would be found out for the impostor she was before they had even left the church.

The bearers made their slow way past her, deposited the narrow coffin at the top of the church, and filed dutifully into the pews at the front, followed by the little gaggle of family members trailing behind.

And the service began.

CHAPTER 10

An hour later, it was over—or almost. The sparse congregation filed out into the driving rain to stand around the grave as the coffin was lowered into the raw earth, and the priest raised his voice to intone blessings over the shriek of the wind off the sea.

It was almost dusk now, and the temperature had dropped even further—and Hal was shivering uncontrollably in her thin coat, but nevertheless she was grateful for the wind and the rain. Under cover of the weather, no one could read her expression as anything other than pinched and pained. Her eyes were watering with genuine tears, as she blinked away the drops that trickled from her hair into her eyes. No one would have expected her to cry—she knew that—but the next test was the wake, back at Trepassen House, and Hal knew that there, she could not escape scrutiny. It was a relief not to have to think about the expression on her face or her defensive body language for just a few minutes—here, huddled around the grave with the wind lashing in the mourners' faces, she could hug herself protectively and blame nothing but the weather.

At last, though, the priest said his final words, and Harding threw a handful of gritty earth from the covered bucket at the side of the grave. It splashed, rather than thudded, onto the wooden coffin lid, and he passed the pail to his brother Abel, who threw a handful in his turn, shaking his head as he did, though Hal could not tell what the gesture meant. Round the circle it went, handful after handful, a few flowers, limp with wet, following the earth into the grave. The last to take the pail was Ezra. He flung the earth almost carelessly, and then turned to Hal, standing in his shadow, just behind his shoulder, trying to efface herself from notice.

He said nothing, just held out the bucket, and Hal took it. As she did, the feeling struck her that there was something profoundly wrong in what she was about to do—blasphemous, almost, in this symbolic act of burying a woman she had no connection with. But the eyes of the family were upon her, and she had no choice.

The earth was clagged with rain now and she had to pull off her glove and dig into the mud with her nails.

It thudded down onto the coffin with a strange finality, and she handed the pail back to the curate.

"Ashes to ashes," said the priest over the noise of the wind and waves, "dust to dust, in sure and certain hope of the resurrection to eternal life . . ."

Hal wiped her muddy palm surreptitiously on her trench coat and tried to shut out his words, but the memories kept intruding—of the kind vicar who had presided over her mother's cremation, of his meaningless words of comfort, and of the promises she could not believe. She felt the mud grit beneath her fingernails and she remembered, with a force that felt like a blow to the chest, the feeling of her mother's ashes, gritting against her palm as she had scattered them on another December day, three years ago. She had gone to Brighton beach, on a day as windy as this, though dry, and she had walked down to the edge of the sea, her bare feet cold against the stones, and stood among the foamy weeds, watching as the ashes had tugged from her fingers and scattered across the sea.

As she stood, looking into the raw, wet mouth of the grave, Hal felt her heart clutch again with the pain of loss, as if an old, half-healed wound had been struck. Was it really worth doing this—putting herself through this again, the grim rituals of mourning and remembrance for what could be nothing more than an ugly lamp or a collection of postcards?

There are two paths ahead of you, they twist and turn . . .

She found her nails were digging into her palms, and she thought of the page of swords, striding out to meet the stormy seas, his sword upraised, his face determined.

The truth was, the two paths were gone now. She had chosen one—and shut off the possibilities of the other as if it had never existed. There was no way back, no point in second-guessing her decision. She had made the choice she needed in order to survive, and now the only way out was to push forwards—deeper into the deception. She could quite literally not afford to fail.

At last the final words were spoken, the priest began picking up his things, and the rest of the family began scattering, moving off towards the cars, their collars raised against the driving wind and rain.

Hal felt a flutter of fear in her stomach. She had to say something—and quickly. She had to ask one of them for a lift—but the thought of approaching these total strangers out of the blue was suddenly almost more terrifying than anything else. It wasn't just the fear of being found out. It was something more basic—more childlike. Whom should she ask? *How?*

"I—" she said, but her throat felt stiff and croaky. "I—is it—"

None of them turned. Harding was in the front, surrounded by his three teenage children and flanked by a woman who must be Mitzi. Hal recognized Richard from Facebook, already fiddling with his phone as he followed his father towards the car park. Abel and Ezra were walking behind, deep in conversation. As she watched, Abel put his arm around his brother, squeezing him tightly as if in consolation, and Ezra shrugged away, a little impatiently.

The others had already scattered to a clutch of cars parked beneath the dripping yews.

She was in danger of being left behind in this deserted graveyard. Panic rose up in her throat.

"Excuse me," she croaked again, more loudly, and then, as before, she felt a hand on her shoulder and turned sharply, to see Mr. Treswick standing there, his umbrella held out.

"Harriet. May I offer you a lift back to Trepassen?"

"Yes, oh yes." Hal felt the words tumbling out, almost incoherently. "Oh, thank you so much, I wasn't sure—"

"There will be no room in the funeral cars, I'm afraid, all the seats in the official cortège are taken up, but if you don't mind sharing my own car . . ."

"N-n-not at all," Hal said. Her teeth were chattering with cold, and she swallowed, trying to steady herself, make her gratitude less naked. "Thank you, Mr. Treswick, I really appreciate it."

"Not at all. Here, you hold the umbrella—mind it doesn't turn inside out, I'm afraid the sea gusts are rather unpredictable—and I will take your case."

"Oh no," Hal protested, "p-please!" but it was too late, somehow the little man had deftly removed the case from where she had let it rest on the graveled path, and the umbrella was in her hand, and he was forging through the rain to the car, parked down by the verge where the taxicab had set her down.

INSIDE THE VOLVO, MR. TRESWICK turned the heating up full, and as the car pulled out into the lane, splashing through the rutted puddles, Hal felt some of the chill begin to leave her fingers. In the graveyard she had thought that she might never be warm again—it was as if the cold had gone right through to her bones. Now the hot air blasting from the vents on the dashboard made her fingers sting and ache with the shock of the thaw, though the chilliness deep inside her seemed impenetrable.

"It's about four miles to Trepassen," Mr. Treswick said conversationally as they wound slowly down the lane to the main road, the wipers frantically swishing back and forth. At the crossroads they stopped while he peered through the gloom up and down the road, trying vainly to see if there was a car coming, and eventually, with a feeling of taking both their lives in his hands, he stamped on the accelerator and the car jolted across the junction and picked up speed.

"I hope Mrs. Warren will have tea waiting for us. Are you staying the night?"

"I—" Hal felt a jolt of guilt. She had not been able to write—there had been no time—and she had no idea what she would do if the invitation to stay was rescinded. "I would love to, yes, but I'm afraid I wasn't able to tell Mrs. Warren I was coming. Your letter only arrived two days ago—I didn't think a reply would get here in time. . . ."

"Oh, I am sorry, I should have put in a telephone number," Mr. Treswick said apologetically. "But no matter, Mrs. Warren will be able to open up a room, I'm sure. I should warn you"—he glanced doubtfully at Hal's wet coat and soaking clothes beneath—"there is no central heating at Trepassen I'm afraid, Mrs. Westaway never got around to having it installed. But there are plenty of fires and hot-water bottles and so on. You should be . . ."—he hesitated—"well, *fairly* comfortable."

"Thank you," Hal said meekly, though something in his tone made her doubt the truth of his words.

"I must say"—Mr. Treswick changed gears as they crested a hill—"I was a little surprised to find out that Maud had had a child."

Maud. So that was the missing daughter's name. M. Westaway—like her mother. Was that where the mistake had originated? Hal felt a silent wash of thankfulness that she had not brought her full birth certificate, followed by a flicker of something else, a kind of alarm. What did Mr. Treswick mean, he was surprised Maud had had a child? Was there something she needed to know? Could she ask, or would her ignorance give her away?

"I . . . what do you mean?" she asked at last.

Mr. Treswick gave a laugh. "Oh, she was very decided as a young woman. Always swore she would never get married, never have children. I remember telling her once, she must have been about twelve at the time, 'You may feel differently when you're grown up, my dear,' and she laughed, and said I was an old fool—she was rather forthright, your mother. She told me children were nothing but padlocks on the patriarchal shackles of marriage. That was the phrase she used—I remember it rather well. I recall thinking at the time that it was rather an unusual turn of phrase, particularly for a child of that age. So I was a little taken aback to learn that she had in fact had a child—and fairly young too, as I understand it?"

"She—she was eighteen," Hal said faintly. "When she had me."

Eighteen. When Hal was a child it had seemed a perfectly reasonable age—grown-up, in fact. Now that she was twenty-one herself, she could not imagine what her mother had been through, the struggle it must have been to have a child so young, and care for it alone.

But the words were barely out of her mouth when she realized her mistake, and felt a rush of cold fury prickle down the back of her neck at what she had just let slip. Damn. *Damn.* What a stupid, amateurish mistake.

It was the first rule of cold reading—be as vague as possible, try not to offer specific information, unless you can retract or twist the meaning if you've got it badly wrong. Always *I'm getting a man's name . . . a name with an* f *in it . . . ?* rather than *I'm hearing from your cousin Fred.* If you must guess at a specific, make it one that's statistically probable—*I'm seeing a blue car . . . ?* Never a green one.

Hal had just committed two grave errors in less than five words. She had given a specific, unnecessary piece of information, and it was one that was statistically unlikely to be right. How many women had children at eighteen? Two percent? Less? She had no idea.

But even setting that aside, she didn't know enough about the facts of this woman's life to make guesses like that. What if Maud would have been in her fifties now, so that elementary maths would tell Mr. Treswick the relationship was impossible? What if she had still been at home at the age of eighteen? Hal had been lulled by the false reassurance of Mr. Treswick's "fairly young, as I understand it"—a piece of information that had seemed to chime so neatly with Hal's own life. But there was fairly young, and fairly young. A twenty-five-year-old mother was "fairly young," these days. She had just slipped up—and badly.

Hal looked nervously across to see if Mr. Treswick had begun frowning, adding up figures in his head. But he didn't seem to have noticed her mistake. In fact, he barely seemed to have heard her remark at all. His mind was traveling down other paths.

"The patriarchal shackles of marriage," he said with a chuckle. "That phrase will always remind me of your mother. Though of course"—he threw a brief glance at her, his eyes bright as a robin's—"she never did marry, I understand?"

"N-no," Hal said. In spite of the chill in her bones, her face felt hot, scorched by the blast from the fan heater. How stupid she had been. From now on she would not offer information—just corroborate what others had already told her.

Though perhaps . . . They turned a corner, the tires shushing in the wet, and Hal pressed her cheek to the cold window and tried to think. Perhaps she hadn't been such a fool to admit her mother's age. It was very possible—probable, even—that she would be caught out at some point. Perhaps it was better to volunteer honest information now, so that if she were caught, she could represent the whole thing as a misunderstanding, luckily picked up, rather than a cold-blooded deception. If she started lying now, there would be no way out later on. Not without prosecution for fraud.

Maud Westaway. If only she had known about the name, she could have googled on the train, found out something about this woman who was supposed to be her mother. What did she look like? How old was she? And what had happened to her?

It was too late now. She could hardly get out her phone and start researching in front of Mr. Treswick. But the idea of having some basic facts to arm herself with, before she faced her "uncles," was enticing. She could not afford to slip up again. Could she creep away when they got to the house? Perhaps if she asked to change into dry clothes . . . ?

She kept silent for the rest of the journey, as did Mr. Treswick, though he shot the odd glance at Hal as the little car ate up the long country miles. It was only as the car began to slow down that Hal sat up, and he raised his voice above the noise of the wipers.

"Here we are." He indicated left, the flashing light turning the raindrops golden. "Trepassen House. Ah, the gates are open. Very good. I must say, I didn't relish the idea of struggling with the latch in this weather."

They turned carefully through the giant wrought-iron gates and began to wend their way up a long, graveled drive.

Far up ahead was a long, low building, and with a jolt, as they came round the corner, Hal realized that she recognized it. An image flashed into her head—tall windows, a sweep of grass falling away—and there it was, appearing before her eyes, like a conjuring trick.

Hal felt her mouth drop open, and for a moment it seemed inexplicable—and then, with a little rush of chagrin, she realized. Of course. It was the postcard she had found online. *We had a very good tea at Trepassen House.* It had been taken from just slightly farther along the lawn, and the jolt of recognition she had experienced was nothing but the perspectives slotting into place. But even as she recognized the image, she was noticing the changes—the ivy and Virginia creeper that had been decorous little trails in that original postcard, but now ran riot over the front of the house, seeming to strangle the bay windows and the columns that supported the porch. The paintwork was no longer the pristine white of the postcard, but cracked and flaking, and the lawns were overgrown, weeds growing between the flags of the terrace.

Hal felt her hopes begin to ebb away a little, along with the righteous certainty she had felt on the train. Where were the ponies, the signs of the foreign holidays, the expensive suits? If there was money here, it had not been spent for a long, long time.

They drove past a copse of yew trees, the rain momentarily stopping as they passed beneath the thick canopy of the branches—and as they did, a flurry of black and white swooped without warning from the tree above, and Mr. Treswick swerved and ground a tire on one of the granite boulders marking the edge of the drive.

"Damnation!" He sounded flustered as he righted their course, and drove more slowly up the final few yards to the house, the rain resuming as they left the shelter of the copse.

"What was it?" Hal asked, looking back over her shoulder. "A gull?"

"No, a magpie. The house is plagued with them—absolutely plagued. They can be surprisingly aggressive." He drove through a vaulted arch and slowed to a halt in a graveled carriage yard to the right of the main frontage. There he turned off the engine and wiped his palms shakily on his trousers. "It's supposed to be the origin of the name, you know. *Piasenn* is the Cornish word for magpie. And *tre* means farm or farmstead. So they say Trepassen is a corruption of Tre Piasenn—Magpie Farm. Whether that's true or not, I have no idea, but it certainly lives up to the name. Another theory holds that it's to do with the Cornish word for the past, *passyen*. Myself, I don't know. I'm no Cornish scholar, I'm afraid." He smoothed his hair and unclipped his seat belt, looking, for the first time since Hal had seen him, more than a little rattled. "I . . . I am not very *fond* of birds—it's something of a phobia. Much as I would love to overcome it, I have not been able to. And the magpies here . . ." He gave a little involuntary shudder. "Well, as I said, they are really rather numerous, and not at all shy. At least"—he reached for his umbrella and gave a small, rather mirthless smile—"at least in this house one has no danger of sorrow."

"Sorrow?" Hal said, startled.

"Why, yes, don't you know the rhyme? One for sorrow, two for joy, and so on? Although joy seems equally unlikely—I've never seen anything less than half a dozen magpies congregated here."

"Yes . . ." Hal said slowly. "Yes, I know the rhyme." Her hand went to her shoulder, and she touched the skin there, beneath the thin coat, remembering, and then let her hand drop. "At least . . . I know the first four lines. Does it go as far as six?"

"Oh yes," Mr. Treswick said, and then frowned. "Let me see . . . one for sorrow, two for joy, three for a girl, four for a boy. What's the next bit—five for silver . . . six I think is gold. Yes, that's right, six for gold."

Six for gold, Hal thought. She bit her lip. If she was superstitious, she might call that an omen. But she was not.

Years of working the cards had not made her more of a believer—if anything, quite the opposite. There were many readers out there who did believe, she had met them. But Hal knew, for she had seen it up close and personal, that signs and symbols were created by people looking for patterns and answers—in and of themselves, they meant nothing.

Now that Mr. Treswick had pointed them out, she could see the magpies, sheltering in the yew tree copse. Two were on the ground, pecking at the berries. Four up in the branches. And the last, the one that had dive-bombed the car, was sitting on the porch roof in the rain, looking balefully down at them.

"What about seven?" she said lightly. "More gold?"

"No," Mr. Treswick said with a laugh. "Alas not." He climbed out of the car and hurried round with the umbrella unfurled. He spoke above the sound of the rain drumming on the fabric. "Seven is the last line of the rhyme. Seven magpies are for a secret never to be told."

Perhaps it was the rain, or the wind that blew up the valley. But Hal could not help shivering as she took her case out of the car boot and followed Mr. Treswick, under cover of his umbrella, into the porch of Trepassen House.

4th December, 1994

I was sick again this morning, skittering down the steep stairs and down the long passageway to the toilet in my nightgown, kneeling on the cold tiled floor to heave up the last remains of yesterday's dinner.

Afterwards, I brushed my teeth, huffing on my hands to make sure my breath didn't have any telltale sourness, but when I opened the door to the corridor, Maud was standing outside, her arms crossed over the ratty old Smiths T-shirt that she wears instead of proper pyjamas.

She said nothing, but there was something in her expression that I didn't like. It was a look of mingled concern and something else, I'm not sure what. I think it might have been . . . pity? The thought made me angry.

She was leaning against the wall, blocking my way, and she didn't move as I came out and shut the bathroom door behind me.

"Sorry." I shook my hair back from my face, trying to look unconcerned. "Were you waiting long?"

"Yes," she said flatly. "Long enough. Are you all right?"

"Of course," I said, pushing past her, forcing her to step backwards against the wall. "Why wouldn't I be?" I called back over my shoulder.

She shrugged, but I know what she meant. I know exactly what she meant. I thought about the expression on her face, the way her flat black eyes followed me as I walked back to my attic. And as I sit here in bed writing this on my knees, watching the magpies swooping low over the snowy garden, I am wondering . . . how far can I trust her?

CHAPTER 11

Mr. Treswick led the way through a side entrance, into a vaulted vestibule tiled with red terra-cotta squares. Hal followed him in, shaking her head as the hiss of the rain was replaced with the hollow drip of water pattering from her coat, and Mr. Treswick's umbrella.

"Mrs. Warren!" he called, his voice echoing along the long corridor. "Oh, Mrs. Warren! It's Mr. Treswick."

There was a silence, and then Hal heard, as though from a great distance, the *click-click, click-click* of heels on the tiled floor, each set of steps followed by an unfamiliar *chink*. She turned her head, and through the glass panes of the door to her left, she saw an old lady dressed all in black half walking, half hobbling along the corridor.

"Is that Mrs. Warren?" she whispered to Mr. Treswick, before she could think better of the question. "But she looks—"

"She must be eighty if she's a day," Mr. Treswick said under his breath. "But she wouldn't hear of retirement while your grandmother was alive."

"Is that you, Bobby?"

Her accent was broad Cornish, and the voice was cracked as a raven's. Mr. Treswick winced, and in spite of her nerves, Hal was a little amused to see a flush of red on his gray-stubbled cheek. He removed his overcoat and coughed.

"It's Robert Treswick, Mrs. Warren," he called down the corridor, but she shook her head.

"Speak up, boy, I can't hear you. All you young people are the same. Mumble mumble."

As she came closer, Hal saw that she was using a cane, and the iron ferrule on the tiles was the *chink* she had heard. It gave her step an odd, uneven rhythm, *click-click . . . chink, click-click . . . chink.*

At long last she reached the door and paused to fumble with her cane, before Mr. Treswick sprang to hold the door open, and she hobbled through.

"So." She ignored Mr. Treswick, and her surprisingly dark, bright eyes settled on Hal. There was an expression in them that Hal couldn't read—but it wasn't warmth. Far from it. A kind of . . . speculation, perhaps? There was absolutely no smile in her voice as she said, "You're the girl. Well, well, well."

"I—" Hal swallowed. Her throat was dry as dust, and she became suddenly aware of her defensive stance—her folded arms, her hair hanging down to shield her eyes. *Think of the client,* her mother's voice in her head. *Think of what they want to see when they come to you.* She wished she had taken out her large thorn earring, but it was too late for that now. She forced a smile, making her face as open and unthreatening as possible. "Yes, that's me."

She held out a hand to shake, but the old lady turned away as if she hadn't seen it, and she was forced to let it drop.

"They didn't tell me if you were coming," Mrs. Warren shot over her shoulder, "but I had a room aired in case. You'll be wanting to change your clothes."

It was a command, not a request, and Hal nodded in meek agreement.

"Follow me," Mrs. Warren said, and Hal caught Mr. Treswick's eye and raised one eyebrow in mute question. He gave a little dry smile and waved his hand towards the stairs, but Mrs. Warren hadn't waited for Hal to acquiesce and was already making her way painfully up the long flight, step by step, her arthritic knuckles clamped to the banister.

"It'll have to be the attic," she said, as Hal hastened up after her, her case bumping each step. There were brass stair-rods across each tread, but so much dust had lodged in the crevices around them, it was almost impossible to see them, or the pattern of the carpet beneath.

"Of course," Hal said breathlessly, as they reached the landing, and Mrs. Warren began another flight, this one carpeted with a more utilitarian stair runner that felt hard and bumpy beneath Hal's feet. "No problem at all."

"There's no point in complaining," Mrs. Warren said grimly, as if Hal had done so. "No warning I had, so you'll have to put up with it."

"It's fine," Hal said. She pushed down the prickle of resentment at Mrs. Warren's manner and smiled again, hoping it showed through in her voice. "Honestly. I wouldn't dream of complaining. I'm very grateful to have a room at all."

They had reached what seemed to be the top landing. There were no more stairs from here—only a tiled passageway with a long row of what seemed to be bedrooms opening off either side. A window must have been open in one of the bedrooms, for there was a cold draft blowing, forceful enough to stir the dust around Hal's ankles as she stood.

"Lavatory is there," Mrs. Warren said shortly, nodding at a door at the far end of the tiled corridor. "The bathroom is a floor below."

The bathroom? Surely there had to be more than one bathroom for this whole house?

But Mrs. Warren had opened one of the doors that Hal had taken to be bedrooms, revealing a narrow staircase set into the wall. She pressed a light switch, and a bare bulb at the top flickered and illuminated a narrow flight, this one bare wood, with no carpet, not even drugget, just a thin strip of lino at the top landing. The old lady started up the steps, her metal-tipped cane thudding against the wood as she climbed.

Hal waited at the foot of the stairs, under the pretense of catching her breath.

There was something she didn't like about that staircase—perhaps it was the narrowness of it, or the lack of natural light, for there were no windows, not even a skylight, or perhaps it was the way that it seemed to be shut away from the rest of the house, the door at the bottom hiding its very existence. But she swallowed, and pushing the door as wide as she could, she hitched up her case and followed Mrs. Warren up the final flight.

"Is this where the servants used to sleep?" she asked, hearing her voice echo in the confined space.

"No," Mrs. Warren said shortly, without turning back. Hal felt snubbed, but when they reached the landing, Mrs. Warren stopped and looked at her, and seemed to relent a little. "Not anymore. They moved the servants' quarters over the kitchen when they rebuilt," she said. "Of course, they're all shut up now, there's only me left and I sleep downstairs, next to Mrs. Westaway's room, in case she needed me in the night."

"I see," Hal said humbly. She shivered. She had never felt more out of place, in her draggled wet coat, her laddered tights, her short black hair drying into spikes from the rain. "She was lucky to have you."

"She was," Mrs. Warren said. Her mouth was a thin line of pinched disapproval. "God knows the family cared little enough for her comfort, though I see you're all happy enough to come down picking like magpies over the spoils now."

"I—I didn't—" Hal started, nettled, but then stopped as Mrs. Warren turned away and hobbled down a short, unlit corridor towards a closed door, rattling the knob with her gnarled hand. What could she say? It was true, after all, at least as far as she herself was concerned. She let her mouth fall shut and waited as Mrs. Warren struggled with the stiff knob, her cane clamped under her arm.

"Damp," Mrs. Warren said shortly over her shoulder, as she tugged at the knob. "Frame swells."

"Can I—" Hal began, but it was too late—as the words left her mouth, the door gave suddenly, and a flood of cold light illuminated the landing.

Mrs. Warren stood back and let Hal pass through. Inside was a narrow little room, painfully bare, with a metal bedstead in one corner, a washstand in the other, and a barred nursery window overlooking the garden. There was no carpet, only bare boards, and a tiny knotted rug by the head of the bed. There was also no radiator, just a small grate filled with coal and kindling already laid out.

The bars gave Hal a strange feeling in the pit of her stomach, though she could not have said why. Perhaps it was the incongruity of finding them up here, in the attic. On the ground floor they might have been needed to keep out intruders. But up here there was only one explanation: these were bars not to keep someone out—but *in*. Only . . . this was not a nursery room, where the bars might be needed to safeguard a clambering toddler. It was a maid's room, far from the rest of the house, totally impractical for a small child.

What kind of person needed to stop their maids from escaping?

"Well, here you are," Mrs. Warren said irritably. "There's matches on the mantelpiece, but we're short of coal, so don't be thinking you can have a fire willy-nilly, now. There's no money to burn. I'll leave you to unpack."

"Th-thank you," Hal said. The little room was extremely cold, and her teeth chattered, though she tried to keep her jaw clenched tight to stop it. "Wh-when should I c-come down?"

"The others aren't here yet," Mrs. Warren said, seeming to answer her question without quite doing so. "No doubt they went around by the coast road, it's always bad this time of year with the storms."

And she turned, before Hal could ask any more questions, and stumped off down the narrow stairs. Hal waited, and heard the door at the bottom slam smartly shut, and then she sank down on the little bed and took in her surroundings.

The room was barely a couple of meters side to side, and the barred window gave it the feeling of a cell, even with the door open. It was also achingly cold. As the air settled around her, Hal realized that she could see her breath if she huffed hard enough. There was a mint-green eiderdown on the bed, and Hal pulled it off the mattress and wrapped it around her shoulders. The fragile satin pulled beneath her fingers so that she was afraid the fabric might disintegrate in her grip, but she was too cold to sit without some kind of warmth.

She thought about lighting the fire, but it seemed pointless when she would have to go downstairs to face the family. And just the thought of asking the disapproving Mrs. Warren for another scuttle of coal made Hal quail, remembering her thinned lips and grim expression.

Did Mrs. Warren dislike *all* the family this much, or was it just Hal? she wondered. Perhaps it was because of the short notice of her arrival—though Mrs. Warren hadn't seemed exactly surprised. Perhaps it was Hal's bedraggled dress and shoes. Or could it be . . . did she suspect something? There had been something Hal couldn't quite pin down in her expression, when she saw Hal, a kind of wary . . . calculation. It was the look, Hal suddenly thought, of a child who sees a cat appear among a flock of pigeons, and stands back to watch the slaughter. What did it mean?

Hal shivered again, in spite of the eiderdown, and then, remembering her vow on the journey over, she pulled her phone out of her bag and opened up the search screen. Her fingers, as she typed the words in the search box, were stiff and reluctant, and not only with cold, and she paused for a long moment before she hit the search button.

Maud Westaway St. Piran missing dead

Then she pressed ENTER.

The little icon whirred for a long time, long enough for Hal to look doubtfully at the coverage bars in the top right-hand corner of the screen. Two out of five. Not great . . . but it should be enough to get some kind of Internet, surely?

At last the results flashed up on the screen, and Hal felt her stomach flip, for there, right at the top of the list, was the piece she had known would come up. It was a newspaper link about her mother's death.

Maud Westaway St. Piran missing dead said the grayed-out text beneath the link, showing that it didn't tick all the search boxes, but that, nonetheless, this piece was the best match.

Hal didn't click. She didn't need to. The information she needed didn't lie in this piece, with its lurid details and sorrowful tone. *Self-styled psychic practitioner,* Hal remembered, and *familiar local figure in her characterful dress,* as though her mother were one step away from a medicated stay in a secure facility, rather than a cheerful, down-to-earth woman making a living for herself and her child in the best way she could.

Great loss to the pier community, though, that was true.

Hal still remembered the way they had gathered round her when she returned to her mother's booth, the mute sympathy on their faces, the way she had found that for months and months afterwards, cups of hot tea would be left quietly outside her kiosk on cold days, how the mistakes in the change at the fish-and-chips stand were somehow always in her favor.

Now she blinked as she scrolled past the links about the crash, her vision blurring as she tried to make out the text in the other pieces. She clicked through to a few, but none of them were related. There was a missing West Highland terrier in St. Piran, and a slew of totally irrelevant links from baby name websites and the St. Piran tourist board.

At last, she shut down the screen, drew the eiderdown around her shoulders, and simply sat, looking out of the little barred window across the rain-spattered garden.

Whoever Maud Westaway had been, whatever had happened to her, she seemed to have gone without a trace.

CHAPTER 12

It was the sound of tires on the gravel outside the window that made Hal's head jerk up, breaking into her thoughts. The satin eiderdown slithered from her shoulders and she snatched for it reflexively, shivering in the sudden gust of cold wind, and then let it fall as she went to the window to see who had arrived.

She could not see the faces of the people below, only the tops of their heads and their umbrellas as they hurried across to the main doors, but she could see the parked cars—they were the two long black sedans, sleek as sharks, that had made up the funeral cortège.

The family had arrived. The real test was about to begin.

She felt suddenly sick with nerves, lightheaded with tension. This was it. A face-to-face encounter with her supposed relatives. Was she really going to do this?

She played people for a living—in her moments of clear-eyed honesty, she knew that. But this was different. This wasn't just telling gullible people what they wanted to hear or already knew. This was a *crime.*

"Bugger tea," Hal heard, floating up the stairwell as she reached the bottom of the narrow attic staircase. "Brandy's what I want—or whiskey, if you can't do that, Mrs. Warren."

Hal heard no reply from Mrs. Warren, but there was a remark from one of the other brothers and a gust of laughter, and she heard one of Harding's children complaining at having to put away his phone.

This was it. *The moment of truth.* The words floated into her head unbidden, and she let out a short laugh. Truth? No. Lies. The moment of lies.

She had been preparing for this her whole life.

If anyone can do this, you can, Hal.

She flexed her fingers, feeling like a boxer before the fight—no, that wasn't quite right, for this was going to be a test of mental agility, not physical. Like a grand master before a chess match, perhaps. She saw herself, as if from above, her hand hovering over a pawn, ready to make the first move.

The cold seemed to be leaving her now, and her face felt flushed and hot with anticipation as she descended the next flight of stairs, her heart beating hard beneath the black dress.

"Let's see if we can't get you some hot chocolate, darling," she heard from a female voice—not Mrs. Warren, for it was clipped and rather monied. Mitzi, presumably? "That morbid wait by the grave was the absolute limit, Harding. Kitty's frozen, where are the bloody radiators in this place?"

"There aren't any, Mit, you know that perfectly well. But I expect there's a fire in the drawing room," Hal heard.

As she rounded the corner of the stairs she saw them all: Harding struggling out of a Barbour jacket; Abel tapping on his phone in the corner of the room, still in his raincoat; Mitzi pulling layers off the children.

Not one of them looked up as she began to make her way down the final flight, until she stepped on a loose board, and Ezra's head came up.

"Hellooo . . ." he drawled, and Hal felt her face flush as all the heads turned towards her, their expressions ranging from curiosity to frank surprise. "I saw you at the funeral, didn't I?"

"Yes," Hal said. She swallowed. Her throat felt dry and sore, almost as if a thorn were stuck there, digging in. "Yes, my—my name is Hal, short for Harriet. Harriet Westaway."

Their faces didn't change until a little dry cough came from behind Harding's shoulder.

"Harriet is . . . Maud's daughter."

It was Mr. Treswick who had spoken, and his quiet voice cut through the chatter in the hallway like a knife through cheese.

The name plainly meant nothing to younger members of the group, nor to Mitzi, who carried on as if he hadn't spoken, shooing her children towards a room up the corridor, complaining audibly as she departed about the smell of damp.

But to the three brothers, it was as if he had sworn, or smashed the empty china vase standing at the foot of the stairs. Harding felt for the chair behind him and sat down abruptly, as if he no longer trusted his legs. Abel gave an audible gasp, and his hand went to his collar. Only Ezra didn't move. He went quite still, and his face turned pale.

"She had—she had a child?" It was Harding who spoke first, the words clotted and thick as though he had to force them out. "Why didn't we know?"

"No one knew," Mr. Treswick said. "Except, evidently, your late mother. Perhaps your sister told her, I am not certain."

But Abel was shaking his head.

"She had a *child*," he said, repeating his brother's words, but with an entirely different emphasis, as if he could not believe the words, or the reality behind them. "She had a *child*? But—but it makes no sense."

Hal felt her stomach shift, and she gripped the banister tightly, feeling her sweaty palm slide against the polished wood.

"It makes no sense!" Abel repeated. "She wasn't—she didn't—"

"Nevertheless," Mr. Treswick said, "here is Harriet."

Hal took a step down into the hallway, feeling her heart beating fast and hard inside her chest, thinking of the part she had to play.

It's natural for you to be nervous, she told herself. *You're meeting your family for the first time. You can use this fear—make it your own.*

"I didn't know I had an uncle," she said, not trying to hide the tremor in her voice, as she held out her hand towards Harding. "L-let alone three."

And he took it, his fingers warm and thick around her cold ones, and shook it, hard, in both of his, as if that handshake could somehow seal a bond between them.

"Well, well, well," he was saying. "Very pleased to meet you, Harriet."

But it was Abel who pulled her into a hug, crushing her glasses into his damp raincoat, so hard that she could feel his heart beating beneath her cheek.

"Welcome home," was all he said, his voice shaking with a kind of painful sincerity. "Oh, Harriet. Welcome *home*."

5th December, 1994

Maud knows. She came to my room last night after I had gone to bed, but I knew before that—I knew from her expression as she watched me over the dinner table, pushing the congealing cod and limp broccoli around my plate with my fork, feeling the nausea rise at the back of my throat.

I knew then, from the look she gave me, and the way she shoved her plate away and stood up, that she had guessed.

"Sit down," her mother snapped. "You do not leave this table without asking permission."

Maud gave her a look close to hate, but she sat back down.

"May I leave the table?" she said, spitting each word out as if it were one of the stray bones from the cod, arrayed around the edge of her plate.

Her mother looked at her, and I saw a flicker of something pass over her face—a desire to thwart, mixed with the knowledge that one day she is going to push Maud too far, and that if Maud defied her, there would be nothing she could do in the end.

"You . . . may," she said at last, though the last word was dragged out. But then as Maud stood, she added, "when you have finished your fish."

"I can't eat it," Maud said. She threw her napkin on the table. "Nor can Maggie. Look at it—it's disgusting. Nothing but bones and tasteless white shit."

I saw the tip of my aunt's nose go white, as it always does when she is furious.

"You will not speak about the food in this house that way," she said.

"I won't lie about it either—God knows there are enough lies in this house already!"

"What does that mean?"

Her mother stood now too, and they faced each other, so alike, and yet so different—Maud is hot where her mother is cold, passionate where her mother is contained, but the bitterness and anger in each face made them look more alike than I ever realised before.

"You know what it means."

With that, Maud picked up the flaccid piece of cod with her fingers and crammed it into her mouth. I thought I heard the bones crunch as she chewed, and I felt the nausea rise up in my throat, making me sweat with the effort of containing it.

"Happy?" Maud said, though the word was barely comprehensible through the suffocating mouthful.

Then, without waiting for an answer, she turned on her heel and left, slamming the dining room door behind her so that the china rattled on the table.

I bent my head over my plate, and trying not to let my shaking hands show, I speared a potato on my fork and put it into my mouth, my eyes blurring.

Don't look at me, *I thought desperately, knowing how my aunt's white-cold anger could redirect onto whoever was unlucky enough to catch her attention.* Don't look at me.

But she didn't. Instead I heard the screech of her chair legs on the parquet, and the slam of the door on the other side of the room, and when I looked up I was blessedly, entirely alone.

It was much later that Maud came to my room. I was sitting in bed in my dressing gown, a hot-water bottle at my feet, sorting my cards. I heard feet on the stairs, and at first my stomach clenched, not sure who it was, but then there came a tap on the wooden door, and I knew.

"Maud?"

"Yes, it's me." Her voice was low, and I could tell she didn't want anyone to hear. "Can I come in?"

"Yes," I whispered back, and the handle turned, and she came into the room, ducking her head beneath the low attic doorway. She was wrapped in a huge cardigan, and her feet were bare. "God, aren't you freezing?" I asked, and she nodded, her teeth chattering. Without speaking I pushed over in the narrow bed and patted the pillow beside me, and she climbed in, her feet like ice as she slid them down past my legs.

"I hate her," was all she said. "I hate her so much. How can you stand to be here?"

I have no other choice, *was what I thought, but I knew that I had as many choices as Maud, maybe more.*

"She acts like it's the 1950s," Maud said bitterly. "No TV, you and me shut up here like fucking nuns, Mrs Warren toiling away in the kitchen—does she realise people don't live like this any more? Other people our age are out there going to gigs, getting drunk, screwing each other—don't you care that we're shut up here in Mother's post-war fantasyland?"

I didn't know what to say. I couldn't tell her that I had never wanted to get drunk or go to gigs. That I never had—even when I had the chance.

"Maybe I fit in with it better than you," I said at last. "Mum always said I was an old-fashioned little thing."

"Tell me about your mum," she said quietly, and I felt a lump rise in my throat—thinking of Mum as she always is in my mind's eye—digging in the garden, with Dad alongside her, humming along to Paul Simon, hoeing the onions or planting bulbs. I tried not to think of those last nightmare months—Mum gasping her last on a ventilator, and Dad's heart attack a few weeks later.

"What's to tell?" I said, trying not to sound as bitter as I felt. "She's dead. They're both dead. End of."

The unfairness of it still makes me gasp—but there's a kind of rightness in it too, that's what I've realised. I was the child of two people completely in love. They were meant to be together—in life, and in death. I just wish that that death hadn't come so soon.

"I want to understand . . ." Maud said, her voice very low. "I want to understand what it must be like not . . . not to hate your mother."

This time, it wasn't the chill of her feet, but the venom in her voice that made me shiver.

My aunt isn't an easy woman—I know that—I knew that before I even came to live here. The fact that she had managed to fight with my father told me everything I needed to know. He was the most mild-mannered man you can imagine. But nothing had prepared me for the reality of what I found here.

"I wish I could get away," she spoke with quiet venom, into her knees. "She let him *go."*

She didn't say who—she didn't have to say. We both knew who she was talking about. Ezra, away at boarding school. He had escaped.

"Is it the boy thing, do you think?" I asked.

Maud shrugged, trying to look unconcerned, but I wasn't fooled. Her cheeks were wet where she had cried after supper.

"Girls aren't worth educating," she said, with a bitter little laugh. "Or not worth paying to educate, anyway. But whatever she thinks, I've got twice his brains. I'll be at Oxford while he's still sitting retakes at some shitty crammer in Surrey. I'm going to show her, this summer. Those exams are my ticket out of here."

I didn't say what I was thinking. Which was—what about me? If Maud leaves, what will I do? Will I be imprisoned here, alone, with her*?*

"I used to hate this room," Maud said softly. "She used to lock us in here as children, for punishment. But now . . . I don't know. It feels like an escape from the rest of the house."

There was a long silence. I tried to imagine it—tried to imagine having a mother who would do that—and what it would do to you as a child to suffer through that—and my imagination failed.

"Can I sleep here tonight?" she asked, and I nodded.

She rolled over, and I switched out the light and turned on my side, my back to her, and we lay in the darkness, feeling the warmth of each other at our spines, and the shift and creak of the mattress whenever the other moved.

I was almost asleep when she spoke, her voice a whisper so soft I wasn't sure at first if she was speaking, or sighing in her sleep.

"Maggie, what are you going to do?"

I didn't answer. I just lay there, staring into the blackness, feeling my heart beating hard in my chest at her words.

She knows.

CHAPTER 13

The next half hour was a blur of questions and evasions, harder than Hal had ever imagined, but strangely exhilarating at the same time.

As she stumbled through the conversation, desperately trying to remember what she had said to whom, she found herself abandoning the chess analogy and returning to the image of herself as a boxer, strapping up her knuckles before clambering into the ring to dodge punches, sidestep questions, and turn awkward inquiries back onto the person opposite her.

And yet, this was no one-to-one sparring match. A single opponent would have been a setup much more within her comfort zone. She was used to that—although this was very far from the controlled environment of her little kiosk. But this confused melee was something entirely different: jumbled voices, cutting across each other, prodding her for answers before she had finished responding to another speaker, butting in with anecdotes and reminiscences. It was so unlike what she was accustomed to that she felt almost punch-drunk, pummeled by the sound.

All her life family had meant one thing—her and her mother. The two of them, bound together, self-sufficient. Growing up, Hal had never felt that there was anything missing, but she had sometimes yearned for the big family holidays of other children at school, the endless ranks of brothers and sisters and cousins to play with, and piles of presents at Christmas and birthdays that came from a large tribe of relatives.

Now—as they crowded around her, talking over each other in jangling voices, asking her about her upbringing, her schooling, her current situation—she found herself wondering how she could ever have envied the other children their uncles and aunts.

Harding was the most difficult—direct question after direct question, barked in that rather sergeant-major voice, like an interrogation. Abel's style was very different, lighter, friendlier; time and again when Hal ran up against something she couldn't answer, he broke in with a chuckle and an anecdote of his own. Ezra said nothing, but Hal felt his eyes upon her, watching.

It was Mitzi who interrupted at last with a laugh that Hal would have found grating under other circumstances.

"Good heavens, boys!" She pushed into the circle of dark suits, swatting Abel on the shoulder and taking Hal's hand. "Leave the poor girl alone for a few minutes! Look at her—she's quite overwhelmed. Can I offer you some tea, Hal?"

"Y-yes," Hal said. "Yes p-please."

On the pier she tried to hide her occasional stammer, and she deliberately kept her voice low and slow, to seem older than her years and emphasize the fact that she was in control, and the querent was on her territory. Here, she realized, as Mitzi led her away from the group, her discomfort was her alibi, and she could use it to her own ends. She shouldn't try to hide her confusion, or her youth—far from it. As she followed Mitzi across the drawing room, she hunched her shoulders to make her already slight frame seem even smaller, let her hair fall over her face like a shy teenager. People tended to underestimate Hal. Sometimes, that could be an advantage.

She let Mitzi usher her to a sofa by the fire, where one of the Westaway grandsons was sitting, jabbing at his phone in a way that made Hal think he must be playing some kind of game. It wasn't Richard. Who was the other one . . . Freddie?

"There you go," Mitzi said comfortingly, as Hal sat down. "Now, can I get you something? Are you old enough for a glass of wine?"

Yes, and have been for several years, Hal thought, but she didn't say that. Drinking here would not be a good idea. Instead she gave a deliberately uncertain laugh.

"I'd prefer that tea you mentioned, thank you."

"I'll be right back," Mitzi said, and tapped her son sharply on the head. "Freddie, turn that off."

Freddie didn't even pretend to put his phone down as his mother left, but he glanced sideways at Hal.

"Hi," Hal said. "I'm Harriet."

"Hi, Harriet. What's your tattoo?"

"My tattoo?" Hal was momentarily surprised, and then realized that the cotton dress had slipped a little, showing one shoulder, and the tip of a wing. "Oh, this one?" She pointed to her back, and he nodded.

"Looks like a bird."

"It's a magpie."

"Cool." He spoke without looking up, apparently negotiating a tricky bit of the game. Then he added, "I want to get a tattoo, but Mum says over her dead body."

"It's illegal before you're eighteen," Hal said briefly. Here at least she was on safe ground. "No reputable tattooist would agree to it, and you don't want to be going to the ones who would. How old are you?"

"Twelve," he said sadly. He shut down his phone and looked up at her for the first time. "Can I see it?"

"Um . . ." She felt an instant sense of intrusion, but she didn't know what else to say. "I—yes. I guess."

She turned, and felt him pull down the cotton of the neckline, exposing the bird, its head cocked to one side. His fingers were cold against her skin, and she tried not to shiver.

"Cool," he said again, enviously this time. "Did you pick it because of this place? You know—all of them." He waved a hand at the trees outside the window, and Hal turned. It was too dark to make out much more than the light from the window glittering on wet boughs, but in her mind's eye she saw again the line of magpies perched on the dripping branches of the yew. She shook her head, pulling the neckline of her dress back up to cover the bird.

"No. My—my mum's n—"

Too late she realized she had let her guard down and had been on the verge of making a horrifying mistake. The truth was that she had got the tattoo in memory of her mother. Margarida. One for sorrow. It had seemed apt at the time. But cold horror washed over her at the realization that she had been about to admit her mother's real name. Stupid, *stupid*.

"Her—her nickname for me was Magpie," she said, after a pause long enough to feel like a chasm opening beneath her feet. As cover stories went, it was beyond lame, but it was the best she could manage on the hop. Regardless, the boy didn't seem to have noticed the yawning pause.

"Is she Dad's sister?" he asked.

Hal nodded. "Yes."

"Well, I guess I should say *was* Dad's sister. She's dead, right?"

"Freddie!" Mitzi came up with a cup of tea, and when she set it down on the table she lightly slapped her son's knee. "That is not—I'm *so* sorry, Harriet. He's a teenage boy—what can I say."

"It's okay," Hal said, truthfully. It wasn't just the nugget of fact he had held out to her, confirming what she had already guessed. It was the fact that she was suddenly on safe ground here. There was no shock in hearing the words from other people—in fact, she preferred the boy's bluntness, rather than the delicate *passed away*, or *fell asleep* that some people used. It wasn't true. Her mother was not asleep, or in the next room. She was dead. No amount of euphemism would soften that fact. And this, at least, was true.

"Yes, she's dead," she said to Freddie. "I got this tattoo in her memory."

"Cool," the boy said again, semiautomatically. He looked awkward now, in the presence of his mother. "Do you have any others?"

"Yes," Hal said, at the same time that Mitzi broke in.

"Freddie, for heaven's sake, stop bothering poor Harriet with personal questions. This isn't appropriate conversation for—"

She stopped, the words *a funeral* unspoken on her lips.

Hal smiled, or tried to, and picked up the tea.

"Really, it's fine." Questions about her tattoos were easier to answer than the ones Abel, Harding, and Ezra had been asking. She felt a shift in her stomach as she saw Harding pat one of his brothers on the shoulder and then follow his wife over to the fire.

"Warming up, Harriet?" he said as he came up to the little knot seated on the sofa. "Very wise. This place is nothing short of perishing, I'm afraid. Mother didn't really believe in modern comforts like central heating."

"Has it—has it been in the family long?" Hal asked. She remembered her mother's advice about conducting readings: *Don't let* them *ask all the questions, ask some of your own. It's easier to direct the conversation if you're in the driving seat, and they'll feel flattered if you show an interest.* "My mother didn't ever talk about this place," she added honestly.

"Oh, donkey's years, I believe," Harding said carelessly. He settled himself with his back to the fire, fanning up the hem of his jacket to let the heat reach his back. "The oldest part of the building is this bit where we're sitting now, which was built in the seventeen hundreds and was quite a modest farm for many years. Then your great-great-grandfather—my mother's grandfather—made rather a lot of money in the late eighteen hundreds from china clay, up near St. Austell, and he used it to completely revamp the place in rather grand style. He kept the Georgian core of the old farmhouse as the reception rooms and main bedrooms, but built a sprawl of wings and servants' quarters in the Arts and Crafts style, turning it into quite an imposing place. However, unfortunately his son wasn't a very good businessman and he lost control of the mine to his business partner. Since then there's been very little money for upkeep, so the house is somewhat frozen in the nineteen twenties. It needs a good million-pound investment to bring it up to spec, certainly not money your average buyer has hanging around, though it's the sort of thing one of the big hotel chains might accomplish. Of course, the land is what's really worth the money now." He looked out of the window, across the rain-swept expanse of grass, and Hal could almost see him calculating—imagining identical new homes sprouting up like mushrooms, hearing the *ker-ching* of cash registers as each new seed germinated into a sale.

Hal nodded, and sipped her tea for want of something to say. Her hands were still cold, in spite of the heat of the fire, but her cheeks felt hot, and all of a sudden she sneezed, and then shivered convulsively.

"Bless you," Abel said.

Harding had taken a step backwards, almost tripping over the fender.

"Oh dear, I hope you haven't caught a cold at the graveside."

"I doubt it," Hal said. "I'm very tough." But she ruined the words by sneezing again. Abel pulled out a beautifully laundered cotton handkerchief and held it out solicitously, but Hal shook her head.

"Biscuit, Hal?" Mitzi said, and Hal took one, remembering that she had not eaten since that morning on the train. But when she put the shortbread in her mouth it tasted dry and stale, and she was not sorry when there was a cough from the other end of the room, and Mr. Treswick raised his voice above the conversation.

"If I might have a moment of your attention, everyone?"

Harding shot a look at Abel, who shrugged, and the two men made their way down the long room towards the lawyer, who was standing beside a grand piano, shuffling papers. Hal half rose from the sofa, but then stood uncertainly, unsure whether the summons included her, until Mr. Treswick said, "You too, Harriet."

He put down his file of papers and walked to the door, opening it to the corridor so that Hal felt the draft of cold air from outside, a sharp contrast to the fire-warmed room.

"Mrs. Warren!" he called, his voice echoing along the passage-way. "Do you have a moment?"

"Are the children needed?" Mitzi said, and Mr. Treswick shook his head.

"No, not unless they would like to listen. But if Ezra could join us . . . where is he, by the way?"

"I think he went outside for a smoke," Abel said. He disappeared for a moment and came back with his brother in tow, rain misted in his dark, curly hair.

"Sorry." Ezra's smile was somehow a little twisted, as if there were a joke only he was party to. "I didn't realize you were going to be pulling the old Hercule Poirot thing, Mr. Treswick. Are you about to reveal Mother's murderer?"

"Not at all," Mr. Treswick said, his face tightly disapproving. He shuffled his papers again and pushed his glasses up his nose with his knuckle, plainly ruffled by Ezra's levity. "And I hardly think that's appropriate given—well. Never mind." He coughed again, rather artificially, and seemed to marshal his thoughts. "Regardless, thank you all for this moment of your time. This won't take very long, but it's my understanding from speaking to Mrs. Westaway that she hadn't discussed her testamentary arrangements with her children. Is that correct?"

Harding was frowning.

"Not discussed, as such, no, but there was a very clear understanding, following my father's death, that she would continue to live in the house until her own passing, at which point it would pass—"

"Well, that is my concern," Mr. Treswick said hastily. "That there should not be any mistaken assumptions. I strongly encourage all clients to discuss their wills with the beneficiaries, but of course not all choose to do so, and it's my understanding that your mother didn't communicate her intentions to anyone."

There was the sound of a cane in the hallway and Mrs. Warren came into the room.

"What is it?" she said, rather crossly. And then, seeing one of Harding's children putting coal onto the fire, "Don't go wasting coal, young man."

"Do you have a moment, Mrs. Warren? I wanted to talk to all beneficiaries of Mrs. Westaway's will, and it seems fairest to do it at the same time."

"Oh," said Mrs. Warren, and a look came over her face that Hal couldn't quite pin down. There was something . . . expectant about it. But Hal didn't think it was greed. More a kind of . . . trepidation. It might almost have been glee. Did Mrs. Warren know something the others did not?

Abel pulled out the piano stool, and the housekeeper seated herself, resting her cane against her lap. Mr. Treswick cleared his throat, picked up the file of papers from the polished piano top, and shuffled them again, quite unnecessarily. Every inch of him, from his polished brogues to his wire-rimmed spectacles, signaled nervous discomfort, and Hal felt the back of her neck prickle. She saw a concerned frown line knitting an anxious furrow between Abel's brows.

"Well, now. I will try to keep this brief—I'm not in favor of the Victorian-style theatrics involved in public will readings, but there is something to be said for transparency in these matters, and the last thing I would want is people committing themselves on a mistaken assumption of—"

"For goodness' sake, spit it out, man," Harding broke in impatiently.

"Harding—" Abel put a placating hand on his brother's arm, but Harding shook it off.

"Don't 'Harding' me, Abel. Clearly there's something he's circling around, and I for one would like to cut to the chase and find out what it is. Did Mother go cracked and leave everything to Battersea Dogs Home or something?"

"Not quite," Mr. Treswick said. His eyes darted to Harding, and then to Hal, to Mrs. Warren, and then back to Harding, and he reordered the papers again and settled his glasses more firmly on the bridge of his nose. "The, um, the long and short of it is this: the estate comprises some three hundred thousand pounds in cash and securities, most of which will be swallowed up by death duties, and the house itself, which is yet to be valued but is by far the most substantial part of the whole, and will certainly run in excess of a million pounds, possibly two, depending on circumstances. Mrs. Westaway left several specific bequests: thirty thousand pounds to Mrs. Warren"—the housekeeper gave a tight nod—"and ten thousand pounds to each of her grandchildren . . ."

At those words, Hal felt her pulse quicken and her cheeks flush.

Ten thousand pounds? *Ten thousand pounds?* Why, she could pay off Mr. Smith, pay the rent, the gas bill . . . she could even afford to take a holiday. A flickering warmth was spreading through her, as though she had drunk something particularly hot and nourishing. She tried not to smile. Tried to remember that there were a lot of hoops still to negotiate. But the words kept repeating themselves inside her head. Ten thousand pounds. Ten thousand *pounds.*

It was all she could do to stay still on the spot, when every particle of her wanted to dance with excitement. Could it be true?

But Mr. Treswick was still speaking.

". . . excepting, that is, her granddaughter Harriet."

Oh.

The sensation was like a balloon, pricked of air, collapsing in on itself into a sad little pile of colored rubber faster than it took to describe.

In that one sentence, it was over. She imagined the ten thousand pounds blowing away into the sea breeze, the notes fluttering over the cliff edge into the Atlantic.

There was a wrench in letting the dream go, but as she watched the notes disappear in her mind's eye, she realized: it had been an absurd fantasy to think that she could get away with this. Farcical, really. Forged birth certificates, fake dates of birth. What had she been thinking?

Well, it was over, but at least she hadn't been found out. She was no worse off than she had been before. As for what she would do about Mr. Smith and his messengers . . . well, she couldn't think about that now. She just had to get through this, and get away.

It felt cruel, though, to have the promise dangled before her for that one moment, only to be snatched away.

As the adrenaline of exhilaration ebbed, a sense of great exhaustion was creeping through her, and Hal put out a hand to steady herself on a chair as Mr. Treswick cleared his throat, preparatory to continuing.

"To Harriet," he said, a little awkwardly, and he shuffled the papers again, as if reluctant to say what was coming, "to, um, Harriet, Mrs. Westaway has left the entire residue of her estate, after payment of death duties."

There was a long silence.

It was Harding who exploded first, his voice breaking into the hush. *"What?"*

"I did realize that this was liable to be something of a shock," Mr. Treswick said diffidently. "That was why I felt it only right to inform you pers—"

"To hell with that!" Harding shouted. "Are you insane?"

"Please don't raise your voice, Mr. Westaway. It's unfortunate that your mother didn't see fit to discuss this with you while she was still—"

"I want to see the wording," Harding said through gritted teeth.

"Wording?"

"The will. The wording of the bequest. We'll challenge it. Mother must have been crazy—when was this monstrosity dated?"

"She made her will two years ago, Mr. Westaway, and I'm afraid that while I appreciate your concern, there is no question of Mrs. Westaway's capacity. She asked her doctor to visit her on the day she made the will, with a view, I believe, towards avoiding any such successful challenge."

"Undue influence, then!"

"I don't believe Mrs. Westaway had ever met her granddaughter, so it's hard to see how that would stand up in co—"

"Give me the damn will!" Harding shouted, and he snatched at the pieces of paper Mr. Treswick held out.

Hal was holding on tight to the back of the chair, her fingers numb and white with pressure, feeling the eyes of Mitzi, Abel, and Ezra on her as Harding scanned down the long document, and began to read aloud.

"*I, Hester Mary Westaway, being of* . . . God, there's pages of this stuff. . . . Ah, here we are: *And to my granddaughter, Harriet Westaway, last known to be resident at Marine View Villas, Brighton, I give the residue of my estate*—Jesus fucking Christ, it's true. Mother must have been mad."

He groped his way to a sofa and sat, heavily, scanning up and down the document as if looking for some kind of explanation, something that would make this madness go away. When he looked up, his face was purple and suffused with blood.

"Who even is this girl? We don't know her from Adam!"

"Harding," Abel said warningly, and he put out a hand to his brother's shoulder. "Calm down. This isn't the time for—"

"And as for you, Treswick, you bloody charlatan. What business had you letting Mother execute a document like this? I should sue you for malpractice!"

"*Harding,*" Mitzi broke in more urgently. "Abel, Mr. Treswick—look at the girl."

"I think she's going to faint," said a voice, tinged with a sort of detached interest, from Hal's right, and she felt all the heads in the room turn towards her, even as the room itself began to disintegrate into fragments.

Hal didn't feel the chair slip from her loosening grip, and Mitzi's cry of alarm came as if from a great way off.

She didn't even feel the thump as she hit the floor.

The nothing washed over her, like a great, thankful wave.

CHAPTER 14

"Harriet."

The voice in Hal's ears was persistent, dredging her up from far below, where she seemed to have been drifting a great while.

"*Harriet.* Come on now, it's time to wake up."

And then, as if to someone else, "Her temperature's still high. Her forehead feels like a radiator."

Hal blinked, screwing up her eyes against a brightness that hurt.

"What—how . . ." Her throat was sore and dry.

"Oh, thank goodness. We were getting worried!" It was a woman's voice, and Hal blinked again and reached for her glasses. She slipped them over her ears, and the room slid into focus. First Mitzi's face, and then behind her the figure of a man—Abel, she thought. Everything came back—St. Piran. The funeral. The house. And—oh God—that scene with Harding . . .

"Here," Mitzi said. There was a rustle, and a glass of water loomed under Hal's nose. "Have some of this. You've been asleep for ages. You must be very dehydrated."

"I—what time is it?"

"Getting on for nine. We were getting quite worried. Abel and I were just discussing whether we should take you to A and E."

"Wh-what happened?"

Looking down, Hal saw she was lying on a couch of some kind, her dress rucked up to her thighs, although, thank God, there was a blanket over her legs. The room was one she didn't recognize—some kind of library, by the looks of it, with honey-colored shelves rising to a high, damp-speckled ceiling, and ranks of peeling leather-bound books, swathed in cobwebs.

"You just keeled over, and when we went to try to help you, you were burning up. It's a good job you're a skinny little thing."

"How are you feeling, Harriet?" It was Abel, speaking for the first time, his light tenor soft and anxious. He came and knelt beside the couch, and touched her gently on the forehead. Hal had to fight not to pull away from the intrusion of his touch, but his knuckles were cool. "Do you want us to call a doctor?"

"A doctor?" Hal struggled up against the sofa cushions, setting dust motes spinning in the golden light of the reading lamp. She imagined Abel picking her up from the floor, her skirt around her hips, and felt her cheeks flare with heat. "God, no. I mean, thank you—but I don't think . . ."

"I'm not sure our chances of getting an out-of-hours GP are very good," Abel said. He stroked his mustache thoughtfully. "But if you're feeling nauseated, perhaps we should try A and E."

"I don't need a doctor," Hal said, trying to sound firm.

"She's still very hot," Mitzi said, talking over Hal as if she hadn't spoken. "Do you think your mother has a thermometer anywhere?"

"Goodness knows," Abel said. He rose, dusting off his knees. "There's probably some lethal Victorian apparatus involving mercury in the medicine cabinet. I'll go and have a look."

"Oh, would you? You're a darling. Rich's iPhone has some app that claims it can take a temperature, but I can't see how it can possibly be accurate."

"I'm fine!" Hal said. She swung her legs to the floor, and was met with a chorus of clucking disapproval from Abel and Mitzi.

"Darling—" Abel put a hand on her shoulder, pressing her back into the couch. "You just went white as a sheet and keeled over. The one thing you are definitely not is fine. Now, if I leave you alone with Mitzi to go and find a thermometer, do you promise not to go running off?"

"I promise," Hal said, only half reluctantly. She put her legs back on the couch, and lay back, shading her eyes from the glare of the lamp.

Mitzi saw the gesture, and bent over.

"Is the light hurting your eyes?"

"A little bit," Hal admitted. "You don't have any painkillers, do you? My head's really hurting."

"I'm not surprised," Mitzi said, a touch of tartness in her voice, as she angled the lamp to the side, pointing it away from Hal's face. "You came down with quite a whack on the parquet. There's an impressive egg on the side of your head. It's a shame you didn't go down the other way—you would have hit the rug, although it's so threadbare I'm not sure it would have done any good. Yes, I have some paracetamol in my handbag, but it's in the other room. Will you be okay while I go and fetch it?"

Hal nodded, and Mitzi stood up.

"Don't do anything silly, now. I don't want you passing out again."

"I won't," Hal said faintly. She didn't mention that the idea of ten minutes alone while Mitzi hunted for her handbag was even more alluring than the painkillers.

As the door shut behind Mitzi, Hal let her head fall back onto the couch and tried to think—to piece together what had happened in the strange, frantic interlude between Mr. Treswick's announcement and her passing out.

Because it didn't make sense. None of this made sense. She was *named*, in this woman's will. Personally named, along with her address. The will was referring to her—there could be no doubt at all.

Could it . . . could it possibly be true? *Was* she Mrs. Westaway's long-lost granddaughter?

A flicker of hope began to burn, almost painful with the intensity of longing.

Be skeptical, Hal, her mother's voice whispered in her ear, *and be doubly skeptical when it's something you* want *to believe.*

And that was the problem. She was telling herself this, not because it was possible, but because she *wanted* it to be so. It could not be true, however much she might want to persuade herself of that fact. Her mother's birth certificate contradicted it absolutely. However Hal twisted the possibilities in her mind, there was no way she could make the connection work. Her mother might possibly be related to this family in some distant way—Westaway wasn't that common a name. But unless Hal ignored the evidence not just of her own birth certificate, but of her mother's too, there was no way she could be Hester Westaway's granddaughter.

Which meant . . . Hal tried to think back to what Mr. Treswick had said in the graveyard. Was it possible that the mistake had occurred not after the will was written, but *before*? Had Hester Westaway hired someone to track down her daughter, and somehow they had got their wires catastrophically crossed?

Hal pressed her fingers into her eyes, feeling the fever flush on her cheeks, and her head throbbed as if it would burst.

"Here we are." The voice came from the doorway, and Hal opened her eyes to see Mitzi walking briskly across the library, a white packet in her hand. "Take two. They should help your temperature as well. Ah, Abel," she said, as one of the bookcases swung back, and her brother-in-law appeared in the opening with something in his hand. "Just in time. Is that the thermometer?"

"Yes." He held it out, the bulb glinting silver in the lamplight. "Somewhat to my own astonishment, I was right. It *is* mercury, so for heaven's sake don't chew on it, Harriet. I don't want to be responsible for poisoning my own niece."

My own niece. Hal felt her cheeks flush involuntarily as he slipped the glass tube beneath her tongue, cool against the heat of her mouth, but she couldn't answer, only close her lips around it and watch as Abel turned to Mitzi.

"Edward rang from a garage near Bodmin. He won't be long now. He was sorry not to come to the service you know, but he was on duty at the hospital, and he never met Mother, so it seemed a little hypocritical to ask him to take a day off."

"Still," Mitzi said, "he is your husband."

"Partner, dear Mitzi, partner. There's a difference, at least in the eyes of human resources. Parents-in-law, you get an automatic entitlement to compassionate leave. Estranged mother of your live-in boyfriend, not so much. Edward is my partner," he added to Hal. "He's a doctor, and I think we'll all feel much happier when he's given you the once-over."

Hal nodded, feeling the glass thermometer chink against her teeth. Mitzi and Abel lapsed into silence, and they all sat, listening to the voices rise and fall from the next room, Abel meditatively stroking his mustache with one finger.

"Has Harding calmed down?" he asked. Mitzi rolled her eyes and shrugged.

"Not a great deal. I'm sorry about my husband," she said, turning to Hal. "It wasn't a very edifying little display, I realize, but you have to appreciate it was a terrible shock. As eldest, I think Harding had naturally assumed . . ."

"It's understandable," Abel said. "Harding spent all his life trying to prove himself to Mother, and now he gets this, from beyond the grave. Poor man."

"Oh, Abel, stop being such a saint!" Mitzi said. "You have an equal right to be upset."

Abel sighed. He shifted his position on the threadbare armchair, tugging at the knees of his trousers to avoid stretching the fabric.

"Well, I wouldn't be human if I didn't admit to a bit of chagrin. But the difference is, Mitzi darling, I've had twenty years to get used to the situation. I resigned myself years ago to Mother's disapproval."

"My mother-in-law cut Abel off without a penny," Mitzi explained to Hal, a touch of righteous disbelief in her voice.

"It was quite a shock at the time," Abel said rather wearily, "but there we go, it was a different era."

"It was 1995!" Mitzi snapped. "Your mother's views were dated even then, Abel. Don't excuse what she did. Personally, in your shoes, I don't think I would have even attended the funeral. There's such a thing as being *too* nice, you—"

"Well, regardless," Abel said, raising his voice and cutting through her, "I didn't expect to get a penny in the will, so it's no shock to me."

"Well, I applaud your levelheadedness. But aren't you surprised for Ezra? Harding always said he was your mother's favorite."

Abel shrugged.

"As a little boy, yes. But you know, as an adult, he cut himself off from all of us, Mother included. I think it was just too . . . after my sister, our sister, after she . . ."

He stopped, trailing off as though the words that followed were too painful to be spoken out loud. When he blinked, Hal saw there were tears on his lashes. She felt a sudden stabbing pain in her side, a physical manifestation of a consuming guilt.

"I'm sorry—" The words were muffled by the thermometer, but they came out almost without her meaning to say them, falling into the silence Abel had left, and his head jerked up.

"Don't be sorry, my dear. Whosever fault it was, it certainly wasn't yours." He dashed at his eyes and looked away from her, towards the shadows of the empty fireplace. "But I will say this, much as I loved Maud, much as I understood why she had to do what she did, she did all of us a bad turn when she ran away, especially Ezra. Twenty years spent wondering if she was alive or dead, and whether she would make contact one day. And now this—this *bombshell.* What *happened* to her, Harriet?"

Hal felt her heart flutter as if a hand had clenched around it, constricting her blood, and for a moment she thought about feigning another faint, but there was no way she could dodge this long-term. She had felt it nudging at the edge of the conversation in the drawing room the entire time the brothers were interrogating her, felt them skirting around the topic, trying to get her to address their half-spoken questions, and she had been saved only by their very English reluctance to bring up something so personal and emotive on first acquaintance. *How did your mother die?* It was a hard thing to ask—and Hal had banked on them finding it so.

But now, in this intimate circle of light cast from the lamp, marooned on the couch, pinned there by the blanket, now there was no escape. Clearly, whatever the truth was, Abel at least didn't know what had happened to his sister. She would have to tell her *own* truth—and if it didn't chime with what Mr. Treswick had found out, then that would be that, and the game would be over.

What she was about to do was crossing a line—not just in terms of the risk she was taking, but also in the way she was about to use her own small tragedy in the service of something mean and dishonest. But there was no way around it.

Once, a long time ago, a teacher at school had called Hal "a little mouse," and the description had offended her, though she hadn't really known why. But now she knew why. Whatever she looked like on the surface, inside, deep in the core of her, she was not a mouse, but something quite different: a rat—small, dark, tenacious, and dogged. And now she felt like a cornered rat, fighting to survive.

She took the thermometer out of her mouth, holding it in her hand, and drew a breath.

"She died," she said quietly. "Just over three years ago, a few days before my eighteenth birthday. There was a car crash. She was killed instantly—a hit-and-run. I was at school. I got a call—"

She stopped, unable to finish, but it was done.

"Oh God," Abel said. His voice was a whisper, and he put his hand up to his face. It was the first time that Hal had seen real grief since she had come here—in spite of Mrs. Westaway's funeral—and she felt her stomach turn at the sudden realization of what she had just done. Abel's pain was real and palpable. It wasn't just the exploitation of her mother's death that sickened her, for with that she was hurting no one but herself. But how casually she had just inflicted her own small tragedy on Abel.

These are real people. She watched Abel's face in the lamplight, with a kind of numbness. *These aren't the imaginary rich yahoos you created on the train. These are real people. This is real grief. These are lives you are playing with here.*

But she could not think like that. She had started this now, and she had no choice but to see it through. She could not go back, to Mr. Smith and his waiting enforcers, and beyond that, to the desperate daily struggle to eat, survive, keep her head above water. . . .

"Oh, Abel, darling," Mitzi said, and her voice was a little throaty.

"I'm sorry," Abel said. He dashed at his eyes again, blinking hard. "I thought—I really thought I'd come to terms with the idea of her death, I mean we hadn't heard from her for so long, obviously we had all assumed . . . but to think that all that time, and she was alive and well . . . and we never knew. Dear God. Poor Ezra."

Poor Ezra? But Hal did not have time to disentangle Abel's remark, for Mitzi was speaking.

"Do you think, Abel," she began, and then stopped. When she carried on, it was hesitantly, as if uncertain of what she was about to say. "Do you think that's . . . why?"

"Why what?"

"Why . . . the will. Do you think your mother realized how she behaved, perhaps . . . ? That she had driven your sister away, and perhaps felt . . . I don't know . . . guilty in some way?"

"A kind of atonement?" Abel asked, and then he shrugged again. "Honestly? I don't think so. God knows, I've never understood

Mother's motives, and in spite of living with her for nearly twenty years, I have precious little insight into her thought processes, but I don't think guilt was an emotion she even registered, let alone understood. I would like to think it was something as positive as atonement, but the truth is . . ."

He stopped, glanced at Hal, and then gave a kind of shaky laugh, as if trying to shrug off the conversation.

"But listen to me, rambling on. Poor Harriet's still clutching that thermometer like grim death. Let's see what it says."

Hal held it out.

"I'm sorry," she said again, and she meant it now. "For all this. I'll be going tomorrow."

But as Abel held the thermometer up to the light, he whistled and shook his head.

"101.5. No question of you going anywhere, young lady."

"A hundred and one!" Mitzi gave a little shriek. "Good Lord. You definitely *cannot* go home tomorrow, Harriet, I won't hear of it. Anyway"—she glanced at Abel, a quick little look, almost of trepidation—"anyway, you will need to stay around. There's so much to discuss. After all—this is your house now."

CHAPTER 15

Your house now.

Your house now.

The words turned sickly in Hal's gut as she lay in the darkness of the attic room, listening to the wind in the trees outside, the crackle of the fire in the grate, and the far-off crash of the sea, trying to come to terms with what had just happened.

She had not had the courage to face Harding, and fortunately Abel and Mitzi had fallen in with her plea for an early bedtime. Abel had helped her up the stairs, lit the fire, and then tactfully withdrawn while she got into her nightclothes, her limbs trembling with a mix of tiredness and fever. Then, after Hal was sitting up in bed, Mitzi had appeared with a bowl of soup on a tray.

"It's only Heinz, I'm afraid," she said as she placed the tray on Hal's bedside table and straightened the contents. "Oh, bother. It's cold already. It was boiling when I left the kitchen, I swear!"

"It's fine, really," Hal said. Her voice was croaky, and her face felt hot from the fire, in spite of the damp chill of the bedclothes. "I'm not that hungry."

"Well, you must eat something, heaven knows you've got little enough to spare. Edward will be here in a few minutes, and he's going to pop up to see you before we sit down to dinner."

"Thank you," Hal said humbly. She felt her cheeks burn, not only with fever and the heat from the grate, but with the thought of what she was doing to this family, and how nice Mitzi and Abel were being over it. Back in Brighton, it had seemed so different—so completely different. Risking everything to snatch a few hundred pounds from a bunch of wealthy strangers—it had seemed somehow rather gallant, a touch of Robin Hood about the whole thing.

But now she was here, in their family home, and the legacy was not a few hundred, nor even the few thousand she had been half daring to hope for, but something terrifyingly huge—and what she was doing seemed anything but gallant.

There was no way she was going to get away with this. The fury in Harding's eye spoke of lawsuits and contested wills and private detectives. But it was too late to turn tail and run away now. She was stuck here—quite literally.

Hal felt her stomach turn and shift and, under Mitzi's watchful eye, she took a spoonful of the soup and forced it down.

There was a knock at the door as she lifted the second spoonful to her lips, and Mitzi stood and opened it. Outside was Abel, his honey-dark hair windswept and tousled—and a handsome, blue-eyed man wearing a rain-spattered overcoat. He had a thick blond mustache that was new, but in spite of that, Hal recognized him from Facebook even before Abel spoke.

"Harriet, this is my partner, Edward."

"Edward!" Mitzi kissed him on both cheeks, before ushering him into the little room. He was tall and broad-shouldered, and he seemed to fill the little space. "Come in and meet Harriet."

"Harriet," Edward said. "Delighted." His voice was clipped, as if from an expensive education, and his overcoat looked well-cut and brand-new, but he pulled it off and draped it carelessly over one arm, before sitting on the end of Hal's bed. "Well, it's a strange way to be meeting a new niece-in-law, but pleased to meet you. Edward Ashby."

He held out a hand, and Hal took it hesitantly, feeling the cold of his skin compared to her own hot hand.

"I won't keep you up, because I'd imagine you're probably longing to get to sleep, but Abel said you had a bit of an episode, is that right?"

"I passed out," Hal said. "But it's nothing serious, I promise." She tried to keep her voice from croaking. "I'd forgotten to eat, you know what it's like."

"I don't, actually," Edward said, with a grin. "My stomach is sacred and I start planning lunch around nine thirty a.m., but I'll take your word for it. Well, you do seem to have a bit of a temperature. Any headaches?"

"Just a bruise where I hit my head," Hal lied. The truth was her head was aching badly, though the paracetamol had helped a little.

"Any nausea?"

"No, none." That at least was the truth.

"And you're eating—that's a good sign. Well, I think you're probably all right, but if you start to feel sick, come and tell someone, okay?"

"Okay," Hal said. She coughed, trying to smother it in her hand.

"Have you taken anything for the temperature?" Edward asked.

"Paracetamol."

"You could take an ibuprofen as well, if you want—I think I've got some." He stood, and patted first his suit pockets, then his overcoat, and finally came out with some pills. They were in an unbranded dispensary bottle, the only label a handwritten pharmacist's scribble that Hal could not make out, but he twisted off the cap and shook two out onto the table.

"Thanks," Hal said. She was longing for them to leave, but she tried to smile.

"Swallow them down," Edward said, rather heartily. "You'll feel better if you do."

Hal looked at the pills. They were white, and completely unmarked. Didn't pills usually have something on them saying the dosage? It came to her, a fleeting, paranoid thought, that these could be anything, from Viagra to sleeping pills. But that was ridiculous, surely.

"Take the pills, Harriet," Abel said. "We don't want your temperature spiking in the night."

Rather reluctantly, Hal put them in her mouth, took a sip of water, and swallowed them down. Edward smiled as she did.

"Well done. And with that, I'll leave you to your soup. Sorry we're meeting under these circs, Harriet," Edward said as he gathered up his overcoat. Hal wasn't sure whether he meant the funeral, her head, or all of it. "But, well—sleep well."

"Good night, Harriet," Abel said. He gave Hal's shoulder a little squeeze that made her flinch, just a touch. She smiled, trying to hide her discomfort.

"Good night, Harriet," Edward echoed. And with that, he winked, and followed Abel out of the room.

"Would you tell Freddie and Kitty it's time to go to bed?" Mitzi called after them both, and Abel nodded, and said something Hal didn't catch in reply.

"Dear Abel," Mitzi said, as their shapes were swallowed by the narrow, dark stairwell down to the main landing. "Such a sweet man. It's such a shame he never had children, he throws it all into his work instead."

"What does he do?" Hal croaked.

"He's a lobbyist on behalf of various children's charities. Rather a well-known one, apparently, if you're in that particular world. But he's also simply one of the nicest people I've ever met—I can't think where he got it from, or how he survived his mother's treatment intact, but there you go. I'm sure it would have reduced anyone else to a bitter shell! But listen to me rabbiting on, distracting you." She touched the soup tray with one finger. "You should be finishing your soup. You've hardly eaten."

"I think I'm too tired to eat much, I'm sorry, M-Mitzi." Hal stumbled over the name, unsure what to call her. Mrs. Westaway? Aunt Mitzi? It seemed more and more wrong, laying claim to a relationship she didn't have. Fortunately Mitzi did not seem to notice, and only sighed and stood up.

"Well, manage what you can, but a good night's sleep is probably what you really need. Sleep well, my dear."

"Thank you," Hal said, or tried to—but she found her throat was stiff, and the words stifled and lost in the noise of Mitzi's feet as she turned and made her way back down the stairs to the others.

After she had gone, Hal pushed away the bowl of cold, congealing soup, switched out the light, and put her hot cheek against the pillow. The fire had died down, leaving only a red glow of coals in the little grate, but there was a gap in the curtains, and the moon shone fitfully in through the bare tree branches, making abstract patterns against the white walls.

My walls, Hal thought dazedly. *My trees.*

They are not yours.

The words whirled in her head, mingling with the yammering voices of the brothers, the thousand questions she needed to find answers for before tomorrow, the hundred whys and what-ifs and hows. . . .

If only, if *only* the legacy had been what she had been hoping for—a couple of thousand pounds, as befitted a long-lost granddaughter. That, she could have claimed with few if any questions, before slipping back into the shadows to resume her old life.

The reality felt like a terrifying millstone, weighing her down as she struggled to free herself from what she had done. There would be no quick claims here—no slipping back to Brighton to strategically "lose touch" with her supposed relatives. Whatever she did, whether she succeeded in fooling Mr. Treswick long-term or not, she was chained to this place now.

But why had Mrs. Westaway chosen to cut out her sons and leave everything to a girl she had never met, daughter of a woman she had not seen for years?

And why had she chosen to do it this way—springing the act upon her family after her own death? Was it cowardice? It didn't seem to fit with the portrait her children were painting—the image Hal was piecing together was of a woman who was indomitable, unyielding, and quite unafraid.

She felt suddenly impossibly tired, her eyes heavy with an exhaustion that seemed to have washed over her all at once.

Closing her eyes, she lay still in the little cot, feeling the cool of the pillow against her cheek, and listening to the sound of the house settling down for the night, feeling the suffocating presence of the Westaways all around. There was a sudden spatter of fresh rain against the glass, and she thought she heard—though perhaps it was her fancy—the far-off sound of waves against a shore.

An image came into Hal's mind—of rising waters, closing above all of their heads, while Mrs. Westaway laughed from beyond the grave—and she opened her eyes, a sudden flood of fear making her skin prickle and shiver.

"Stop it," she whispered aloud. It was a trick her mother had taught her when she was a little girl—when the nightmares became too real, sometimes saying the thing out loud was enough to break the spell, silence the voices inside your own head, in favor of a real-life voice.

The image receded—back to whatever paranoid fantasy it had come from. But the flavor of it lingered . . . an old, bitter woman, gone beyond harm herself, and abandoning the living to their fate.

What had Hal got herself mixed up in? And what had she started?

CHAPTER 16

When Hal awoke, the attic room was bright with sunlight, and she lay still for a long time, blinking and disoriented. There was a strange heaviness upon her, and she had to fight off the thickness of sleep and force herself to sit up, yawning and gritty-eyed, trying to remember where she was.

Her situation came back with an unsettling rush.

She was not safe at home, in her tiny flat in Marine View Villas, waiting to make her way down to the pier for the day's work—she was in Cornwall, in this strange cold house. And even before memory came fully back, she knew from the uneasy tightness in her gut that she was in deep, deep trouble.

For a few moments she sat quietly, letting the events of the day before come back, feeling the ache in her limbs, which were heavy and limp and reluctant to obey her. She was tired, no, not just tired, more than that—wrung out, thickheaded, as if the fog of sleep were still clinging in the corners of her mind.

As she forced her legs over the side of the bed, she remembered Edward handing her those blank, unmarked pills, and his insistence that she take them, and she shivered—not just from cold. But surely not. He was a doctor, after all. And besides, what would be the point?

More likely she was just suffering the hangover of the chill she had caught at the grave, and the effects of bumping her head. Cautiously, she put her hand up to the bruise beneath her hair, but although it felt a little tender, there was no swelling. She felt cold, but not the strange, trembly hot-cold of the night before. This was just normal, winter's morning cold, her feet shrinking from the chilly bare boards as she padded across the room to her suitcase, where her phone sat charging.

7:27 a.m. Early, but not stupidly so. There was also an unread text message in her inbox, from a number she didn't recognize. Someone at the pier?

Hal fumbled for her glasses, slipped them on, and then pressed the text message icon.

FIVE DAYS, was all it said.

No sign-off. But Hal did not need to wonder who it was from.

Gone was the sleep-fuddled dread. Instead she was suddenly wide awake, her skin prickling with fear, as if at any moment the man with the lisp and the steel-toe-capped boots might come through the door, drag her out of the narrow bed, punch her in the face. *Broken teeth . . . broken bones.*

She found she was shivering.

They can't find you here. You're safe here.

The words slowed her heart, and she repeated them like a mantra until her shaking fingers were steady enough to unzip her case.

You're safe. Just get through today. One step at a time.

One step at a time. Okay. The little room was unbelievably cold, her breath huffing white as she pulled on jeans and a T-shirt. At the bottom of her case was her jumper. It was bundled up with a wad of other clothes, and Hal dragged it out hastily, not noticing the tin that was caught in its folds. It fell with a thud at her feet, the lid flew off, and the tarot cards scattered across the floor, like brightly colored autumn leaves.

On top was the card she had cut before the journey—the page of swords—his head cocked, staring defiantly out of the frame with a little half smile that could have been anything from a challenge to resignation. It was a card Hal had seen a million times, and she knew every detail, from the bird at his feet to the tiny tear in the top right-hand corner. But as she gathered it up along with the others, she paused for a moment, held by something in his face, trying to analyze what that could be.

Whatever it was that had stopped her, it eluded her, and she dropped the cards on the bed and, with a shiver, unfolded the jumper and pulled it over her head.

The familiar warmth wrapped her like a hug, and when she had put on her socks and pulled on her knee-high biker boots, she felt in a strange way armored, more ready to face the rest of the family as herself, rather than the impostor she had somehow become yesterday.

Finally she raked her fingers through her hair, picked up her mobile phone from the bedside table, and looked around to see if there was anything she had forgotten.

In the stark morning light the room looked somehow different, less spooky, perhaps, but sharper, bleaker, even less forgiving. All the details she had noticed yesterday were picked out in sharp relief—the metal bars across the window black-painted, like the metal bedstead; the tiny grate, no bigger than a shoe box; the damp-speckled paint on the ceiling. In daylight, she could see that what she had taken for a shadow at the top of the sash window was in fact a sizable gap where it hadn't been properly closed. As she got closer, she could feel the draft from the cold air whistling through—no wonder the room was so cold.

Hal put a hand through the bars and shoved at the frame, trying to close the sash properly, but it seemed to be stuck, and the position of the bars prevented her from pushing with any effective force.

Nevertheless, she wriggled both hands through the bars and tried again, crouching to try to get a better angle, and as she did, something glinting on the glass caught her eye. It was a scratch on the glass—in fact, more than one. It was writing.

Hal straightened, trying to make out the letters. They were tucked behind one of the bars and hard to see, but as she tilted her head to one side, suddenly the low morning sunlight caught the marks at just the right angle, illuminating them so that they glowed as if written in white fire.

HELP ME, it said, in tiny crabbed capitals.

Hal's heart quickened. For a long moment she just stood there, staring at the writing, trying to understand what it meant.

Who had written this? A maid? A child? And how long ago?

It wasn't a cry for help. There was no hope of the message being seen from outside—or even from the inside, angled as the letters were. If anything they were hidden, deliberately, behind the bars. Hal herself would never have seen them if she hadn't stood in this exact spot.

No, this was something . . . something else. Not so much a desire to be heard, but more the expression of a thought too terrifying to keep inside.

She thought of her mother—telling her to speak aloud, to dispel the nightmares inside her head; remembered her own whispered *STOP IT,* a mantra to chase away demons. Was this the same thing? Were these scratches the marks of someone trying to anchor themselves to reality, chase away the whispering voices of fear inside?

HELP ME.

In spite of the jumper, Hal was suddenly cold—very cold, with the kind of chill that comes from within, and inside her head was a voice she could hear, repeating the words again and again.

HELP ME.

In her mind's eye Hal could see a girl, just like herself, alone in this room. There were bars on the window, and a locked door.

Except . . . the door was not locked. Not for her, at any rate. And whatever had happened up here, this was not her concern. This was not her family, and not her secret, and she had better things to worry about than some long-gone girl with a penchant for dramatic gestures.

Whatever had happened in this room, whatever the past of this house, it didn't matter. What mattered now was getting through today without giving herself away, and finding as much information as she could about Maud. Once she had that—a birth date, perhaps, even a middle name, if she could somehow come up with a plausible way of finding the information—she could escape back to Brighton and forge a birth certificate that would convince Mr. Treswick. Touch wood.

Touch wood. She knew what her mother would have said to that. In fact, she could picture her so exactly, the wry shake of her head, the smile quirking at the corner of her mouth. Suddenly Hal longed for her so much that it was like a physical pain around her heart.

Never believe it, Hal. Never believe your own lies.

Because superstition was a trap—that was what she had learned, in the years of plying her trade on the pier. Touching wood, crossing fingers, counting magpies—they were lies, all of them. False promises, designed to give the illusion of control and meaning in a world in which the only destiny came from yourself. *You can't predict the future, Hal,* her mother had reminded her, time and time again. *You can't influence fate, or change what's out of your control. But you can choose what you yourself do with the cards you're dealt.*

That was the truth, Hal knew. The painful, uncompromising truth. It was what she wanted to shout at clients, at the ones who came back again and again looking for answers that she could not give. *There is no higher meaning. Sometimes things happen for no reason. Fate is cruel, and arbitrary. Touching wood, lucky charms, none of it will help you see the car you never saw coming, or avoid the tumor you didn't realize you had. Quite the opposite, in fact. For in that moment that you turn your head to look for the second magpie, in the hope of changing your fortune from sorrow to joy—that's when you take your attention away from the things you* can *change, the crossing light, the speeding car, the moment you should have turned back.*

The people who came to her booth were seeking meaning and control—but they were looking in the wrong place. When they gave themselves over to superstition, they were giving up on shaping their own destiny.

Well, if there was one thing Hal had learned, it was that she would not be caught in that trap. She would shape her own life. She would change her own fortune. She would make her own luck.

CHAPTER 17

The drawing room where they had sat last night was empty, the ashes in the grate cold, three abandoned whiskey glasses on the table. But the hum of a vacuum cleaner sounded from somewhere deep inside the house, and Hal followed the sound, along a tiled corridor lined with stuffed birds of prey poised beneath dusty glass, and through a room laid for breakfast. There were boxes of cereal, a tub of margarine, and a bag of cheap sliced bread laid out next to an ancient toaster.

Beyond that was a conservatory full of grapevines and orange trees—or at least, it had been, at one time. There were no orange trees left, but the labels on the pots still bore their names—Cara Cara, Valencia, Moro. A few vines remained, their thick, gnarled stems rising from the ground, but they had almost all died. The leaves were yellowed, and a few bunches of raisin-like grapes clung to the stalks. The only living things were the thin strands of grass that clung tenaciously between the bricks of the floor. It was very cold, a chilly draft blowing from somewhere and making the withered leaves on the dead vines flutter and rustle; looking up, Hal saw that one of the panes in the roof had smashed, and the wind was blowing through.

The vacuum cleaner was loud now—and coming from the room on the other side of the conservatory, so Hal pushed through the dead vines and opened the door at the far end.

The room was some kind of sitting room, very dark, and furnished with a Victorian level of clutter—all tasseled curtains and side tables and overstuffed sofas. In the middle of the room, standing on the hearthrug, was Mrs. Warren, her stick laid to one side, pushing the hoover back and forth with grim determination. For a moment Hal thought about retreating, but then she reconsidered. She still needed information on Maud, and this might prove the perfect opportunity—a quiet interlude, one-on-one . . . it would be much easier to control the conversation, bring it round to what she wanted to know. And she could use Mrs. Warren's age and slight deafness to her advantage—old ladies usually loved to reminisce, and it would be easy to cover any slips by pretending Mrs. Warren had misheard what she had said.

Hal coughed, but the housekeeper did not hear her over the sound of the motor, and at last she cleared her throat and spoke.

"Hello? Hello, Mrs. Warren?"

The old lady swung round, the hoover still going, and then switched it off.

"What are you doing here?" Her expression was accusing. Hal felt herself quail a little in spite of herself.

"I—I'm sorry, I heard the hoover, and I—"

"This is my sitting room, private, d'you see?"

"I didn't know." A mixture of defensiveness and annoyance rose up inside her. "I'm sorry, but I couldn't have known it—"

"You *should* have known," the old lady snapped. She clicked the hoover back into its upright position, and picked up her stick. "Coming here, swanning around like you owned the place—"

"I wasn't!" Hal said, goaded out of politeness. "I wouldn't do that at all—I just didn't kn—"

"You ask, do you hear me? You don't go poking into things that don't concern you." Mrs. Warren stopped, pursing her lips shut as though she would have said more, but had thought better of it, and glared at Hal with undisguised hostility.

"Look, I said I'm sorry," Hal said. She crossed her arms protectively across her chest, nettled by the injustice of it—and yet unable to defend herself, because she could not afford to antagonize someone she might need to mine for information. Besides, at bottom the old lady was right. She *was* an intruder, however much she might pretend otherwise. "I'll go back to the other wing. I was—" A sudden inspiration came. "I was just going to ask if you needed any help."

She smiled, pleased with her own quick-wittedness, but it faded from her lips as she saw Mrs. Warren draw herself up to her not-very-full height, her expression venomous.

"Well, *aren't* we the gracious little lady. I may be getting on, but I'm not quite in my dotage, and I don't need help from the likes of *you*." Mrs. Warren managed to make the final words sound like an insult. "Breakfast will be at eight."

And she turned and switched on the hoover again.

Hal retreated quietly, closing the door behind her, and went back into the conservatory, feeling ruffled by the encounter. How could Mrs. Warren have taken her last words so personally? It was as if she had *wanted* to take offense.

Aren't we the gracious little lady.

The implication stung—the more so because it was so untrue. If it had been Richard or Kitty at the door, then she could have understood. But Hal's upbringing had been about as far from being born with a silver spoon as you could possibly get. She thought of her own childhood, of pushing their ancient, coughing hoover around the living room after school, before her mother got home from the pier, wanting to take some of the load off where she could. The second-hand clothes her mother had picked over at the charity shops, the boys' shoes she had been forced to wear when there were no girls' ones in her size. *You know what?* her mother had said, pleading with Hal with her eyes to like them. *I think they're cooler anyway. They suit you.* And Hal had smiled and nodded and worn them with as much pride as she could muster. *I prefer them,* she'd told the girls at school. *They're better for running and jumping and playing football.*

It had come to be true in the end.

You know nothing about me! she wanted to shout back through the sitting room door.

She walked back slowly through the conservatory, wondering what to do until the others came down. Outside she could see, dimly, through the green mold on the panes, the lawn stretching down to the sea, and beyond it the windswept yews, the ones farthest from the house half bent over by the continual sea wind. The magpies were strutting on the lawn, and Hal thought of the rhyme that Mr. Treswick had recited yesterday. She couldn't make out the number of birds through the clouded glass, but there must be at least seven, maybe more, and it seemed suddenly right—in this house full of secrets.

Well, it was very plain she wasn't going to get any answers from Mrs. Warren. The hoover was still humming from behind the sitting room door, but Hal no longer had any faith in her ability to plumb the housekeeper for information, even when she emerged. And the rest of the house was quiet. But perhaps she could use this interlude to her advantage.

Stepping softly, she opened the third door leading out from the conservatory. It led into a small hallway, with a toilet opening off one side of it, the cistern dripping hollowly, and on the other side of it a door, firmly closed.

Hal glanced behind her, thinking of Mrs. Warren's accusations of poking and prying, but the vacuum cleaner was still going, and with a defiant spurt of adrenaline she reached out and turned the handle. She slipped inside, and closed the door behind her, as quietly as she could.

It was a study—but one that had plainly not been used in many years. Dust was thick on the books, cobwebs skeined across the desk blotter, and the telephone that rested on the desk was yellowed Bakelite of the kind Hal had only seen in films. There was a cracked leather book on the desk embossed with the words *Diary Planner* in faded gilt lettering, and very, very gently, Hal opened the cover. *Desk diary and day planner 1979,* she read. It was older than Hal herself. When she let the cover fall back, it made a sound like a soft thud, and a little cloud of dust rose up.

Whose room had this been? It was profoundly masculine in a way Hal couldn't quite define, and she could not imagine Mrs. Westaway using it, somehow. Was it Mr. Westaway's? What had happened to him?

She leafed through the desk diary for a few pages, hoping something useful might leap out at her—*Maud's birthday* seemed too good to hope for, but there might be some nugget of information she could use to her advantage. But the writing was so crabbed it was hard to make anything out, and those notes she did decipher were resolutely unpromising and businesslike—*CF meeting . . . Telephone Webber . . . 12.30 Mr Woeburn, Barclays.*

Hal closed it gently and turned her attention to the rest of the study. Opposite the desk were shelves of books, rising to the ceiling, as dusty and cobwebbed as everything else—all except, Hal suddenly noticed, for one volume, tucked away at the far top right, a slim anonymous book with a buttercup-yellow spine.

Beneath it was a set of wooden steps, designed for reaching the top shelves, and looking closer Hal could see that there was a footprint in the dust—still dusty itself, to be sure, but not the thirty years of dust covering the rest of the study.

Hal cocked her head, listening to the vacuum cleaner going back and forth, back and forth, and then climbed up the steps to retrieve the book, trying to set her feet as closely as possible within the other person's prints.

It was a photograph album—she could tell that as soon as she took it down. As she opened it the thick pages creaked gently, the plastic film that covered the pictures unsticking with reluctance.

The first page held a black-and-white snapshot of a fat blond baby in an old-fashioned stroller and a miniature Aran sweater, staring blurrily out to the camera. There was a lawn behind him, falling away to the sea, and Hal recognized the view as the top terrace at Trepassen, just outside the drawing room. *Harding, 1965* was written in neat pencil across one corner.

Hal turned the pages, feeling like a time traveler tiptoeing through the past. There was a little boy aged about two on the beach below the house, and another of him sat on the lap of a stiff, formal-looking man with a bristly mustache. The boy was presumably Harding, but who was the man? Mr. Westaway?

More photographs, a color snap of the same little boy, a little older this time, on a blue tricycle. *H, June 1969,* read the caption. Next came Harding in a school uniform, knock-kneed in his gray shorts, and then another baby appeared, red-faced and newborn. Maud? For a second Hal felt her heart leap as she looked to the penciled caption beneath for a date. But no—it read *Abel Leonard born 13th March 1972.* On the facing page was a black-and-white picture of the same baby lying on a hearthrug, kicking his little legs. *A.L. 3 months,* said the caption.

But before she could turn the page, a noise made her freeze. There were voices filtering in through the hallway—not Mrs. Warren, by the sound of it, but members of the family. And they were coming closer.

She must *not* be found in here, poking through the family papers.

Hastily, Hal shoved the book back into place and scrambled down the ladder, less careful this time about where she put her feet, and then stood at the bottom, holding her breath as she tried to work out where the voices were coming from. At first her heart was thudding too much to make it out. Then she heard, "Mrs. Warren! How might one obtain some coffee?" and realized they were coming from the breakfast room.

Quickly Hal slipped out of the study, closing the door behind her, and hurried through the little hallway. She was just in time—no sooner had she entered the conservatory than the door to the breakfast room opened and Harding's head stuck out.

"Mrs.—" He broke off. "Oh, Harriet."

"Yes," Hal said, slightly breathlessly. There was dust on her fingers, she saw, from the study, and she wiped them surreptitiously on the back of her jeans. "I was just passing the time in here until eight—Mrs. Warren said breakfast would be served then."

"Well, you'd better come through," Harding said. There was something awkward in his manner, and he coughed and picked an imaginary speck of dust off his blue golfing pullover before adding, "About last night, Harriet, naturally the news was a shock, but I hope you didn't—"

"Please," Hal managed. She felt a betraying flush rise up her cheeks. "There's no need—"

But Harding was going to say his piece, no matter what, and Hal had no choice but to stand and endure a rather pompous little speech that basically amounted to an apology for his remarks last night.

"That's not to say," he finished up, "that I don't still have some concerns about Mother's state of mind. But I was wrong—very wrong—to suggest that that was any reflection on you, Harriet. If you have any involvement in this at all, it's as an innocent bystander. Well, there we go." He coughed and brushed at his sweater again. "Passing on to more pleasant things, I hope you're feeling better?"

"Oh—oh yes," Hal said, though her cheeks were still flushed. "Thank you. I feel completely fine. I'll be able to travel today."

"Travel today?" Harding raised his eyebrows. "There's no question of that, my dear. Mr. Treswick needs to see all the beneficiaries in his office in Penzance, and in any case, there's a great deal we need to sort out here."

At the mention of the appointment with the lawyer, Hal felt her stomach lurch, as sickeningly as if the ground had dropped away beneath her feet. Of course she had known that there would be hoops and formalities, but somehow in her fantasies about how this would pan out, she had always imagined herself sending in her documents by post from a safe remove. That was before, though—when she had been imagining a legacy of a few thousand at most.

Now, with the entire estate hinging on her identity . . .

The prospect of having to go in person and actually stand there, heart thumping, while her papers were looked over, was not comforting. There would probably be questions too—specific ones that Harding, Abel, and Ezra had been too polite to put to her at their mother's wake, and she would have no time to figure out plausible answers or pick her wording. What if Mr. Treswick realized his mistake while she was actually in his office? Would he call the police?

She opened her mouth to reply, but before she could find the right words, the door behind them slammed open, and Mrs. Warren appeared, stick in hand.

"Oh, Mrs. Warren," Harding said, with an ingratiating smile. "We were just discussing breakfast. How kind of you to put out the toaster and so on—where can one obtain tea and coffee?"

"It's not yet eight," Mrs. Warren said stonily. Harding blinked, and Hal could tell he was doing his best not to look put-out.

"Well, I appreciate that, but it's seven fifty-five—"

"What Harding means . . ." came a voice from behind them, and Hal turned to see Ezra standing in the doorway. He was unshaven and looked almost hungover, his clothes rumpled and his hair standing up on end; but as Hal watched, his mouth quirked into the most charmingly wry smile she could remember encountering, transforming his whole expression. "What he meant to say is, couldn't we persuade you, Mrs. Warren, to let us take some of the work off your hands and see to our own tea?"

"Well," Mrs. Warren said. She smoothed her hair with her free hand. "I don't know about that, Mr. Ezra." Her Cornish burr sounded suddenly stronger. "My kitchen is my kitchen. But I'll see what I can do."

She turned and disappeared back through the door at the end of the conservatory, and Ezra winked at Hal.

"Harriet. Good to see you vertical. That was quite a performance you put in last night."

"I—" Hal felt herself flush. *Quite a performance.* The reference was clearly to her fainting fit, but the word was uncomfortably close to the truth. "I'm feeling much better."

"Unusual to see *you* vertical at this hour, if it comes to that," Harding said sourly.

"And very fortunate for you and your morning tea that I am, Harding. What's the saying, something about flies and honey?"

"Flies be damned, she's a cantankerous old bat. I don't know why Mother put up with her all these years. I notice *she's* walked away with her thirty thousand intact."

"That's hardly the point," Ezra said. His smile had disappeared, and he looked at Harding with something pretty close to naked dislike. "And lower your voice, unless you want to have cold soup for the rest of the stay."

"What do you mean, it's hardly the point?"

"I mean, she was basically a carer to Mother for about fifteen years, for a peppercorn wage. You think we could have got a live-in nurse for the kind of money Mother paid Mrs. Warren? Thirty thousand seems like a pretty cheap price to pay to me."

"It's pretty rich to say 'we' could have got a nurse," Harding said irritably. "I can't see what you would know about the matter, given we haven't seen you on these shores for the best part of twenty years. At least Abel had an excuse for cutting and running. Those of us who stuck around to see through our responsibilities—"

"You always were a sanctimonious shit," Ezra said. He grinned, making a joke of the words, but there was no charm or humor in his expression this time, more the quality of a wolf baring its teeth. She held her breath, unsure of where this was going, but Harding didn't reply; he simply rolled his eyes and turned away from his brother towards the breakfast room. When he got to the door, he held it open for Hal, standing punctiliously back until she had passed through.

Inside, Mitzi, Richard, and the two other children were seated at the end of the long table. Abel and Edward were nowhere to be seen.

"Harriet darling," Mitzi said. She had put on lipstick this morning, and her mouth was incongruously cheerful against the muted, faded shades of the room, and the bleached morning light. "How are you feeling today?"

"Fine, thank you, Mitzi," Hal said. She took the seat that Harding pulled out for her, between himself and Ezra, and sat down. "I'm not sure what happened last night—a mixture of cold and no food, I think."

"Not to mention the shock," Mitzi said. She pursed her lips disapprovingly as she reached for the muesli. "I don't know what Mr. Treswick was thinking, springing the whole will situation on us like that."

"Well, he had to tell us at some point," Ezra said. He seemed to have recovered from his flash of irritation with Harding, and the smile was back in place, and more convincing now. "He probably thought it was better to rip the bandage off in one go, so to speak. Get it over with."

"He should have prepared us," Mitzi said stubbornly. "Particularly poor Harding."

"Why poor Harding?" Ezra asked. He grinned across the table at Mitzi. "The rest of us are just as snubbed as him, you know. Or is it that much of a shock to be lumped in with us paupers?"

"Ezra," Mitzi said, with the air of someone having her patience tested. "You haven't been here, but Harding was certainly led to expect—"

"Tough when you've already put down the deposit on a new Land Rover," Ezra said sympathetically.

"Now, look here," Harding said, at the same time that Mitzi snapped, "Ezra, you are being deliberately provocative."

Ezra only laughed, throwing back his head so that Hal could see the unshaven line of his jaw, and the hollow of his collarbone where his shirt was open at the neck.

Then he stood, threw down his napkin, and stretched until his shirttails came loose.

"Fuck it," he said laconically, leaning across the table and picking up the piece of toast Richard was buttering on his plate. "This is a little more hypocrisy than I can cope with at breakfast. I'm going out."

"Out where?" Mitzi demanded, but Ezra didn't seem to have heard her question. He took a giant bite of Richard's toast, tossed the crust onto the table, and then strode out into the hall.

"He's impossible!" Mitzi exploded, as the door slammed behind him. "Harding—are you going to let him get away with that?"

"Dammit, Mit. What do you want me to do?" Harding pushed away his plate. "Anyway, he's right."

"What do you mean? He stole Richard's toast! And how dare he accuse you of hypocrisy!"

"Oh, for God's sake." Harding stood, marched over to the toaster, and shoved in two more slices of bread. "Happy? The toast is hardly the most important thing here."

"Accusing you of hypocrisy, then—what cheek!"

"I think that was a general remark, Mit—and much as I find him deeply irritating, he's not wrong on that particular point, is he? All of us in that church yesterday, with our carefully glum faces—and I doubt there was one person there who was sorry she was gone."

"How dare you." The voice came from the doorway, and all heads at the table turned, to see Mrs. Warren standing in the doorway, a coffee jug trembling in one hand. "How *dare* you, you little sniveling good-for-nowt."

"Mrs. Warren," Harding said stiffly. He drew himself up to his full height. "What I said was intended for my wife, and in any case—"

"Don't you 'Mrs. Warren' me, you despicable little arsehole," she snarled, her Cornish accent somehow making the last word into a kind of foreign invective.

"Mrs.—" Harding began, but he didn't get to finish. Mrs. Warren set down the coffeepot on the table with a crack that sent drops spattering across their plates, and slapped him around the back of the head, like a recalcitrant child.

Hal's face felt frozen in shock. The whole scene was surreal—Harding standing there like a pompous schoolboy caught swearing in the corridor; Mrs. Warren, her face twisted with fury; Mitzi, Richard, and the other children wide-eyed with shock.

"Mrs. Warren!" Harding bellowed furiously, rubbing the back of his head, and at the same time his daughter called out, "Daddy!" and then, when her father did not respond, more urgently, "*Daddy!* The toast!"

They all turned to look at the ancient toaster on the end of the table, to see smoke pouring out of the opening at the top. As Hal watched in horror, the blackened slices burst into flames.

"That goddamn thing!" Harding roared. "It's a death trap—Mother should have thrown it away years ago." He marched across to the wall socket, pulled out the plug, and then threw a place mat over the smoking toaster. The flames went out. A strong smell of singed cotton joined the scent of burned toast, and Mitzi let out a shuddering breath.

"Oh, for heaven's sake! Is there nothing reliable in this house? Mrs. Warren, can you—"

But then she stopped, breaking off in exasperation. Mrs. Warren had gone.

CHAPTER 18

The rest of breakfast had a stifled, edgy quality, as if no one wanted to refer to Mrs. Warren's outburst and Ezra's disappearance; and although she knew she should have been using the time to winkle out vital facts about Maud before her interview with Mr. Treswick, Hal found herself bolting down her toast, and then excusing herself from the table as fast as possible.

In the hall outside she paused for a moment, trying to decide what to do. She had no desire to go back up to that coffin-like bedroom, but wandering around the house as if she already owned the place felt painfully presumptuous.

She needed to get out, clear her head, try to work out her next move.

Farther up the corridor she could see a door to the garden standing open, presumably where Ezra had made his exit, and she followed the stiff breeze and crunched her way out onto the gravel at the front of the house. Ahead of her was a wide sweep of drive, dotted with weeds and self-seeded saplings. To the left was a block of low buildings—garages, or perhaps former stables, she thought—but the smell of cigarette smoke filtering around the corner told her that that was where Ezra had gone, and she had no desire to face him just now. In fact, she needed a break from them all.

Instead she turned right, past a rather dismal shrubbery with a strong scent of cats, and round to the façade she had seen on that postcard, the long low house, the lawn falling away to the sea. *We had a very good tea at Trepassen House. . . .*

What had happened to that house, and that family? The picture-postcard tranquility she had seen in that photograph, tea on the lawn, like something from an Agatha Christie novel, all that had vanished—swallowed up in decay and something stranger and more worrying. It was not just the sense she had of a house long neglected. It was something darker, the feeling of a place hiding secrets, where people had been terribly unhappy, and no one had come to comfort them.

Wrapped in her thoughts, Hal crunched across the frosted lawn, feeling the frozen blades of grass crackle beneath her boots. The air was crisp and cold, and she huffed out, watching her white breath disappear. When she stopped to look back at the house, she realized how far she had come, and how large the grounds really were—from her attic room it had been hard to see where the garden ended and the surrounding countryside began; but now that she had walked almost to the copse at the bottom of the lawn she was a good couple of hundred yards from the house, and she could see that the copse itself formed part of the grounds—a cluster of trees with something at the center. Hal thought she could see something dark glinting through the trees. Could it be water?

"Admiring your domain?"

The voice, coming from behind her up the slope, made Hal jump, and she jerked her head around to see Abel walking down across the lawn, his hands in his pockets.

"No!"

The word slipped out defensively, before Hal had properly considered her reply, and she felt her cheeks flush with something that was not just cold; but Abel only laughed. He pulled at his mustache.

"I'm not Harding, you don't need to worry about me on that score—there's no ill feeling on my part, I assure you. I had no expectations anyway."

Hal wrapped her arms around herself, unsure of what to say. It struck her that for someone who kept stressing how very unconcerned he was about being cut off, Abel talked about it a lot. She remembered Mitzi's words in the library: *Oh, Abel, stop being such a saint!* Was anyone really that selfless? Could someone survive being disinherited by their only parent and honestly feel no bitterness at all?

Abel seemed to feel her equivocation, or at least her discomfort about the topic, for he changed the subject.

"But tell me, what happened at breakfast?"

"At breakfast?" Hal faltered. She remembered Harding and Ezra's near fight, and felt herself hedging, unwilling to get caught in the complicated web of resentments and loyalties she sensed between the brothers. "I—I'm not sure what you mean. Harding and Ezra had . . . well . . . a bit of a . . . disagreement."

"Oh, you needn't worry about them," Abel said with a laugh. He fell into step beside her. "They've been sparring since Ezra could first talk. By the way, if we head to the left here, I can show you the maze."

"There's a maze?"

"Not a very good one. It's over there." He pointed away from the copse of trees, towards the far side of the lawn. "But that wasn't what I meant, actually—I was talking about the plumes of smoke floating up the stairs."

"Oh, that!" Hal said. She echoed his laugh, relieved to be on less touchy ground. "The toaster caught fire."

"Oh, was that it. I thought perhaps Mrs. Warren had tried to burn the house down rather than let it pass to the unworthy."

Hal felt her cheeks flush in sudden shock at the word, and Abel's face changed.

"Oh God, Harriet, I'm sorry—that was incredibly crass of me. I didn't mean you—I just meant—well, look, Mrs. Warren's always had a touch of the Mrs. Danvers about her. I don't think she would have been happy with any of us inheriting—except maybe Ezra."

"It's okay," Hal said stiffly. She could hardly admit how close to the bone Abel's remark had struck. "Why does she like Ezra so much?" she managed after a moment's awkward silence.

Abel blew into his hands, sending a cloud of white breath gusting ahead of them, as if thinking about her question.

"Who knows," he said at last. "There's no reason—on paper, at least. He's always been charming, but heaven knows, Mrs. Warren is pretty resistant to stuff like that. He was always Mother's favorite too. Youngest child syndrome, maybe. Youngest *boy*, at least. Your mother was actually the youngest, of course—by a few hours, anyway."

"They were twins?" Hal said unguardedly, and then wanted to bite her tongue off. She had *got* to stop saying the first thing that came into her head. She had never thought of herself as a particularly garrulous person—quite the reverse, in fact; people who knew her often remarked on how self-contained she was, how little she volunteered. But she had not understood before coming here how impossible any conversation at all would be, how every chance remark could be a trap. It wasn't just a case of not giving away too much of herself, and concealing the gaps in her knowledge—every step she took was on false ground that could give way at any moment. She could not afford to forget that.

Fortunately, though, Abel didn't seem to have noticed the oddness of her question. He only nodded.

"Fraternal, of course. They were . . . they were very close. I was four years older, and Harding older still—he's eight years older than me, so he was away at school by the time they could walk. But Maud and Ezra . . . that's why, I think, he never really got over her disappearance. He was always a tempestuous personality, but after she ran away . . . I don't know, Harriet. Something changed. It was like all that fire turned inwards, onto himself. He spent years looking for her, you know."

"I'm so sorry," Hal said. Her throat was stiff and sore with falsehood.

Abel put a gentle hand on her shoulder. She felt as if his touch should have burned her, but it did not.

"She—she was a remarkable woman," he said softly. "I don't know how much she told you about her childhood, but it can't have been easy being here with Mother after Harding and I had broken away. Ezra was at boarding school for most of the time, and even when he was at home, he somehow always managed to escape the worst of it, but . . . well, my mother wasn't an easy person to cope with at the best of times, and she got stranger and more irascible as she got older. I think in the end Mrs. Warren was really the only person who could stand to be in her company—and I'm not sure she really got away unscathed. But listen." He stopped, cleared his throat, and drew a breath, then smiled determinedly. "The reason I came to find you—I found something in my room, and I thought you . . . well. I thought you might like it."

They had stopped walking, and Abel reached in his pocket and pulled out a crumpled photograph, folded and dog-eared, and yellowed with that strange golden haze that always seemed to come over photographs a few decades old.

"I'm sorry, it's not in very good condition, but—well, you'll see."

Hal took the piece of paper from Abel, and bent over it, trying to make it out.

When she did, her breath caught in her throat, and she almost choked.

"Harriet?" Abel said uncertainly. "I'm sorry—maybe this isn't—"

But Hal couldn't speak. She could only stare at the photograph in her hand, pressing her fingers together, so that their shaking couldn't betray her shock.

For there, on the lawn outside Trepassen House, was a little group of four people—two girls, a boy, and a slightly older man in his early twenties.

The man was Abel—his honey-colored hair cut into a painfully nineties Brit-Pop crop, and his clothes very far from the expensively cut outfit he was wearing today, but unmistakably him.

The boy was Ezra, his black hair and curving smile making him instantly recognizable—and sitting next to him was a fair-haired girl wearing battered Doc Martens, laughing at him. She must be his long-lost twin sister—the missing Maud.

But the fourth member of the group—the last girl, sitting on her own a little way from the others, her dark eyes looking directly at the camera and at the person taking the photograph . . . that girl was Hal's mother.

Hal found she was not breathing, and she made herself inhale, long and slow, and let it out again, trying not to let her trembling breath give away how badly shocked she was.

Her mother had been here—but when? *How?*

"Harriet?" Abel said at last. "Are you okay? I'm sorry—it must still be very raw for you."

"Y-yes," Hal managed, though her voice was a whisper of its usual self. She swallowed, and forced herself to hold the photograph out towards Abel. "Abel—there's you, Ezra, and m-my mother, but—" She swallowed again, trying hard to work out how to phrase this, how to ask the question she needed to know, without giving everything away. "Who's the other girl?"

"Maggie?" Abel took the photograph from her fingers, and smiled fondly at the little group, forever seated in the sunshine, frozen in their teens and twenties, forever young. "Goodness. Little Maggie Westaway. I'd almost forgotten about her. She was . . . well, I suppose a sort of distant cousin. Her real name was Margarida too, I believe, like Maud, though we never called either of them that—too much of a mouthful. She used to call Mother her aunt, but I think in fact her father was my father's . . . nephew, or cousin? Something of that kind. Her parents died when she was in her teens, a lot like you, Hal, and she came here to finish her final year at school. Poor thing. I don't think it was a very happy time for her."

Hal looked at the girl sitting on the grass, at her unflinching dark eyes, and she saw what Abel meant. There was something wary and equivocal in the girl's gaze. She was the only member of the little group who was not smiling.

"I see," Hal managed. She tried to steady the trembling in her legs and keep her muscles from betraying her. "Thank—thank you for sharing this with me. It means a lot."

"It's for you," Abel said. He held out the picture, and Hal took it, wonderingly. She let her finger trace over her mother's face.

"Really? Are you sure?"

"Yes, of course. I don't need it—I have enough memories of that time, and they're not all of them very good ones. But this was a lovely day, I remember we all went swimming in the lake. It was before—well, never mind. But I'd like you to have it."

"Thank you," Hal said. She folded the photograph carefully along the existing line and pushed it gently into her pocket, and then she remembered her manners, and made herself smile. "Thank you, Abel, I'll treasure it."

And then she turned and walked away up the frozen slope towards the house, unable to keep up the pretense any longer.

AS HAL HURRIED UP THE stairs towards the attic, she could feel the shape of the photograph in her jeans pocket, and she had to stop herself from putting her hand over it, as if to hide it from sight.

Her mother. Dear God, her *mother*.

Hal was panting as she climbed the last set of steps to the attic bedroom, and inside she shut the door, pulled the photograph out of her pocket, and sank to the floor with her back against the door, staring at the little image.

It all made sense—the coincidence over the names, Mr. Treswick's mistake—the only strange thing was that Abel himself hadn't guessed the truth on seeing the photo. For it was so painfully clear now that Hal had the evidence in front of her own eyes.

Maggie, Abel had called her mother. Hal herself had never heard her mother use the nickname—but it made sense. It was an obvious shortening for Margarida. *A family name,* her mother had said once, when she'd asked why her grandparents had chosen such an odd, hard-to-spell name. And then she had shut down the conversation, as she often did when Hal wanted her to talk about her childhood and her long-dead parents.

Her real name was Margarida too, like Maud.

Two cousins—both called Margarida Westaway. And in looking for one, Mr. Treswick had stumbled upon the other, without realizing. Had he even known of the other Margarida's existence? Presumably not, or he would have made sure to find the right person when he searched. But if all he had was a name, and an unusual name at that . . . If you found Joan Smith, you would make damn sure you'd found the right one. But Margarida Westaway—he could be forgiven for assuming he had found the right woman.

But now that she was over the first shock of seeing her mother—young, fearless, *here*—the disquiet began to sink in.

The question that had beat in her head as she hurried up the stairs was how Abel could possibly have seen that photograph and not joined the dots—and now, as Hal stared down at the faded, yellowed picture, the thought recurred, more unsettlingly. For the other Margarida, the *real* Margarida, the one sitting on the lawn next to Ezra, was fair, like Harding and Abel. Hal's mother was dark, like Hal herself.

All her life, Hal had heard people remark on her likeness to her mother, and she had never really been able to see what they were talking about, beyond their obviously similar coloring. But now . . .

looking at the photographic evidence in front of her, her mother at an age so close to her own . . . now Hal could see it only too clearly. From the suspicious dark eyes, the color of espresso coffee, to the straight black hair, the hawkish nose, even the defiant tilt of her mother's chin—Hal saw herself.

Here, right in front of her, was concrete evidence of the truth—and of the mistake that had been made. How long would it be before Abel—or someone else—realized that?

Restlessly, Hal stood and walked to the window, looking out. The day had grown overcast, and far away in the distance she could see a gray mass, flecked with white, rising to meet the sky. It might have been a cloud, but Hal thought—though she could not be sure—that it was probably the sea.

All of a sudden she felt a powerful urge to get out, get away—and she found herself gripping the bars as if she could prize them apart and escape the confines of the little room and the prison she had created for herself with this situation.

Because, as she shoved the photograph away in her pocket for the second time, Hal realized that the evidence in the picture was only half the issue. The real problem was something far worse.

In taking that photo, in asking the questions she had in the way that she had, Hal had crossed a line. She was no longer simply the passive recipient of Mr. Treswick's error, swept up in a mistaken assumption, with no provable wrongdoing on her part.

No. In that moment of accepting the photograph, she had begun to actively deceive the Westaways, in a way that could be tracked back to her and proven. And the potential result of her deception was no longer a few thousand pounds, but a whole estate—stolen from under the noses of Hester Westaway's rightful heirs.

Up to this point, Hal thought, she might at a stretch have claimed ignorance or confusion. She could have cited Mr. Treswick's letter coming out of the blue, the fact that she had never met her grandparents—she could have painted herself as an innocent bystander caught in a mix-up, a trusting young woman, too shy to question the discrepancies in what she had been told.

But now, by taking this photograph and failing to mention that the *other* woman in the picture was her real mother, she had begun something very different.

She had begun to commit an active, traceable fraud.

6th December, 1994

I couldn't sleep last night. I lay awake, my hands over my stomach, trying to press it back to flatness, and I thought about the night it happened. It was late in August, when the days were longer and hotter than I could ever have imagined, and the sky was that fierce Cornish blue.

The boys were back from school and university, filling the house with an unaccustomed noise and energy that felt strange after the stifled silence I had grown used to these last few months. My aunt had gone up to London for some reason, and Mrs Warren had gone into Penzance to see her sister, and without their dark, crow-like presence the atmosphere felt light and full of happiness.

It was Maud who came up to find me in my room, where I was reading—she burst in, holding a towel and her bright red swimming costume in one hand, and her sunglasses in the other.

"Get a move on, Maggie!" she said, plucking the book out of my hand and tossing it onto the bed, losing my place, I noticed with a flash of irritation. "We're going swimming in the lake!"

I didn't want to—that's the strange thing to remember. I don't mind pools or the sea, but I've never liked lake swimming—the slimy reeds, and the mush at the bottom, and the mouldering branches that catch at your feet. But Maud is a hard person to say no to, and at last I let her pull me downstairs to where the boys were waiting, Ezra holding a set of oars.

In the crumbling boathouse Maud untied the rickety flat-bottomed skiff, and we rowed out to the island, the lake water dap-

pled and brown beneath the hull of the boat. Maud tied the boat to a makeshift jetty and we climbed out. It was Maud who went in first—a flash of scarlet against the gold-brown waters as she dived, long and shallow, from the end of the rotting wooden platform.

"Come on, Ed," she shouted, and he stood up, grinned at me, and then followed her to the water's edge, and took a running jump.

I wasn't sure if I would go in—I was content to watch the others, laughing and playing in the water, splashing each other and shrieking. But the sun grew hotter and hotter, and at last I stood, shading my eyes, considering.

"Come in!" Abel yelled. "It's glorious."

I walked to the end of the jetty, feeling the damp wood fraying against my bare toes, and I dipped—just dipped—the tips of my toes in the water, watching with pleasure the scarlet polish I had borrowed from Maud glowing bright beneath the water.

And then—almost before I knew what had happened—a hand seized my ankle, and I felt a tug, and I stumbled forwards to prevent myself from going over backwards—and I was in, the golden waters closing over my head, the mud swirling up around me—and it was more beautiful and terrifying than I could ever have imagined.

I didn't see who pulled me in—but I felt him, beneath the water, his skin against mine, our arms grappling, half fighting. And in that moment when we both surfaced I felt it—his fingers brushed my breast, making me shiver and gasp in a way that wasn't just the shock of the water.

Our eyes met—blue and dark—and he grinned, and my stomach flipped and clenched with a hunger I had never known—and I knew then that I loved him—and that I would give him anything, even myself.

After we rowed back, we walked up to the house and had tea on the lawn, wrapped in towels, and then we stretched out to bask in the sunshine.

"Take a photo . . ." Maud said lazily, as she stretched, her tanned limbs honey-gold against the faded blue towel. "I want to remember today."

He gave a groan, but he stood obediently and went to fetch his camera, and set it up. I watched him as he stood behind it, adjusting the focus, fiddling with the lens cap.

"Why so serious?" he said as he looked up, and I realised that I was frowning in concentration, trying to fix his face in my memory. He flashed me that irresistible smile, and I felt my own mouth curve in helpless sympathy.

Later, long after supper, when the sun was going down, Mrs Warren had gone to bed and the others were playing billiards on the faded green baize, laughing in the way they never did when my aunt was home. Ezra had brought his stereo down from his room and the tape deck blasted out James, REM, and the Pixies by turns, filling the room with the clash of guitars and drums.

I could never play billiards—the cue never did what I wanted, the balls flipping off the cushions with a life of their own. Maud said I wasn't trying, that it was perfectly simple to match up cause and effect, and work out where the ball would end up, but it wasn't true. I had some gene missing, I think. Whatever it was that enabled Maud to see that if a ball were hit from this angle, it would ricochet over there, I didn't have.

So I left them to it and wandered out onto the lawn in front of the old part of the house. I was sitting, watching the sun beginning to dip towards the horizon, and thinking about how beautiful this place was, in spite of it all, when I felt a touch on my shoulder, and I turned, and saw him standing there, beautiful and bronzed, his hair falling in his eyes.

"Come for a walk with me," he said. And I nodded, and followed him, across the fields and through sunken paths, down to the sea. And we lay on the warm sand and watched as the sun sunk into the waves in a blaze of red and gold, and I didn't say anything, because I was so afraid to break this perfect moment—so afraid that he would get up and leave forever, and that everything would be back to normal.

But he didn't. He lay next to me, watching the sky in a silence that felt like the breath you take before you say something very important. As the last streak of sun disappeared beneath the horizon, he turned to me and I thought he was going to speak—but he didn't. Instead he slipped the strap of my sundress down my shoulder. And I thought— This is it. This is what I have been waiting all my life to feel, this is what those girls at school used to talk about, this is what the songs mean, and the poems were written for. This is it. *He* is it.

But the sun has gone now, and it's winter, and I feel very cold. And I am no longer sure if I was right.

CHAPTER 19

Hal wasn't sure how long she had been sitting there, staring at the photograph, trying to work out what she should do. But at last she heard, very faintly, the sound of the clock in the hall downstairs chiming eleven, and she stood, stretching out her cramped, chilly limbs.

The urge to run back to Brighton and hide from the nightmare she had created was still strong—except that they knew where to find her. Mr. Treswick had her address, and he would come and track her down and start asking questions. And besides . . . Her stomach clenched at the memory of Mr. Smith's awaiting enforcers, her crushed belongings. Hal had never thought of herself as a coward, but she was, she knew that now. She thought of the man's voice, his slow soft lisp . . . *broken teeth . . . broken bones sometimes . . .* and she knew she did not have the courage to face him again.

No. She could not go back there without the money.

Could she run away for good—from everyone? But where would she go, and how, without money? She didn't even have the money for a taxi back to Penzance, let alone the cash needed for a fresh start in a strange city.

Well, whatever she decided, she couldn't hide up here forever. She would have to go down and face the family at some point.

Flexing her cold fingers, Hal opened the door.

Standing outside, perfectly still in the darkness of the hallway, was a figure, dark clothes disintegrating into the shadows, standing motionless just inches from Hal's face.

Hal gasped and took a step backwards into the room, her hand pressed to her chest.

"Jesus—what—"

She found her hands were shaking, and caught at the metal bedstead to steady herself.

"Yes?" The voice of the figure in the shadows was cracked, with a flat Cornish burr. As her fright subsided, Hal felt anger flood in its wake.

"Mrs. Warren? What the hell are you doing snooping outside my room?"

"'Tain't your room," Mrs. Warren said bitterly. She took a step forwards, over the threshold, sweeping Hal's meager possessions with a contemptuous look. "And it never will be, if I've anything to do with it."

"What do you mean?"

"You know."

Hal pushed her hands inside her pockets to hide their trembling. She would not show this old woman she was afraid.

"Get out of my way."

"Just as you like. I came up to tell you, he wants you downstairs."

"Who's 'he'?" Hal said. She tried to keep her voice steady, and it came out colder and sharper than she meant.

"Harding. He's in the drawing room."

Hal could not bring herself to say thank you, but she nodded, once, and Mrs. Warren turned to retreat into the shadows of the hallway.

Hal followed her, and was just shutting the door of her room behind her, when Mrs. Warren spoke, jerking her head back over her shoulder towards the room and the scattering of Hal's belongings.

"*She* was into all that muck."

"What?" Hal stopped with her hand on the knob, the door just ajar, a crack of room showing through the gap.

"Them cards. Tarry or whatever she called it. Pagan stuff, it was, devils and naked men. If it was up to me, I wouldn't have had them in the house. I would have burned them all. Disgusting things."

"Who?" Hal said, but Mrs. Warren only continued slowly down the corridor as if she hadn't heard, and Hal found herself bounding after her retreating back, grabbing the old woman's wrist, harder than she meant, forcing her to turn back to face her. "*Who?* Who are you talking about?"

"Maggie." Mrs. Warren spat the name like a swearword, her vehemence sending little flecks of spittle into Hal's face. "And if you know what's good for you, you'll ask me no more questions. Now, let go of me."

"Wha—" Hal gasped. The words hit like a slap in the face, and the questions rose up inside her, churning too quick to be caught. But the one that beat inside Hal's skull was unsayable: Did she *know*?

Before Hal could do more than gasp, Mrs. Warren had wrenched her wrist out of Hal's grip, with a strength Hal would not have given her credit for, and hurried away down the stairs, silent and malevolent.

Hal let out a long, shuddering breath and then went back inside the bedroom, her heart beating fast enough to make her feel dizzy with it.

Maggie. Her mother's nickname. Maggie. Her mother who had been *here*, more than twenty years ago. What had Mrs. Warren meant in bringing her up, here, now? Was it a threat? Did she know the truth? But if so, why had she stood by and said nothing?

There were no answers—and at last, for want of anything else, Hal picked up the tarot cards and began to pack them back into the tin. Mrs. Warren's threat echoed in her head. She wouldn't really dare to burn them, would she? It seemed ridiculous—and yet there was something about the venom in her voice that made Hal think it might be a real possibility.

There was no lock on the bedroom door, or on the case, so all Hal could do was pack the cards away inside their tin, push them deep into her suitcase, and hope for the best.

What had made her pack them in the first place? It wasn't as though she believed.

Hal zipped up the case and turned to leave the room—but then, with a sudden misgiving, she stopped, opened the case, and pushed the tin into her back pocket, alongside the photograph. Let Mrs. Warren snoop. Let her come and look through every pocket of the case. It was only as she reached the top of the narrow, windowless stairs that a thought came to her—a memory of yesterday, of the *tap, tap* of Mrs. Warren's cane on the wooden steps of the secret staircase.

But the woman standing outside her doorway just now had held no cane, and her approach had been utterly silent.

The thought made Hal shiver for no reason that she could put her finger on, and she wished again that there was a lock on the bedroom door. She had never felt the need for one before coming here, but the thought of that bitter old woman, creeping silently about the house at night, opening the door to Hal's room . . .

Hal paused, looking back along the narrow, dark corridor, remembering the way Mrs. Warren had stood there in the darkness. What was she doing? Listening? *Watching?*

She was about to carry on downstairs when something caught her eye, a darkness in the dark, and she made her way back to stand in front of the closed door, running her fingers over the wood, feeling, rather than seeing, how very wrong she had been.

There was a lock on the door. Two, in fact. They were long, thick bolts, top and bottom.

But they were on the outside.

CHAPTER 20

There was no sign of Mrs. Warren when Hal finally descended, and for a moment she stood in the front hallway, trying to get her bearings and remember which of the wooden doors hid the drawing room. She had passed it on her way to breakfast, but then the door had stood open. Now they were all closed, and the long, monotonous hallway with its featureless tiled floor and identical doors was surprisingly disorienting.

Hal tried one at random—but it opened onto a dim, paneled dining room, far grander than the breakfast room they had used that morning. The tall windows were shuttered, thin gray shafts of light piercing the shadows, and a vast table draped with calico dust sheets stretched the length of the room. Above her head hung two huge shapes swathed in gray that at first, in the darkness, Hal thought were giant wasps' nests. She ducked reflexively, before her eyes adjusted and she realized they must be chandeliers, encased in some sort of protective covering.

Her footsteps swirled in the dust, and backing out slowly, she closed the door quietly behind her and made her way up the corridor.

At the next doorway she put her hand out to knock—but before her knuckles could make contact with the wood, she heard a voice coming from inside, and paused for a moment, unsure if she was about to interrupt a private conversation.

". . . conniving little gold digger." It was a man's voice, one of the brothers, Hal thought. But she could not be sure of which.

"Oh, really, you are impossible." A woman's voice, Mitzi's, clipped with impatience. "She's an orphan, no doubt your mother felt sorry for her."

"First of all, we have no proof of that whatsoever, we know nothing about this girl, we have no idea who her father is or was, or whether he's still in the picture. For all we know, he could have put Mother up to this. And second"—it was Harding, Hal realized, as he raised his voice to speak over Mitzi's exasperated protests—"second, Mitzi, if you had known my mother in the least, you would realize how very unlikely it would be for her to be motivated by anything as charitable as pity for an orphan."

"Oh, Harding, what nonsense. Your mother was a lonely old woman, and perhaps if you'd been willing to let bygones be bygones the children and I might have got to know her a little better, and this whole situation—"

"My mother was a bitter, cruel harpy," Harding shouted. "And any reluctance to let you and the children be exposed to her venom was entirely out of concern for you, so don't you *dare* suggest that this situation is my fault, Mitzi."

"I wasn't suggesting that for a moment," Mitzi said, and a placatory note had crept into her voice, beneath the irritation. "I understand your motives were good, darling. But I just think that perhaps it's not really surprising at this point if your mother chose to pass over two sons who were completely estranged, and a third who kept his wife and children away for nearly twenty years. I can't blame your mother for being a little hurt. I certainly would be! When was the last time we were down here? Richard can't have been more than seven."

"Seven, yes, and she told him he was a sniveling little coward when he burned his finger on the grate—remember?"

"I'm not saying she didn't have her faults—"

"Mitzi, you are not listening to me. My mother was a bitter, poisonous woman and her one aim in life was to spread that poison as far and wide as she could. It's exactly like her to continue to spread division from beyond the grave. The sole surprise is that she didn't leave the entire place to Ezra in the hope that he, Abel, and I would end up in a bitter dispute over all this, and the whole estate would get swallowed up in legal fees."

"Oh, Harding, that's absurd—"

"I should have seen it coming," Harding said, and Hal had the feeling he was no longer even really listening to his wife. "She wrote to me, d'you know that? About a month ago. No word of her illness, of course, that would have been too simple, too straightforward. Oh no. She wrote her usual letter, full of complaints, but her sign-off was different—that's what should have told me."

"Different, how?"

"She signed off, always, *your mother*. Always. Even when I was at boarding school, crying my eyes out every night. All the other boys' mothers signed off with *love and kisses*, and *ever your adoring mummy*, and *a thousand hugs*. All that sort of tripe. But Mother—no. *Your mother*. That was it. No love. No kisses. Just a cold statement of fact. A perfect metaphor, in fact, for her life."

"And the last time? Did she add something?"

"Yes," Harding said. And he paused, a brooding silence that made Hal hold her breath, wondering what was coming. Not the love that Harding had waited all his life for, surely? The silence stretched, until Hal thought she must have missed whatever Harding was about to say, or that he had thought better of it, and she raised her hand, ready to knock and announce her presence, but finally Harding spoke.

"She finished, *après moi, le déluge*. That was all. No name. No sign-off. Just those four words."

"*Après* what?" Mitzi sounded completely nonplussed. "After the . . . the rain? What on earth does it mean?"

But before Hal could hear Harding's answer, she heard a voice at her back.

"Eavesdropping?"

Hal spun round, her heart thumping.

It was Harding's daughter, what was her name? Kitty. She was standing in the corridor, twirling her long blond hair around one finger, and chewing something. When Hal didn't speak, she held out a packet in one hand.

"Tangfastic?"

"I—" Hal swallowed. She spoke low, not wanting Harding and Mitzi to hear from inside the room. "I wasn't—I mean, I didn't mean to—I was about to go into the room, but they seemed—"

"Hey, no shade from me." The girl threw up her free hand, the charm bracelet on her wrist jangling. "It's the only way I ever find out anything around here." She pulled out a jelly shape from the packet, examined it critically, and then popped it in her mouth. "Look, I kept meaning to ask, what *are* you?"

"I—I, what?" Hal swallowed again. Her mouth felt dry, and she flexed her cold fingers inside her pockets, digging her nails into her palms, trying to anchor herself. She was uncomfortably aware that the Pandora bracelet Kitty was wearing on her left wrist probably cost more than her own entire outfit, possibly more than her whole wardrobe. "What am I? I'm not sure what you—"

"I mean, like, I know you're some kind of relation, but Dad hasn't really explained the connection. Are you the missing aunt? No, wait, you're too young, right?"

"Oh! Right. No—" She blinked, trying to remember what exactly she was supposed to be doing here. The photograph of her mother lounging on the lawn outside the drawing room flashed through her mind, and she screwed her eyes shut for a moment against the image, rubbing her forehead as if to vanquish her mother's face.

She must not think about her mother. She had to remember who she was supposed to be—not who she was. Maud was Harding's sister, which meant . . .

"I guess I'm . . . your cousin?"

"Oh, right, so your mum was the one who ran away?"

"I—I suppose so, yes. She—she didn't really talk about it."

"So cool," the girl said enviously. She pushed another Haribo into her mouth, and spoke around it. "Not gonna lie, there's been points where I've seriously considered it, but I reckon you need to be at least eighteen to pull it off, otherwise you're pretty much guaranteed to end up on the streets, and there's no way I'm turning tricks for some pedo pimp."

"Um—" Hal found herself completely at a loss. This girl was self-assured in a way that Hal had never been. "I— How old *are* you?"

"Fourteen. Rich is nearly sixteen. Freddie's twelve. He's a total dickwad, so I wouldn't bother with him. Rich is okay if you can get him to take his headphones off. And hey, I'm at a girls' school, I need to keep on his good side, right? He's my shortcut to hot older boys."

"I never really thought about it like that," Hal said faintly.

"Have you got a boyfriend?" Kitty asked. Hal shook her head.

"Girlfriend?"

"No, I—I've not really been in the right place for dating for the last couple of years."

"Gotcha," Kitty said wisely. She nodded and put another Haribo in her mouth. "You should try a dating app. They can match you up by location."

"That wasn't really what I—" Hal began, but then the drawing room door opened and both their heads turned, to see Mitzi standing there.

"Oh, girls. I thought I heard voices. Kitty, if you want to come into Penzance, you need to get your shoes on, and tell Richard to hurry up. Harriet, if you have a moment, your uncle would like to speak with you."

Hal nodded, and looked past Mitzi to where Harding was standing in the drawing room, his back to the door, looking out to the cloud-dark sky and rain-soaked lawns. The sea in the distance was invisible in the mist.

Mitzi stood back, ushering Hal inside, and then closed the door, and Hal heard her trotting purposefully away up the corridor, lecturing Kitty as she went.

Hal stood waiting nervously for Harding to turn around, but he did not. Instead he spoke, still facing the view in front of him.

"Harriet, thank you for agreeing to meet with me."

For a moment, Hal could not think what to say in reply. The incongruity of the phrase struck her—as though they were both businessmen discussing a merger, rather than—rather than what?

"I—you're welcome," she managed at last, and took a hesitant step forwards into the room.

But Harding was speaking over her, as if he were determined to get through his piece and would not be derailed from his course.

"As you may have gathered from Mr. Treswick last night, there is quite a lot of paperwork we need to go through before he can start to move forward on the process of obtaining probate."

"I, well, yes," Hal said. She felt her stomach twist at the mention of paperwork. What could she do? Could she delay the meeting? Or would it be better to go and find out what they needed from her, and then claim she had forgotten it? "Although I didn't know, I mean, I didn't bring—"

"There is a great deal we need to discuss," Harding said. "All this"—he waved his hand at the expanse of green lawns falling away in front of the windows—"all this is a great responsibility, and there are a lot of decisions you will need to make, Harriet, and fairly quickly. But that will come later—in the meantime, we have an appointment with Mr. Treswick in Penzance in"—he glanced at his watch—"just under forty minutes, and it will be fairly tight to get there. You don't have a car here?"

Forty minutes? Hal felt her mouth drop open in horror. This was all moving much too fast. She needed time to research—to work out what Mr. Treswick was likely to ask. What if they wanted her to complete forms, and she tripped up over some minor detail? Then she realized that Harding was waiting for an answer to his question, and swallowed.

"I—no—" she managed faintly.

"No matter. We'll squeeze you in. There's a fold-down seat in the boot."

"But, Unc—" She stumbled over the word, unable to make herself articulate it, and began again: "Look, there's something I must—"

"Later, Harriet," Harding said briskly. His moment of reflection had passed, and he turned, clapping Hal on the shoulder so that she staggered, and then opened the door to the hallway. "There will be plenty of time to talk on the journey, but for now, we must get going or we'll be late for Mr. Treswick. The appointment is at noon so we are already cutting it rather fine."

With a sinking heart, Hal followed Harding into the corridor, and from there out to the front of the house, where the car was waiting, the three children belted in the back.

"Just a moment, Harriet, while I get the boot seat set up," Harding said, but his face changed as the big estate boot swung open. "Mitzi? Where are the fold-down seats?"

"What?" Mitzi looked over her shoulder. The engine was already running, and her impatience was plain. "What are you talking about, Harding?"

"The boot seats. Where are they? Harriet is traveling with us."

"But she can't—there's no room. We took the seats out to make room for the cases, remember?"

"Oh, for heaven's sakes. Does no one in this family plan more than two steps ahead?" Harding said testily. "Well, there's a simple answer: Freddie will have to stay behind."

"Firstly, darling"—Mitzi's voice was brittle as cut glass—"it was *your* idea to remove the seats, if you remember. And secondly, Freddie can't stay behind, he's a beneficiary. Mr. Treswick needs to see his ID."

"Oh, for God's sake!" Harding said explosively. Hal felt a little flicker of hope ignite inside her. Was it possible she would not be able to attend after all?

She was just about to offer to remain at the house when a voice came from behind her.

"Good morning, all."

Hal and Harding both turned, and Hal heard Harding's sigh, a plosive noise, like a whale coming up for air.

"Ezra," he said flatly.

He was standing, hands in his pockets, grinning widely.

"Hello, dear brother. And hello again, Harriet. Nice to see Harding is putting you firmly in the crumple zone. Have you investigated what happens to the estate if Harriet doesn't survive the trip, Harding?"

"Ezra!" Harding snapped. "That is an *entirely* inappropriate joke to make. And no, Harriet won't be traveling in the boot, as someone"—he ignored Mitzi's eye-rolling sigh of exasperation from the driver's seat—"forgot to pack the spare seats. We were just discussing how to proceed."

"Well, I can solve that," Ezra said. "I've got to go into Penzance myself. I need to transfer some money while I'm here. I'll give Harriet a lift."

"Oh." Harding seemed—Hal couldn't quite put her finger on it—almost disappointed at having his bubble of irritation pricked. Or perhaps it was annoyance at having to be beholden to his brother. "Well. That is a . . . neat solution. Excellent."

He shut the boot with a slam and smoothed his Barbour jacket over his stomach.

"Right. Well. Do you know where we are heading, Ezra?"

"Very much so." Ezra twirled his car keys on his finger. "I may have been out of the country for a while, but Penzance isn't so vast that I'm likely to lose my sense of direction. See you there, Harding."

"Very good. Do you have my mobile number?"

"I don't," Ezra said carelessly. "But given I've survived this long without it, I'm sure we'll manage."

Harding gave an exaggerated sigh, and pulled his wallet out of the inner pocket of his Barbour. Inside was a small stack of business cards. He pulled one off the top, and handed it to Hal.

"I will entrust *you* with this, Harriet, as I have very little confidence in Ezra's organizational abilities. Don't lose it. And don't be late." He opened the passenger door and climbed inside the car. "The appointment is at tw—"

But his last words were drowned in the scrunch of tires on gravel as Mitzi accelerated. Hal heard a faint, "Bye, Harriet!" from her window, and then the car disappeared out of the gate and down the drive, a cloud of magpies rising indignantly from the trees as they passed below.

CHAPTER 21

"So . . ." Ezra's voice, as he led the way through the arched gate and around the side of the stable block, to a yard blowing with weeds and grasses, was a long, drawn-out drawl. "You are my . . . niece, I suppose it would be?"

"Yes," Hal said. The word was almost lost in the scrunch of their feet on gravel, and the sound of the wind in the trees, and when Ezra didn't turn she said it again, more loudly, trying for more conviction this time. "Yes."

"Well, well," Ezra said. He shook his head, but did not elaborate, and instead held out his car key towards the low, dark sports car parked beneath the trees on the other side of the yard. It gave a little *beep-beep* and the lights flashed once, to show that it was unlocked. As they drew closer, Ezra gave a short, mirthless laugh, and looked up at the tree above.

"Little bastards," he said. "Mother should have had them poisoned."

For a moment Hal could not work out what he was talking about. She followed his gaze up to the branches above, and saw once again the magpies hunched against the sea wind, their bright beady eyes following her movement. It was only when she looked down at the car that she realized what Ezra had meant. From the back, the car looked fine, but as Hal came closer, she could see that the windscreen and the expensive matte paintwork of the bonnet, the parts of the car parked beneath the cover of the trees, were thickly spread with a layer of dense black droppings, halfway between bird guano and something more like a rabbit's.

"What *is* it?" Hal asked, even as she looked up at the birds overhead, and then grimaced. "Sorry, stupid question."

"You guessed right," Ezra said, a little grimly. "I should have remembered not to park here. Clearly Harding did. Right, there will now be a short pause while I go for a bucket. I'm sorry, it'll make us late for the appointment, but I can't see to drive, and it etches the paintwork if you leave it on. Stay here, and I'll be back as soon as I can."

"Don't worry," Hal said. She watched Ezra as he turned and walked back across the courtyard, leaving her alone with the car, and the cawing of the birds.

A few minutes later he returned with a bucket of warm water.

"Stand back," he said briefly, and Hal stepped hastily out of the way just in time for Ezra to sluice the car, making the birds above screech and cackle as they rose into the air and then resettled.

"That's as good as it'll get without a proper car wash," he said at last. "I suggest you get in, and we'll make good our escape while we can."

AS THEY PASSED THROUGH THE wrought-iron gates onto the open road, Hal felt as if an enormous weight had lifted from her shoulders, but she didn't realize that she had let out an audible sigh of relief until Ezra turned to look at her, the corner of his mouth twisted into a wry acknowledgment.

"Glad I'm not the only one."

"Oh." Hal felt herself flush. "I didn't mean—"

"Please. I'm not one for hypocrisy. It's a horrible place. Why do you think we all got out as soon as we could?"

"I'm sorry," Hal said. She didn't quite know what to say. "It—it's strange, because it's such a beautiful building, in some ways."

"It's just a house," Ezra said briefly. "It was never a home—not even when I lived there."

Hal said nothing. Harding's words to Mitzi echoed in the back of her head: *My mother was a bitter, poisonous woman and her one aim in life was to spread that poison as far and wide as she could. . . .* Ezra had grown up with that poison. They all had.

Was Harding right? Was the decision to leave the house to Hal his mother's last act of vengeance?

"I have no interest in that place," Ezra said. He glanced over his shoulder as they came up to a blind bend, hugging the curve of the road. "I only came back to see my mother buried. I am telling you this, Harriet, so that you understand there's no hard feelings on my part about my mother's will. Understand? My only wish in all this is to leave this place now and for good. You can do what you like with it, as far as I'm concerned. Sell it. Tear it down. I really don't care."

"I understand," Hal said quietly. There was a silence in the car, while she searched for something to say, something to forestall the questions that would come if she let the silence stretch out too long. *Control the conversation,* she heard her mother's voice in her ear. *Make sure you are in the driving seat, not the client.* She felt a sudden overwhelming rush of longing to know about her mother's past, about her connection to this place. What had it been like, coming here as an orphan cousin? Had her mother felt the same oppression that Ezra had described, that Hal herself had felt? How long had she stayed? A week? A month? A year?

If only she could ask Ezra. He must have known her. The photograph, warm in Hal's back pocket, was evidence of that—evidence that they had met, spoken.

"Your—your car," Hal said at last, struggling for a remark. "It's a left-hand drive, I've just realized. Do you live abroad?"

"I do," Ezra said. For a minute he seemed disinclined to say more, but then he added, "I live in the south of France, near Nice. I own a small photographic gallery down there."

"How lovely," Hal said, and the envy in her voice was no fabrication. "I went to Nice once, on a school trip. It was beautiful."

"It's a nice place, yes," Ezra said shortly.

"Have you lived there long?" Hal asked.

"Twenty years or so," Ezra said. Hal did the maths in her head as he stepped on the accelerator to pass a parked car. He could not be more than forty, which meant he must have left England almost as soon as he left school. London had not been far enough for him.

"You live in Brighton, don't you?" he asked, glancing across at her. Hal nodded.

"Yes. It's nice too, the beach isn't as spectacular as Nice, but . . . I don't know. I can't imagine living far from the sea."

"Me either."

They continued in silence for a while. It was only when they reached the outskirts of Penzance that something occurred to Hal and she broke the quiet in the car.

"Un—" The phrase felt strange and false on her tongue, but she forced it out. "Uncle Ezra, do you—do you speak French?"

He glanced across from the road, his expression a little quizzical, with an element of some skepticism Hal couldn't quite pin down.

"I do. Why do you ask?"

"I wondered . . . I heard a phrase . . . *après moi, le déluge.* What does it mean? It's something about a flood, isn't it?"

"Literally, yes." Ezra shot her a look, and then indicated a turn in front of a lorry. After they had completed the turn, he spoke again. "But it's a famous saying in France. It's usually attributed to Louis Quinze, who was the last king before the Revolution came and destroyed his son. The literal meaning is, as you say, 'after me comes the flood'—but the real meaning is something more profound and ambiguous. . . . It means either, 'after I go, everything will collapse into chaos, because I have been the only person holding up the dam,' or else something even darker."

"Even darker?" Hal said. She gave a small laugh. "That's pretty dark already."

"It depends how you take it, though. Does it mean, 'I am dying, I have done all I can to prevent this, but now it must take its course,' or does it mean . . ." He paused, waiting for a gap in the traffic, and Hal realized she understood what he was saying.

"I suppose there's a sense of . . . not just knowing what may come, but willing it to happen," she said. "Acknowledging your part in precipitating it. Is that what you're saying?"

"Exactly."

Hal could not quite work out what to say in reply to this. The thought came to her again: an old woman, knowing the end was coming near, rubbing her hands as she drew up the will that was to set her nearest and dearest at each other's throats. Had it really been as calculatingly vicious as that?

There was no love lost between Harding and Ezra, you didn't have to be a cold reader to work that out. But what was her own part in all this?

They drove the last mile or so in silence, Hal lost in her own thoughts, until at last Ezra drew into a car park and stopped the car, pulling up the hand brake with a crunch and killing the engine.

"Well, here we are. There's just one hitch."

"What's that?"

"It's twelve twenty. I think we've missed the appointment."

"Oh." Hal said. She glanced at the clock on the dashboard, and felt a sudden sickening mix of emotions wash over her—a queasy relief at not having to face Mr. Treswick today, and trepidation at the thought of Harding's reaction, and at the knowledge that she had only postponed the encounter. "Fuck." It was out before she had considered it, and she bit her lip. The word was not in keeping with the image she was trying to present to the Westaways—meek, unassuming little Harriet, butter wouldn't melt. Swearing wasn't part of the deal, and she felt as cross with herself as if she'd sworn at a client. The pink on her cheeks was real, though it was a flush of annoyance at her own unguardedness, rather than shame. "Sorry, that was—"

"Oh, for God's sake, you're an adult. I'm not your keeper. And while we're at it, can we stop with the Uncle Ezra business? I'm not your uncle."

Hal flinched in spite of herself, and perhaps Ezra noticed, for he rephrased.

"I didn't mean that as coldly as it sounded. But we've never met. *Uncle* implies a relationship that we don't have—and as I said before, Harding has the monopoly on hypocrisy in this family. I'm done with all that."

"Okay. . . ." Hal said slowly. "So . . . what should I call you?"

"Ezra will do fine," he said. He opened his car door.

"Wait," Hal said impetuously. She put out a hand towards the gear stick, not quite touching his. "If—if we're swapping names . . ."

"Yes?"

"Everyone here calls me Harriet, but that's not what my—" She stopped. She had been about to say, *that's not what my mother called me,* but somehow the word stuck in her throat. "That's not what my friends call me," she finished.

Ezra raised one eyebrow, interrogatively. "And that is . . . ?" he prompted.

"Hal," Hal said. Her heart was beating, as though she had given away a great piece of herself. There was no logic to it—these people knew her real name, who she was, even where she lived, thanks to Mr. Treswick. Compared to what she had done already, there was nothing identifying or risky about sharing a nickname; yet it felt like a leap of faith in a way that nothing else had. "They call me Hal."

"Hal," Ezra said. He said it slowly, as if rolling the word around his mouth, tasting it. "Hal." Then his tanned face broke into a broad grin—generous, beguiling, quite different from his usual, rather sardonic expression. "I like it. Well, shall we go and report in for a telling off?"

"Yes," Hal said. She drew a deep breath, and opened the door of the car. The tin of tarot cards felt hard in her back pocket, and she thought of the page, and of the storm clouds roiling behind him, and the rough waves at his feet, the rising waters. *Après moi, le déluge. . . .*

"Yes. Let's go."

CHAPTER 22

"Marvelous." Harding's voice was sarcastic. "You do realize what you've just ensured, don't you, Harriet?"

"Me?" Hal felt a wave of annoyance at the injustice of his remark wash over her, and swallowed it back, remembering her role as a meek, biddable niece. She was arranging her face in an expression of contrition when Ezra broke in, sounding bored.

"Harding, if anyone is at fault here, it's me. Or rather those fucking magpies."

"Magpies be damned. Today is Friday, in case you haven't noticed. The solicitors' offices are closed tomorrow and Sunday. Your tardiness has just ensured that we will all have to hang around until Monday to continue the discussions."

"Let me guess," Ezra said, and there was an edge in his voice that Hal remembered from breakfast, "you'll be docking my pocket money and taking away my Xbox privileges?"

"Monday? Surely not!" Mitzi interrupted. "Why can't we come back this afternoon?"

They were standing outside Mr. Treswick's office, on a narrow little back street with a view looking down towards the choppy harbor waters.

"Unfortunately Mr. Treswick has an unavoidable appointment in Truro this afternoon—that was the whole point of meeting before lunch—so he won't be available until Monday morning at the earliest. And although the identification documents could no doubt be dealt with by post, there are papers to sign and a huge amount to discuss, which can really only be accomplished face-to-face. Not least the vexed question of Mrs. Warren."

"But the children need to be back at school on Monday!" Mitzi protested. Harding sighed heavily.

"Well, I very much regret it, but I think the only sensible solution is for you and the children to return, and for Ezra, Abel, Harriet, and myself to stay until this is sorted out."

"Speak for yourself," Ezra said. He sounded bored again, his irritation back under control, though Hal had the impression his temper was still there, like a dog barely kept at heel. "I don't intend to hang around, and I don't suppose Abel does either. We're not named in the will. Why should we?"

"Unfortunately," Harding said, rather testily, "it appears that you are. As am I. As is Abel. Not as beneficiaries, but a little talk just now with Mr. Treswick's receptionist revealed a delightful little nugget that he omitted to mention. For some reason Mother saw fit to make the three of us joint executors, along with Mr. Treswick himself."

"What?" Ezra's face was incredulous.

"You heard me."

"You must be joking! It's almost like she *wanted* us here, tearing at each other's throats."

"I have no doubt she did," Harding said. "In fact, I'd go as far as to say this whole situation was probably engineered with precisely that outcome in mind."

"I won't do it," Ezra said. His face was set, his dark brows knitted, giving him a saturnine look. "I'll—renounce it, or whatever the bloody word is. You can't be forced to act as executor."

"In the longer term, I'm sure you're right," Harding said irritably.

"But it would be a courtesy to inform Mr. Treswick of that fact—and I'm sure there will be some formalities associated with giving up the role. I highly doubt you can simply get back into your Saab and speed back to Nice without a word to anyone."

"That fucking bitch," Ezra said viciously, and in the ensuing silence Hal heard Freddie snigger, loud and clear. "And you can shut up as well," Ezra snarled.

"Ezra!" Mitzi gasped. Freddie's jaw had dropped and his face was blank with shock. Behind him, Hal saw that Kitty was stifling her own laugh with her hand.

There was a moment's silence; then Mitzi hoisted her handbag on her shoulder and drew herself up to her not-very-full height.

"Well. That is *quite* enough. Richard, Katherine, Frederick, come, please."

"But—" Richard began.

"I said, we are leaving," Mitzi barked. "We'll go and find a place for lunch. Harding—I will text you when we've found a café."

Harding gave a *harrumph* that might have been acquiescence or might have been annoyance, and Mitzi stalked away, up the narrow street, her children in tow.

Hal suppressed the urge to run after them—or, even better, to keep on running, past the little group, up the high street, and into Penzance station, to board a train back to her old life and never return here again. As she watched, the little group turned the corner at the top of the street and disappeared.

"Fuck," Ezra said. He ran a hand over his unshaven face, and then through his hair, ruffling it up so that it stood on end, the curls sticking out in all directions. "*Fuck*. Harding, I'm sorry. That was out of order. The kid—it was just the wrong—"

Harding shrugged.

"It's not me you need to apologize to, though I daresay a spot of groveling to Mitzi wouldn't go amiss. But I imagine Freddie's heard worse at school, so I'm sure he'll survive."

"I'm *sorry*," Ezra said again. And then, "*Shit*."

"Look," Harding said, a touch of impatience in his voice, "I'm not concerned about Freddie right now. You lost your temper. It's not the end of the world. I'm more concerned about what we do about this damned business with Mr. Treswick. I want this over as much as you do, Ezra. But running away is only going to create more problems. If you insist on leaving, obviously I can't prevent you. But I would suggest that it will probably be a lot quicker, in the long run, to sort this out here and now, rather than shuttling papers and identification documents back and forth across the Channel. Harriet"—he turned to her—"I'm very sorry for this inconvenience, but I take it you will be able to negotiate a day off work, given the circumstances?"

"I—I'm not sure," Hal said, feeling both their eyes on her. The image flashed into her head again of herself as a rat, backed into a corner, scrabbling for a way out.

"If your employer would like to speak to someone about this—"

"No, it's fine," Hal said hastily. "I'm self-employed, anyway. I only have myself to think about."

She should probably phone Mr. White, ask someone to put a note up on the kiosk to explain the situation to any clients who dropped past. But he could hardly kick up a fuss for a family bereavement. And mid-week in early December, no one would miss her except possibly Reg.

"Self-employed?" Harding raised his eyebrows as he buttoned his coat. "I realize I've never asked, Harriet, what *do* you do?"

"I'm—I work on a pier," Hal said awkwardly. She disliked this question. Her profession came up sometimes with new acquaintances, and invariably it made her into the center of attention in a way that she did not enjoy. The responses varied depending on the social situation. In passing conversation, it could be anything from polite interest to veiled amusement. At parties and in pubs, it was more often guffawing skepticism, or clamorous requests for a reading. She had quickly learned not to say "psychic" because of the aggressive demands to produce an instant prediction there and then. "Tell me what I'm thinking," Hal remembered one man in a pub saying, almost shoving his face into hers. "Go on. Tell me what I'm thinking if you're a bloody Mystic Mog."

He'd looked down at her small breasts, and Hal had thought, *I know what you're thinking.* But she didn't say it.

Now, if pressed for details, she simply said she did tarot readings, and then when people asked for one she was able to laugh and say that she didn't have her cards.

For a moment she thought that Harding might be about to ask questions, but fortunately at that second his phone buzzed, and when he pulled it out of his pocket, his face brightened.

"Ah, it's Mit. She's found a café. Well, Harriet. Shall we?"

IN THE CAR BACK TO Trepassen, Hal was silent. Ezra had not joined them for lunch, pleading the meeting with his bank, and she had waited for a good hour at the prearranged spot in the car park, long after Mitzi and Harding had driven away. When Ezra had finally turned up, there was a smell of whiskey on his breath. His driving seemed unaffected, however, though Hal had not been able to stop herself from wincing when he pulled out in front of a fast-moving Land Rover.

They were almost back to Trepassen House when Ezra spoke.

"Are you okay? You're very quiet."

"Sorry," Hal said. She forced herself to sit up straighter, paint a slightly nervous smile on her lips. *Remember—you're a mouse, not a rat. Little mousy Harriet.* "I was just . . . thinking."

"About . . . ?"

"It's . . ." She paused, trying to think of something that would be the truth, but not the truth, but the words came out almost in spite of herself. "It's just . . . Harding, and his family. I don't think they realize how lucky they are . . . in some ways."

Ezra said nothing, but he cocked another glance at her, and then shifted down a gear for a tight bend.

"They are lucky," he said at last. "And you're right, they don't know it. Maybe that's what made me lash out at poor Freddie." He rubbed his hand over his face and sighed, and Hal smelled again the faint scent of whiskey. "Whatever Harding's faults—and God knows he's got them—he's a better parent than most."

"My mother was a wonderful parent," Hal said. Her voice shook despite herself, and she clenched her jaw, thinking, *I will not cry. Not now. Not here. I will not use her death to get his sympathy.* But she could not stop a single tear tracing its way down her nose. She scrubbed it away fiercely. "At least, whatever I've lost, I had her for eighteen years. I wouldn't have changed a thing, in all that time."

Ezra changed gear again and then said, with a perceptible effort, "Harriet, Abel told me about—" He swallowed hard. "About what, what happened to Maud, the car accident. He said that—"

He stopped, and Hal saw that his face was twisted with grief.

"I never knew." His voice was hoarse, and Hal had the sense that here at last was someone whose grief was as real and encompassing and raw as her own. "I searched for her for years, and I never knew that all that time she was alive and well and living just across the Channel, and it—God, it kills me. I'm so, so angry with her. How could she?"

"I don't know," Hal whispered. And she felt again the tearing sense of betrayal at the lie she was perpetuating here. She had not understood, when she set foot on that train, what she was setting in motion. The lies about herself, about her own background, the game with Mr. Treswick—all that felt like a game. But this playing with people's past tragedies, none of this was what she had signed up for.

What must it be like to lose your twin, your other half?

"I'm sorry," she said, her voice husky with the strain of holding back tears. "I shouldn't have brought her up—I didn't mean—"

She stopped, and Ezra shook his head, but not admonishingly. Instead the gesture seemed to express something neither of them could say.

"What about your father?" he asked at last, and then cleared his throat.

They had come out of the sunken lane and were onto the cliff road that wound inland to Trepassen. Hal found herself staring out of the window at the dark expanse of sea, flint-colored and strange, so different from Brighton's chalk-milky waters.

"I never knew him," she said. Her voice was steady now. This part wasn't painful, at least. There were no betrayals in telling this story, and it was a question she'd answered many times before. "He was a one-night stand. My mother never knew his name."

"So he could be out there, somewhere?" Ezra asked.

Hal shrugged.

"I suppose so. But I can't see any prospect of finding him, even if I wanted to."

"You don't want to, then?"

"Not really. You don't miss what you never had."

It was true, in a way. But even as she said it, Hal thought of Harding at lunch, his arm around Kitty, holding her tightly against the breeze from the door. And she knew . . . it was only half true.

8th December, 1994

Abel came home from Oxford today. Term ended last weekend, but he came home the long way, via a friend's house in Wales, trailing his feet. I don't blame him for his reluctance. Harding, who I still haven't met, sent a brisk message saying the accountancy firm he works for in London couldn't spare him, and that he would not be returning for Christmas. And Ezra's school doesn't break up for another week.

The first I knew of his arrival was Maud pricking up her head, like a collie that has caught a noise. We were sitting in the drawing room, the only warm room in the whole house apart from my aunt's sitting room. We were huddled close to the fire, me playing patience, Maud reading and listening to something on her Walkman. I was frowning over a particularly knotty spread, when suddenly she pulled off her headphones.

"Jesus," she said. "We must look like something out of Little Fucking Women. What—"

She broke off abruptly, and listened for a moment. Then, before I could ask what she had heard, she was running out of the drawing room, down the corridor towards the front door.

"Al!" I heard, and his answering shout, and I followed, in time to see her rush into his arms. He picked her up, spinning her around in a giant bear hug while she screeched out laughing protests.

"Hi, Abel," I said, suddenly shy, and he nodded at me over the top of Maud's head as he deposited her down on the hallway rug.

"Hi, Maggie."

And then that was it. The kind of greeting you'd give a stranger, or a passing acquaintance. He picked up his case, slung one arm around Maud's shoulders, and went back to talking to her about his term, about some girl he was seeing, and I felt . . . I don't know what. A kind of furious grief, I suppose. Disappointment that after all that happened over the summer, he couldn't bring himself to ask how I was, or what was happening in my life. It had felt like we were so close, all of us, in those lazy summer days. And over the weeks and months that followed, Maud and I had become even closer—closer than sisters. But now it was very plain, to Abel at least, I am an outsider in this family. Perhaps I always will be.

The thought was unsettling, and I turned away, back down the chilly corridor to the comparative warmth of the drawing room, turning over possibilities in my mind.

Soon the truth will come out whether I want it to or not. The question is, when it does, will they close ranks against me?

I thought, when I came here, that I was finding a second family, a replacement for the one I had lost. But now . . . now I'm no longer sure. Seeing Maud in Abel's arms like that, laughing together, excluding me even without meaning to . . . well, it was a reminder of a truth I should never have forgotten: whatever else we have shared, blood is thicker than water. And if they close ranks against me, I have nowhere else to go.

CHAPTER 23

It was awkward getting out of Ezra's car, and Hal stumbled, and as she did, she felt the tin slide from her back pocket and land with a thud on the gravel, spilling open.

"Damn!"

She bent, scrabbling up the feathered old cards before they were caught by the wind and whipped away.

Ezra slammed his door and came round her side of the car to help.

"Dropped something?" he asked, and then leaned down and picked up one of the cards, looking at it curiously. As he did, his face changed, almost as if he had seen a ghost, and then he seemed to catch hold of himself, and gave a laugh.

"Tarot!"

"It's what I do," Hal said shortly. There was a card slipped under the wheel of the Saab, and she tried to tease it out without ripping the edge on the gravel. "I'm a tarot reader on the pier in Brighton."

"No way!" He was laughing properly now. "Really? You kept that quiet."

"Not really." She bent and peered under the chassis of the car. There were two more cards beneath, and she grabbed the first, but could not reach the second. "Could you—can you reach that card right in the middle there? Between the wheels?"

Ezra bent and looked, and then stretched a long arm beneath the body of the car, scrabbling with his fingers.

"Got it."

But when he stood, brushing himself off, and looked at the object he was holding, Hal saw that it wasn't a card. It was the photograph that Abel had given her.

"Huh." He held it in his hands for a moment, brushing a fragment of gravel off the fragile folds. "Where did you get this?"

"Abel gave it to me." Hal bit her lip. "He—he thought . . . he thought I might want it. Because I don't have many photos of my mother."

"I see." Ezra said nothing more, just stared down at the photograph, and Hal saw his thumb very gently brush the face of his sister, sitting beside him, laughing at him. "You—" He swallowed painfully. "You must miss her."

"Yes. Yes, I do."

Her throat hurt with the truth of it. Time healed, they said, but it wasn't true, or not completely. The first raw wound of loss had closed and silvered over, yes, but the scar it had left would never heal. It would always be there, aching and tender.

Ezra brushed again at an imaginary speck of sand, and then, almost reluctantly, Hal thought, he handed the picture to her with a smile that held something of her own barely covered grief.

"I do too," he said. And then he turned and headed into the house, as though there were nothing more he could bear to say.

CHAPTER 24

"So, in view of all that, it looks like we are stuck until Monday," Harding said wearily, slumping back on the drawing room sofa. He picked a cup of tea off the tray that Mitzi had just put in front of him and took a gulp.

"You are kidding me." Abel put his head in his hands. "I can't stay away until Tuesday. I've got client meetings on Monday afternoon."

"Well, I suggest you postpone them," Harding said irritably. He smoothed his shirt, which was gaping across the middle, exposing soft white skin like uncooked dough. "Might I add, it's partly your fault for not being present at the meeting in the first place. Between you and Ezra, I have the feeling that I'm the only person trying to sort out this mare's nest."

"I had no idea Mother had made me her bloody executor!" Abel said. "What in God's name possessed her?"

"What in God's name possessed her to do *any* of this," Harding snapped. "Including disinheriting all of her children."

"Spite, pure and simple," Ezra said from the corner of the room. He rose, took a cup from the tray and a digestive biscuit from the plate. "I've no doubt the one thing that amused her on her deathbed was the thought of the unpleasantness she was leaving behind."

Abel nodded bitterly.

"I could believe that. She probably thought that a protracted legal wrangle swallowing up all the estate's resources would keep the unpleasantness going for years."

Protracted legal wrangle. The words made Hal's stomach seem to drop away, and she felt a spike of fear course through her. There was no way any papers she could forge would survive such a process. It would all come out—the truth about her mother, her grandmother—everything.

But there was no way back now—she had gone too far. There was no longer any possibility she could credibly pass off this deception as an honest mistake.

She imagined herself in a court of law, the prosecuting barrister saying, with false confusion, "Run this past me again, Miss Westaway. It was your honest belief that your maternal grandmother had changed her name from Marion to Hester and moved from a modest council house in Surrey to an estate in Cornwall *after her own death*?"

Hal felt the confession rising up inside her again. *Impostor. I'm an impostor.*

There was only one way out. It wouldn't save her from Mr. Smith—but then nothing would, that was becoming clear. Even if, by some miracle, she managed to get hold of fake papers good enough to pass muster, and to bluff her way through the interviews, there would be no money in time for his deadline.

No. She would just have to cut her losses and get out, while she still could.

She stood, shoving her hands in her pockets to prevent them from shaking.

"Listen, I've been thinking—"

"Not now, Harriet," Harding said. He dunked his biscuit in his tea, and then tutted as the edge crumbled.

"Yes, now!" Hal said firmly. She felt a kind of desperation choke her—the knowledge that she was blundering deeper with every day that passed, and that soon there might be no escape route at all. "I've been thinking—about the legacy—I don't—"

She stopped—searching for words, searching for the right way to say this. But before she had found her tongue, Ezra cut into the silence.

"Look, Abel's right. Very probably Mother *did* want us to spend the money on litigation and quarreling. I can't see any other reason for her doing this. But let's be honest—do any of us deserve a penny from her?" He looked at Harding, then at Abel. Abel shrugged. "Do we *want* a penny? I certainly don't. Isn't the best thing just to foil Mother's wish and let it go?"

From the corner of the sofa, Kitty began humming the *Frozen* theme.

Abel laughed.

"Let it go. I like it, Kitty. There's something rather . . . freeing about the idea. Well, for my part, I never expected anything, and I certainly don't want Trepassen like a millstone around my neck. I'd be glad for it to go to Harriet."

"No!" Hal said desperately. The words burst out of her, and she spoke without thinking, without holding back what she really meant. "You don't understand—I don't—I don't *want* this."

"I *beg* your pardon?" Harding turned towards her, one brow raised.

"I don't want—*this*." Hal waved her hand at the house, the grounds outside the window. "This isn't what I thought I was signing up for when I came here. When I got Mr. Treswick's letter, yes, I admit, I was hoping for a legacy." The words tumbled out, spoken from the heart, too rapidly to consider whether she was doing the wise thing. "But not this—not *everything*. I never wanted such a huge responsibility—all I ever wanted was to pay my heating bill and some of my debts. Isn't there any way I can—I don't know—can't I renounce this?"

There was a long silence, broken only by Kitty still humming "Let It Go" beneath her breath, and the subdued hiss of Freddie's earphones.

"Well," Mitzi said at last, her tone bright and rather brittle, "I call that very handsome of you, Harriet."

"It . . . it's certainly something to consider," Harding said. He stood, tucked his shirt more firmly into his pleated trousers, and paced to the window. "I believe there is something called a deed of variation, which enables beneficiaries of a will—providing everyone involved agrees—to vary their shares of the inheritance . . . but we must of course consider whether that would be morally right, given Mother's wishes—"

"I don't want her money," Ezra said bluntly. "I don't want it from her, and I don't want it from Harriet."

"Look," Abel said. He put his arm around Hal's shoulders, squeezing her tight. "It's a lovely gesture, there's no doubt about it, and I'm very proud of Harriet for suggesting it. But it's not something to be decided lightly. I suggest we all sleep on this—not least Harriet—and perhaps we"—he glanced at his brothers—"ought to talk about this separately. And then discuss, before we meet Mr. Treswick on Monday. Agreed?"

"Agreed," Harding said. "Harriet?"

"Okay," Hal said. She realized that her fists were clenched inside the sleeves of her jumper, the muscles tensely resisting Abel's hug. "But I'm not going to change my mind."

CHAPTER 25

It was several hours later, and Hal was walking the grounds in the growing dusk, trying to work out what the hell to do. Her sense of intrepid Robin Hood daring had completely vanished, and she felt only a growing panic, swelling inside her, threatening to suffocate her.

Abel had tried to take her aside after the tea and talk to her, but she had broken away, unable to take his well-meaning concern. The pats on the arm, the platitudes, the overaffectionate hugs, they were all making her feel stifled, and she had made an excuse about feeling tired and wanting to go up to her room, and he had let her go.

When she had got up there, though, the feeling of suffocation had only increased, and she lay in the narrow metal cot, with the bars looming over her like a prison cell. She could not stop thinking about the bolts on the door, and the tiny, crabbed *HELP ME* on the glass of the window. What had happened here? Why had her mother never mentioned this part of her life? Had something so terrible happened that she could not bear to talk about it?

In the end, she had got up and tiptoed quietly down the stairs, past the drawing room, where Mitzi was holding forth to her children about homework and revision, and out into the twilit garden.

Dew was falling, turning the grass silver in the light from the drawing room windows, and when she looked back up the hill she could see the trail she had left, and feel the wetness of her jeans, the damp seeping through her boots.

She walked without purpose or aim, until she found herself back at the copse of trees she had seen the first day, the one she had noticed before Abel pointed out the maze.

This time, she could see clearly through the trees the glimmer of water, and she made her way along the overgrown path, weaving past nettles and brambles, to the shore of a small lake. Once, she thought, it might have been a lovely spot. But now, with night falling and the winter coming, there was something terribly sad about it, the lake choked and peat-colored with rotting leaves, the shores impassable banks of black mud. In the center was a little island with a scraggle of trees and bushes, and across the other side was a dark shape, some kind of building, Hal thought, though her eyes struggled to make it out in the dim light.

She took off her glasses, polishing them to try to make out the shape better in the gloaming, when she heard a crack behind her and whipped around to see a tall figure silhouetted against the lights of the house.

"Who—" she managed, her heart thudding in her chest, and she heard a laugh, deep and amused.

"Sorry." It was a man's voice, and as the figure came closer, she scrabbled her glasses back on with shaking hands, and recognized the face. It was Edward. "I didn't mean to startle you. It's dinner—didn't you hear the gong?"

"How—" Hal found she was trembling, her shock out of all proportion to Edward's looming presence on the dark path. "How did you kn-know I was here?"

"I followed your footsteps in the dew. What on earth possessed you to come here? It's a pretty depressing spot."

"I don't know," Hal said. Her heart in her chest was still thumping, but it was slowing. "I—I wanted a walk. I needed to get out."

"I'm not surprised," Edward said. He put his hands in his pockets, digging for something, and for a minute Hal wondered what it was, but then he pulled out a cigarette, tapped his forefinger to his nose, and lit up. "Don't tell Abel. He doesn't like it."

The smoke drifted up, pale against the darkening sky, and Hal found herself wondering about this man. She had barely seen him since his appearance last night. What had he been doing?

"Shall we head up?" she asked, and he nodded.

"Slowly, though, I need to finish this." He took another drag, and Hal began to pick her way back towards the lawn. It had grown much darker since she came down this way, and it was hard to see the path now. She felt a nettle swipe at her arm and winced, drawing in her breath with a hiss of pain.

"Bramble?" said Edward from behind her.

"Nettle," Hal said briefly. She sucked at the side of her hand, feeling the bumps of the sting with her tongue. It was going to hurt.

"Ouch," Edward said laconically, and Hal heard the crackle and flare of his cigarette as he inhaled.

"Tell me," she said, more as a way of distracting herself from her stinging hand than from real curiosity, "what's the building on the other side of the lake?"

"Oh . . . it used to be a boathouse," Edward said. "Back in the day. I doubt you could get a boat across the lake now, too weed-choked." He threw his cigarette butt behind him, and Hal heard it sizzle as it made contact with the water, sinking into the murky depths. "It needs to be dredged. It stinks in the summer."

"I thought you never came here?" Hal asked in surprise. The words were out before she could think better of them, but Edward didn't seem to have taken offense at her questioning. She heard him laugh, softly, behind her in the darkness.

"Bit of poetic license on Abel's part. His mother did cut him off, you know. I think that for several years at least the whole 'darken my doorstep' stuff was quite real. But they had a bit of a rapprochement in recent years."

"People often mellow as they get older, don't they," Hal said carefully. They came out of the trees, and Edward fell into step beside her.

"Maybe," he said. "But I don't think that was it. The impression I got was that Hester had become, if anything, more unpleasant. But Abel . . . well, he's an odd soul. Rather too forgiving for his own good. He can't bear to feel there's bad blood between himself and other people. He'd do almost anything—swallow any amount of insults, walk over hot coals, generally abase himself—rather than feel there's animosity. It's not his most attractive trait, but it does make for an easy life in some ways. The last few years he came down here quite a bit."

Hal was not sure what to say to that. The thought crossed her mind that Edward didn't seem to like his partner very much. But perhaps it was just the effect of a long-term relationship.

As they crossed the lawn, Hal could see that the dining room was still shuttered and dark, and she was rather relieved when they reached the graveled path and Edward turned left, leading them along the façade to the conservatory she had seen earlier that day, and in through it to the room where they had eaten breakfast.

The others were waiting, Harding seated in the wing chair at the head of the table, Freddie slouched low in his seat, playing on his DS, and the other two children surreptitiously checking their phones under cover of the tablecloth. Mitzi was seated between Abel and a chair that had Edward's jacket slung over the back of it, discussing her plans for the journey home. Only Ezra was not yet there.

Hal sat quietly in a spare place next to Richard and tried to disappear into the background, but she had scarcely pulled in her chair when the door to the conservatory opened and Mrs. Warren limped in holding a huge crock of stew.

"Oh, Mrs. Warren!" Mitzi said. She jumped up. "Let me help you."

"'Let me help you,' she says." Mrs. Warren put on a mincing version of Mitzi's cut-glass vowels. She banged the pot down on the table, thin gravy slopping onto the cloth. "Didn't hear none of that when I spent all afternoon chopping."

"Mrs. Warren," Harding said stiffly, "that was rather uncalled for. My wife was out attempting to sort out the business of my mother's will, along with the rest of us. And if you feel the work of catering is too much for you, you have only to say and we'll be glad to help you out."

"I'm not having strangers messing about in my kitchen," Mrs. Warren retorted.

"Really, Mrs. Warren, we're hardly strangers!" Harding snapped, but Mrs. Warren had turned and left the room. "For heaven's sake, she's becoming impossible!"

The door banged shut.

"She's very old, darling," Mitzi said placatingly. "And she looked after your mother fairly devotedly. I think we can cut her a little slack on those grounds, don't you?"

"I agree, Mit, but we must begin to get our heads around the problem of what we do with—"

He broke off as Mrs. Warren came back in with a plate of baked potatoes, which she thumped down, and then turned to leave without a word.

Mitzi sighed, and beckoned to Freddie for his plate.

"Come on then, let's get this served up before it goes cold."

The stew was gray and unappetizing, and Freddie's face, as his mother handed him back a plate of gnarled brown lumps and a watery wash of liquid, was dismayed.

"Urgh, Mum, this looks gross."

"Well, it's supper, Freddie, so you'll have to manage. Take a baked potato," Mitzi said. She took Kitty's plate and began ladling. Kitty picked up a potato with her fingers, and pulled a face as she put it on the side of her plate.

"Those potatoes are rock-hard. They look like dinosaur eggs."

"For goodness' sake!" Mitzi snapped. She put a plate down in front of Richard and then began to help Edward.

"I must say, it does smell a little unappetizing," Edward ventured as she passed the plate to him. He took a piece of meat—beef, was Hal's guess, though it could have been anything from mutton to venison—and chewed cautiously. "Do you think I dare ask for some mustard?" He spoke around the lump in his mouth.

"Personally, I wouldn't risk it," Abel said. He was sawing at his meat with rather grim determination, and he put a piece in his mouth, grimacing slightly. "It's actually not too bad," he managed.

"What did I miss?" The voice came from the doorway, and Hal turned to see Ezra standing there, shoulder propped against the doorframe.

"Oh, it's you," Harding said, rather sourly. "How nice of you to deign to join us."

"I didn't miss much, judging by Abel's face," Ezra said. He pulled the chair out next to Hal and sat down, resting his tanned forearms on the table. "So. What's for supper then?"

"Gray vomit and dinosaur eggs," Kitty said with a giggle.

"Kitty!" Harding thundered. "I'm thoroughly fed up with you today."

"Oh, for goodness' sake, Harding." Mitzi slammed a plate in front of him. "Leave the child alone. It's not her fault you're in a foul mood."

"I am not in a foul mood," Harding snarled. "I am simply asking for basic manners at the dinner table."

"Look, Mrs. Warren is very old, and she's done her best," Abel began, but Ezra interrupted him.

"Oh, give it a rest, Abel. The girl's right. Mrs. Warren's cooking has *always* been terrible; it's just that as kids, we only had boarding school dinners to compare it to, so we didn't realize quite how bad it was. Harding's lot are lucky enough to have higher standards of comparison."

Hal's bowl had made its way down to her, and she poked cautiously at the gray lump of meat, and abandoned the stew in favor of the baked potato. The skin was wrinkled, but when she sliced into it, she could feel the middle was raw.

"Well, I'm not eating it," Kitty said firmly. She pushed her plate away. "I saw Mum buying Hobnobs in Penzance today."

THERE WAS NO DESSERT, BUT after dinner they made their way through to the drawing room, where a lukewarm pot of coffee stood on a table in front of the fire. Mitzi left the room and returned with three packets of biscuits, which she opened up and distributed. Her children fell on them like starving orphans. Hal picked out a chocolate digestive and dipped it into the cup of coffee Edward poured for her. The taste, as she put the crumbling corner in her mouth, was pure home, and for a moment she was transported back to her childhood, to Sunday mornings in her mother's bed, surreptitiously dipping cookies into her mother's morning coffee.

"Are you all right, Harriet?" Mitzi's voice broke into her thoughts. "You looked very pensive there, for a moment."

Hal swallowed her mouthful, then forced a smile.

"Yes, I'm fine. Sorry. I was just thinking."

"I found out something about Hal today," Ezra said unexpectedly, from the other side of the room. He picked up his coffee and sipped it, his eyes resting on Hal as he swallowed. "Something she's been keeping rather quiet."

Hal looked up, startled, and felt her heart speed up a little. She went back over the conversation in the car, the things she had said about her mother. Had she let something slip? Her hand, as she set the coffee cup down on its saucer, shook a little, so that the china rattled together with a tinkling sound.

"What's that?" she managed at last.

"Oh . . . I think you know, Hal," Ezra said. There was mischief in his smile. "Why don't you go ahead and tell them."

This is it, Hal thought. *He knows. He's found something out, and he is giving me a chance to confess before he tells them about my past.*

"You're right," Hal said. She swallowed, her mouth suddenly dry. "There is—there is something I didn't tell you. Uncle Harding—I—"

Ezra put something down on the coffee table between them.

It was a tin of Golden Virginia tobacco.

Hal felt the blood rush to her face as she realized her mistake, the huge blunder she had almost just made.

"Harriet is a tarot reader," Ezra said. "Aren't you, Hal?"

"Oh!" Mingled relief and anticlimax flooded through her. She felt a strong desire to laugh. "I didn't realize that's what you were going to— Yes. It's true."

"A tarot reader?" Mitzi exclaimed. She clapped her hands. "But how exotic! Harriet, whyever didn't you tell us?"

"I don't know," Hal said truthfully. "I suppose . . . some people are a little bit odd about it." She thought back to Mrs. Warren, the fury that had boiled up in her face when she saw the cards.

"You know," Abel said, "you know . . . it's funny. I would never have thought Maud's daughter would end up doing something like that. She was terribly skeptical."

Hal glanced up at him, but there was nothing combative in his tone or expression. His face was only a little sad, as if remembering back to happier times.

"She was . . . well, I'm sure you know this better than we do, but she was a very rational person," he continued. "She had no time for what I think she would have called 'bullshit.' Sorry, Harriet," he added hastily, patting her arm. "I don't mean that to sound as rude as it probably comes across. I hope I haven't offended you."

"It's okay," Hal said. She smiled, almost in spite of herself. "I'm not offended. And actually . . . I don't really believe in it myself."

"Really?" Mitzi said, her voice slightly doubtful. "How does that work, then? Don't you feel guilty taking people's money if you think it's all rubbish?"

Hal felt her cheeks flush. She rarely admitted this to people she didn't know—certainly never to clients. It felt like a doctor admitting that he had no faith in conventional medicine, or a psychiatrist dissing Freud.

"That probably sounded more cynical than I meant it to—but . . . I'm not superstitious. I don't believe in knocking on wood, or crossing fingers, or crystal gazing, or any of that. I don't think the cards have any special occult power, though I'm not sure I'd say that outright to a client. But they do . . ." She found herself struggling to articulate something she rarely dissected, even to herself. "They do still have meaning—even if you know nothing about tarot, you can see the richness of the symbolism and the imagery. The ideas they represent . . . they're universal forces that bear on all our lives. I suppose what I believe is not that the cards can tell you anything you don't already know, or that they have magical answers to your questions, but that they give you . . . they give you the space to question . . . ? Does that make sense? Whether the statements I make in a reading are true or false, they give the sitter an opportunity to reflect on those forces, to analyze their instincts. I don't know if I'm explaining this right."

But Mitzi was nodding, a frown drawn between her neat brows.

"Yeees . . ." she said slowly. "Yes, I can see that."

"So will you do one?" Kitty asked. She sat up, her eyes wide with anticipation. "Do me! Oh please, do me first!"

"Kitty," Mitzi scolded. "Harriet is not at work."

"Nonsense," Ezra said. He grinned across at Hal. "She didn't have to bring her cards, did she?"

Hal folded her arms, uncomfortably unsure what to say. After all, it was true. She had chosen to bring her cards, *those* cards in particular. But she didn't want to give a reading, not here, not now, with these cards. For reading the cards was revealing—and not only for the client. Hal knew that she gave away almost as much about herself in the remarks she made as she found out about her clients.

But Kitty was looking at her pleadingly, her hands clasped with anticipation, and Hal didn't have the heart to refuse, or the skill to do it gracefully, in this house where she was a guest.

"Okay," she said at last. "I'll do one for you, Kitty."

"Awesome!" Kitty said excitedly. "What do you need? Do you need a special table or anything?"

Hal shook her head.

"No, an ordinary table is just fine. Sit opposite me."

Kitty knelt on the rug opposite, and Hal opened the tin, and drew out her cards.

"Oooh . . ." Kitty breathed, as Hal spread them on the table. Her eyes darted from one card to another: the two of wands . . . the Hermit . . . the queen of cups . . . "What's that one?" she asked, pointing at the Star.

"This one?" Hal picked it up. In her deck, the Star was a woman bathing in a forest pool at night, pouring water over herself beneath the light of the stars. It was a beautiful card, serene and tranquil. "It's the Star," Hal said. "It means . . . renewal of faith, peace, communing with yourself, serenity. Or reversed, it means the opposite—discouragement, dwelling on the bad things in life."

"And what about this one?" Kitty pointed towards a card at the edge of the deck. It showed a girl crawling across a snowy landscape. Snowflakes fell from a dark sky, their tranquility a sharp contrast to the scene below, where the young woman was poised in her endless struggle. Her bloodied fingers had scored deep grooves in the snow as she dragged herself towards some unseen goal, and in her back were nine daggers, each of a different kind, some long, some short, some polished with finely wrought hilts, others no better than wooden stakes. The tenth, a piece of glass, or perhaps ice, was in her own hand.

"That's the ten of swords," Hal said. She knew the card off by heart, but now she picked it up, studying it afresh, before turning it so that Kitty could better see the image. It was one of the darkest cards in the pack, and it was one that always made Hal flinch a little when it came up in a reading. "It means . . . betrayal, backstabbing, ending . . . but it can also mean that an ordeal is coming to a close. That you'll be given peace, though the price may not be one you want to pay."

"Because she's going to die, you mean?" Kitty's eyes were wide.

"On the card, yes," Hal said. "But you shouldn't take them literally. Now . . ." She picked up the cards, shuffled them together. "I'm going to spread the deck out facedown, and then ask you to choose ten cards. Don't touch the cards—just show me with your finger."

There was something comforting in the familiar ritual. Hal could do a Celtic Cross reading almost in her sleep, and as she laid the cards out and ran through the familiar commands and explanations she always used, she felt her own mind clear.

It was true what she had told Mitzi. She didn't believe in anything mystical, but she did believe in the power of the cards to reveal something about the querent, both to the reader and to the sitter themselves.

She didn't ask Kitty what her question was, but she knew from her bright, blushing face what it would be—something about a boy, no doubt. Or maybe a girl. There was no fear in Kitty's face, no doubt or desperation, as there was when people were asking questions about life or death, about the safety of a child, or the health of a parent.

To Kitty, this was just a bit of fun. He loves me, he loves me not. And that was as it should be, at her age.

When they came to the final card of the reading, the "outcome" card, Hal turned it over, and saw that it was the Lovers, upright, a naked man and woman entwined, his hand upon her breast, bathed in sunlight. And she knew immediately, from the scarlet blush that mounted up Kitty's neck and flushed her cheeks, that she had been right.

"This card," Hal said, smiling in spite of herself, so infectious was Kitty's embarrassed delight, "this card represents the outcome—it's the overriding card of the whole reading, and it's the closest that the cards come to a direct answer to your question. You have chosen the Lovers—a trump card, one of the strongest in the deck. And it means love. Love and union and relationships. What this card is saying, here, in this position, is there will be love and, yes, happiness in your future. I see a very important relationship, one that will be very dear to you, and bring you much joy. But," something made her add, looking at Mitzi's suddenly rather pursed mouth, "this card also means choice—the choice between right and wrong, the high road and the low. This card shows the balance between all the different forces in your life, and indicates the importance of choosing the right course—one that will keep all those forces in their proper proportions. Romantic love is just one element—and it won't always lead you right. You must be careful not to let it dominate everything else in your life. Satisfaction from other sources—work, or family, for example—is just as important, and can bring you just as much happiness. And what this card is telling me is that you will always be loved—" She swallowed for a moment, thinking of Mitzi and Harding and the warm cocoon of security wrapped around their children. "You will always have someone there for you. You can strike out into the world, secure in that love, secure that love will find you."

She stopped, and there was a short pause, and then a little round of applause from the others.

"What a lovely reading, Harriet," Mitzi said. Kitty was pink and radiant, and Hal was suddenly pleased that she had agreed to do this.

"Anyone else?" she said, almost jokingly, and she was surprised when Abel grinned and put up his hand.

"Go on," he said. "Do me."

Hal looked at the clock on the mantelpiece. It was getting on for ten, and Kitty's reading had taken longer than she had realized.

"Okay," she said. "But I'll do you a quicker version of the reading—the Celtic Cross takes rather a long time. This one is simpler, it's called a three-card spread. You can use it in lots of different ways, to answer a question, or to feel your way through a dilemma, or even to explore your past lives, if you believe in that sort of thing, but for now let's just do a past, present, future reading. That's nice and simple—it's a reading people often begin with when they're starting out."

She shuffled the cards, and again went through the familiar patter—asking Abel to think of a question, getting him to cut the cards and choose just three this time. Then she laid them out, facedown—past, present, future—and waited for a moment, gathering her thoughts, listening to the hush that had descended on the room, the crackle of the fire, the sound of the wind in the chimney, and the *tick, tick* of the clock on the mantel.

At last, when her thoughts were still and clear, Hal turned the first one, the past card. There was a moment when the watchers circled around, all crowded in to look—and then a ripple of laughter broke out, as they recognized the image from Kitty's reading. It was the Lovers. Hal smiled, but she shook her head.

"I know what you're thinking—that this is the same card that Kitty drew, and that I'll say the same things, but this is inverse—you've drawn it upside down."

"What does that mean?" Abel asked. Hal watched him looking at the card, trying to read his reaction. It was hard to decipher, but she thought there was something a little mocking about it. His mouth was serious, but compressed as if he were hiding a smile. Hal didn't mind people who didn't take the readings seriously—she didn't like hostility, but amusement was fine. Now she frowned, looking at the image, trying to clarify her thoughts and crystallize them into words.

"You heard me talk to Kitty about the fact that the Lovers represent choice," she began. "Well, this is a card full of stark opposites—male and female, sky and earth, the fire of the sun and water of the river behind them, the high road of the mountain and the low road of the valley. In the past you've had a choice—and a pretty stark one. It was a crossroads in your life—a decision where you . . ." She paused, seeing Abel's hands tighten, his fingers going to a ring on the fourth finger of his right hand, heard the slight clearing of his throat showing she had touched on a nerve. He twisted the ring as she continued. "I think perhaps it was to do with . . . a relationship? You made your choice, and at the time it seemed like the right, the only decision . . . but now—"

She stopped, suddenly realizing the dangerous path this reading was leading her down.

Abel's expression had lost its mocking amusement, and behind him, Hal saw Edward stir uneasily; she bit her lip, wondering if she had already said too much.

To cover the moment of confusion, Hal turned over the next card. It was the ten of swords, and Hal saw Abel push his chair back a little from the table, cross his legs defensively. Something was very wrong here—she could feel the tension emanating from him, and she knew she had to tread carefully, for she had stumbled on something she didn't understand and it was in danger of blowing up in her face.

"This . . . this is the present," she said slowly. "The problem you're wrestling with at the moment. It concerns . . . a betrayal—"

She broke off. Abel had stood up and pushed past her, not waiting for the end of the reading.

"I'm sorry, Hal," he flung over his shoulder, "but I don't think I can do this."

The drawing room door slammed shut behind him.

"Oh God." It was Edward, his face white and anguished. He shot a look at Hal, something between anger and upset. "Thank you *very* much," he said, and then yanked Abel's chair out of the way and ran after his partner into the hallway. "Abel!" Hal heard from far down the corridor as his feet receded. "Abel, come back!"

Mitzi looked first at Ezra, then Harding, and blew out a long breath.

"Oh dear."

"What?" Hal looked around the circle of faces, dismay rising in her. "What did I say?"

"You weren't to know, Harriet," Mitzi said. She got up, and picked up the chair that Edward had toppled in his haste to follow Abel. "Although quite why Abel reacted like that I don't know. . . ."

"What Hal said was completely general," Ezra said. "If Al hadn't reacted like a hysterical teenager—"

"Go to bed, children," Mitzi said firmly. There was a chorus of protest from Richard, Kitty, and Freddie, which she quelled by adding, "Just this once, you can take your phones up with you. I'll come to collect them at lights out. Go!"

She waited until the children had left the room, dragging their feet, and then shut the door behind them and turned to Hal.

"Harriet, I wouldn't normally gossip about this, but I think at this point it's better that you know. As far as I understand it, Abel proposed marriage to Edward last year, but then . . ."

She faltered and looked across at Harding, who threw up his hands as if to say *Don't look at me! You started this.*

"But then it turned out Edward had been fucking some woman for about four years," Ezra finished, rather brutally. "There. I've said it. That *is* what happened, isn't it?"

Mitzi nodded, rather sadly.

"Yes, that's my understanding too. I had a rather confused conversation with Edward about it last year when he was drunk, where he tried to represent it as some sort of wild oats, but really of course the time for all that is well past. It's one thing to do that sort of thing as an eighteen-year-old, quite different when you're a fortysomething man in a long-term relationship. Anyway, to cut a long story short, I think they went through a really very rocky time. I had thought it was all sorted out, but evidently this brought up some painful memories. You weren't to know, Harriet."

"Oh no," Hal said wretchedly. She put her head in her hands. "I'm so sorry. I wish I hadn't done this."

"It was my fault," Ezra said. He shook his head. "I shouldn't have asked you to read. I'm sorry, Hal."

"You keep calling her that," Mitzi said lightly. Her effort to change the subject was a little forced and obvious, but Hal welcomed it nonetheless. She held out the tin, and Hal gathered the cards together and slipped them inside. "Is it a nickname?"

"Yes," Hal said. "It—it's what my mother used to call me."

"You must miss her enormously," Mitzi said. She put out a hand, and tucked a stray lock of hair behind Hal's ear. To her horror, Hal felt tears welling up inside her. She turned away, pretending to search for a stray card, swallowing hard against the sudden lump in her throat and blinking away the swimming tears in her eyes.

"I—I do—" she managed. Her voice was croaky, despite her efforts.

"Oh, Hal, darling, come here," Mitzi said. She held out her arms, and almost in spite of herself, Hal found herself swept into a hug.

It was incredibly alien—Mitzi's slim, wiry frame, no taller than Hal's own; the scent of her perfume and hair spray strong in Hal's nostrils; the painful impression of her chunky necklace against Hal's ribs. But there was something so simple, so instinctually maternal about the gesture, that she could not bring herself to break away.

"I just wanted to say," Mitzi whispered into her ear, not trying to hide what she was saying, but meaning it for Hal rather than for general discussion, "that you were a complete darling to say what you did earlier, about the deed of variation. Whatever you decide—and you mustn't let yourself get swept up in all this nonsense, or to feel responsible for what your grandmother did—it was very noble of you to think of it."

"Thank you," Hal managed. Her throat felt stiff and hoarse, and she let her fingers rest on Mitzi's shoulders, half wanting to free herself, half unable to stop herself from hugging her back.

"We *aren't* going to let you disinherit yourself," Mitzi said sternly, as she released Hal. "There is no question of that. And regardless of what happens, you have a family now, so don't you forget it."

Hal nodded, forcing a smile, in spite of the tears that still threatened to fall. And then she picked up the tin full of cards, made her excuses, and escaped up the stairs to bed.

11th December, 1994

My aunt knows. I don't know how—but she knows. Did Maud tell her? It seems impossible—I'm as certain as I can be that she wouldn't say anything, not after her promise. Lizzie, perhaps? From the way she looks at me I have a horrible feeling she may be putting two and two together. But I can't believe . . .

In the end, it doesn't really matter. She has found out.

She came to my room as I was getting ready for bed, bursting in without knocking.

"Is it true?"

I was half-undressed, and I clasped my shirt to my chest, trying to cover my swollen breasts and stomach, under pretense of shyness. I shook my head, pretending I didn't know what she meant, and she drew back her hand and slapped me, making my head jerk backwards, leaving my ears ringing and my cheek flaming with the shock of the smack. The shirt fell to the floor, and I saw her looking at me, at my changed body, and her lip curled, as she realised she didn't need to ask the question.

"You disgusting little slut. I took you in, and this is how you pay me back?"

"Who told you?" I said bitterly. I picked up the shirt and put it back on, wincing against the stinging pain in my cheek.

"That's none of your business. Who is he?" she demanded, and when I didn't answer straightaway, she grabbed my shoulders and shook me like a rat, making my teeth rattle. "Who's the boy who did this?" she shouted.

I shook my head again, trying not to cringe away from her fury, trying not to show my fear. My aunt has always intimidated me—but I had never seen her like this, and suddenly I understood how Maud hated her so much.

"I w-won't t-tell you," I managed, though it was hard to speak. I can't let her know. Her anger would be unspeakable and I would never see him again.

She stared down at me for a long moment, and then she turned on her heel.

"I can't trust you. You've shown that. You'll stay in your room and I will have supper brought up to you. You can stay here and think about what you have done and the shame you've brought on this family."

She slammed the door shut, and I heard a kind of scraping sound, as if someone were scratching something across the top and bottom of the door. It took me a minute to understand, and even when the truth dawned on me, it was with a kind of cold disbelief. Was she—was she locking me in?

"Aunt Hester?" I said, and then as I heard her heels click away down the corridor, I ran to the door, rattling the handle, banging on it with my fists. It didn't open. "Aunt Hester? You can't do this!"

But there was no answer. If she heard me, she said nothing.

Still in disbelief, I tried to force the door, leaning against it with all my strength, but the bolts held.

"Maud!" I screamed. "Lizzie?"

I waited. There was no answering call, only the slam of a door. I wasn't sure which one, but I thought it could be the door at the foot of the attic stairs. A sense of complete hopelessness stole over me as I realised. It was almost eight. Lizzie would have gone home, long since. And Maud—I don't know where she was. In bed? Downstairs? Either way, it wasn't likely my voice would carry all the way through two sets of doors, and down the maze of corridors of this rambling house.

I didn't call for Mrs Warren. There would be no point in that. Even if she heard, she wouldn't come.

I went to the window, looking out between the bars into the quiet, moonlit night—its tranquillity a terrible contrast to my raw throat and my fingers, bruised from hammering.

And a realisation came over me.

I am trapped. I am completely trapped. She could send Maud away to school, sack Lizzie, and keep me here for . . . for how long? For as long as she wants—that's the truth. She could keep me until the baby comes. Or she could starve me until I lose it.

The truth of this makes something inside me turn weak and soft with fear. I should be strong—strong for myself and strong for my child. But I am not. This house hides secrets, I know that now. I've been here long enough to hear the stories, of the unhappy maid who hung herself in the scullery, and the little boy who drowned in the lake.

My aunt is someone. And I am no one. I have no friends here. How easy it would be to say that I simply . . . left. Ran away in the night. No one would raise a fuss. Maud might ask questions, but Mrs Warren would swear to have seen me leave, I'm sure of it.

If she chooses to, she can simply lock the door and throw away the key. And there would be nothing I could do.

I sank to my knees by the window, the moonlight flooding the room, and I put my hands to my face, feeling the wetness of tears, and the cool hardness of the ring I still wear, my mother's engagement ring. It's a diamond—just a very small one. And as I knelt there in the moonlight, something came to me, a desire to leave a mark, however small, something she cannot erase, no matter what she does to me.

I took off the ring, and very slowly I scratched upon the glass, watching the moonlight illuminate the letters like white fire. HELP . . . ME . . .

CHAPTER 26

Up in her room, Hal lay flat on her back, her forearm flung over her eyes to shut out the moonlight, and she could not sleep.

It was not just the moonlight, painfully bright through the thin curtains. It was not even the reading that weighed upon her, or not only the reading. It was everything. Abel's expression as he fled. Edward's exasperation. Mitzi's whispered remarks as she held Hal close . . .

The deed of variation. The thought of it was like a noose around Hal's neck, not yet tight, but slowly tightening, and already making it hard to breathe. When she had suggested it, it seemed like such a simple solution—she would refuse the bequest, melt away back to Brighton, disappear out of their lives.

But Mitzi's last words—so kindly meant—made it clear that that was never going to happen. Even if she renounced this legacy, she would still be trapped in a web of bureaucracy and forms and ID—this tangle of family loyalties and resentments, dragging her under as it had the others. But what could she do? The only way out of it was to admit to her fraud.

Hal sighed, and turned from her back onto her front, pressing her face into the crisp white pillowcase to try to get away from the moonlight that pierced the thin curtains. It cast long dark shadows of the bars across the bed, and as she shut her eyes, she had a sudden, jolting image of herself as she would look to someone standing across the room—like the girl from the ten of swords.

Betrayal. Backstabbing. Defeat.

A prickle of fear ran through her, and suddenly Hal could no longer bear to lie still. She sat up, shivering in the cold, and then got out of bed and paced to the window. There she stood, looking out through the bars across the moonlit landscape.

It looked so different by night. The emerald greens and rain-washed blues were turned to a thousand shades of black, the moonlight serving only to cast long, warped shadows that, without her glasses, made familiar shapes blurred and strange. Even the sounds were different. The roar of the occasional car along the coast road had gone, the cawing of the magpies had fallen silent—and all Hal could hear was the far-off crash of the waves, and the hoot of an owl, hunting. Hal closed her fingers on the window bars and rested her forehead on the glass, wishing, wishing she were a hundred miles away, at home in Brighton, out of this nightmare tangle of lies and guesses.

HELP ME

The letters stood out clear and bright in the moonlight, and Hal suddenly knew, without a shadow of a doubt, that they had been scratched on just such a night as this, by someone even more desperate than her.

Perhaps this other girl had not been as lucky. Perhaps for her the shackles had been not just emotional, but literal. Perhaps she had sat here looking out over the frosty lawn, wondering how or even *if* she could escape.

Well, Hal was not trapped. Not yet. There was still time.

As quietly as she could, she pulled off her pajamas and got back into her jeans, top, and hooded sweater. Then she dragged her case out from under the bed, lifting it so that it made as little noise as possible on the bare boards.

Her spare clothes were already inside, neatly divided into clean and worn. Aside from that, there was only her wash-bag, book, and laptop to pack.

Hal's hands were trembling as she pushed them inside and zipped up the case. Was she really going to do this?

You owe them nothing, she told herself. *You've taken nothing. Not yet.*

And, after all, what was the worst they could do? They had her address, but it didn't seem likely she would be able to stay there for long, not now that Mr. Smith's minders had tracked her down. Perhaps the best thing to do would be to disappear completely—simply scoop up her things, the most important papers, her mother's photographs—and walk away into a new life. There were other towns. Other piers.

The idea of starting again was frightening, and Hal thought of the huddled bodies on the pavements in Brighton, people just like her who had taken a leap—and slipped, falling between the cracks to end up homeless and friendless and alone.

It was a risk—a real risk. Hal had no safety net—and if she fell, there was no one to catch her. For a moment Mr. Treswick had seemed to promise a very different existence, one with savings, and safety, and security. But that moment, that promise, had gone. And whether it was Mitzi's words to her today or the scratches on the windowpane, something inside Hal had crystallized into a cold, hard realization: she had to get away.

Everything was packed—almost. The final thing Hal did was to settle her glasses on her nose and pick up her tarot cards, shoving the tin into her back pocket.

Then she turned the handle of the door and pushed.

Nothing happened.

Hal felt her breath catch in her throat, and her heart seemed suddenly to be beating painfully hard.

The bolts. The bolts on the outside.

But no—it wasn't possible. She would have heard. Surely she would have heard? And who—*why?*

A fluttering panic rose up inside her.

Forcing herself to breathe slowly and steadily, Hal set the case quietly on the floor, wiped her sweating palms on the back pockets of her jeans, and tried again.

The handle was turning, but the door still didn't open to her shove. It was bowing at the top, but stuck at the bottom.

Hal's breath was coming quicker now, but she made herself slow down—think rationally. *There's no reason for anyone to lock you in. You're only panicking because you saw the bolts. Yesterday this wouldn't even have occurred to you. Remember what Mrs. Warren said—damp makes the frame swell.*

Taking a deep breath, she turned the door handle and pushed until a crack appeared around the edge. Then she put her foot against the part that was still sticking and leaned, slow and steady, with as much force as she dared, trying not to make any sudden movements that might wake the sleepers below.

There was a long, protesting *creeeak*, and then the door gave with a bang that sent Hal stumbling forwards, her hand over her mouth.

She waited for the protesting voices, the sound of feet on the stairs . . . but nothing happened, and at last she plucked up the courage to pick up her case and tiptoe out. As she left the bare little room, she could not stop herself looking back at the door, checking to see if . . .

But no. She was being paranoid. The bolts were drawn back, undamaged. It was just as Mrs. Warren had said—the damp, and nothing more.

Still, though. The kind of house that had locks on the outside of the doors was not one Hal wanted to sleep in any longer.

Holding the case in front of her like a shield so that she could fit down the narrow flight, she went as quietly and quickly as she could to the hallway below, and the one below that, and from there down the long curving staircase to the ground floor, and freedom.

13th December, 1994

I have to get away.

I HAVE to get away.

The words I scratched on the window are like a taunt, now. An admission of defeat. Because no one is going to help me except myself.

It is three days since I was locked in here, and apart from a hurried, whispered conversation with Maud, I have seen no one except my aunt. She brings up trays at odd times, and sometimes not at all, leaving me terrified and hungry.

And always—always the same question. Who is he. Who is he. Who is he.

Today, when I shook my head, she hit me again, so that my head snapped back with such a force that I heard my neck crunch, and the hot flare in my cheekbone blossomed across my face and into my ear, making it ring with pain.

I staggered backwards into the bedframe and I looked up at her, holding on to the metal with one hand, the other pressed to my face, as if to hold the bones together. For a moment she looked almost frightened—not of me, but of what she had done, what she might *have done. She had, I think, lost control—perhaps for the first time since I had known her.*

Then she turned on her heel and left and I heard the scraping of the bolts before she clattered down the stairs.

I sank down on the bed. My hands were shaking, and I felt a wave of cramps in my stomach, followed by a wash of sickness. At first I thought I might be losing the baby, but I sat quietly, waiting, and the pains subsided, though the heat in my cheek and the screech of tinnitus in my ear remained.

I wanted to write in my diary—to do as I always do when things get too much—let it out onto the page, like a kind of bloodletting, letting the ink and paper soak up all the grief and anger and fear until I can cope again.

But when I got the book out of its hiding place under the loose board, I looked at it with fresh eyes.

I can't tell her the truth. Not just because if I do, I will never see him again. But because I am seriously beginning to fear that if I do, she may kill me for real. And for the first time, after today, I truly think she is capable of it.

She can't make me tell her—but if she searches my room, she doesn't need to. It's all here.

So after I've finished this entry, I'm going to make a fire, and then I'm going to rip out every single page about him, score out his name, tear out every reference and burn them.

Because, whatever she does to me, she can't make me confess. I just have to hold on until I've seen him—and after that we'll decide what to do, together. Somehow, I will get word to him. I can pass a letter to Maud, perhaps. After all, I have paper here, and pens. And I can trust her—at least . . . at least, I hope I can.

He will come, when he gets that letter, surely? He'll come. He has to. And then—we'll go somewhere, run away—together. We'll figure it out.

I just have to hold on to that thought.

I just have to hold on.

CHAPTER 27

The stairs creaked painfully as Hal made her way downwards, holding her breath at every sound, at the screech of an owl hunting in the garden, at the *drip, drip* of a far-off tap.

At last she reached the passageway on the ground floor, and, holding her suitcase rather than risk the rattling wheels, she tiptoed as quietly as she could towards the entrance hall, where the glass panes above the door cast moon-bright crescents on the panels opposite.

The door was bolted, top and bottom, and Hal struggled with the stiff fastenings, but after what seemed like a silent, trembling age, she worked them out of the shafts and turned the door handle.

It was locked. And there was no key. Hal looked around the entrance hall—beneath the silver salver that held letters and bills. Behind the dusty vase of dried leaves. On the lintel of the door. No key. *No key.*

Her heart was beating fast now. Leaving had become, instead of a longing, an imperative. If she was found here now, stealing out of the house like a thief in the night, it was quite likely someone would call the police. But it no longer mattered. The only thing that mattered was getting away.

Hal scanned the hallway, and then picked up the case and retreated into the drawing room. The tall windows in there were closed and shuttered, but on the inside, and after a long moment of struggling with the bar, it gave with a sudden thump, and the shutter swung open. Behind it, the window itself was fastened with just a simple latch, and Hal lifted it, her heart racing with a mix of relief and anticipation. The panes opened into the room, letting in a gust of frosty air, and she peered out into the night, making sure that she was not about to step out into a six-foot drop.

There was a drop—but only a couple of feet, to the veranda below, and she carefully lowered her case out, then dropped to her knees to clamber out herself.

She was halfway there, one leg over the sill, when a voice spoke from the darkness of the other end of the room.

"That's right. Sneak away in the night. Coward."

Hal's head shot up, her blood suddenly racing with fear.

"Who's there?" she demanded, the fright making her voice more aggressive than she had meant, but the speaker at the other end of the room only laughed, and walked into the shaft of moonlight.

In truth, Hal hadn't really needed to ask. She had known who it was—who else would be prowling so silently through the darkened rooms in the middle of the night?

Mrs. Warren.

"You can't stop me," Hal said. She put her chin up defiantly. "I'm going."

"Who said I'm stopping you?" Mrs. Warren said. Her lip was curled, and there was a kind of scornful laugh in her voice. "I told you to leave once, and I'll say it again. Good riddance. Good riddance to you, and your trash mother before you."

"How dare you." Hal found her voice was shaking—not with fear, but with anger. "What do you know about my mother?"

"More than you," Mrs. Warren said. She leaned towards Hal, her voice full of a venom that made Hal shrink back. "Little milk-

and-water coward. She was a conniving little gold digger, just like you."

Hal scrambled backwards out of the window, and staggered to her knees on the paving. She was so angry, she felt a ringing in her ears, a kind of hissing fury. It was a mixture of fury . . . and shock.

"Don't you dare talk about my mother that way. You don't know what she went through to bring me up—"

"Don't talk to me about what you don't know anything about," Mrs. Warren spat. "Get out. You should never have come back here."

With that, she swung the window shut, so that Hal had to snatch her fingers out of the way, just before the heavy frame banged to.

She caught a glimpse of a face, filled with a poisonous hate, and then the shutter slammed closed too, and she heard the bang and scrape of the bar being pulled across.

Hal stood for a moment, her heart beating hard in her chest. She found that her arms were wrapped around herself, as if trying to shield herself from something—though from what, she didn't know. As her heart slowed, she let her arms drop to her sides, and forced herself to breathe slowly and more deeply.

Thank God. Thank God she was out of that horrible house, and away from that horrible woman. Let them write. Let them come after her, for all she cared. They couldn't make her return. They couldn't make her show them anything. She could move—change addresses—change her name, if that was what it took.

About one thing, Mrs. Warren was right, she thought, as she picked up the case and began the long walk down the drive to the main road, to try to hitch a lift to Penzance. She should never have come.

IT WAS ONLY LATER, MUCH later, after a lift on a lorry on its way to St. Ives and a lecture from the driver about personal safety, when she was huddled in the doorway of Penzance station, her coat around her, waiting for the doors to open and the first train to London to arrive, that she had time to reflect on Mrs. Warren's words, to unpick the realization beneath the hissed invective.

Conniving little gold digger.

Good riddance to you, and your trash mother before you.

Those words could mean only one thing: Mrs. Warren knew. She knew the truth.

She knew that Hal's mother was not Mrs. Westaway's daughter, but the dark-eyed cuckoo cousin, taken in as an orphan.

And she knew, therefore, that Hal herself was an impostor.

But she had said nothing. *Why?*

The puzzle had been in the back of Hal's mind since last night, twisting and turning in her imagination, shaping and morphing into a dozen different possibilities. But it was only when the doors of the station opened and Hal rose stiffly, stretching out her chilled, cramped limbs and trying to smile at the station attendant, that Mrs. Warren's last words spoke again inside her head, like a bitter echo.

She should never have come. That was right. But it wasn't quite what Mrs. Warren had said.

What she had said was, *You should never have come* back.

CHAPTER 28

The words stayed with Hal, niggling at her on the long journey back to London.

Come *back*. What had she meant? Was it a slip of the tongue?

Was it possible that she had been to Trepassen as a child, too young to remember? But if so, Mrs. Warren must know full well the truth about her mother. In which case, why had she not said anything? Was she hiding something of her own?

Suddenly Hal longed to be back in Brighton. Not just to be home—but to look through the box of documents beneath her bed.

There was so much in there that she had never looked at—boxes of papers and old letters, diaries, postcards—things Hal had found too painful to read after her mother's death, but that she could not bear to throw away. She had bundled them up and stored them, out of sight and out of mind, ready for a day when she would have a reason to go through them.

And now that day had come. For one thing Hal was sure of. Her mother *did* have a connection to that house. And so did Hal. She was not Mrs. Westaway's granddaughter, that was certain. But she *was* a relation. And if her mother was connected to that place, so was she, and she was determined to find out what that connection was.

IT WAS THE MIDDLE OF the afternoon when Hal reached her flat, footsore from carrying her case all the way from Brighton station. She had no money for a cab, and her bus pass had expired.

As she drew closer to Marine View Villas, she found her heart was thumping hard in her chest—and not just from the long walk. Words hissed in her ear in time with her footsteps: *Broken teeth . . . broken bones . . .*

"Stop it." She said the words aloud, crossing the road, and a boy of about fifteen looked sourly round at her.

"I'm eighteen, innit. You can't tell me what to do."

Hal shook her head, wanting to tell him that whatever he'd been talking about, it didn't matter to her. But he was gone, and she was turning into her road, her heart going at a sickening rate now.

When she got to the narrow front door, there was no sign that it had been forced, but instead of unlocking it, she rang the bell for the ground-floor flat.

The man who answered it looked surprised, as well he might. Hal had never seen him before.

"Yes? Can I help?"

"Oh . . . I'm sorry." Hal felt discomfited. She had been planning to ask Jeremy, who lived here, to accompany her up to her flat. "I didn't realize—is Jeremy here?"

"Is he the guy who lived here before? I don't know. I only just moved in this week. Are you a friend of his?"

"Yes—no. Not really," Hal said. She hitched her case up, feeling her feet aching. "I live here, upstairs."

"Oh. Right. Well, remember your key next time, eh? I was having a kip."

"I've got my key," Hal said. "It's not that. I just wondered—look, you haven't seen anyone hanging around here, have you? A bald man, bouncer type?"

"Don't think so," the man said briefly. He had lost interest now, and had retreated back to his own front door, plainly wanting to get back to his bed. "Ex, is he?"

"No." Hal shifted her grip on the case, wondering how honest she could be. "No, I . . . I owe him some money, actually. And he's not been very . . . understanding."

"Ohhh . . ." The guy held up his hands, showing Hal his palms, really backing away now. "Look, I'm not getting mixed up in that, love. Your money, your business."

"I'm not asking you to get mixed up," Hal said crossly. "I just want to know, did you see anyone?"

"No," the man said, and he closed his flat door in her face.

Hal shrugged and sighed. It was not very reassuring, but it was as good as she was going to get.

As she climbed the stairs to her attic flat, she held her suitcase in front of her like a shield once again, and the image came to her, fresh and sharp, of that narrow staircase back in Cornwall, and a girl disappearing upwards, into darkness. When she shivered, it was not entirely at the thought of what might be waiting upstairs.

At the top she paused, trying to still her breathing, listening for any sound behind her front door. It was shut, and locked, and showed no signs of being forced, but then it had looked okay last time too. Clearly they had got in once, they could do so again.

When she bent and peered beneath the doorway, only a cool breeze blew in her face. There was no sign of any movement showing through the narrow crack, no feet standing silently behind the door.

At last, holding her phone like a weapon, her finger poised over the nine, she put her key into the lock as silently as she could, and then twisted and opened it with one swift movement, kicking the door hard back against the wall of the living room with a bang that echoed in the quiet hallway.

The room stood empty, silent, the only sound Hal's pounding heart. No feet came running. Nevertheless, she didn't put down her phone until she had checked every nook and cranny, from the bathroom, to her wardrobe, right down to the alcove behind the living room door where she kept the hoover.

Then, and only then, did her heart begin to slow, and she shut the front door, drawing the chain and bolt across, and let herself sink down on the sofa to rub her shaking hands over her face.

She could not stay here, that much was obvious.

Hal rarely cried, but as she sat there on the worn old sofa that she had jumped on as a child, in front of the cold gas fire her mother had lit so many afternoons after school, she felt her throat close with unshed tears, and a few self-pitying drops traced down her nose. But then she took a deep breath and scrubbed them away. This wouldn't do. It wouldn't help. She had to move on.

But before she did, she needed to find the truth, the answers to the questions she had been asking herself ever since Mr. Treswick's letter had come through. She was sick of lies and lying. It was time for the truth.

Hal's stomach was rumbling, so she made herself a piece of toast, and took it through into her bedroom. Then she pulled the box out from under the bed, tipped the contents upside down onto the rug, and began to sift through.

Upended like this, the first pieces of paper were the oldest—expired passports, exam certificates, old letters, photographs—though the dates were jumbled, the contents moved from drawer to drawer too many times to be strictly chronologically ordered. Hal opened an envelope at random, but it was nothing very interesting, just some of her mother's old bank statements.

Beneath it there was a sheaf of baby photographs—herself, presumably, about six months old, smiling up at an unseen photographer.

Another envelope contained the original rent contract for the flat, the ink faded, the staple in the corner beginning to rust. It was dated January 1995, a few months before Hal's birth. Sixty pounds a week, her mother had agreed. It seemed impossibly low, even back then, and Hal thought she might almost have laughed, had she not been so close to tears.

She couldn't do that. She couldn't give way to self-pity. Tomorrow she would make a plan—find somewhere to go—but in the meantime she had to focus on the task at hand. She could not take all this with her, she'd have enough to do with packing her clothes and other essentials. So then—a pile for stuff that could be recycled. And for the stuff that she needed to keep, she could make one pile for personal papers relating to her mother, a pile for the flat, a pile of essentials—passports, birth certificates, anything that she might need to start her new life. And then finally on the bed she would put anything relating to Cornwall and Trepassen House, however tangentially. Perhaps there would be something there, some connection to the Westaways that would give her the foothold she needed to get out of this mess.

The first thing to go on the bed was a postcard. The writing side was blank, but the picture, when she turned it over, made Hal sit up. It featured Penzance. She recognized the harbor. The postcard was divided into four quarters, with Penzance on the bottom left, St. Michael's Mount on the top right, and two photographs of unidentified headlands that Hal didn't recognize on the other sections. The link might be a slim one, but it *was* evidence, however thin.

But what made Hal's heart really miss a beat were letters—a sheaf of them, tied up with string. They were addressed to Margarida Westaway, at an address in Brighton Hal didn't recognize, and the postmark was Penzance. Hal peered inside the first one, but there was no return address, and the ink was so faded she had trouble making out the words.

I am sending this to you via Lizzie . . . something Hal couldn't make out . . . *please don't worry about the deposit—I have a little money left from my parents and beyond that I'll—oh, God, I don't know. I'll tell fortunes on Brighton Pier, or read palms on the seafront.*

Anything to get away. There were more, several more. But it would take her hours to go through them and decipher the crabbed, faded writing. Resolutely she put them on the bed and carried on sifting.

She was only halfway down the box when she came across something wrapped in an old tea towel. It felt like a book. Hal frowned and picked it up, but the thing unraveled, and into her lap fell—yes, a book. But not a printed book. A diary.

Gently, Hal picked it up and began to leaf through the pages. Great chunks had been ripped out—frayed stubs of paper all that was left of their existence—and the pages that were left were hanging by a thread, unanchored by the loss of their neighbors. The first whole entry was one towards the end of November, but judging by where it came in the book, Hal thought that the diary itself must have been started in October or September, perhaps even earlier. Only fragments of those months remained, though. The rest of the pages—less than half, by Hal's estimate—were thickly covered with writing, but even there, sections were scrawled over, names erased, whole paragraphs scratched out.

The entries came to an end on December 13, and after that the pages were whole, but blank. Only one single page, right at the end of the diary, had been removed. It was as if the diarist had simply stopped.

Hal leafed slowly back to the beginning, past fragments of text, running her fingers over the thickly scored-out sections. Who had done this? Was it the writer of the diary? Or someone else, scared of what evidence might be found within its pages?

And more to the point, whose diary was it? The writing looked a little like her mother's—but an immature, unformed version—and there was no name inside the front cover.

At last she came to the first whole section, and began to read.

29th November, 1994, Hal read, frowning to make out the faint, discolored letters, the scrawling hand. *The magpies are back. . . .*

CHAPTER 29

It was almost dark when Hal finally looked up from the papers, and she realized, blinking, how the light had faded, so that she had been squinting to make out the letters on the torn and butchered pages.

But at last she knew—she had the answers she had been looking for—or some of them, at least.

The writer of the diary was Hal's mother. And she was pregnant—with Hal herself. It must be. The dates matched exactly—Hal had been born just five months after the final entry.

But as she walked through to the living room, switching the light on as she went, Hal was thinking back over what she had read. She turned on the kettle, and while it came to the boil she leafed back through the fragile pages until she came to the entry she was looking for, the one dated December 6. And as she reread it, a cold certainty hardened in Hal's stomach.

Her mother *had* known who her father was. And not just that, Hal had been conceived *there*, at Trepassen.

Everything her mother had told her—the story about the Spanish student, the one-night stand—it had all been lies.

In so many ways, the diary explained everything. The mix-up with the names. The reason Mrs. Westaway had never told Mr. Treswick about a black sheep cousin with the same name as her own daughter. She had cut off her niece, a disgrace to the family, and no one had spoken of her again.

But in other ways, it explained nothing.

Why had her mother lied?

And who *was* her father?

If only, Hal found herself thinking, as she flicked through the torn, disintegrating pages, *if* only *you hadn't destroyed his name, everything about him. Why?*

So often she had heard her mother's voice inside her head—lecturing, admonishing, encouraging—but now, when she needed her most, her voice was silent.

"Why?" Hal said aloud, hearing the despair in her own voice, the way the single word echoed in the silent flat. "*Why?* Why did you do it?" It was a cry for help, but there was no answer, only the imperceptible ticking of the clock, and the crackle as her fingers tightened on the diary in her hand.

The symbolism was painfully obvious—*if there is an answer, Hal, it's in your hands.* She could almost hear her mother's voice, a little mocking. And she felt rage flood her, at having the truth dangled in front of her and then snatched away, just as the legacy had shimmered there like a beautiful mirage for a moment before disappearing into nothingness.

But the answer was not there. If it was, it lay in the torn-out sections. Even in the passages that remained, her mother had blacked out names and paragraphs.

And she *had* no time. She had to leave tomorrow, before Mr. Smith's men noticed that the girl they were hunting was back.

Slow down. Her mother's voice again, softer this time. *Think clearly.*

Slow down? she wanted to shout. I *can't* slow down.

More haste, less speed.

Very well, then. She had to puzzle this out, slowly and logically.

There could not be that many suspects. Who could have been at Trepassen, that long summer? The brothers?

The entry of December 6 was still open on her lap, describing the night her mother assumed she had conceived. Hal read it through again, and again, and this time she stopped at one phrase: *Our eyes met—blue and dark.*

Hal's mother had dark eyes, like her own. Which meant that whoever she'd slept with must have been a blue-eyed man.

Ezra had dark eyes—uncompromisingly so.

Abel . . . well, that was more difficult. He was fair, but his eyes . . . Hal shut her own, trying to remember. Grayish? Hazel?

Blue eyes could look gray in the right light, but try as she might, she could not picture Abel's kind, bearded face with blue eyes, nor could she imagine him in her mother's arms. He would have *said* something, surely?

In desperation she pulled the picture from her pocket—the one Abel had given her, taken the very afternoon that her mother had been writing about.

There was Ezra, his dark head thrown back, laughing with an openness so at odds with his present-day cynicism that Hal thought her heart might break a little, his dark eyes just slits of merriment. There beside him was his twin, Maud, her fair hair cascading down her back.

And there, too, was Abel, his dark-blond hair glinting in the sun. She peered closer, trying to make out his face, beneath the faded color and the frayed folds of age, as if she could see through the paper to the past, and the people left behind.

Could it be? Could she be Abel's child?

In which case . . . she stopped, feeling something cold against the back of her neck, like a chilly hand laid there. If she was Abel's daughter, the legacy might hold up. Was that why Mrs. Warren had said nothing? Because the legacy *did* belong to Hal?

The thought should have been a welcome one, but for some reason it made her feel like the bottom of her stomach had fallen away.

Before she folded up the picture to put it away, she looked very deliberately at the fourth person in the frame, at the one whose eyes she had been avoiding—at her mother, her dark eyes uncompromising, staring out at her through the years.

What are you trying to say? Hal thought desperately. She felt her hands close on the old, fragile paper, the flecks of pigment disintegrating beneath her fingertips.

What are you trying to tell me?

It was as if her mother were looking out at her from the past, right *at* her.

But no.

Not at her.

At . . .

Hal's fingers were shaking as she put the photograph down, very gently, and began flicking back through the pages of the diary, back, back . . . no, too far . . . forward . . .

And there, at last, there it was.

In the crumbling boathouse Maud untied the rickety flat-bottomed skiff, and we rowed out to the island, the lake water dappled and brown beneath the hull of the boat. Maud tied the boat to a makeshift jetty and we climbed out. It was Maud who went in first—a flash of scarlet against the gold-brown waters as she dived, long and shallow, from the end of the rotting wooden platform.

"Come on, Ed," she shouted, and he stood up, grinned at me, and then followed her to the water's edge, and took a running jump.

And then, just a few lines later:

"Take a photo . . ." Maud said lazily, as she stretched, her tanned limbs honey-gold against the faded blue towel. "I want to remember today."

He gave a groan, but he stood obediently and went to fetch his camera, and set it up. I watched him as he stood behind it, adjusting the focus, fiddling with the lens cap.

"Why so serious?" he said as he looked up, and I realised that I was frowning in concentration, trying to fix his face in my memory.

Hal had imagined only four people in that scene: her mother, Maud, Ezra, and Abel—the four people in the photograph's frame. But it was not quite the truth. Someone must have been *taking* the picture. And it was the person her mother was looking at. The same person she had gone down to the beach with later that evening. Her lover. Hal's father.

Hal stared at the photograph, meeting her mother's fierce, direct gaze—and for the first time she read the intensity in those eyes as something else. Not suspicion. Not antagonism. But—longing.

Of all the people in the photograph, her mother was the one who stared directly at the photographer, challenging him—whoever he was—with her eyes, locking his gaze.

Hal had read that look quite differently—she had seen the connection between her mother and the viewer as their own relationship, as if her mother were gazing out of the past at her.

But now she understood. It was not she herself that her mother was looking at—for how could she? It was the photographer. It was Hal's father. Ed.

CHAPTER 30

That night, Hal's bed had never felt softer or more welcoming.

She slid under the covers and shut her eyes, but sleep didn't come. It wasn't that she was not tired—she was, almost to the point of nausea. It wasn't even the thought of Mr. Smith's men. She had dragged a chest of drawers across the front door, and she didn't think that even they would come in the middle of the night, risking waking all her neighbors, and the consequent 999 calls.

What stopped her from sleeping was that every time she shut her eyes, she was back—between the pages of the diary, in the claustrophobia of that little room. The picture was so vivid: the narrow attic, the barred windows, the two metal bolts, top and bottom . . . when she shut her eyes, they rose up in front of her mind's eye, as if she were back there herself, and she felt a kind of sick dread. Not just for her mother—who, after all, had escaped, and made her way here, to Brighton, and made a life for herself and her child away from Trepassen. But for those other children—for Abel and Ezra, locked in that room as children, as punishment for whatever childish misdeeds they'd committed. And most of all for Maud.

The first few times Hal had read the entries, she had been looking for her mother—trying to picture the person behind the words, and compare them to her own memories. Then she had read it again, scouring it for mentions of the boy who might be her father. Ed. Edward? She found herself remembering that cool, handsome face, the appraising blue eyes, trying to pick out any features that might have belonged to her.

Come on, Ed. The words rang inside her head as though her mother had shouted them aloud in the little room.

Ed. It was a common enough name. There must be dozens of Edwards, Edgars, and Edwins scattered around Cornwall. And yet . . .

All evening she had gone round and round, combing for other mentions that might give evidence either way, arguing for and against, back and forth. But her mother had kept her word, and apart from that small slip, every reference to her father's name had been ripped out, or scored through.

Now, though, in the stillness of the night, as Hal went back again and again over words she had committed to memory, she found herself looking for mentions not of Ed, but of Maud.

Her own mother was oddly shadowy—perhaps it was because she spent so many of the entries describing others, but it was hard to match the uncertain, romantic girl writing this diary with the strong, practical woman she had become, after years of single motherhood. Without the evidence of her own eyes, Hal could never have imagined her mother writing with such heat and yearning about a man. Perhaps this was the first, and last, time.

But Maud—Maud was different, somehow. Though she only flitted through the pages, she felt like a constant presence in the diary; and as the clock ticked past midnight, and the rain spattered at the window, Hal found herself scouring her memory for references to Maud.

It was not just the fact that it was Maud's legacy that she, Hal, had been handed on a plate. It was that there was something about her that spoke directly to Hal. Perhaps it was her fierce determination, her refusal to be quashed, her desire to break free. Perhaps it was her wry humor, or her generosity. For Maud's love and concern for her cousin ran like a thread of gold in the dark throughout the diary, and even across the gap of twenty years, Hal found herself smiling at her remarks. What was it she had said about the tarot cards? *Load of wafty BS,* that was it. It was so close to what Hal sometimes found herself thinking when she met the more earnest practitioners that she had almost laughed aloud when she read it.

But what had happened to her? To Maud—to the real Margarida? Where was she now? And why did no one talk about her? Was she dead? Or had she made good her vow to escape?

Perhaps she had disappeared abroad, changed her name, made a new life for herself. Hal hoped so. For Maud's own sake, but also because she knew the truth of what had happened in those torn-out pages. She knew the truth about Hal's mother, and her father.

Abel, Ezra, Harding, Mr. Treswick—thanks to Hal, they all believed that Maud had died in a car crash, three hot summers ago. Only Hal knew the truth—that it was not Maud who had died, but Maggie, her cousin.

It was possible, even probable, that Maud was still alive, still out there, still holding on to the truth of what had happened to her cousin, and the secret of Hal's own identity.

But to find her, Hal was going to have to go back. Back to Trepassen, where she could start again, pick up the threads of Maud's life from the beginning. And there was only one way that Hal could think of doing that.

CHAPTER 31

The next day was Sunday. It was eight when Hal dragged her duvet to the living room and curled up on the sofa with a cup of coffee in one hand, and a pile of letters in her lap.

On top of them was Harding's business card.

She waited until nine thirty before she dialed the number, but it went through to voice mail, and she could not stop a small spurt of relief when she heard the smooth female voice of the automated message.

"This is the voice mailbox of—"

And then in Harding's own voice, slightly pompous and half a tone deeper than his natural register: "Harding Westaway."

"Please leave a message after the tone," continued the woman, and there was a *bleep*.

Hal coughed.

"Um . . . Uncle Harding, it—it's Hal. Harriet. I am so sorry for running out yesterday, but the fact is—"

She swallowed again. She had spent the time since getting up trying to decide what to say, and in the end she had decided there was only one thing she *could* say, only one thing that made sense of her actions. The truth.

"The fact is, I—I've been pretty freaked out by all of this. Whatever I was expecting when I came down to Cornwall, it wasn't what Mr. Treswick read out, and I've found it very hard to come to terms with my grandmother's will. On Friday night I couldn't sleep, and I'm afraid I—I just—"

Beeep. And the message cut out, indicating that she had taken too long to explain herself.

"To send the message, press one. To rerecord the message, press two," said the female voice.

Hal swore quietly, pressed one, and then hung up and redialed. This time it went through to voice mail almost immediately.

"Sorry, I took too long and the message cut out. Look, the long and the short of it is, I'm very sorry I left without talking to you first, but I've had some time to think and—and I'd like to come back. Not just because I appreciate you probably need me present for the interview with Mr. Treswick, but also—well—I have a lot of questions about my mother and about why my grandmother chose to do this and—well, that's it, really. I hope you'll forgive me. Please call me back on this number and let me know. Bye. And sorry again."

When she put down the phone, she felt her stomach turn with a feeling halfway between nervousness and sickness. Was she mad—to go back?

Perhaps. But she could not stay here—not with Mr. Smith's men waiting for her, and not without knowing the truth of her own past. If she burned these bridges now, then she might never be able to find out what had happened at Trepassen. Who her father really was.

Why had her mother lied about her father's identity?

Last night she had been too busy searching in the diary for answers—answers she had not found. But now the question was beginning to press upon her like a guilty secret, demanding her attention. For some reason, her mother had chosen not just to keep Hal in the dark about the identity of her own father, but to go further: to spin a whole tale of falsehoods. The Spanish student—the one-night stand. None of it had existed. But why? Why go to such lengths to keep Hal in the dark about something she had every right to know?

Before she could unpack the conundrum any further, her phone buzzed against her leg, the shrill sound of the ringer following with a millisecond delay. She looked at the screen, and her stomach flipped. Harding.

"He-hello?"

"Harriet!" Harding's voice was full of a kind of hectoring relief. "I've just listened to your messages. Young lady, you gave everyone here a severe fright."

"I know," Hal said. "I'm sorry." She was sorry, genuinely sorry. "I just—it's like I said in my message, I was overwhelmed by it all. It's hard to go from having no one and being answerable to no one to—well."

"You could at least have left a note," Harding said. "Mitzi got the shock of her life when she went up to wake you and found your bed empty and your belongings gone. We had no idea what had happened."

"I saw Mrs. Warren as I was leaving. Didn't she tell you?" The memory of that strange, disjointed encounter was dreamlike. Had it really happened? Had Mrs. Warren really said the things Hal remembered? *Good riddance to you, and your trash mother before you.* It seemed impossible.

There was a disconcerted silence.

"Mrs. Warren, you say?" Harding said at last. "No. No, she said nothing. How very odd."

"Oh." Hal felt wrong-footed. She had assumed Mrs. Warren would have got her side of the story in first—Hal creeping out like a thief in the night, probably with the family silver under her arm. "I just assumed . . . well, I should have phoned earlier. I'm sorry, Uncle Harding."

Uncle Harding. It was strange how the words slipped out so automatically. A few days ago they had been so hard to say—she had practically had to force the title *uncle* out of her mouth. Now it was becoming habit. She was beginning to believe her own lies.

"Well, we will say no more about it, my dear," Harding said, a little pompously. "But for goodness' sake, don't run away in the middle of the night again. We'd only just found you after all these years and—well—" He stopped and gave a kind of harrumphing cough, covering up the emotion that Hal sensed lurking beneath the matter-of-fact façade. "I don't think your aunt, for one, could stand the strain. She was beside herself yesterday, with no idea where you were and no means of contacting you. Now—did you say you were coming back?"

"Yes," Hal said. She swallowed. With her free hand she picked up the topmost letter from the pile in her lap, folding it back into the creases of the envelope it had lain in for so many years. "Yes, I am."

CHAPTER 32

Hal had not considered how she would pay for the ticket back to Penzance until she got to the ticket office at Brighton station, and her card was refused. As she dragged her case away from the counter, her face scarlet with embarrassment, she ran through her options in her head, and could see only one—to try the app again, and hope that the website would process the ticket without checking in with her bank. It seemed a slim hope, but she had no others.

In a quiet corner beside the coffee stand she pulled out her phone, and was about to open up the app, when she saw an unread text message from Harding.

Dear Harriet, it read, a little stiffly, *after consultation with Mr Treswick, we would like to advance you your fare back to Trepassen, as the travel is necessary to sort out estate business. I enclose a code for a prepaid ticket that should function at any of the machines at Brighton. Please call me if there are any problems. Uncle Harding. PS Abel will meet you at Penzance.*

As Hal closed down the message she had the strangest feeling—a mixture of warmth and suffocation. It felt as though a snug scarf were being wrapped around her stiff and unwilling body, but just a little too tightly.

Remember who you are, she thought, knowing she should have been typing an effusive thank-you text. *Remember that meek, grateful little mouse of a niece.*

But as the reality of her own past began to clash with the fiction she had created, it was becoming harder and harder to maintain that role. Harder and harder not to slip up. Was she crazy to go back?

As the train sped west, the sky darkening all the time, Hal knew she should have been reading, researching, googling names, preparing to plunge herself back into her part. There was so much she needed to know. Had Maud got to Oxford? What had happened to her after that?

But somehow she could not find the will. She let her head rest against the scratched glass of the window, and stared out at the countryside flashing past. It was cold, and getting colder as they left London and passed into the countryside, the bare trees rimed with frost, the grass white, and puddles black with ice. On any other day Hal would have found it beautiful, but today all she could think about was everything she had left behind and that, perhaps, she would never see again—the flat where she had grown up, all of her past. She was moving forwards now, with every mile the train covered, forwards into an unknown future, her only belongings the case of clothes and papers at her side.

But she was also going back, into her own past—and of all the unanswered questions that jostled at the back of her mind, there was one in particular that Hal kept returning to, poking and prodding with increasing unease, like a tongue returning again and again to a sore tooth.

Why had her mother lied?

The diary, everything in it, that was clear enough. Maggie could not tell her aunt the identity of her baby's father, and risk never seeing him again.

But why had she lied to Hal herself?

Hal had been turning the question over and over in her head with increasing urgency, but she could think of only one reason—to protect her.

But from what?

It was dark when the train pulled into Penzance, and Hal was almost asleep, but she roused herself and picked up her case, feeling the weight of all the extra clothes and papers she had crammed into it. As she stepped off the train onto the platform, she had the strangest sense of déjà vu, mixed with the unsettling realization of how far everything had changed. There was the station platform, with the big clock and the echoing announcements, and there she was herself, with her torn jeans and shabby hand-me-down case, and her hair falling in her eyes.

But there too was Abel, standing on the platform, looking up at the arrivals board, and when he saw Hal standing on the other side of the barrier his face broke into a smile, and he waved his car keys in the air.

When Hal was through the barrier she found herself engulfed in a completely unexpected hug, and then Abel released her, and grinned, his tanned face creasing into lines of relief.

"Harriet! It's so good to see you. You gave everyone quite a fright. We'd barely got used to having you around and then—well." He broke off, his face twisting in a rueful smile. "Let's just say, it's good to know you're okay."

"I'm sorry." Hal found herself studying his face from the side as they walked slowly up the platform. *Do you know my father?* she wanted to ask. *Is he Edward?* But the words were unthinkable. "I didn't mean to make everyone worry. And I'm sorry my train was delayed." She glanced up at the clock. Nearly half past nine. The train had been supposed to arrive at eight thirty. "Were you waiting long?"

Abel shook his head.

"Awhile, but don't worry. To be honest, I was glad of the excuse to get out—I had a surprisingly good coffee in the station café. I'm not sure I could have taken another one of Mrs. Warren's cups of gray dishwater."

In the station light, Abel's eyes were uncompromisingly gray themselves, but Hal couldn't stop herself checking again when they reached the car park, trying to make out their color beneath the floodlights as Abel paused to unlock a sleek black Audi.

He caught her staring, and Hal flushed and looked down.

"Something on my chin?" he asked, with a laugh. Hal shook her head.

"I'm sorry. No—it's just, I . . ." She swallowed and felt her cheeks flush. "I'm still trying to get used to the idea that I have all this family. It's so hard to compute."

"I can only imagine," Abel said lightly. "We're finding it a bit of an adjustment ourselves, and there's only one of you. It must be ten times stranger for you, finding a whole family you never knew." He opened Hal's door and took her case, before shutting her inside. When he came round to the driver's side, he shut the door, turning out the internal light and throwing everything into shadows, illuminated only by the green glow of the dashboard.

"Abel," she said slowly as they pulled out of the space. "I—I wanted to thank you again, for that photo of my mother. I don't have very many pictures of her at my age and it means . . . well, it means a lot to me, that's all."

"That's all right," Abel said easily. He glanced in the rearview mirror, and then put the car into gear. "You're very welcome. I don't have many pictures of that time either, unfortunately. I had more, but they didn't always come with very happy memories, so I didn't keep as many as I should. But I'll have a check when I go home, see if I can find any more. If there's any with your mother in, you're welcome to keep them."

"Thank you," Hal said quietly. They were winding through the narrow streets behind the station when she plucked up her courage.

"Abel, can I ask something?"

"Of course."

"Who—who took that photo? The one you gave me?"

"Who took it?" Abel frowned. "I'm not certain. Why do you ask?"

"Oh . . ." Hal's stomach turned as they rounded a corner slightly too fast. "I don't know. I just wondered."

"I honestly can't remember. . . ." Abel said. He was still frowning, and he rubbed at the bridge of his nose as though giving himself time to answer. "I think . . . yes, I'm almost sure it was Ezra."

Hal swallowed, feeling like she was taking her life in her hands.

"It wasn't . . . it wasn't . . . Edward, was it?"

"Edward?" Abel glanced sideways at her in the darkness of the car, the unearthly green light from the LEDs on the dashboard making his expression strange and hard to read. "Why on earth would you say that?"

His voice was suddenly completely unlike that of the warm, solicitous man she had grown to know over the last few days. There was something cold and bitter in it, and Hal felt herself grow very still, like a mouse that has seen a snake rise up from the grass. She knew suddenly and with certainty that it would be very, very stupid to mention the diary.

"I—" She had no need to make her voice sound small. It was already a squeak in her throat. "I—I don't know. I just wondered."

"It was Ezra," Abel said flatly, turning back to the road, closing off the discussion.

But that could not be true, Hal thought, as the car swung around the corner. Ezra was in the photograph.

"It's just—" she tried again, but Abel cut her off, and this time his voice was cold with what sounded like anger.

"Harriet, that's enough. It wasn't Edward. I didn't know him back then. End of story."

You are lying, she thought. *His name is in the diary. You must be lying. But why?*

CHAPTER 33

When they arrived at Trepassen House, Abel parked the car and Hal followed him round the house to the main entrance. There were no lights visible, and the house looked almost deserted, the blank windows like black, expressionless eyes. Hal had a sudden premonition of how it might look in twenty, thirty years' time—the roof caved in, the windows cracked and broken, leaves gusting across the rotting parquet.

"We're back," Abel shouted as they entered the main door, his voice echoing along the corridor, and Hal felt her stomach flip, before she could analyze why. But when the drawing room door opened and Harding's head came out, she realized. It was Mrs. Warren she was afraid of. Before she had time to dissect the realization, she found herself in Harding's stiff embrace, her cheek against his tweed-upholstered shoulder, as he patted her awkwardly and uncomfortably firmly on the back of the head, like a cross between a Labrador and a child.

"Well, well, well," he said, and then again, "Well, well, well." When he pulled back, Hal was astonished to see that his jowly face was ruddy with some kind of suppressed emotion, and his eyes were watering.

He dashed at them, and coughed. "Mitzi will—*hrumph*! She will be very sorry to have missed you, but she has already left to drive the children back home. They have school tomorrow."

"I'm sorry," Hal said humbly. "I'm sorry to have missed her too."

"Edward had to leave too," Abel said. Hal felt a sharp pang of something, quite different from the vague guilt she had felt at the sound of Mitzi's name. She realized that she had been hanging on to something—the prospect of seeing Edward, looking into his eyes, trying to find something of herself in his face.

"I'm sorry," she said again. "Is he—will he be coming back?"

"I doubt it," Abel said. His face was rather grim, and he seemed to realize it suddenly, and make an effort to shake it off. As he took Hal's coat he forced a smile, a rather insincere one. "Unless we get held up here for another weekend, which I sincerely hope we won't."

"Have you eaten?" Harding put in. "I'm afraid we have all had supper some time ago, but there's tea in the drawing room and I could ask Mrs. Warren for a sandwich. . . ."

He trailed off a little doubtfully, and Hal shook her head emphatically.

"No, please, I'm absolutely fine. I ate on the train."

"Well, come through and have some tea, at least. Warm yourself up before you go to bed."

Hal nodded, and Harding ushered her into the drawing room, where tea was waiting on the coffee table.

The fire was burning low in the grate, and the lamps on the side tables were lit, giving the room a golden glow that somehow covered up the cobwebs and the cracks in the paneling, the dirt and the frayed curtains, the damp and neglect. The room looked, for the first time, almost homelike, and Hal was suddenly overwhelmed with a sense of longing. It was not exactly a longing to stay here, for Trepassen was too gothic and gloomy to ever feel like a truly welcoming place. It had the sense of a house where people had suffered in silence, where meals had been eaten in tension and fear, where secrets had been concealed, and where unhappiness had reigned more often than contentment.

But it was, perhaps, a longing to stay a part of this family. For all his pomposity, the wetness at the corner of Harding's eye had touched Hal more than she could express. But it was not just Harding. Ezra, Abel, Mitzi, the children—each in their own way had welcomed Hal, had opened themselves to her, trustingly—and she had repaid them . . . how? With lies.

Only Mrs. Warren, Hal thought, unsettlingly. Only she had never trusted Hal.

The thought niggled at the back of her mind as she accepted the cup of tea that Harding poured, and cautiously dipped in a rich tea biscuit. Since those hissed midnight accusations, Hal had been turning Mrs. Warren's words over and over in her mind, and she kept coming back to the same uneasy conclusion. Mrs. Warren . . . knew.

But had she kept quiet? The only explanation, and it was not a very comforting one, was that Mrs. Warren had something to hide herself. . . .

The clock on the mantel chimed as Hal swallowed the last of the tea, and she, Harding, and Abel all looked up.

"Good Lord," Harding said. "Half past ten. I had no idea it was so late."

"I'm sorry," Hal said. "I've probably kept you up. My train was delayed."

"No, no. You didn't keep me up," Harding said. He stretched, his checked shirt pulling up from his belt and exposing a little slice of doughlike middle. "I assure you. But today has been . . . well, let's just say I'm finding this whole weekend more than a little wearing, and with Mitzi and the children away it's a chance to catch up on my beauty sleep. So I think, if you don't mind, Harriet, it will be up the stairs to Bedfordshire for me."

"I'll turn in too," Abel said with a yawn. "Where's Ezra?"

"God knows. He disappeared after supper. Probably out walking. You know what he's like."

"Did he take a key?"

"Again, I refer the honorable gentleman to my previous answer," Harding said, a little irritably this time. "God knows. This is Ezra we're talking about."

"I'll leave the front door unlocked," Abel said with another yawn. He rose, brushing imaginary lint off his trouser legs. "Lord knows, there's little enough to steal. Right. Good night, Hal. Can I give you a hand with your case?"

"Good night," Hal said. "And no, don't worry, I can manage myself."

THE NARROW STAIRCASE THAT LED up to the attic was unlit, and Hal searched for a long time before she found the switch.

But when she clicked it, nothing happened. She clicked it again, but still no light. Her phone was somewhere deep at the bottom of her bag, and with her hands full of luggage, in the end she was forced to make her way upwards in darkness.

There were no windows on the attic landing, and the darkness, as she climbed, was absolute, an inky, sooty blackness so intense that she could almost taste it. When she reached the top she put down her case and felt with her fingertips for the turn of the corridor and the door to the attic room—her room, it was beginning to feel like, though the idea gave her a strange, queasy feeling, as if history were looping round and coming full circle.

This time, although it was stiff, the door gave with a sharp tug, and she fumbled forwards into the room, feeling for the light switch.

When she flicked it, there was again no light, and this time Hal felt a surge of irritation. Had the whole circuit gone? What the hell?

It didn't matter so much in here, for the curtains were open, and enough moonlight came in to enable her to find her way to the bed, undress, and crawl between the cold sheets.

She was almost asleep, watching moon shadows moving on the wall, when she noticed something.

It was not a fuse. Someone had taken the bulb out of the light fitting in the center of the room, deliberately leaving her in the dark.

All that hung there now was an empty socket.

CHAPTER 34

"Can I ask a question?" Hal asked over breakfast. She took a piece of toast from the pile in the center of the table and was about to spread it with marmalade, but when she unscrewed the top of the jar there was a thick crust of mold over the jelly, and she felt her appetite diminish.

"What?" Harding looked up from his own toast, which he was briskly plying with butter. "A question? Of course. What is it?"

"St. Piran village. How far is it?"

"Oh . . . matter of four miles. Why do you ask?"

"I thought . . ." Hal swallowed, and twisted her fingers in the fraying edge of her jumper. "I thought I might go for a walk this morning. Do we have time? When are we seeing Mr. Treswick?"

"Unfortunately, not until tomorrow," Harding said. He cut his toast in half, a little more forcefully than the action required, and his knife screeched on the plate, making Hal wince. "It seems he is a busy man. So you are free to do whatever you wish today. But it's not a very nice walk, I warn you. The fields are being plowed at this time of year, so walking across them is rather hard work and distinctly muddy. You'd do better along the main road, but it means dodging the traffic."

"I don't mind," Hal said. "I just—I feel like I need some fresh air. Is it . . . is it hard to find?"

"Not especially," Abel said. "But I'm not sure if you're dressed for it." He looked at her a little doubtfully. The snappy chill of the night before was gone and he was back to his usual solicitous manner, but Hal couldn't help wondering if the cold irritation was still there beneath the caring veneer. Which face was the real Abel Westaway? "It's very nippy out there. We don't get snow in this part of Cornwall very much, but we had a frost last night."

"I'll be fine," Hal said. She put her hands in the pocket of her hoodie and hunched her neck into the collar. "I'm very tough."

"Well, you don't look it," Abel said, and he flashed a little avuncular wink. "Listen, if you're really going to go, take my walking jacket. It's the red one on the peg by the front door. It'll be too big for you, but at least it's windproof, and if it comes on to rain you won't get drenched. There's rain forecast for this afternoon. But if you get to St. Piran and it starts tipping it down, or if your legs are giving out, give me a ring, and I'll come and collect you from outside the post office."

"All right," Hal said. She stood up. "I might go now—get started while it's dry. Is that okay?"

"Fine by me," Abel said. He put up his hands, and gave her a quick, wry smile that crinkled the skin at the corners of his eyes. In the morning light, they looked suddenly rather blue. "I'm not your father."

OUTSIDE THE FRONT DOOR, HAL got out her phone and opened up maps, and into it she put an address: 4 Cliff Cottages, St. Piran, Cornwall.

The dial whirled as her phone calculated the distance and walking time, and then a route flashed up—down the drive and onto the main road.

She turned into the frosty wind, and pushed the phone deep into the pocket of Abel's walking coat, and then set out, the wind in her face, the phone warm in her grip.

I'm not your father.

Why had he said that? It was so uncomfortably close to her own speculations that she had not been able to find a reply—and had only gaped, and then left the room hurriedly, hiding her shock. Did he know something? Had he and Ezra been talking? Hal had not thought much of Ezra's casual inquiry in the car on the way back from Penzance, but now his words came back to her, and she found herself wondering about how much the brothers really knew.

Abel's comment had been a perfectly reasonable remark, on the face of it, just as Ezra's question was a perfectly reasonable thing to ask. People wanted to know where you came from, who you were. It was something Hal had dealt with her whole life: "Where's your dad?" "What does he do?" Questions that every child in the playground asked, trying to size you up. Even, most vexatiously, "Why don't you have a father?"

Grown-ups tended to phrase the inquiry more tentatively—"Do you have family near?" or "Are your parents around?"—but it came down to the same thing.

Who are you? Why don't you know?

The questions had never seemed to matter much when Hal's mother was alive. Back then, she had known who she was—or so she thought. But now they chimed so closely with her own thoughts, she wanted to scream.

For that was the worst of it. Not the lack of a father. Not even the not knowing.

But the lies.

How could you lie to me? she thought as she tramped down the long, winding drive, past the twisted yews with the magpies watching her as she went beneath, through the forbidding iron gates.

You did know and you lied to me, and you stopped me from asking the questions I had a right to have answered.

She had never hated her mother—never. Not when there was no money, and the other children had heelies and Pokémon cards, and she had sensible shoes and drawings she'd done herself on little scraps of paper. Not when the electricity money ran out and they sat by candlelight for a week, cooking on a gas canister borrowed from a friend. Not when her shoes ran into holes, and her mother was late home from the pier and missed parents' evenings and class plays because she could not afford to turn down a client.

She had understood—this was not of her mother's choosing either. And what little they had, they shared—good times and bad. When there was money, there were treats. When there was hardship, they endured it together. She was doing her best. She was doing it for Hal.

But this—this revelation . . . this was not something she had done for Hal. This was something she had kept to herself—knowledge she could have shared, but had instead hugged to herself, guarding it.

And why? What could be so bad about the man who had held the camera that day, the man whose eyes her mother held so steadily, the man she had loved?

In her jeans pocket was the sheaf of letters—the letters, postmarked from Penzance, that she had found beneath the bed. It had taken her a long time to decipher them, but at last she had read them all. They were letters between Maud and Maggie, and they were planning to run away. They were not dated, but from the sequence of events Hal thought that the last one was the one on top—the one she had read part of when she first opened the packet. Now she got it out of her back pocket as she walked steadily along the coast road, the wind in her face, chapping at her lips, and she bit her lip, and tasted salt.

Dear Maud, I am sending this to you via Lizzie, as I don't dare to put this in with the rest of the post. I am so glad you've found us a flat. Please don't worry about the deposit—I have a little money left from my parents and beyond that I'll—oh, God, I don't know. I'll tell fortunes on Brighton Pier, or read palms on the seafront. Anything to get away. I never thought I would write this, but I am afraid—really afraid.

Write back via Lizzie, her address is at the bottom. She'll bring it up when she comes to clean—but if it comes to the house YOU KNOW WHO will open it, and all hell will break loose.

I love you. And please hurry. I can't cope with it here much longer.

Mxx

There was an address on the bottom: 4 Cliff Cottages, St. Piran, Cornwall. The address now in Hal's phone.

The paper fluttered in the wind as Hal folded it up, but the words stayed with her. *I am afraid—really afraid.*

She had held them inside her all of that long train journey, rattling in her head in time with the wheels of the train.

When she had first read the letter, curled up on the sofa with her phone in her lap, it was her great-aunt she had imagined, standing in the door of the little room, drawing the bolts. Or maybe Mrs. Warren, with her hissed invective and her hatred. But now, Hal wondered. For her mother had been . . . not fearless, perhaps, but full of courage. Hal could not remember a time when she'd turned away from something because she was frightened. Because it was stupid—yes. Because it was risky, and she had a child to protect and bring up, certainly. But just because she was afraid—no, that never. If something was difficult but necessary, Hal's mother faced it.

What had made her so afraid that she had run far away from Cornwall to the other side of the country, and never spoken of that time again?

Hal wondered. And as the sky darkened with snow clouds and the chill deepened, she realized something. She was afraid too. Not just of what she was about to do. But of what she might find at the end of it.

CHAPTER 35

St. Piran turned out to be not so much a village as a collection of buildings blown together like driftwood along the roads and lanes that wound down to the sea. Here was a farm, hardy little sheep crouched low against hedgerows, shielding themselves from the wind. There was a petrol station, shuttered up and closed with a cardboard sign in the window: RING BILL NANCARROW OR KNOCK ON COTTAGE FOR KEY TO PUMP.

The church where the funeral had been held was nowhere to be seen, but as she traipsed down the main road Hal heard a far-off church bell tolling the hour—ten slow strikes, rather mournful.

At last, Hal saw a red pillar-box and beside it a solitary phone box, sticking out into the road, and as she rounded the bend she saw the post office Abel had described. Inside the pocket of Abel's coat, her phone buzzed, indicating a turning; pulling out her phone, she checked the route again and saw that she was supposed to turn left down a little unmade road, past a modest row of brick-built council houses, with sensible gardens, low roofs, and storm porches closed against the sea winds. CLIFF COTTAGES, read the sign at the corner as she turned into the road, and Hal felt her heart speed up.

Number four had a neat square of frosty grass in front of it, and a crazy-paving path up to the front door, and Hal found her hands were trembling, not just with cold, as she licked her lips and tucked her hair behind her ear, and walked up the garden path to ring the bell.

Somewhere inside the house a novelty chime sounded, and Hal waited, her heart beating hard as she heard the sound of shuffling footsteps and saw a shape appearing through the glass patterned door.

"Hello?" The woman who stepped into the storm porch was in her forties or fifties, very plump, with rolls of curly hair dyed a slightly improbable shade of yellow that almost matched the wet rubber gloves she was still wearing. But there was something kind about her face, and Hal found herself relaxing a little in spite of her nerves. She swallowed, wishing she had rehearsed what she was about to say.

"Hello . . . I . . . um . . . so sorry to disturb you, but do you know someone called Lizzie?"

"I'm Lizzie, yes," the woman said. She folded her arms. "What can I do for you, my love?"

Hal felt her heart quicken, hopefully.

"I . . ." She licked her lips again, tasting the salt that seemed to permeate everything around here. "I—I think you knew my mother."

ON THE WAY DOWN TO Cornwall, Hal had gone back and forth over the problem of what to say, and how to phrase her questions. She had thought of imaginary cousins . . . fake names . . . even of resurrecting Lil Smith as an alias.

But when the door opened, and Lizzie had been there in person, with her plump kindly face, and her Cornish accent soft and rich as clotted cream, somehow all of that had fled, and she had found herself saying the last thing she had intended. The truth.

Now she was sitting in Lizzie's living room, and the story was tumbling out, so fast that Hal barely had time to consider it.

Her mother's death, the lack of money. The letter from Mr. Treswick, and the improbable hope that this mistake might actually be real—followed by the growing conviction that it was not. The disquieting discovery of the photograph, and the bolts on the attic door, and the midnight flight back to Brighton. And then, finally, the diary in her mother's papers, and the letters, and the care-of address that had led her here.

"Oh, my lover." Lizzie's round, red face was full of concern as Hal came to a halt, and she sat back against a cushion, and fanned herself. "Oh my days, what a right old pickle you've got yourself into. And you ent told them?"

Hal shook her head. "But I will. I know that. I have to. I just—I don't . . ." She stopped. "I wanted to find out all I could before I burned my bridges."

"Well, I'll tell you all I can, but 'tain't much. It's so long ago, and I never saw neither of 'em after they left, so I can't tell you much beyond what happened here. Your ma, she arrived . . . when must it have been . . . 1994, I suppose it was. Late spring or early summer, I remember her arrived in the taxi from Penzance station and it was a right cold day, and those bloody magpies were wheeling and circling and making a nuisance of 'emselves as usual. She was a lovely girl, your ma. Pretty, and kind, and always happy for a chat. Whereas her cousins . . . I don't know. They always kept themselves to themselves. It was always very them-and-us, with the villagers. I suppose for so long it had been all of 'em up there in the big house and all of us down here, they was used to it. But your ma being brought up somewhere else, she saw it different. We were always talking when I was supposed to be cleaning, and Mrs. Warren—my, she had a sharp tongue, she'd come along and snap at me with her tea cloth. Fair hurt, it did! And she'd say, 'Back to work, Lizzie, they don't pay you to stand there gabbing.'

"But I always felt . . . well, I suppose the truth of it was, your ma was lonely. She'd lost her mother and father, and she'd come here expecting to find family, and what did she get? The old maid's room in the rafters, and the cold shoulder from her aunt and cousins."

"But . . . but not from Maud?" Hal said. "In the diary, it reads as if Maud is her friend?"

"Later, yes. But Maud . . . oh, she was a funny one, right from a little girl. I started cleaning up there when I was fifteen, you know, and she must have been about five or six when I started. And I remember her standing there watching me with her hands on her hips, and I say to her, wanting to make friends, like, 'I like your dress, Maud, it's very pretty.' And she tosses her head, and says, 'I'd rather be complimented for my mind than my clothes.' And I couldn't help it—I just burst out laughing. Mortal offended she was. She didn't speak to me for weeks after. But when you got to know her, underneath that prickly surface, she was a kind little thing, and fierce when she felt something was wrong. I'd been there a few years when there was trouble over some missing money and Mrs. Warren was interrogating all the staff, and I was the last one to have cleaned the room where it was supposed to have been. And I was all prepared for the sack, but Maud she comes marching into the kitchen, like an avenging angel, ignoring Mrs. Warren telling her to get out, and she says, 'God damn it, Mrs. Warren, it was Abel took that money and you know it. We all know he steals from Mother's purse. So leave Lizzie alone.' And then she stormed out. She couldn't have been more than ten. But listen to me, rattling on. This isn't what you want to know."

"No . . ." Hal said slowly. "No, it's fine. To be honest . . . my mother never talked about her time here. It's sort of . . . fascinating to find out all this. I never knew she had a cousin with the same name, let alone about Abel and Ezra and Harding and all the others. I wish she'd told me. I don't know why she didn't."

"I don't think it was a very happy time for her," Lizzie said, and the light went out of her kind eyes, her face suddenly sad. "She came here after her parents died, and then it wasn't more than a few months before she got into trouble—with you, I suppose it must have been.

Of course, we didn't know anything about it at first, at least I didn't. But by December there was starting to be talk. She'd been sick all through the autumn, and tongues started wagging, and by the time Advent came around, she was beginning to show. She was only a slip of a thing, and for all the baggy clothes she'd begun to wear, you could see something wasn't right. And she had that look to her—I can't explain it, but you'll know it. Something a little bit puffy around the face, a way of holding herself when she thought no one was looking. I'd seen it before, and I knew. I think the only person who didn't suspect anything was Mrs. Westaway, and when she found out—oh, it was like the plagues of Egypt descended on that house. Doors slamming, and poor little Maggie confined to her room for weeks on end. She couldn't stand to look at her, Mrs. Westaway said, and there were trays sent up and down, and she was barely allowed out. Maud took her meals up whenever she was allowed, and I used to see her coming back down and it looked as if she'd been crying. We all tiptoed around for weeks in the run-up to Christmas, wondering what was going to happen, and who the father was. Someone at her school, we reckoned, though if she knew, she never did say."

"But it wasn't," Hal broke in urgently. "She did know, and that's partly why I came here. I was hoping you could help me work it out. It was someone who came to stay at Trepassen House that summer, it must have been in August. A blue-eyed man, or a boy maybe. Do you know who it could be?"

"Came to stay?" Lizzie was frowning. "I don't know about that. I can't remember more than two or three times the children had friends to stay. Ezra, he had a school friend back once, I think, though I can't remember if it was that summer or the summer before. I don't remember his eyes. And Abel, he had some friends from university who lived in Cornwall and North Devon, sometimes one of them would come for the day, especially when Mrs. Westaway was out. The house was a different place when she wasn't around. I'm sorry," she added, seeing Hal's expression. "I wish I could help you more, but I'd be lying if I said

I remembered. And I only came up a couple of times a week, as the children got older. Mrs. Westaway just didn't have the money for daily help, by then, and I had my own kids anyway."

"Don't worry," Hal said, though she felt her heart deflate like a pricked balloon, a great reservoir of hope that she didn't know she'd been holding on to leaching away. "Tell me about . . . tell me about what happened after. With the letters."

"Well. That was the real scandal then. So Maud was invited to interview at an Oxford college in December, and while she was away things got very bad between Mrs. Westaway and your mother. I'm ashamed to say it, but I was glad to get out of the house when I left each day. I'd hear Mrs. Westaway screaming at her, though they were up in the attics, threatening her with all sorts if she didn't give up the name of the father, and your mother crying and pleading. Once I saw her on the way to the bathroom and she had a black eye and a split lip. I wish now I'd done something but . . ." She trailed off, and Hal saw her blink and rub at the corner of her eye. "Well, Maud came back and it was like she'd seen the light or something. She told me she had an unconditional offer from wherever it was, some women's college, I think, so that she didn't need to study anymore, near enough. But she told me not to tell her mother, and in January she got invited back for another interview—or said she did. Afterwards, I wondered if there really was another interview, or if it was just an excuse to get away. And that was when the letters began. Maggie was here, writing to Maud—sometimes in Oxford, and sometimes in Brighton. And Maud was there, writing back, and I felt like a ruddy postman I can tell you, shipping the letters up and down. But by then I was really afraid for your ma, afraid that Mrs. Westaway would go too far, and hit her hard enough to give her a miscarriage or summat. So I was glad to do what I could to help."

"You don't know what any of the letters said?" Hal asked. She almost held her breath, waiting for the reply, but Lizzie shook her head.

"No, I didn't open them. Only one I saw—and that because your ma didn't have an envelope, and she asked me to put it in one for her. It was the last one."

"Wh-what did it say?"

Lizzie looked down at her lap, her pink fingers fretting anxiously with the rubber gloves she held there.

"I didn't read it," she said at last. "I'm not that sort of person. But it was folded in a way I couldn't help but see one line, and it stuck in my head in a way I've never been able to shake. It said, *I've told him, Maud. It was worse than I ever imagined. Please, please hurry. I am afraid of what might happen now.*"

There was a long silence, Lizzie reliving those memories, Hal turning the words over and over in her mind, feeling the chilly dread within her growing.

"Who—" she said at last, and then stopped.

"Who was the 'him' in the letter?" Lizzie asked, and Hal nodded dumbly. Lizzie shrugged, her plump, cheerful face grave and rather sad. "I don't know. But I always assumed . . ." She bit her lip, and Hal knew what she was about to say, before the words were spoken. "I always assumed she'd told your father about her pregnancy at last, and it was him she was afraid of. I'm sorry, my darling."

"So . . ." Hal found her lips were dry and she licked them, and took a sip of the tea Lizzie had set before her when they sat down, though it had gone cold in the cup. "So . . . what happened next? I know my mother did move to Brighton and had me. What about Maud?"

"Well, that set the cat among the pigeons," Lizzie said. Her face broke into a smile, and she took a long draft of her own tea and set the cup down. "It was maybe late January, or early February. Maud had come back from Oxford or wherever she was supposed to be, but I knew that wasn't the end of it. There were letters coming back and forth, and Maud whispering on the phone in the hallway, jumping like a thief when I came round the corner. Anyone else, I would have thought it was a boy, but I knew enough to know it wasn't that.

"I wasn't there the night they left, but I came up the next day to clean and the house was in an uproar. The girls were gone in the night, they'd taken only their clothes, seemingly, and not so much as a note left. Mrs. Westaway was tearing apart the attic room and Maud's bedroom, saying things I hope never to hear again—foul things about both of them, her own daughter too. But they never called the police, I know that, for my brother-in-law was in the force and he said they never had no official report of the girls going. Perhaps she was afraid of what would come out, I don't know. So in the end, I suppose, in a way, she let them go. Maud, or maybe Maggie, I was never sure, sent one letter to the house—I know, for I saw the envelope lying on the hall table and I recognized the handwriting from all those days and weeks ferrying papers back and forth—they had rather similar writing, but it was definitely one or the other. I don't know what it said, but I saw Mrs. Westaway read it through the crack in the drawing room door. She read it, and then she tore it up and threw the scraps in the fire, and then she spat after them."

"And that was it?" Hal said uncertainly. "You never heard from them again?"

"That was it," Lizzie said. "Almost, at least. I got a postcard from Brighton one day in March. All it said was *Thank you, Mx* and no return address, but I knew who it was from."

"And they never came back," Hal said. She shook her head wonderingly, but Lizzie shook her head in reply.

"No, I didn't say that. I never heard from them again, but Maggie, she came back."

"*What?* When?"

"After she had you. I wasn't there, so I don't know what happened, but I know she came back, for Bill Thomas ran a taxi from Penzance in those days—he's long dead now—and he took her up to the house, and told me afterwards. He said he dropped her off and asked if he should wait, but she said no, she would call when she wanted to be collected. He said she had a look on her face like a maid going into battle. 'A Joan of Arc look' was what he called it."

"But why?" Hal found herself frowning, shaking her head. "Why would she go back, when she tried so hard to get away?"

"I don't know, my darling. All I know is, that really was the last I heard of her. Of either of them. Neither of them ever returned again, after that, and I never heard a word from them again. I often thought about them—and about that baby, you, I suppose it would have been! I often wondered how they were doing. You say your ma became a fortune-teller?"

"Tarot," Hal said. She felt a little numb, battered by all the information that Lizzie had imparted. "She had a booth on the West Pier in Brighton."

"That's no surprise," Lizzie said. Her broad face broke into a smile. "Oh, but she loved her tarot cards, treated them like fine china, she did. And many's the time she read for me. Three children, she said I'd have, and three children I did. And what about Maud? I always thought she'd go on to become some university professor at a women's college. History, it was, she wanted to study, I remember. She said to me, 'There's nothing you can't learn from history to tell you how to deal with the present, Lizzie. That's why I like it. However evil men are now, there's always been worse.' So that's what I'm guessing." She took another sip of her tea, her blue eyes twinkling at Hal over the cup. "Professor of history at the University of London, that's my betting. Am I right?"

"I don't know," Hal said. Her throat had closed, and her voice, when she managed to speak, was stiff and croaky. "I never met Maud, at least not that I can remember. My mother never even mentioned her name."

"So she just . . . disappeared?" Lizzie said. She raised her eyebrows, faint blond shadows almost disappearing into her yellow fringe.

"I suppose so," Hal said. "But wherever she went, she must have gone before I could even remember her face."

CHAPTER 36

The walk back to Trepassen House took Hal much longer than the outward one. She had refused the offer of a lift from Lizzie, and partly the slowness was because the walk was uphill, and the rain had started making the verges slippery, forcing her to stop and wait for a gap in the traffic every time she passed a deep verge-side puddle, or risk getting drenched by the splash-back.

Partly, though, the plain truth was that she was deliberately walking slowly, trying to sort out the tumble of thoughts before she had to face Harding and his brothers with the truth.

She had to come clean—she had known that, even before Lizzie had spoken the words. She had known it, Hal thought, even before she left for Brighton. She had been running away from the whole situation—from the confession she knew she must make.

She tried to imagine the words.

I lied.

I have been lying to you since I got here.

My mother was not your sister.

She felt sick at the thought—there had been something about the relief with which Harding and Abel had welcomed her back yesterday, almost as if she had been their own sister, come home at last. And now she was going to tear that all away from them again—plunge them back into the decades-long uncertainty they had endured before Hal walked into their lives. How would they react?

Harding would rage and bluster. Abel would shake his head—Hal could almost see the disappointment in his eyes. Ezra? Ezra she didn't know. He was perhaps the only one of the three she could imagine taking the news with equanimity, maybe even laughing. But then she thought of the barely suppressed rage and grief she had witnessed beneath the surface when he spoke of his sister's disappearance . . . and suddenly she was not so sure.

Whatever happened, though, however angry they were with Hal herself, Harding at least would be relieved, once the news had sunk in. For Hal's bequest would fail, and . . . then what? The money would return to the pot, presumably, and would be treated as if their mother had never made a will.

Thank goodness Mitzi wasn't there—for the thought of confessing in front of Mitzi, who had been so kind . . . Hal almost doubted she could have brought herself to do it.

But Lizzie knew—and with that came a kind of relief, for there was no going back, no way Hal could chicken out now. She had to push through with this, make her apologies, and . . . then what? Go to see Mr. Treswick, she supposed, to explain the whole situation.

But beneath those thoughts were layered other, more disturbing ones. For behind all this lay one simple, immutable fact: Maud was still missing—and no one seemed to know what had happened to her.

Sometime after February 1995 she had slipped out of sight of her mother, brothers, and cousin, and disappeared. Had she gone of her own volition? Or was the truth something else, something more sinister?

Hal thought of her as she walked, of the fiercely intelligent child that both Lizzie and Mr. Treswick remembered with such amused awe. Of the girl in Maggie's diaries, who had fought with Mrs. Westaway and guarded Maggie's secrets. And of the woman she had wanted to become—free, educated, independent. Had she made it? Was that the truth—that she had helped her cousin free herself from Trepassen House, and then disappeared in her own turn, to make her life somewhere else? It was possible. But it seemed so unlikely—and so strange, that in all the years, Hal's mother had never even mentioned her name. However much Maggie had wanted to leave the unhappiness of Trepassen behind her, it seemed unbelievably callous to have erased the existence of a woman who had done so much to help her.

But the only other possibility was even more disturbing—that Margarida Westaway was dead.

CHAPTER 37

Hal was soaked and shivering by the time she got to the big wrought-iron gates. She was profoundly grateful that Abel had made her take his walking jacket, but the hood was too big to stay up. However tight she pulled the drawstring, the wind blew it back and sent the rain running down the back of her neck to soak her T-shirt.

For a mile or so she tried holding it in place with one hand, but even with her fingers scrunched as far as she could get into the cuffs of the coat, it left her hands cold and blue, and in the end she abandoned the hood, and shoved her hands deep into the pockets of the coat.

When Hal pushed open the gate, the hinges shrieked, a low, mournful sound that cut through the patter of the rain, and made her shiver in a way that wasn't just cold. There was something about the long, low note that made the skin on the back of Hal's neck crawl. It was as though the house itself were dying in pain.

By the time she got up to the house, there was a little sleet mixed in with the rain, the tiny shards of ice stinging her cheek and making her eyes water, and in spite of her trepidation, she was glad to reach the shelter of the porch, where the wind dropped and she could shake off the worst of the water. Inside, she took off Abel's coat, watching as the water pooled on the tiles, and feeling the sensation painfully returning to her chapped fingers, stinging as the blood began to return. From the drawing room she could hear male voices, and taking a deep breath, she put the coat on the peg and made her way across the hallway to the half-open door.

"Hal?" Abel looked around as Hal entered diffidently. "Bloody hell, you look like a drowned rat. Why didn't you call me?"

"I was enjoying the walk," Hal said. She moved closer to the fire, trying to mask the chattering of her teeth. It was not quite a lie. She had not enjoyed the walk, not exactly, but she had not wanted a lift. She'd needed the time to clear her head, work out what she was going to say.

Across the room Ezra was sprawled on the sofa, replying to something on his phone, but he looked up as Hal passed him, and gave a snorting laugh.

"I've never seen anyone look quite so impressively bedraggled. I'm afraid you've missed lunch, but we could probably brave Mrs. Warren's lair for a cup of tea if you need something to warm you up. Or the water in the immersion tank should be hot, if you want a bath?"

"I'll do that," Hal said, grateful for the excuse. Part of her wanted to get this over and done with, but another, more cowardly part was clutching at any straw to postpone the cataclysm that was sure to follow. "Wh-where's Harding?"

"In his room, I think. Having a nap, is my guess. Why?"

"Oh . . . just wondered."

THE BATHROOM WAS UPSTAIRS—JUST one for the entire house, with a huge claw-footed tub streaked green with copper rust, and a lavatory in one corner with a chain that clanked and screeched when Hal pulled it, reminding her of the metallic groan of the gates.

But the water, when she turned the brass taps, was hot, and the pressure was good, and when she at last lowered herself into the scalding heat, she felt something inside her release, a tension that she hadn't known she was holding on to.

Uncle Harding—I'm not who you think I am.

No. Absurdly dramatic. But how could she say it? How could she bring it up?

When I went back home, I discovered something. . . .

And then the story of the diary, as though she had just come to this dawning realization.

The trouble with that was that it was a lie.

So what, then?

Harding, Ezra, Abel—I set out to defraud you.

Maybe the words would come, when she was faced with them all. Closing her eyes, she submerged herself beneath the water, so that her ears filled with the sound of her own pulse and the *drip, drip* of the tap, driving out all the other voices.

"HARRIET?"

Hal jumped and turned, clutching the towel to herself, as Harding's head came out of the doorway of one of the rooms. At the sight of her, damp and pink from her bath, bare shoulders rising from a swath of towel, he looked almost as horrified as Hal felt.

"Oh! My dear, I'm so sorry."

"I had a bath," Hal said, unnecessarily. She felt the corner of the towel slip, and hitched it up, holding her damp clothes in front of herself like a shield. "I was just going up to get dressed."

"Of course, of course," Harding said, waving a hand to indicate that she should feel free to go, though when Hal turned he spoke again, forcing her to turn back, shivering as she did, in the sudden draft. "Oh, Harriet, I'm so sorry—there was one thing I wanted to say, before we met with the others. I won't keep you, but I wanted—well, your offer to perform a deed of variation was very generous, but I'm sorry to say that Abel, Ezra, and I discussed it, and Ezra is being rather difficult about it. He's an executor, you know, and as such he has to agree to any such deed, and he feels, rather strongly, that Mother's wishes should be honored, however perverse and disruptive. I must say it seems an extraordinary position to me, given he never showed the least interest in her wishes when she was alive, but—well—there it is. We'll discuss it with Mr. Treswick tomorrow, anyway."

Hal shivered again, unable to prevent it, and Harding seemed belatedly to realize the cold.

"Oh dear, I am sorry, I'm keeping you dripping in the corridor. Don't mind me, I'll see you downstairs for a gin and tonic, perhaps?"

Hal nodded, stiff with the knowledge of all that she had left unspoken; and then, unable to think what else to say that was not an addition to all the lies she had already told, she turned and made her way up the stairs to the attic room.

IT WAS PERHAPS HALF AN hour later when she pushed open the door to the drawing room and found all three brothers sitting around the coffee table, in front of a roaring log fire.

There was a bottle of whiskey on the table between them, and four tumblers—one unfilled.

"Harriet!" Harding said heartily. His face was flushed, with a mix of heat and whiskey, Hal suspected. "Come in and have a drink. I'm afraid my offer of gin and tonic turned out to be premature—there's no tonic in the house. But I did take the precaution of buying a bottle of whiskey when I was in Penzance earlier, so we do at least have that."

"Thanks," Hal said, "but I don't really—"

She stopped. She didn't drink, not anymore. There had been too many oblivious nights after her mother's death, too many times when one glass had dissolved into many. But now she had a sudden, powerful yearning for something, however small, to nerve her for what she was about to do.

"Actually, thanks," she said, and Harding poured her a generous, overgenerous, measure, and pushed the tumbler across the table to her.

He refilled his brothers' glasses at the same time and then raised his own.

"A toast," he said, meeting Harriet's eyes. "A toast to . . ." He paused, and then gave a short laugh. "To family."

Hal's stomach tightened, but she was saved from answering by Ezra's derisive snort. He shook his head.

"I'm not bloody drinking to that. To freedom."

Abel gave a chuckle and picked up his own tumbler. "Freedom seems a little harsh. I'll drink to . . ." He raised his glass, thinking. "To closure. To seeing Mr. Treswick tomorrow and getting home to Edward ASAP. Hal?"

The acrid smell of the whiskey stung her nostrils, and she swirled it, looking down into the tawny, glinting depths.

"I'll drink to . . ." Words crowded in—unsayable words. Truth. Lies. Secrets. Her throat tightened. There was only one toast that she could find in her heart, the crowding, painful truth, waiting to be blurted out. "To my mother," she said huskily.

There was a long pause. The whiskey in Hal's glass trembled as she looked around the circle of faces. Harding's mustache quivered as he raised his glass.

"To Maud," he said, his voice harsh with suppressed emotion. The whiskey caught the light, winking solemnly.

Abel swallowed hard, and raised his own tumbler.

"To Maud," he said, very softly, his voice so low Hal would not have been sure of the word if she had not known what it was already.

Ezra said nothing, but he raised his glass, and his dark eyes were bright with a grief Hal found almost too painful to look at.

For a moment they sat, all four of them, glasses raised in silent remembrance, and then all of a sudden, Hal could bear it no longer. In one movement, she threw back her head and gulped the whiskey down in three long swallows.

There was a short silence, and then Harding burst out with a kind of shakily relieved laughter, and Ezra clapped a slow round of applause.

"Well done, Harriet!" Abel said drily. "I wouldn't have thought you had it in you, you little mouse."

There it was again. *Little mousy Harriet.* But it was not true. It had never been true. After her mother's death, she had made herself small and insignificant, but the façade that she showed to the world was not the truth of her.

Inside there was an iron strength—the same strength, Hal realized, that had enabled her mother to escape Trepassen, start again in a strange town, pregnant and alone, and build a life for her baby daughter. At the heart of Hal, beneath the unassuming layers and drab clothes, was a deep, resilient core that would keep fighting, and fighting, and fighting. Mice hid and scuttled. They froze in the face of danger. They allowed themselves to be made prey.

Whatever Hal was, she was not a mouse.

And she would not be anybody's prey.

Uncle Harding, I'm not who you think I am.

When she put the glass down, it rattled against the tray, and she cleared her throat, her cheeks burning with the consciousness of what she was about to do. She remembered Mrs. Warren's look that first night . . . the look of someone watching a flock of pigeons, who sees a cat suddenly creeping from the shadows of a nearby tree. The look of someone who stands back . . . and waits.

"Well—" Harding began, but Hal interrupted him, knowing that if she did not do this now, she might never do it.

"Wait, I—I have something to say."

Harding blinked, slightly put out, and the corner of Ezra's mouth quirked as if he was amused to see his brother discomfited.

"Oh, well, please." Harding waved a hand. "Be my guest."

"I—" Hal bit her lip. She had been turning this moment over and over in her mind ever since she left Cliff Cottages, but the right words had not come, and suddenly she knew that it was because there *were* no right words, there was nothing she could say that would make this okay.

"I have something to tell you," she said again, and then she stood up, not quite knowing why, but feeling unable to stay slack and safe in the corner of the sofa. She felt like she was about to fight, to defend herself from attack. The muscles in her neck and shoulders hurt with tension.

"I found out something when I was back in Brighton. I hadn't been sure before, but I went through my mother's papers and I found out—"

She swallowed, her mouth suddenly dry, wishing she had not drained the whiskey so fast, but had saved a sip for now. Harding was frowning; Abel was suddenly tense, leaning forwards in his chair, his expression full of a kind of apprehension. Only Ezra looked unconcerned. He had folded his arms and was regarding her with interest, like someone watching an experiment play out.

"Well?" Harding said, with a little impatience in his voice. "What did you find? Spit it out, Harriet."

"Margarida Westaway—your sister—she was not my mother," Hal said.

She felt a great weight roll off her, but there was no relief in its passing, only an aching pain, and a kind of dread as she waited for the crash as it dropped.

There was a long silence.

"I—*what*?" Harding said at last. He was staring at Hal, his plump, ruddy face scarlet with the heat of the fire, or with shock at Hal's speech, she was not sure which. "I beg your pardon?"

"I'm not your niece," Hal said. She swallowed again. There were tears coming up from somewhere deep inside, and it would have been so easy to let them out—play for their sympathy—but the knowledge made her force them back down. She would not play the victim here. She was done with dissembling.

"I should have realized before—there were . . . things . . . they didn't add up. But it was only when I went home, I looked in my mother's papers to try to get to the bottom of it, and I found . . . I found diaries . . . letters . . . making it clear there had been a terrible mix-up. My mother wasn't your sister. She was Maggie."

"Oh my God." It was Abel who spoke, his voice flat and blank with shock. He put his head in his hands, as if to try to contain thoughts that threatened to burst out. "Oh my God. Hal—but this is—this is—" He stopped, shaking his head like someone punch-drunk, trying to shrug off blows. "Why didn't we *see*?"

"But—but wait, this means the will is invalid," Harding burst out.

"For God's sake!" Ezra said. He gave a derisive laugh. "Money! Is that all you can think of? The will is hardly the most important thing."

"It's what brought Harriet here in the first place, so I would say it's quite important, yes!" Harding shot back. "And the money isn't the point at all. I deeply resent what you're implying there, Ezra. It's about—it's about—oh dear God, just when we were beginning to get the whole benighted situation sorted out—what in hell's name was Mother thinking?"

"A good question," Abel said in a low voice. He was slumped in his seat, his head still in his hands.

"But—but your name was in the will," Harding said slowly. He had the air of someone whose first shock was beginning to wear off, who was retracing his footsteps . . . trying to piece things together. "Or—wait, are you telling us—are you not Harriet Westaway at all? Who are you really?"

"No!" Hal said quickly. "No, no, I *am* Harriet. I promise you. And my mother really is Margarida Westaway. But I think your mother must have asked Mr. Treswick to trace her daughter." Hal's face felt stiff, and her fingers cold, in spite of the fire. "And somehow the threads became crossed, and he found my mother instead, without realizing the mix-up. I think he must have reported back to your mother that he had found your sister and that she had died, but that she'd had a daughter. And so she put my name in the will—not realizing that I wasn't her granddaughter at all."

"How did *you* not realize?" Abel said, but there was no anger in his voice, only bewilderment. He looked up at Hal, his eyes full of a puzzled pain that she didn't fully understand. "Surely there were things that didn't add up—things that made you think—"

He stopped. Hal felt herself grow still and careful. This was it. This was the dangerous part. Because he was right.

She forced herself to stop pacing, and to sit, and her mother's voice was in her head. *When you're tempted to answer in a hurry—slow down. Make them wait for you. Give yourself time to think. It's when we hurry that we're most prone to stumble.*

"Well . . ." she said slowly. The sofa springs squeaked as she shifted her weight uncomfortably, and the wind howled in the chimney. "Well . . . there were things. Not at first—but later . . . but you have to understand . . . my name, it was there in the will. And Mum never spoke much about her childhood. She never mentioned any brothers, or a house in Cornwall, but then there was so much she never talked about. She didn't talk about her parents either, or my father. I just took it for granted that this was another part of her I didn't know. And I wanted so much . . ." Her voice faltered, no artifice here as she fought hard against the tremor in her voice, for this was the truth. "I wanted *so much* for it to be true. I wanted this—all of this—" She waved her hand at the room, at the fire and the house and the men sitting around her, looking at her with varying degrees of puzzled exasperation and bewilderment. "Family. Security. A *home.* I wanted it all so much, Mr. Treswick's letter felt like—it felt like an answer to a prayer. I think—I think I shut my eyes to my doubts."

"I can understand that," Abel said heavily. He stood and rubbed his hands over his face, looking suddenly very old, much older than his fortysomething years. "Dear God, what a mess. At least you've told us now."

"Well, I for one will be having *stern* words with Mr. Treswick tomorrow," Harding said angrily. His face was a worrisome shade of purple. "This is damn close to some sort of—of professional negligence on his part! Lord knows how we'll sort out this legal tangle. Thank God it came out before we obtained probate!"

"Jesus," Ezra said under his breath. "Can we stop banging on about the bloody will? Presumably you'll get the bloody money now, isn't that enough?"

"I resent—" Harding began more hotly, but was interrupted by a tremendous resounding clanging that made everyone jump convulsively, and Harding slam down his whiskey glass as the noise died away.

"For God's sake, Mrs. Warren!" he bellowed, opening the drawing room door. "We are *all* in here. Was there really any need for that?"

She came to the door, hands on hips.

"Dinner's ready."

"Thank you," Harding said, rather ungraciously. He folded his arms, and then looked at Abel, seeming to ask him an unspoken question. Hal couldn't quite read Harding's face, but Abel evidently understood, for he shrugged and nodded, rather reluctantly.

"Mrs. Warren," Harding said heavily. "Before we go into the dining room, there's something we should explain, as it concerns you too. It's come to light"—he shot a glance at Hal—"that Mr. Treswick made a rather unfortunate error in drawing up Mother's will. Harriet is *not* Maud's daughter, she is in fact Maggie's child, something Harriet only discovered when she went through her mother's papers. God knows how Mr. Treswick made such a regrettable error, but obviously in light of it the will is invalid. I'm not sure what will happen—I presume intestacy rules will have to be followed. But there it is."

"I never thought she was," Mrs. Warren said. She crossed her arms, her stick beneath her elbow. Harding blinked.

"I beg your pardon?"

"A-course she's Maggie's child. No one with any sense woulda thought otherwise."

"What? But why didn't you *say* something?"

Mrs. Warren smiled, and her eyes, in the dim light of the fire, seemed to Hal to glitter like stones.

"Well?" Harding demanded again. "Are you saying you knew this for certain and you said nothing?"

"Not for certain. But it was common sense. And none of my business, anyway."

"Well!" This time it was an explosion of disbelief, but Mrs. Warren had already turned and was stumping down the long, tiled corridor, her cane *click-click*ing as she went.

"Did you hear that?" Harding asked the silent group in the room, but no one answered.

At last Ezra walked out, his shoulders hunched in mutinous silence. Abel shook his head and followed. Harding turned too, and Hal was left alone.

Her hands were still trembling, and she paused for a minute, warming them in front of the fire, trying to get the feeling back into her numb fingertips.

She was just about to leave when a piece of coal in the grate suddenly flared and spat, throwing out a flaming splinter onto the rug. Hal was about to stamp on it when she realized her feet were bare—she had taken off her soaked shoes at the door. Instead she took up the poker and flicked the coal back towards the stone-flagged hearth, scratching out the last sparks with the tip.

There was a smoking hole in the rug, and a scorch in the board beneath, but nothing to be done about either, and looking down, Hal saw that it was not the first. There were three or four holes even larger, one where the fire had eaten quite a little way into the board. With a sigh, she put the fireguard in place and turned to leave, only to find Mrs. Warren standing in the doorway, barring the way.

"Excuse me," Hal said, but Mrs. Warren didn't move, and for a brief moment Hal had a fantastic notion that she was going to have to call for help, or escape out of the window again. But when she took a step towards the doorway, Mrs. Warren pressed herself back against the frame, and allowed Hal to pass through, though she had to edge her way, to avoid tripping on Mrs. Warren's cane.

It was only when she was past and starting up the corridor, the tiles chill beneath her feet, that the woman spoke, her voice so low that Hal had to turn back.

"What did you say?" Hal asked, but Mrs. Warren had disappeared inside the drawing room, and the heavy door slammed shut behind her, cutting Hal's question off short.

But Hal was sure—at least, almost sure—that she had caught the words, hissed low as they were beneath the sound of the wind in the chimney.

"Get out—if you know what's good for you. While you still can . . ."

CHAPTER 38

Hal went to bed early that night, and whether it was the strain of the day or the long walk to Cliff Cottages, she fell asleep almost at once.

She awoke stiff and with the sense of having slept a long time, but it was still not dawn, and when she got up and went to the window, shivering in the cold night air, the moon was still high. Her breath was white against the pane, and the sky had cleared, and in the moonlight she could make out the glitter of frost on the lawn.

Her mouth was dry and she reached for the glass beside her bed, but when she picked it up, it was empty. In her tiredness she must have forgotten to fill it the night before. The chilly walk through the dark landing down to the bathroom below was not enticing, and Hal decided to ignore the thirst. She got back into bed and shut her eyes, but the dryness in her mouth niggled at her, keeping sleep at bay, until at last she gave up, swung her legs out of bed, and picked up the glass. Wrapping her fleece around her, she went cautiously out into the corridor.

It was pitch-black outside, the lino freezing under her bare feet, and she tried the switch on the wall, but as she did, she remembered too late that she hadn't told anyone about the missing bulb.

Sure enough, the switch clicked fruitlessly, and Hal sighed and went back to the attic room to pick up her phone. The thin tunnel of light from its torch made the corridor feel, if anything, even darker, but at least she could see the black, yawning opening to the stairs.

She was only one step down, when her foot caught on something.

Hal clutched, instinctively, for a banister—but there was none there. She felt her fingers scratch at the bare wall, and then the horrible stomach-wrenching lurch as the phone flew from her hand, and she realized she was falling, with nothing she could do to stop herself.

She landed with a crunch in the hallway below, thudding her head against the floor, and rolled to a stop against the wall, where she lay, gasping, winded, waiting for the sound of running footsteps, questions, solicitous inquiries. But none came.

"I'm—I'm okay!" she called shakily, but there was no response, only the noise of the wind, and beneath it the far-off sound of a muffled snore, coming from somewhere below.

Cautiously, Hal sat up. She felt for her glasses, before realizing she hadn't put them on in the first place. They were still on her bedside table, which was something at least to be thankful for. She'd almost rather have a broken arm than broken glasses, so far from home. Her phone was on the bottom step of the stairs, facedown, the torch still shining up to the ceiling, and when Hal picked it up the screen was cracked, but the phone itself still seemed to be working.

The water glass, on the other hand, had smashed—there were shards scattered on the floor, and her hand was bleeding, but there was no blood coming from the place where her head had hit the floor, and when she flexed her arms, no bones seemed to be broken. As she got shakily to her feet, dizziness swept over her, but she didn't fall, only steadied herself against the wall, and it passed.

It was almost unbelievable luck that she hadn't broken an arm, or even her neck. The wall of the corridor was only feet away from the bottom of the stairs. If she had hit it with her skull, she would have been dead.

A wave of trembling sickness washed over her. Delayed shock, she thought numbly, and she sank down onto the bottom step, feeling her head throb where she'd hit it against the floor, and the uncontrollable shaking in her arms and legs. She was no longer thirsty, and in any case, the idea of picking her way through the shards of shattered glass in bare feet felt impossible. She wanted only to crawl back into bed where it was safe and warm, and let the trembling in her limbs subside.

Slowly she got to her hands and knees, and not quite trusting herself to go upright, she crawled up the stairs, her phone in her hand.

In almost any other position she might have missed it—but as it was, the light from the phone fell straight onto it. It was one step down from the top. A rusty nail, driven into the skirting board at ankle height, a length of snapped string still trailing from it.

Hal felt her breath catch in her throat, and she stopped, frozen, the beam from her phone shining onto the innocuous little thing.

Then she got hold of herself, and forced herself to swing the beam to the other side of the stairs.

There was its twin, driven into the same place, only this one had been wrenched almost out of place by the force of her fall.

She hadn't tripped. This was no accident.

Someone had driven in those nails, and strung the string across the top step, taking advantage of the fused bulb at the top of the stairs to ensure that she wouldn't see, even in daylight, what had been done.

It hadn't been there when she went up to bed, she was sure of it. She couldn't have passed up the stairs without tripping over it.

Which meant that someone had come up here, while she was sleeping, to set the trap.

But no . . . she wasn't thinking clearly—they could not have hammered in the nails. She would have heard them. Which meant . . . it meant that this had been premeditated. The nails had been there all along, waiting for the removal of the bulb, and the string to be set up. Someone had been intending this. They had prepared for her to return, back from Brighton, and they had guarded against it.

Hal's heart seemed to slow inside her chest, a great stillness settling over her.

She should have been panicking. But it was as though something had hold of her inside, and was squeezing . . . squeezing. . . .

She crawled rather than walked the last few steps into the attic room, and shut the door, before subsiding with her back against the wooden panels. Her head was in her hands, and she was thinking, not for the first time, of the bolts on the outside, and of the silent malevolence of the person who had come up those stairs, just a few hours earlier, and set a trap designed to kill.

As she closed her eyes and pressed her forehead into her knees, an image floated into Hal's head unbidden.

It was the eight of swords. A woman, blindfolded, bound, surrounded by a prison of blades, and the ground at her feet bloodred as though she were already bleeding from cuts that could never free her.

The cards tell you nothing you don't already know. It was her mother's voice, steady in her ear. *They have no power, remember that. They can't reveal any secrets or dictate the future. All they can do is show you what you already know.*

Oh, but now she knew, all right.

The walls of the trap were closing around her, sharp enough to maim.

Now she knew that someone hated her enough to kill her. But *why*?

Because it didn't make sense. A few hours before, she might have thought that it was an attempt by one of the brothers to regain his share of the inheritance he had thought was his. Because Hal was—had been—the residuary legatee. If she died, her share of the money obeyed the laws of intestacy, which meant that, in the absence of a husband, it would be divided among Mrs. Westaway's children.

But now that she had admitted the truth, Harding, Ezra, and Abel had nothing left to fear from her. The money would revert to them whatever happened to her.

So why, then? Why now?

Get out—if you know what's good for you.

Après moi, le déluge. . . .

What did it mean?

Hal's head, where she had hit it, felt ready to burst, and it throbbed until she thought she might cry out from the pain of it.

Whatever she had done, whatever she had meant, Mrs. Westaway had started something with this legacy, and Hal was blindly following the sequence of events she had set off. Only, like the woman on the eight of swords, she was hedged about with dangers she could not even see.

At last, almost blind with the throbbing pain that had begun to envelop her entire skull, Hal crawled into bed, letting her aching head rest slowly on the cool pillow, closing her eyes, and pulling the blankets up to her chin as though they could protect her against the threats she felt crowding around.

She was almost asleep when a name came to her, like a suggestion whispered into an ear.

Margarida . . .

The word trickled slowly, like cool dark water, through the recesses of Hal's skull, and in its wake, in spite of her tiredness, her mind began working, making connections.

Hal had claimed that her mother was Margarida Westaway—the girl called Maud in her mother's diary. And, because of that claim, certain facts had been taken for granted. The fact that Maud had run away from Cornwall. The fact that she had moved to Brighton and had a daughter. And the fact that she had died in a car crash, just three years ago.

But the truth was very different.

The question was, *how* different.

And how far would someone go to keep the true facts from coming out?

One thing was certain: this was no longer about the money, for Hal had kissed good-bye to that with her confession. There was something deeper and stranger at stake here—something that someone would kill to conceal.

She should have been afraid, and part of her was. But deep down, in the core of herself, the secret predatory self that she kept hidden and locked away, Hal knew. She would not run again. Someone had tried to scare her away once, and it had almost worked. But it would not work again.

Now she wanted answers. What had set her mother running so long ago? Why had she gone to such lengths to lie about her father? And what had happened to Maud?

And most of all—what *was* this secret, the secret that lay at the heart of all of this mystery, that someone was ready to kill to protect?

Hal wanted answers to all those questions, and more. And she was ready to fight.

CHAPTER 39

There was no question of going back to sleep, and at last Hal could bear it no longer.

Her phone on the bedside table said 5:05. Too early to get up, but she could not lie there in the darkness for two more hours. She sat up and reached for her glasses, the movement making the back of her head throb painfully, but at last she had them settled on her nose, and she fired up her phone, frowning at the little cracked screen as she tried to work out what to search.

Something had happened to Maud Westaway—something that someone in this house knew, and did not want anyone to find out. Was it Mrs. Warren?

Hal thought again of her face last night, of the wicked gloating pleasure, and the bald admission that she had known all along of Hal's deception. Whatever it was, Hal thought, she would not put Mrs. Warren past knowing about it and keeping it secret for her own twisted reasons.

But trying to work out who in the house was concealing something was a blind alley, because the truth was, everyone had something to hide, Hal knew that well from her tarot readings. Everyone had secrets, things that they did not want to reveal and would go to great—sometimes extraordinary—lengths to conceal.

What she had to do was try to work out what the secrets were—and what her own part in them was. Someone had been prepared to kill her to stop her revealing what she knew. And what was that?

Hal rubbed her knuckles into her eyes, trying to think clearly.

Because of her evidence, everyone had assumed Maud was dead, that much was clear. And they had assumed, too, that she had died in a car crash. So there were two possibilities. The first was that Maud *was* dead—but not in a car crash, and someone wanted to cover up what had really happened to her.

That was alarming enough—the idea that Hal might have stumbled onto a potential murder.

But the second possibility was in a way even more worrying. For the other possibility was that Maud was alive—and that someone in this house was hell-bent on concealing that fact. But why? Could it be the money again? The will? If the legacy to Hal failed, would the money revert back to the pot, or would it travel back up the line that would have inherited it, back to Maud? Or was it something else that someone was trying to conceal—something Maud knew, or could reveal?

There was no way of knowing. But either way, the first step was finding out which possibility she was dealing with.

Finding out whether someone was alive or dead was surprisingly hard—Hal knew that from a client who had come back time and time again, begging Hal to tell her whether her missing husband was still alive, in spite of Hal's increasingly emphatic insistence that she did not know.

It was always the way. The people who were skeptics would never be convinced—and the people who believed would never be persuaded otherwise. Hal was used to that—used to the resigned disbelief when she told people that she could not answer their questions or change the facts of their lives, as if she had powers she was concealing but chose not to admit for some perverse agenda of her own. She knew the source of their disbelief: it was a reluctance to come to terms with the fact that they would never get the answers and outcomes they craved. But most people, however unwillingly, accepted that Hal would not change fate for them, even if they did not accept that she *could* not. They went away secretly believing that if Hal would not oblige, there would be others out there who could, if they only searched hard enough.

This woman, however, had been different.

She had come back time and time again, phoning under different names when Hal stopped accepting appointments from her, turning up without warning and banging on the glass, so that Hal learned to dread the clutch of her lean fingers and the desperation in her hollowed eyes.

At last, more from a desire to be rid of her than any kind of charity, Hal had taken down the husband's name and last known address, and had herself turned to the Internet to try to give the woman the answers she needed—only to run up against an almost complete lack of information. The man wasn't on Facebook, and it seemed impossible to search for a death certificate without knowing the date of death. Hal had assumed that the records would be computerized, and that a simple search of the man's name and perhaps his date of birth would throw up anything on record—but it seemed not. For historic records, such a facility existed—but for anything in the last fifty years, you needed to know the exact details of death not just to obtain a death certificate, but simply to find out if such a certificate existed.

It seemed that without knowing *when* someone had died, there was no way of finding out *if* they even had.

But Hal had no date of death. If Maud *was* dead, her brothers knew nothing of the true facts of what had happened, and Mr. Treswick's searches had not uncovered the fact. The alternative, then, was to prove the opposite—that she was still alive. But how?

The only lead Hal had was the Oxford college that Lizzie had mentioned. An unconditional offer from Oxford, she had said. And later, that she thought it was a women's college. Hal opened up Google on her phone. In 1995 there had been only one women's college left in Oxford—St. Hilda's, though Somerville had only just become coeducational the year before. It was possible that Maud might have called it a women's college in her description to Lizzie.

A few minutes of searching threw up a database of alumni for both colleges, but it was searchable only by people who were themselves former members of the specific college. Oxford itself would confirm a candidate's degree and class to an employer, but took twenty-one days to respond to requests.

Hal sighed, but wrote down the numbers of the colleges. Perhaps if she spoke to a real person, she could blag the information she needed. Or she could pretend to be Maud herself, and perhaps whether they spoke to her or not would reveal whether she was a former member of the college.

Really, though, where did that get her? Two, three years on from Maud's disappearance from Trepassen? It still left a huge gulf of years after that on which Hal had no information whatsoever. And out of the only people she could have asked, one had just tried to kill her.

In the cold light of day, it was hard to realize and remember. Had it really happened? The bump on her head was clear enough, but the nails, and the piece of string—had she *really* seen what she had thought?

It was almost seven now, and Hal stood, shivering as the covers fell away, and pulled on her clothes, cold as the floor they had been lying on. Outside in the hallway she took a deep breath, and switched on the torch on her mobile phone.

The nails were still there, rusted and bent, on either side of the stairs.

But the string had gone.

Hal frowned. She was certain she remembered it—a piece of unremarkable garden twine, dark against the drab boards, fastened at one end around the left-hand nail. But it wasn't there anymore; only a pale loose thread from the lino on the landing trailed down.

Had someone come up and cleared it away? Or was it possible she had mistaken the lino thread in the darkness?

She switched off the phone and walked slowly and carefully down the stairs, watching her steps for shards of the broken glass, and thinking as she did. Last night, her one thought had been to show Harding, Abel, and Ezra the evidence of what someone had tried to do. Now she was reconsidering. The nails were bent and rusted, and even to Hal's eye they looked as if they could have been there for some time. And as for the string . . . she could just hear Harding's skepticism: *Really, Harriet? Isn't it possible you just caught your foot in that trailing thread from the lino? Regrettably careless, certainly, but hardly a plot to kill. . . .*

And the answer was . . . yes. It was possible. Though Hal was as certain as she could be that that was not what had happened.

DOWNSTAIRS, HAL STEPPED LIGHTLY OFF the carpeted flight of stairs onto the cold tiles of the entrance hall. As she did, a clock somewhere deep inside the house ground into action and began to strike. Hal counted off the chimes. One . . . two . . . three . . . four . . . five . . . six . . . seven.

The silence, afterwards, was a little unnerving, but the feeling faded as she pushed open the drawing room door. It was empty—just as they had left it last night, the whiskey glasses scattered across the table.

Four cups. In tarot, the four of cups meant inwardness. It meant not noticing what was under your nose, failing to grasp the opportunities that were being presented. In Hal's deck the card was a young woman lying under a tree, apparently asleep, or meditating. Three empty cups lay on the ground in front of her, and a fourth was being offered to her lips by a disembodied hand. But the woman didn't drink. She didn't even notice what was being shown to her.

What was it that she was failing to notice?

Breakfast would not be served until eight, and Hal didn't relish the thought of bumping into Mrs. Warren, as she had the first morning, so she pushed her feet into her shoes, still damp from their soaking yesterday, put up the hood of her fleece, and gently undid the drawing room window, stepping outside into the chilly dawn air.

THE NIGHT HAD BEEN CLEAR, and very cold, and the temperature overnight had gone well below freezing. The grass beneath Hal's feet was thick with frost, and it crunched gently as she walked, her breath a cloud of white, tinged with the faintest of pink by the rising sun.

Outside in the cold, bracing air, her panicked certainty of last night had begun to recede, leaving her feeling a little foolish. A blown lightbulb, which someone had got halfway through replacing and then forgotten. A couple of nails, probably left over from when a carpet runner had covered the stairs, and a single thread, both seen by the wavering light of a mobile phone—it wasn't much to build a conspiracy theory on. And besides, it didn't make *sense.* Even if Maud was dead, and even if someone wanted to prevent that fact from coming out, what would be the sense in trying to kill Hal? She had already revealed the truth—that her mother wasn't Maud. There was nothing left to disclose. Tripping her down the stairs would be a pointless risk, and achieve nothing. The horse had bolted—and there was no stable door to close.

In the slowly brightening dawn, her fears of the night before suddenly seemed not just laughable but impossible, and she felt her cheeks flush a little as she remembered her panicked crawl back to her room, and the thumping of her heart as she sat against the door with her knees to her chest.

Oh, Hal . . . Her mother's voice in her ear. *Always so dramatic . . .*

She shook her head.

She had been walking aimlessly, letting her feet take her where they wanted, and now, as she looked back over her shoulder to the house, she realized quite how far she had come.

For a moment she stood, looking back at the green sea of lawn between herself and the house, and beyond that, the tangle of stables and outbuildings, glass houses and kitchen plots.

How many homes could you build in this one garden? How many people could you house, and how many jobs could you create?

And here it all was, all this land, all this beauty, ring-fenced, first for one dying old woman, and now for her heirs.

Well, it was no longer her problem. Ezra, Harding, and Abel could fight over it now. What would they do—sell it? Perhaps it would become a hotel, with the grounds given over to swimming pools and glamping yurts. Or perhaps someone would knock the house down and build a golf course, with rolling green as far as the eye could see, a grass-green sea meeting the blue of the horizon.

Today the far-off sea was gray, tipped with white horses, and the wind was fresh in Hal's face as she walked, always downhill.

She had been planning to get as far as the boundary and then cut back round to the house, but when she looked away from the headland, she realized that her feet had led her inexorably back to the path they always seemed to take—the clump of trees, with the dark water glimmering through.

This time, however, Hal looked at the water with different eyes. It was not just any lake that lay within the dense, overgrown copse. It was *the* lake. The one her mother had written about in her diary.

And there, between the bare, frosted trunks, she could see the shape of the boathouse.

She changed direction, heading down towards it, curious now.

The trees that surrounded it were a mix of beech, oak, and yew, only the yew still green. The others were bare, a few brown leaves clinging to the branches, fluttering in the wind that came up the valley. As Hal picked her way down the overgrown path, pushing aside brambles and stepping across nettles, she found the words of the diary running through her head—the description of them taking the boats out that day. *"Come on, Ed," she shouted, and he stood up, grinned at me, and then followed her to the water's edge, and took a running jump.*

Ed. Edward. Could it really be true? She remembered how Edward had come to meet her that evening at the lake, his laconic voice: *Oh . . . it used to be a boathouse . . . back in the day.* And she thought, too, of the way Abel had deliberately steered her away from it that first morning, before she had even known what it was. Was there something they did not want her to see?

The door was closed and seemed to be locked, but Hal could see through the cracks in the blackened, gappy planks. The building was open to the lake on the water side, and there were two platforms on either side, and in between a strip of dark water.

She was leaning on the door, peering through a gap between two of the planks, when suddenly the rotten wood gave and the door burst inwards, sending Hal stumbling inside, slipping on the wet, slimy platform so that she staggered, trying to save herself from shooting into the water, and fell to her knees, barely inches from the lake surface.

She knelt there, panting, steadying herself. The fall had jarred bones already bruised from last night, making her grit her teeth with pain, but as she sat back on her heels nothing seemed to be broken.

Was she safe? Hal looked down at the jetty planks beneath her feet, at the lapping, leaf-strewn water, thin shards of ice floating on the surface. She wasn't sure. This place looked ready to collapse into the lake at the slightest provocation, and she would not have been surprised if her foot had gone straight through the planks into the water beneath. At least it was shallow. Cautiously, she picked up one of the sticks that had fallen through the holes in the roof, and pushing aside the fragile, broken sheets of ice, she tested the depth. Barely a foot before the stick jagged on something hard beneath the water, a smooth shape that showed pale as Hal pushed away the leaf mold with her stick.

As she peered closer through the dark, slightly peaty water, she recognized the shape of a boat, hull up beneath the water. Black, rotting leaf debris had settled over it, masking it, but her stick had stirred up the water, and faint streaks of white showed where she had trailed the tip. As her eyes got used to the dim light and the way the water slanted the perspective, Hal made out something else—a jagged hole near the keel. Had someone sunk it deliberately?

All of a sudden, this didn't feel like the place her mother had described in her diary, the place where she had laughed and swum and played with her cousins, and with the boy she was about to fall in love with. It felt . . . The realization came to Hal suddenly, like a cold touch on the shoulder. It felt like a place where something had died.

Hal shuddered, and stepping as lightly as she could, she stood and moved backwards, through the broken door, and back out into the cold morning light. The air tasted fresh and sea-clean after the scent of brackish water and rotten wood in the boathouse, and she breathed it deeply. As she did, her phone pinged with a reminder, and she pulled it out of her pocket to check, though the lurch in her stomach told her what she already knew.

11.30—appt with Mr Treswick.

God. Well, there was no point in putting it off. And even a kind of relief to think that in a few hours the whole business would be laid to rest. She just had to hope that Mr. Treswick would be as accepting of her part in the "mix-up" as Harding, Abel, and Ezra had been . . . or appeared to be, at least.

Hal shivered, pushing her hands deep into the pockets of her fleece. Suddenly toast and coffee—even Mrs. Warren's coffee—seemed very welcome, and she walked quickly up the hill to the house, her frosty breath streaming over her shoulder.

Behind her, the boathouse door swung quietly closed, but she did not look back.

CHAPTER 40

"Oh dear." Mr. Treswick removed his glasses and polished them, though they were quite clean already, from what Hal could make out. "Oh dear, oh dear. This is most awkward."

"Please." Hal put out a hand. "Please, it's my fault. I should have—I should have said something earlier."

"I blame myself, very much," Mr. Treswick was saying, as if he hadn't heard. "I must say, it absolutely never occurred to me that Maggie's name was Margarida too. I knew of course that there had been a cousin, but everyone referred to her as Maggie, and I'm afraid I simply assumed her full name was Margaret. Oh dear, this is extremely problematic."

"But the legacy cannot stand, presumably?" Harding said impatiently. "That's surely the main thing?"

"I will have to take advice," Mr. Treswick said. "My instinct is to say that no, it does not stand, since Mrs. Westaway clearly meant the legacy to pass to her daughter's child. But the fact that Harriet is named along with her address . . . oh dear. This is very knotty indeed."

"Well . . ." Ezra rose and stretched, so that Harriet heard his spine and shoulders cracking. "We've done all we can to sort this out for the moment, so I suggest we leave it to the lawyers now."

"I will be in touch with you all," Mr. Treswick said slowly. His brow was furrowed, and Hal felt deeply sorry for him, as he lifted his glasses to rub at the place where the rests pinched the sides of his nose. "There may be quite some disentangling to do, I'm afraid."

"I'm so sorry," Hal said, and she had no need to fake the miserable compunction in her tone. She wished, more than anything, that there was a way to tell him of her own complicity in this, without ending up as part of a prosecution, but she couldn't risk it. Better to cling to the shaky pretense that this was all an innocent mistake, though she was beginning to wonder how long that edifice could hold up. "Good-bye, Mr. Treswick."

"Good-bye, Harriet."

She nodded and stood, and he took her hand. At first she thought he was going to shake it, but he did not; he simply held it, rather gently, and when at last she smiled and pulled away, she thought for a moment that he did not want to let her go. It was a disquieting thought, the memory of his dry, old fingers holding hers rather insistently, and it stayed with her as she followed Harding down the hallway back to reception, wondering . . . wondering. . . .

At the end of the corridor, Hal looked back, and she saw that he was still there, standing in the doorway of his office, his gaze somber, and Hal found herself pondering his expression as she passed through the doorway after Harding, back into the bright, crowded little reception area.

The door swung shut behind her, but she could not resist one last glance back as it closed, to see him still standing there, his arms crossed, his brow furrowed. She could not escape the idea that there was something else Mr. Treswick would have said, if he could. Something more. But what?

CHAPTER 41

"Well," Harding said, as they exited the lawyer's office and stood uncertainly in the street outside. "Can I buy anyone lunch? Or, perhaps more to the point, a pint?"

"Not me," Ezra said. He looked up at the sky, which was heavy and yellow, with the promise of snow. "I've got a crossing booked from Folkestone tonight. I need to get back and start packing."

"Tonight?" Harding blinked. He looked a little piqued as he buttoned up his jacket against the cold wind. "Well, I think you could have warned us. I doubt Mrs. Warren will appreciate your running out like this."

"Jesus!" Ezra said. He hadn't shaved that day, and his four o'clock shadow extended down his throat below the neckline of his T-shirt. Hal thought he looked a sharp contrast to Abel's groomed handsomeness, and Harding's bluff middle age. "Will you piss off with the emotional blackmail, Harding. I've got a business to get back to."

"We've *all* got responsibilities—"

"I didn't even want to bloody come!" Ezra said. There was something a little dangerous in his voice, and Hal had the impression that he was holding himself back.

"Oh, for God's sake," Abel snapped. Hal had the sudden image of a bubbling anger beneath the smiling, good-natured façade, as if something inside Abel were reaching boiling point and making the kind, compliant exterior increasingly hard to maintain. "I don't know why you're acting like you're uniquely pissed off to be here."

"Keep out of it, Abel," Ezra growled, but Abel shook his head.

"No. I know Maud was your twin and this has stirred up a lot of painful stuff for you, but she was my sister too. You don't get a monopoly on grief and difficult upbringings—in fact, you know what? You had a far easier time of it growing up than either Maud or me."

"What do you mean?"

"You were her favorite, you know that full well," Abel said, a little bitterly.

"If Mother had a favorite, she didn't let me know about it," Ezra said shortly.

Abel gave a laugh. "Utter bollocks. You know you could twist her around your little finger. Same as Mrs. Warren. Maud and I got pasted for things you escaped with scot-free. *You* could have got away with murder."

"Abel, shut up," Ezra said curtly.

"Telling you truths you don't want to hear?"

"You know nothing." He shoved his hands into his pockets. "You don't know what it was like for me those last years, after Maud ran away. You were off in the city shagging whoever your current toyboy was—"

"Oh, so we're resorting to homophobic slurs now, are we?" Abel said.

"I have no problem with you shagging whoever you want," Ezra said, his voice dangerous and level. "I'm just making the point you weren't bloody there, so don't tell me what it was like."

"Children, children," Harding said, with a rather forced laugh. "That's quite enough. Now, come on. Of course you're quite right to leave whenever you want to, Ezra. No one is suggesting otherwise. Just that it would be a good idea to keep us all apprised of your plans."

"Well, in the spirit of keeping you both apprised, I'll probably head off tonight as well," Abel said. He shivered a little at the cutting wind that was blowing down the narrow alley. "There's snow forecast, apparently, and I want to make a start before the roads get shut down. I can't afford another day out of the office either, and . . . well . . . I need to see Edward. Sort some things out." There was a short, awkward silence. "Do you want a lift back to London, Harding? I know Mitzi took the car."

"Thank you," Harding said, a little stiffly. "That would be very kind."

They had reached the car park now, and Abel pulled out his keys and pressed the remote unlock.

"What about me?" Hal said, rather faintly.

"I'm sorry?" Harding turned to her, and then blinked. "Oh. Harriet, of course. What time is your train?"

"I don't know," Hal said. "I haven't checked the timetable. But I need—"

The word stuck in her throat, but she forced herself on. "I mean, I don't have any way of getting to the station."

"I'll drop you off en route," Ezra said briefly. "But I warn you, I want to be away by four. Is that too early?"

He unlocked his car.

"Thanks," Hal said. "Any time is fine, honestly. I think there are trains roughly every hour until about six."

Ezra nodded. Then without another word, he got into the car, fired the engine, and drove off.

Beside Hal, Abel let out a gusting breath of exasperation as he watched his brother's car drive away.

"Oh dear. I'm sorry, Hal. I . . . we've never really got on, the three of us. We're too different, and I don't think we've ever got over a childhood of Mother playing us off against each other. I don't know what Ezra thinks, maybe he honestly doesn't believe Mother favored him, but to everyone else it was pretty clear that as far as she was concerned, he could walk on water, and she didn't try to hide it from the rest of us. It was no fun growing up with that."

"It—honestly—it's none of my business," Hal said awkwardly.

"Quite," Harding said crisply. He put an arm around Hal's shoulders. "I think the last thing Harriet needs to take home with her is memories of our dirty washing. Well, my dear, this has certainly been a very odd business, but I hope now that our branches of the family have found each other, you'll stay in touch."

"I will. I promise," Hal said, though she had a horrible feeling she did not have much choice, given Mr. Treswick's worried look as she left.

"Now," Harding said briskly. "Let's all get out of this perishing wind and back to Trepassen to break the news to Mrs. Warren."

CHAPTER 42

"Where *is* Mrs. Warren?"

The words floated up the stairwell towards Hal as she bumped her case down the final flight, and she felt a little prickle of something—trepidation, perhaps.

All the time, while packing, she had had to fight the urge to cram her belongings into her case any old how, so strong was the sense that the old woman might be making her way up the stairs for one final confrontation.

Strange fantasies tripped through Hal's mind—someone sliding the bolts closed on the bedroom door and locking her in, or barricading the door at the foot of the stairs. Ezra's impatient good-byes, *Well, I can't wait for Harriet any longer.* The others dispersing before the snow hit—leaving her alone, in the darkening house, with a vengeful old woman. . . .

So strong was the feeling that she had left the bedroom door open while she packed, the better to hear the *tap, tap* of her stick on the stairs—though even as she did, she reminded herself of that morning she had found Mrs. Warren waiting in darkness outside her door, the silence of her approach.

Was Mrs. Warren really the frail old lady everyone assumed, or was that walking stick simply another layer of deception? Whatever the truth, it was clear she could move quietly when she chose.

Now Hal was packed and ready, her coat on, and the sky was dark with snow, and she wanted nothing more than to get away.

Abel and Harding were standing in the hallway when she rounded the corner of the landing, and Abel turned his face up towards Hal as she bumped the case down the stairs.

"You haven't seen her, have you, Hal?"

"No." She joined them in the shadow of the staircase. "Not since last night."

Even at breakfast she had not been there—the coffeepot had been steaming on a mat when they arrived in the breakfast room, the toast and cereal laid out, no sign of Mrs. Warren.

"Ezra's gone to find her," Harding said. "He's the only person likely to come out of her lair alive."

But at that moment there was the sound of a door slamming far up the corridor, and they turned to see Ezra striding towards them, shaking his head.

"I tried the door of her room. It's locked, and she's not answering. Must be asleep or gone into town. Would you say good-bye for me?" he said to Harding, who nodded.

"If I see her, but we'll be leaving right after you two. She'll be sorry not to say good-bye."

"Probably, but it can't be helped. The forecast is getting worse, I don't want to wait. Good-bye, Harding." They shared a slightly awkward man-hug, more a backslap than an embrace, and then Ezra turned to Abel.

"Bye, Abel."

"Good-bye," Abel said, "and look, I'm sorry if I spoke out of turn."

"I—well, I'm sorry too," Ezra said, rather stiffly, and Abel held out his arms.

"Hug it out?"

Ezra looked profoundly uncomfortable as his brother put his arms around him, and Hal had the impression of an unyielding, unwilling mass, but he put his arm around his brother and squeezed, almost in spite of himself.

Then it was Hal's turn. She embraced each of the brothers in turn, feeling Harding's unaccustomed paunchy softness beneath the Barbour, and Abel's lean hard ribs under his soft sweater, the surprising strength of his grip as he hugged her.

"Good-bye, my dear," Harding said.

"Good-bye, little Harriet," Abel said. "Keep in touch."

And then Hal was climbing into Ezra's car, and the engine was growling, and they were off, down the driveway, the magpies rising up in a cloud behind them as the first speckles of snow began to fall.

AT FIRST, THE DRIVE WAS quick, and Hal sat in silence, her head resting against the window, and tried not to think about what she would do when she got back to Brighton.

A strange feeling was prickling in the pit of her stomach. Part of it was trepidation—an unwillingness to face the plethora of choices she would have to confront when she stepped off the train at Brighton station. She could go home for a couple of nights perhaps, but any longer than that and Mr. Smith's men would come knocking.

But beneath the worries was something else, something that tugged at her heart when she thought of Abel and Harding and Ezra, and the feeling of their arms around her. It was homesickness almost, a visceral longing so sharp it was like a pain inside her. But it was not for any home she had ever had. It was, perhaps, a longing for what might have been. For that alternate existence where she had family to fall back on, a safety net. She had never realized how alone she was, until she had glimpsed the alternative.

But she shook herself. She could not think like this. What she had lost had never been hers, and she had to be positive. She had turned her back on a fraud, had got herself out of a nightmarish situation.

And—remembering the trailing thread on the stairs, and the paranoia of that restless, horrible night—she was safe. At least for the moment.

Had it been real? She still didn't know. But the more she thought about it, the more she could not believe it was one of the brothers. An image kept coming back to her: Mrs. Warren, silently standing outside her door, her stick nowhere in sight. She could move swiftly and quietly, Hal was certain of it. She could walk without her stick. It was not impossible. Perhaps she had escaped more than just prosecution.

The sky seemed to darken with her mood, and as they pulled up outside Penzance station, the snow was no longer melting straight onto the windscreen. Instead, as Ezra turned off the lashing wipers, it began to stick, speckling the glass, and sliding down to form little drifts at the bottom.

"Well . . ." Hal said, rather awkwardly. "Thank you, Ezra. For the lift. I guess . . . I mean, I suppose this is good-bye. . . ."

"I'm not coming back, if that's what you mean," Ezra said. He looked out of the window at the falling snow. "I've done my bit by Harding. My life is elsewhere now, and I need to get on with it, not keep looking back here."

"I can understand that," Hal said. There was a heaviness around her heart, but also, as she thought of the leap her mother had made, and Ezra too after his twin had disappeared, a kind of hope. If they could leave everything, start anew in another place, another country even in Ezra's case, perhaps she could too?

"Well . . . good-bye," she said again, and fumbled with the door handle. As she dragged her case across the slushy tarmac, she did not look back.

Inside the station, everything was strangely quiet. There were few staff, and even fewer passengers, barring a couple of students sleeping on rucksacks, covered with coats. A train was standing at one of the platforms, but the lights were switched off.

Hal frowned, puzzled, but it was only when she turned to look at the departure board that her stomach turned over.

Canceled. Canceled. Canceled.

Train after train. London. Exeter. Plymouth. Nothing was running.

"Excuse me—" She ran panting across the slippery forecourt, and touched one of the station attendants on the arm. "What's going on? Why are all the trains canceled?"

"Ent you heard?" the man said, rather astonished. "Heavy snow up the coast. There's been a blockage on the line near Plymouth. Can't no trains get through until it's cleared, which won't be today."

"But—" Hal felt her face grow even paler. "But—but you don't understand. I don't have anywhere to go. I have to get back."

"Ent no trains leaving today," the man repeated firmly, shaking his head. "And probably not tomorrow neither."

"Shit."

Before she had realized what she was going to do, Hal had picked up her heavy case and was slipping and sliding back across the wet tiles to the entrance of the station, where Ezra had dropped her off.

"Ezra!" she cried. The snow was barely slush, but it was enough to bind in the wheels of her case, slowing her down.

"Ezra, wait!"

But his car was no longer there.

For a minute she just stood, staring into the falling snow, fighting off the panic that was threatening to overwhelm her. What could she do? Phone Harding? But he and Abel would have already left, more than likely, going the opposite way.

There was little point in getting out her purse—she knew what it contained, which was a few pound coins and an expired bus pass.

She was alone, without any money, in a strange town, and the temperature was dropping. What could she *do*?

Without quite knowing why, Hal found herself crouching down, balancing on the tips of her toes as she wrapped her arms around herself and pressed her face to her knees, making herself as small as possible, as if trying to keep every particle of warmth she still had left in her shivering body, as if to physically contain the fear that was suddenly growing and growing inside her.

She was still crouched there in the snow, gripping the handle of her case as though it was the only thing that could keep her safe, when a car horn beeped loudly, making her jump to her feet and almost lose her balance in the snow.

It had grown very dark—too dark to perceive anything more than a dazzle of headlights and the growl of an engine.

And so it was with a flood of relief almost overwhelming in its warmth and physicality that she heard the sound of an electric window and Ezra's laconic voice saying, "What the hell are you doing crouched in the snow like the little match girl?"

"Ezra!" Hal stumbled through the slush, her feet slipping, towards the car. "Oh, Ezra, I'm so glad to see you—what are you doing here?"

"I had to turn the car to head back to the road. More to the point, though, what are you doing?"

"The line's closed. No trains are running. I thought I was stranded."

"Hmm . . ." She could see his face now in the light from the dashboard, brow furrowed, thinking. "That is a problem . . . you'd better hop in."

"But where will you take me?"

"We'll figure it out. I can drop you at Plymouth, maybe, if the track from there is okay. Or . . . you live in Brighton, don't you?"

Hal nodded.

"It's not a million miles out of my way, if the worst comes to it."

"Really?" Hal felt a hot wave of relief wash over her. "But—but I can't ask you to do that, Ezra. And I don't have any money for petrol."

He only shook his head.

"Just get in, would you? It's perishing out here. And we need to get going."

CHAPTER 43

Ezra drove in silence for the most part, the snow growing heavier and heavier as they made their slow way north. Soon the deep-sunk single-track country lanes were covered with white, and Ezra slowed to a crawl as he rounded the tight bends, making only slightly better time on the main roads, where lorries had already carved dark tracks.

As they approached Bodmin Moor, the snow grew thicker, and condensation began to mist the inside of the windscreen in spite of the heaters. Up ahead, the traffic slowed, drivers dropping their speed as the visibility grew poorer and the slush began to build up at the sides of the road. Ezra started to tap his fingers on the steering wheel, and Hal shot a sideways look at him. He was frowning deeply, his dark eyebrows knitted, and his eyes flickered from the windscreen, spattered with falling snow, to the speedometer, hovering around thirty, to the clock, and then back to the windscreen.

At last, without warning, he pulled into the left-hand lane and began to indicate.

"Are we stopping?" Hal asked, surprised. It was gone six. They had been driving for almost three hours. Ezra nodded.

"Yes, I think so. My eyes are getting tired. I think we'd better stop for coffee . . . maybe a bite to eat. Hopefully it'll be better going by the time we start again. At least they'll probably have salted the roads."

The slip road was dusted with white, crossed with the tracks of motorists who had made the same decision, and he drove slowly, parking the car in an empty space near the service station. Hal got out, stretching her legs, and looked up in wonderment at the dark sky above, the flakes spiraling down. In Brighton, snow rarely settled, and she could not remember the last time they had had a fall this heavy.

"Come on." Ezra hunched his shoulders into his jacket. "Don't stand there, you'll freeze. Let's get inside."

THE SERVICE STATION WAS QUIET, full of empty tables covered in the debris of the day, and they didn't have to queue. Hal tried to pay for the coffee, but Ezra shook his head and pushed his credit card across the counter.

"Don't be silly. You don't have to be a—" He stopped, suddenly awkward.

"What?" Hal asked, feeling defensive.

Ezra carried the coffees to an empty table before he answered.

"You're young," he said at last. "And broke. Young people shouldn't pay for drinks. I firmly believe that."

Hal laughed, but took the cup he proffered.

"You're not offended?" he asked, sipping at his black Americano. Hal shook her head.

"No. I *am* young, and broke. I can't be offended at the truth."

"Thank God for proper coffee after Mrs. Warren's muck," Ezra said with a lopsided, rather dry smile. They sipped in silence, and then he said, "I just wanted to say I . . . I wouldn't blame you. If you had known."

Hal's heart seemed to slow and still inside her, and she put down her cappuccino.

"What . . . what do you mean?" she said at last.

"Forget it," Ezra said. He swallowed another gulp of his coffee. Hal saw the muscles in his throat move beneath his stubble. "It's none of my business. I just meant . . ." He stopped, drank again, and then said, "If you had known, about . . . about your mother not being . . . I wouldn't have blamed you . . . for not saying something straightaway."

"I don't know what you mean," Hal said, but she felt a tide of blood beginning to climb from her breast up her throat to her cheeks, a great flush of guilt, like a tidal wave of shame.

"That's okay, then," Ezra said. He looked out of the window at the falling snow, deliberately not meeting her eyes, giving her time to compose herself.

"So . . ." he said after a minute or two, speaking still as if to the night sky outside. "You're Maggie's child. I'm still getting used to that fact. Did you . . . did you know . . . that she lived here for a while? With us, I mean."

Hal felt her breath catch.

"Before I came here, I didn't know that, no. But Abel told me about a cousin Maggie. That's what made me add two and two together afterwards. I—I wish she'd told me about Trepassen."

He looked back at her, meeting her eyes. His were dark and full of understanding.

"It wasn't a very happy time for any of us. I can understand why she would want to forget about it."

"Ezra." Hal felt a lump in her throat, and she took a deep breath. "Ezra, can I show you something?"

He nodded, puzzled, and Hal dug in her pocket and pulled out her tarot tin. Inside was the photograph Abel had given her, folded in half. She unfolded it carefully, and watched as Ezra's face split in a smile of recognition, though there was something sad in his eyes too. He reached out, and touched the cheek of his twin, very gently, as if she could feel it through the paper.

"Ezra, did you—do you know . . . who took this photo?"

He looked up at her, frowning slightly, as though he had been somewhere very far away, and the effort was in dragging his thoughts back to the present day.

"Sorry, what did you say?"

"Who took this photo?"

"I'm not sure if I remember," he said slowly. "Why do you ask?"

"Because—" Hal took a deep breath. "Because I think—I think he might be my father." The words felt like a confession, and she felt a great release of some kind of tension she had been hardly aware of holding back, but they provoked no reaction in Ezra; he just continued to look at her, puzzled.

"Why do you say that?"

"I found my mother's diary," Hal said. "She talks about this day—about the person taking the photograph. That's all I know about him—that and the fact that he had blue eyes."

"Blue eyes?" Ezra said. He frowned again, not following her logic. "But yours are dark. How did you work that out?"

"It's in the diary too," Hal said. It was such a relief to talk it over with someone that she felt the words tumbling out in her eagerness to explain. "There's this line she writes, his blue eyes meeting her dark ones. And she mentions someone called Ed, says that he was there the day the photograph was taken. I asked Abel, but he said there was no one else there apart from the four of you—but—"

She broke off. Ezra's face had changed. He looked fully in the here and now, and there was a touch of something Hal could not place in his expression. She thought it might be a kind of dread.

"But that's not true," he said, very slowly. Hal nodded. She felt something inside her grow quite still, waiting.

"Oh God," Ezra said. He put his face in his hands. "Abel. What have you done?"

"So . . . he *was* lying?"

"Yes. But I don't know why he would protect him."

"Protect who?" Hal asked. She was almost certain she already knew, but she needed to hear the name—hear it from the lips of someone who had been there, someone who could tell her for *sure.*

"Edward."

Hal felt her stomach turn inside her, as if she were on the Twister at the foot of the pier and it had flipped her in a great arc above the sea, one of those sickening twists that left you gasping.

So it *was* true.

She swallowed. It was so strange. All the pieces had pointed to him—the name in the diary, the blue eyes . . . and yet . . . and yet she felt no connection to him, and now that Ezra had confirmed her suspicions she felt nothing except a kind of sickness.

He is my father, she thought, trying to make it real. *Edward is my father—why would my mother lie about it all these years?*

Why had he said nothing? Abel must know the truth after all—or suspect it, at least—or else why would he have lied to protect his lover from Hal's inquiries?

But why lie? Why should Edward hide his identity from his own daughter?

Unless . . . unless there was something else he was hiding. . . .

"Edward," she managed, her lips dry. "He was definitely there? He was the one taking the photograph?"

Ezra nodded.

"So he's my . . ." But she could not say the word aloud. She shut her eyes, pressing her fingers to her temples, trying to *see* him. There was nothing of herself in his face—but perhaps that was not surprising. When she opened her eyes and stared down at the photograph on the table, it was her own face she saw, in her mother's. She was her mother's daughter, through and through.

It was as if her mother had erased her father's DNA through sheer force of will.

"Hal—don't," Ezra said awkwardly. He looked profoundly uncomfortable and ill-equipped to be having this conversation, and

Hal could tell that every atom of him would have rather got up and walked into the night, but that he was steeling himself to see this through. "Don't jump to conclusions, it's just a picture."

But Hal had spent too long reading the diary, too long puzzling it out, to believe him. It was the only way it made sense. Edward—the man taking the picture—was her father. And for some reason Abel was desperate to conceal that fact. Desperate enough to tell a lie he must have known would come home to roost at some point.

"I don't get it," Hal said. She looked down. Her fingers were crushing the paper cup of coffee, and she forced them to release. "Why would he lie?"

"I don't know." They sat in silence for a long minute, and then Ezra, with an effort, put out his hand to Hal's shoulder. "Hal, are—are you okay?"

"I'm not sure," she whispered, and for a moment he rested his hand there and she felt the warmth of his fingers striking through her jacket, and she had a great urge to turn and cry into his shoulder. There was silence as she struggled to master herself.

Then Ezra let his hand drop and the moment was broken. He picked up his cup and took a long gulp of coffee, then made a face.

"God, I wish I could have a proper drink. I'd kill for a glass of red, right now."

"There's a restaurant over the other side of the food court," Hal said, but he shook his head.

"Better not. I'm tired enough. Though of course there's nothing stopping you, if you want one."

"I don't," Hal said, rather awkwardly. "Drink, I mean."

Ezra picked up the paper cup and sipped again, looking at her over the top with his dark eyes. They were nearly coal-black, a brown so deep that the pupil and iris merged almost into one.

"What's the story behind that, then?"

"No story," Hal said, automatically defensive, and then she felt bad. There was no truth to hide anymore, no point in holding her cards close to her chest. And this man had been kind, and had told her the truth where others had lied, and was going above and beyond his duty to try to get her home. She owed it to him to repay his honesty in kind. "Well, a bit of a story, to be honest. I mean, I'm not in AA or anything like that, but I just found . . . it was after my mother died. Drinking stopped being fun, somehow. It became . . . it was a way of coping, for a bit. And I don't like crutches."

"I can understand that," Ezra said quietly. He looked down at the paper cup, seeming to study something in the peaty depths. "Maggie was always very independent. I don't think she really liked living with us for that reason. It was, well, a kind of charity, I suppose, and Mother never let her forget it. There was always this unspoken feeling that she needed to earn her place by being grateful, or some kind of bullshit."

"What—" Hal felt her breath catch in her throat. "What was she like, Ezra, when you knew her?"

Ezra smiled. He did not look up at Hal, but there was something a little sad in his expression as he stared down into his coffee cup, swirling the dregs thoughtfully.

"She was . . . she was fun. Kind. I liked her very much."

"Ezra, do you—" She swallowed. Suddenly she wanted that glass of wine very much indeed. As much as Ezra did, perhaps. "Do you think I should . . . say something? To Edward?"

"I don't know," Ezra said. His face was suddenly very grave.

"Why didn't he say anything?"

"He may not know, I guess."

"But *she* knew. My mother, I mean. Why wouldn't *she* have said anything?"

"Hal, I don't know," Ezra said, and suddenly his face was twisted with an emotion that he seemed to be trying to master, and failing. "Hal, look, I wouldn't normally interfere, but I can't stand by and—what I'm trying to say—" He stopped and ran his hands through his hair. "Harriet." The use of her full name stopped her somehow, in her tracks. "Please, please, leave this."

"*Leave* it? What do you mean?"

"Leave it alone. It's in the past. Your mother clearly didn't tell you this deliberately—and I don't know why she chose to keep it secret, but she must have had her reasons, and maybe they were good ones."

"But—" Hal leaned forwards in her chair. "But don't you understand? I have to *know*. This is my *father* we're talking about. Don't you think I have a right to know about him?"

Ezra said nothing.

"And it's not just my mother—it's—it's everything. What happened to Maud? Why did she and my mother run away together, and why did Maud disappear?"

"Hal, I don't *know*," Ezra said heavily. He stood up and paced to the tall glass wall at the front of the service station, his shape silhouetted against the falling snow and the lamps in the car park. They had dimmed the lights in the food court now, and Hal had the feeling they were getting ready to close.

"Is Maud dead?" she persisted. "Is she hiding?"

"I don't know!" Ezra cried, and this time it was more a shout of fury. Across the food court, a boy in a uniform stopped sweeping up crumbs and looked towards them, his expression puzzled and alarmed.

For a moment Hal felt a prickle of fear, but then Ezra rested his forehead very gently on the windowpane, and his shoulders seemed to sag in a kind of despair, and she understood.

Of course. She had been so blindly focused on her own need for answers that she had forgotten—this was his past too. Maud was his twin, the person he had been closest to in all the world, and she had cut him off too, without explanation, and disappeared. He had lived with that uncertainty for longer than Hal had lived with hers.

"Oh God, Ezra." She stood too, walked towards him, and put out her hand, but let it fall, not quite daring to touch his shoulder. "I'm sorry, I didn't think—she's your sister, you must—"

"I miss her so much," he said. There was an anguish in his voice that Hal had never heard before, a depth of feeling she would not have believed from his dry, sarcastic everyday demeanor. "God, I miss her, like a hole in me. And I'm so fucking angry. I'm angry all the time."

And suddenly Hal understood the source of Ezra's lightness, his perpetual sarcasm, the dry smile that always seemed to hover around his lips. He laughed, because if he did not, something inside him would break free, a raging loss that he had been containing for twenty years.

"I'm so sorry." Hal felt a lump in her throat. She thought of her own mother, of the fury she herself had felt at the way she had been snatched away, so abruptly, so meaninglessly. But at least she knew. At least she had been able to stroke her mother's hair, to bury her, to say good-bye. At least she knew what had happened.

"When I heard about the car accident, I thought—" He stopped, and Hal saw him draw a deep, shuddering breath, and then force himself on. "I thought that was it, that I knew what had happened, and however much it hurt that I'd never see her again, I thought that at least if we—if we knew—"

He broke off, and Hal realized afresh what she had done to this family with her little deception, and the way that it had grown and grown out of all proportion to what she had intended. What she had done to *Ezra*, to this man standing in front of her now, holding himself together with such pains.

"I'm sorry," she whispered again. She sank back onto the hard plastic chair at the coffee table, and put her head in her hands, wishing she could tell him exactly how sorry, but she could never do that, not without confessing what she had done. "Ezra, I'm—I'm so sorry."

"It makes me so angry—the *waste.* Maggie. Maud. Mown down in front of your own house—what a fucking waste of a life."

"Ezra—"

"It's all right," he said at last, though she could tell from his voice and the way that he scrubbed at his eyes with his sleeve that it was not. He drew a long breath, and turned around to face her, even managing a twisted smile.

Across the food court the boy had started sweeping again, and the servers at the hot food counter had turned off its lights.

Hal found she could not speak, but she nodded. Ezra closed his eyes for a moment, and suddenly she had a great urge to put her arm around him, tell him that it would be okay, that they would find the truth about his sister, but she knew she could not do that. It was not a promise she could make.

"Due to the inclement weather"—the announcement broke into their silence, tinny and echoing in the high rafters—"and road closures, this service station will be closing in thirty minutes for health and safety reasons. All customers are requested to complete their purchases and return to their cars within the next thirty minutes. We apologize for any inconvenience."

"Well . . ." Ezra cleared his throat, and picked up his jacket from the back of the plastic chair. "We should probably get going anyway. It's getting late, and we've got a long way still to go. Do you want anything else?"

Hal shook her head, and Ezra said, "I'll get us a couple of sandwiches at the shop, we won't have time to stop again."

OUTSIDE THE SNOW HAD NOT stopped falling; if anything, it was coming down faster. Ezra shook his head as they climbed into the sports car and buckled in.

They drove in silence for perhaps twenty minutes. The roads were not busy, but as the visibility worsened the traffic in front of them slowed. A few miles farther on, Hal put her hand out towards Ezra's arm and he nodded.

"I've seen it."

It was a long line of stationary red lights in the distance, faintly visible through the falling snow. He was pressing on the brakes, slowing the car as it caught up with the jam, and then they stopped completely, the yellow wink of hazard indicators flashing all around them as the cars behind caught up and signaled the delay.

Ezra put the hand brake on and then sat, staring into the distance. Hal, too, was lost in her own thoughts, mulling over the conversation at the service station. After what seemed like a long time, but might have been anything from five to twenty-five minutes, a driver up ahead leaned on his horn, a long mournful *beeeeeep,* like a foghorn sounding across the hills, and then another took it up, and another.

Ezra glanced at the clock, then back at the line of stationary traffic, and then he seemed to make a decision.

"I'm going to turn around," he said. "They must have closed the road over the moor. We'll try going round, via St. Neot. The snow might be worse, but this traffic is going nowhere. I think we'll make better time."

"Okay," Hal said. There was a brief flurry of horns as he executed an awkward turn, and then they were making their slow way down the road away from Bodmin, back along the route they had come.

Hal yawned. The car was warm, the heater comfortable, and she pulled off her coat and crumpled it up beneath her head, where it rested against the window. Then she closed her eyes, and let herself drift off into sleep.

HER DREAMS WERE TROUBLED, A confused tangle of chasing through the long corridors at Trepassen with Mrs. Warren's stick tap-tapping ominously in her wake, and however fast she ran, she could never outpace it. Then somehow she was at the head of the stairs again, and though she knew the thread was there, stretched across it, she tripped and fell, and as she looked back over her shoulder she saw Edward, standing there at the top, his head thrown back, laughing at her. She had time to think, *I'm going to die,* but when she fell, it was not with the bone-crunching impact she had feared, but with a splash, into cold, cold water, dappled with leaves and dead insects. When she surfaced, the smell of the boathouse was in her nostrils, the scent of stagnant water and rotting wood, and the slime of the leaves was beneath her and around her as she thrashed in the frozen water.

Help! she tried to scream, but the icy water rushed in, choking her.

She awoke with a shock and a beating heart to darkness, and for a moment she couldn't remember where she was, but then she saw. She was in Ezra's car. They were in a lay-by beside a deeply sunken lane, and the snow was still falling, and Ezra had turned the engine off.

"Are we stopping again?" Hal's mouth was dry, and the words came thickly.

"I'm afraid so," Ezra said heavily. He rubbed his eyes, as if he too was very tired. "This fucking snow. I'm sorry, we're not going to get through. It's gone eight and we're not even at Plymouth."

"Oh God, I'm so sorry. What about your crossing?"

Ezra shook his head.

"There's no way I'll make it. I've rung and they've said I can pay a fee to change the ticket to tomorrow."

"So—so what do we do?"

Ezra didn't reply straightaway, just nodded back along the way they had come. Hal bit her lip. The snow continued to fall with a soft patter on the glass of the windscreen.

"I'm sorry," Ezra said, seeing her expression. "I did think about trying to push through, at least to Brighton, but I'm just too tired—and it's too dangerous, none of these roads have been gritted."

"So . . . we go back . . . ? To—" She swallowed. "To Trepassen?"

"I think we have to. It won't take as long going back, the roads going south are pretty quiet. We can try again tomorrow."

"Okay," Hal said. She felt something shift inside her at the thought of returning to the cold house, and Mrs. Warren's waiting figure, rocking by her fireside, mistress once again of all she surveyed. It was not an inviting prospect. But what was the alternative—a B&B? She had no money for a room, and she could not very well ask Ezra to pay.

"Okay," she said again, trying to make herself sound—and feel—more positive. "Back to Trepassen it is, then."

"It's not likely to be a very warm welcome," Ezra said, as he turned the key in the ignition and the engine roared out into the quiet. "But at least we won't freeze."

CHAPTER 44

Returning to Trepassen felt strange, like putting on the heavy pack that you'd downed a few hours earlier, the blisters from the straps still raw. Or sliding your feet back into wet shoes that were once soggily clammy, and had become in the interim downright unpleasant.

The gate onto the road was still ajar, but as they turned up the drive, Hal saw that the long stretch of whiteness was unmarked. No car had passed this way for many hours. Either Abel and Harding had thought better of leaving, or they had left soon after Hal and Ezra, and had not returned.

"There's no lights on," Ezra said beneath his breath as they wound round the last bend of the drive. The white marker rocks were hard to see, except in the places beneath the trees where the canopy had protected the road from the snowfall, and he had to slow to a crawl to ensure he didn't slide off the path. "Mrs. Warren must be in bed."

Good, was all Hal could think, though she did not say it.

They parked in front of the porch, and Ezra turned off the engine, and they both sat for a moment. Hal had an image of two athletes before a fight, strapping up knuckles, snapping mouth guards into place. Except it was not Ezra she was fighting.

"Ready?" he said, with a short laugh. Hal didn't smile in return. She only nodded, and they stepped out into the falling snow.

The door was locked, but Ezra lifted one of the flat stones that formed the sheltered seating of the porch, and beneath it Hal saw a huge, blackened key—a thing from another era, at least six inches long. He fitted it into the lock and turned it cautiously, and they stepped inside, into the dark, breathing house.

"Mrs. Warren?" Ezra called softly, and then when there was no answer, a little more loudly, "Mrs. Warren? It's just me, Ezra."

"Do you think Harding and Abel have gone?" Hal whispered. Ezra nodded.

"Harding texted while you were asleep. They made it across Bodmin Moor before the road closed and holed up at a travel lodge near Exeter."

"I'm so sorry," Hal said. She felt a stab of guilt. "It's my fault—if you hadn't gone via Penzance . . ."

"No use crying over spilt milk," Ezra said shortly, but the suppressed rage Hal had seen earlier seemed to have vanished, and there was only resignation in his tone. "Look, Hal, it's very late, and I don't know about you, but I'm shattered. Are you okay for me to head up?"

"Of course," Hal said. "I'll go to bed too."

There was a short, awkward silence, and then Ezra pulled her into a clumsy hug, almost too hard, that scraped her face on his jacket, and left her bones bruised.

"Good night, Hal. And tomorrow . . ."

He stopped.

"Tomorrow?" Hal echoed.

"Let's just get going as early as possible, okay?"

"Okay," she agreed. They climbed the first flight of stairs together, and then at the landing, they went their separate ways.

WHEN HAL OPENED THE DOOR to the attic chamber, the little room was just as she had left it—curtains pulled back, so that the pale snowy light filtered through the barred windows, covers thrown back, even down to the blown bulb on the landing.

There were a few pieces of coal left in the scuttle, and with the comforting knowledge that she would not be around for very long in the morning to face Mrs. Warren's censure, Hal screwed up a page of newspaper, placed the coals in the grate, and put a match to the fire.

As it flared up, she sat, hunched in front of it, thinking about her mother crouching here so long ago, tearing the pages from her diary, and everything Hal had learned since finding it.

Edward. Could it really be true?

It must be—but when she thought of him, of his smooth blond hair, carefully coiffed mustache—she felt nothing. No sense of connection. Just a faint loathing for the man who had impregnated her mother and then left her, ignored her letters, leaving her to the mercy of a woman like Mrs. Westaway.

Part of her wanted to push the knowledge aside and move on, into the future, as Ezra had suggested. But the questions still niggled. Why had Abel lied so transparently? Had he banked on her not asking the same questions of Ezra?

If *only* her mother hadn't scrubbed all the mentions of Hal's father from the diary.

Hal sat, staring into the flames, too tired to rouse herself sufficiently to go to bed. She was almost beyond thought now—and she had the strangest feeling that history had looped around, putting her here, in her mother's place, where Maggie herself had crouched so long ago, watching the flames burn the name of her lover to ashes, so that she, Hal, could discover a truth that had been buried long ago. But what was that truth?

Not just the name of her father.

There had been something else . . . something Ezra had said that was bothering her, but she could not pinpoint what it was. Was it during their conversation in the service station? She cast her mind back, running through everything he had said, but whatever it was, it kept slipping through her fingertips, a truth too insubstantial to catch hold of.

At last she stood, stretching her stiff limbs, the air of the room cool on her cheeks after the heat of the fire. Her case lay at the foot of the bed. In the pocket was the old tobacco tin, and she opened it and drew out her cards. Shivering a little, she cut the deck.

The card that stared up at her was the Moon, inverted.

Hal frowned. The Moon meant intuition, and trusting your intuition. It was a guiding light, but one that could be unreliable—for it was not always there, and sometimes when you needed it most, the night would be impenetrably dark.

Inverted, it meant deception, and especially self-deception. It meant the intuition that could lead you astray, down a false path.

Don't fall into the trap of believing your own lies . . . Her mother's voice in her ear, warning, always warning. *You want to believe as much as they do.*

And she did. She did want to believe. After her mother's death, she had found herself dealing out the cards night after night, trying to make sense of it all, trying to find answers where there were none. She had spent hours poring over her mother's cards, running her hands over them, looking for meaning.

But always that voice of skepticism in her ear, her mother's voice: *There is no meaning, apart from what you want to see, and what you are afraid of turning up.*

She put her hands over her ears, as if she could shut out that voice of whispered sense and logic.

When had her mother become so cynical?

The girl in the diary, with her superstition and her obsessive reading of the cards, she was like a different person from the woman who had taken herself to the pier every day to read for fools and strangers. Tarot had been a job for Hal's mother—nothing more. It had been something she was good at, but she had never believed, however convincing her patter was to strangers, and she had never hidden that skepticism from

Hal. How had she turned from this questing, openhearted young girl into the disillusioned, weary woman Hal remembered?

They're not magic, sweetheart, she had said to Hal once, in answer to her question. Hal could not have been more than four or five. *You can play with them all you like. They're just pretty pictures. But people like to pretend that life has . . . meaning, I suppose. It makes them feel happy, to think that they're part of a bigger story.*

Then why, Hal had asked, confused, did people come to see her every day? Why did they pay money if none of it was true? *It's like going to see a play,* she had explained. *People want to believe it's true. My job is to pretend it is.*

The girl in the diary had not been pretending. She had been in love—with the power of the cards, and the power of fate. She had believed. What had that changed? What had happened to make her stop believing in that power?

There is something I'm not seeing, Hal thought, and she picked up the Moon card and stared down at it, at the shadowy face in the bright orb. *Something I'm missing.*

But whatever it was, it lay just out of reach, and at last she put the cards away, and slid between the sheets, fully clothed, to try to sleep.

She was almost asleep, drifting in the strange no-man's-land between waking and dreaming, the firelight making patterns on the insides of her lids, when an image came to her.

A book. A buttercup-yellow book with no lettering on the cover or spine.

It wasn't hers, and she could not place where it had come from, and yet . . . and yet it was somehow familiar. She had seen it before. But where?

Hal sat up, feeling the chill air of the room at the back of her neck, and she pressed her fingers to her closed lids, trying to picture it, where she had seen it, why her subconscious was needling her now.

She had almost given up and was about to lie back down and put it down to a tired imagination, when something came back to her in a sudden rush. Not a picture—but a smell. The smell of dust, of cobwebs, of fraying leather. The feeling of thick, sticky plastic between her fingers. And she knew.

It had been that first morning at Trepassen. The study, frozen in time, and the book on the high shelf that she had started to look through, only to be interrupted.

The photographs. Perhaps they would show her something she was missing. Edward, maybe, as he had been as a young man. Or even her mother.

And more than the photographs—the footstep in the dust.

Someone, that very first morning at Trepassen, or perhaps a week before, had been in that study to look at the pictures. It might have been nostalgia, but Hal thought that of all the people she had ever met, the Westaways had not a bone of nostalgia in their bodies. The past for them was not a happy place, full of golden memories, but a minefield charged with pain. No—if Abel, Ezra, Harding, Edward, or any of the others had got down that album, it had been for some other, very practical reason. And suddenly Hal wanted to know that reason very much.

There was something in that album that someone had wanted to see, or check, or remove. But why?

And if she and Ezra left first thing tomorrow, she might never have another chance to find out.

Swinging her legs out of bed, Hal pulled her coat back on as some protection from the chilly night air, and shoved her bare feet back into her cold shoes. Then she pushed open the attic door, and tiptoed quietly down the stairs.

At the first landing she paused, listening, but no sound of snores reached her ears. If Ezra was asleep—and he must be, for he had looked exhausted enough to fall asleep on his feet—he was a silent sleeper.

And then she was down in the hallway, in the dark.

Hal did not dare to turn on a light, but the house was no longer the unfamiliar maze of that first morning, and she did not need one; the faint light coming in through the hall windows was enough for her to pick her way past the drawing room, past the library and the billiard room and the boot closet. She pushed through a dividing door, and there on her left was the breakfast room, the dirty dishes still laid out on the table. The sight made Hal stop in her tracks—had Mrs. Warren done *anything* since they left? But she could not stop now to wonder about that.

The next part was the most dangerous, for it took her right past Mrs. Warren's sitting room, and Hal had no idea where she slept. *If* she slept. Somehow she would not have put it past her to be still awake at midnight, rocking in her chair in front of the hissing fire.

The stone floor of the orangery was cold, and too noisy to risk. However, there was no way round it—it was the only route to the study, or the only one Hal knew, at least. In the end, she bent and took off her shoes, tiptoeing across the frosty flags, wincing at the chill striking up into her bare soles.

And then she was through, and in the little vestibule on the far side, and her hand was on the study door.

WHEN SHE ENTERED THE STUDY, Hal had, for the second time, the strangest sense of having stepped back in time. The dust of years was soft beneath her feet as she stepped across the fraying carpet, the only resistance the minute crunch of small insects or gusted leaves, crushed beneath her toes.

The room was shrouded in darkness, and Hal had no choice but to fumble for the switch of the green-shaded desk lamp. It was very old, the cord fraying and fabric-covered, prewar at the least, she thought, but when she found the brass switch and clicked it, it came on without protest, illuminating the room in a soft, verdant glow.

There were the steps, untouched since her last visit, the footprint upon them clearly visible. And there, at the top, was the book she had hurriedly replaced, still sticking out at a very slight angle into the room.

Her heart beating in her mouth, Hal set her foot onto the library steps, in the footprint of that other person, and stepped up, up, and up once again, until her hand closed on the soft yellow spine, and she slid the book out into her waiting arms.

BACK DOWN AT THE DESK, Hal sat in the wing-backed chair and angled the desk lamp towards the book. Then, with a sense almost of trepidation, she opened the softly creaking spine.

The pictures were just as clear and old-fashioned as she remembered. Harding as a baby, chubby-necked in his scratchy-looking sweater, Harding riding on the shiny tricycle, and then a few pages later Abel's first appearance: *A.L. 3 months.*

But this time the caption rang a bell. Al. Why was that? Hal was racking her brains when it came to her suddenly—the entry in her mother's diary, Maud calling her brother Al. Hal had not thought of it at the time, but now it made sense.

She flicked forwards through the album, faster now, through pictures of Abel toddling on the beach, playing with a ball; through a holiday in France, or perhaps Italy, Harding and Abel sitting serious-faced on the steps of some European church, ice creams in their fists; through a family Christmas, and then . . .

Two little babies, swaddled side by side. *Margarida Miriam (l) and Ezra Daniel, 2 days old.*

They were asleep, eyes tight closed, and with their eyes shut she would not have been able to tell which was which, without the caption. How strange, that two twins who had looked so similar in babyhood, had grown up so unlike each other. Their faces were peaceful, turned to each other as they must have turned in their mother's womb, no hint of the strife and pain that was to come.

Maud.

Hal let her gaze rest on the tranquil little face, cherubic in repose.

Where are you, Maud? she wanted to ask. Dead? Running? Hiding? But how could she do that—how could she leave her brothers, her *twin* in pain for so many years?

She turned the page, to see Maud as a fat-legged toddler pushing a battered wooden dog across a hearthrug, and beside her Ezra, playing with a huge bear, almost larger than himself. The next few pages were just of Ezra—age four, on a brand-new bicycle, shining in the sun. Age five, grinning a gap-toothed smile. Hal shook her head, remembering Abel's bitter remark about Ezra being his mother's favorite.

She was about to turn the page, in search of another picture of Maud—but suddenly it was too painful to carry on, watching this little girl growing towards whatever oblivion had snatched her up, and Hal sighed and closed the album, pressing her fingers into her eyes, pushing back the ache in her head, and her heart.

Whatever answers she was looking for, she had been foolish to think they would be here. She should put it back where it came from, go to bed, to sleep, and follow Ezra's advice to forget the past—give up this stupid obsession with finding out what had happened, so many years ago.

But who *had* got the album down, that first morning? One of the brothers? Edward? He had barely arrived, but he might have *just* had time. The only other option was Mrs. Warren, and that was stranger still.

One thing was for sure—the truth about her mother did not lie within these pages. Unless—

She stopped, the thought snagging at her, and then opened her eyes, her blurred vision refocusing painfully on the buttercup-yellow cover in front of her. Once again, she picked it up and leafed slowly forwards through the pages, her stomach clenched with uncertainty, unsure of what she was about to see.

The confirmation came slowly—not from a single picture, but shimmering into focus, like a Polaroid photo developing in the light, features appearing from an unformed blur.

First there was a round, childish face sharpening into features that were painfully familiar, baby-blue eyes deepening and darkening into black ones. Limbs lengthening, skin tanning, an expression that changed slowly from openhearted trust to wariness.

And then at last, the final photograph in the book—*The Twins' 11th birthday*—there she was. Staring out of the page through a dark, tangled fringe, her dark eyes alight with the bright reflection of the candles, so like her brother that Hal wondered how she had ever managed to miss it.

Margarida. Maud. Hal's mother.

CHAPTER 45

If Hal had not already been sitting down, she would have had to grope for a chair.

Her mother was Maud. *Maud.* There was no other explanation. The girl in those photographs, Ezra's twin, growing up alongside him at Trepassen, *was* Hal's mother. It was unmistakable.

And yet—it made *no* sense.

It had to be true. The pictures in the book did not lie. There was her mother's face, shimmering into focus in front of her very eyes, page after page, from babyhood through to first school days, into her almost-teenage self, all the time growing towards the woman Hal knew painfully well. Her mother was *not* Maggie.

Which meant . . . It meant that Hester Westaway *was* her grandmother.

It meant that the will was valid.

But what about the birth certificate? What about the diary? What about—

And then Hal realized, and it was like the moon coming out from behind a cloud. All those shapes that had been formless black confusion in the clouded darkness were illuminated, falling into their rightful places in a landscape that suddenly made sense. She could not be sure. But if she was right . . . if she was right, she had been looking at this upside down the whole time.

If she was right, nothing was as she had thought it was.

If she was right, she had made a terrible, terrible mistake.

The snow outside was still falling, and Hal pulled her coat closer around her as she turned the pages. But it was not only the cold that made her shiver this time. It was a sense of foreboding suddenly gathering around her—of the weight of the secrets of the past, and the dam that she was about to break. The deluge.

This time, as she leafed through the fading pictures with their yellowed coverings, this time there was no sense of wonder or nostalgia. This time, she felt as if she were plunging down a rabbit hole into the past.

Because the child in the photographs, laughing and playing with her twin brother in the grounds of Trepassen, was not Hal's aunt. It was her mother—her dark eyes unmistakably like Hal's own—but not Hal's own.

Which meant that Maggie, the girl who had come to Trepassen, who had written that diary, who had got pregnant, who had run away and disappeared—was a stranger. Yet Hal *was* Maggie's daughter. There was no other explanation. However Hal worked the maths in her head, the result was the same—Maud could not have been pregnant at the time of Hal's birth. And Maggie was.

There was only one possibility, and it had been staring her in the face ever since she opened Mr. Treswick's letter, but she had been too blind to see it.

Hal's mother—the woman who had loved her, and brought her up, and cared for her—was not the woman who had given birth to her.

But what had happened? *How* had it happened?

Hal put her hands to her head. She felt as if she were carrying a load, immensely heavy, and immensely fragile and dangerous. She had the sense of herself tiptoeing along a narrow tightrope, and in her arms a bomb, ticking gently, and about to go off at any moment.

Because if this meant what she thought it did . . .

But she was getting ahead of herself.

Don't rush—her mother's voice in her head. *Build your story. Lay it out—card by card.*

Card by card, then.

So. What did Hal know for sure?

She knew that Maggie had escaped—that much was clear from the diary, and from Maud's letters. Maud had helped her get away sometime in January or February, and the two of them had come to Brighton to make a life together. There, in the peace and quiet of the little flat, Maggie had given birth to her baby daughter, and Maud . . . Maud could not have gone home. Lizzie had made that clear. She had never seen her family again, from the moment she walked out. So she must have stayed with her cousin, taking care of her, biding her time, hugging her acceptance letter from Oxford and waiting for autumn when she would take up her place at last.

But then, for whatever reason, Maggie had gone back to Trepassen. *Something* had drawn her back—and whatever it was, it must have been a good reason, for her to return to the place she had tried so hard to escape from. She had packed her bags, left her baby with her cousin, and taken the train down to Trepassen alone, with a "Joan of Arc look" upon her face, "like a maid going into battle," as Lizzie had said.

Was it money that had driven her back? The realization that, try as they might, two young women not yet out of school could barely afford to feed and clothe themselves, let alone a baby? *I have a little money left from my parents,* she had told Maud in her letter. But that little money would not have lasted long, even supplemented with earnings from the pier, not with Maud soon off to university, and no childcare for Hal. Perhaps she had gone to fight for support for her child.

Whatever it was, it had gone terribly wrong. Maggie—not Maud—had disappeared. She had left Hal motherless, and left Maud to pick up the pieces of her life—her flat, her little booth on the pier . . . and her child.

In one respect, it must have been easy, with *Margarida Westaway* on the birth certificate and on the flat lease, and on the sign above the door at the pier. Her mother *was* Margarida Westaway—she had the passport and birth certificate to prove it. There was no dispute there. Maud had simply slipped into her cousin's life.

But Hal's heart ached at the thought of how hard it must have been too. Maud had given up everything—that freedom she had fought so hard for, her university place, her hard-won future—she had given it all up, for Hal. She had picked up her cousin's child, and she had taken over the booth on the pier for one reason and one reason only—to put food on the table, because she had no other option.

No wonder the open, questing girl in the diary had read like a different person from the cynical, skeptical woman who had raised Hal. They *were* different women. It was not that Maggie had changed her mind; it was that Maud had never done so.

What was it Maggie had said, quoting Maud? *Load of wafty BS*, that was it. It had struck a chord with Hal, and she had laughed and connected with the remark in a way that she had not quite understood. But now she did.

Now she understood why Maud had shone so clearly out of the pages, that connection she had felt, reaching back through the years.

It was because they *were* connected. Maud was not just a distant relative—she was the only mother Hal had ever known. The person she had loved beyond her own life, beyond reason, beyond bearing, when she had lost her.

Urgent questions beat inside Hal's heart. How. *Why*.

But she had to take this step by step . . . with the slow, measured pace of a reading. She had to turn each card as it came, consider it, find its place in the story.

And the next card . . . the next card was one that made Hal feel terribly uneasy in a way that she couldn't completely pin down.

For the next card was not a card at all: it was a photograph. *The* photograph. The one that Abel had given her that first day at Trepassen.

Hal pulled the Golden Virginia tin out of her pocket and prized it open. The photograph was there on top, folded in half, and she unfolded it, staring at the picture with fresh eyes.

There was Maud—staring out at the camera, with that defiant gaze. But there, too, was Maggie. Maggie who had written the diary. And she wasn't looking at the camera. She was looking at Ezra, with her blue, blue eyes.

Blue eyes met dark . . .

She had had it the wrong way round, all this time.

Hal had not inherited her dark eyes from her mother, for her mother was blond.

She had inherited them from her father. The man who had set up the camera on its tripod, started the timer, and returned to take his place in the photo.

Ezra. Daniel.

Ed.

Ezra was her father.

CHAPTER 46

Hal's phone was upstairs in the attic, and she wore no watch, but she was sure from the stillness of the house that it must be gone midnight, probably long gone.

But there was no way she could go back to bed with this weight of truth heavy inside her, and the questions churning and churning.

There was only one person she could go to—one person who might tell her the truth.

Mrs. Warren.

And she had to go now, before Ezra woke up. If she left it until dawn . . .

Hal picked up the album, pushed back the chair, and stood, trying to summon her courage, remembering the thread across the stairs, the hissed invective in Mrs. Warren's voice—*Get out—if you know what's good for you . . .*

Like Joan of Arc, her mother had been. Like a maid going into battle.

Well, she had not inherited much from Maggie. Not her features, not her eyes or her hair, not even her sense of humor and skepticism. But perhaps she had inherited her mother's courage.

Hal took a deep breath, steadying herself, trying to quiet the questions clamoring inside her—and then she opened the study door and stepped softly through the orangery to knock at the door of Mrs. Warren's sitting room.

There was no answer at first, and Hal knocked a little harder, and as she did the door swung inwards, unlatched, and she saw that the gas fire in the little sitting room was on, and that the lamp on the table was burning.

Had Mrs. Warren fallen asleep in her chair?

It was pushed in front of the fire, close up, a blanket slung over the back of it making a dark shape that could have been a hunched old lady—but when Hal went cautiously forwards, her free hand outstretched in the flickering darkness, it only rocked away and then back, unmoored, and she saw that it was empty except for a couple of cushions.

"Mrs. Warren?" Hal called quietly. She tried not to let her voice shake, but there was something very eerie about the silence, broken only by the low rise and fall of a radio, and the *creak, creak* of the rocking chair upon the boards.

After the study, the sitting room was stiflingly overheated, and Hal wiped her brow, feeling sweat prickle across the back of her neck.

The sound of the radio was coming from behind a door at the back of the sitting room, and Hal took a cautious step towards it, but as she did so she nudged a little side table covered with pictures, and they fell, half a dozen of them.

"Shit!"

She grabbed for it, steadying the table before it could topple, but the pictures were like dominoes, clattering down in sequence, and Hal stood, frozen for a moment, her heart in her mouth, feeling its panicked thumping.

"Mrs. Warren?" she managed, her voice shaking. "I'm sorry, it's only me, Hal."

But no one came, and with trembling hands she began to right the pictures, one after the other.

As she did, she saw, with a growing sense of disquiet, what they were.

Ezra. All of them.

Ezra as a baby, in Mrs. Warren's arms, his soft hand reaching out for her cheek.

Ezra as a toddler, running across the lawn.

Ezra as a young man, almost unbearably handsome, his smile flashing out, unguarded and full of wry mischief.

Ezra, Ezra, Ezra—a shrine, almost, to a lost little boy.

There was one of the three brothers together on the mantelpiece. None of Maggie, though that, perhaps, was not surprising. Not a single one of Maud. And none, save for that one picture with Ezra in her arms, of Mrs. Warren herself.

It was as if all the love in that twisted old heart, all the caring and gentleness, had settled on a single person, concentrated into a beam of adoration so ferocious that Hal felt that it could have burned the skin.

"Mrs. Warren," she said again, a lump in her throat now, though whether it was pity or fear, she could not have said. "Mrs. Warren, wake up, please, I need to speak to you."

But nothing. Silence.

Hal's hands were shaking as she crept, inch by inch, across the firelit room, towards the door at the back, holding the yellow album out in front of her now, like a shield. She imagined pushing it open, the hunched figure standing behind in silence and darkness, just as she had that night outside the attic, waiting, watching.

"Mrs. Warren!" There was a note of pleading in her voice now, almost a sob. "Please. Wake up."

She was at the door now. Nothing. No sound, no movement.

Her hand was on the panel.

And then she pushed, and the door swung open, showing a narrow bedroom with a single iron cot bedstead, a flowered flannel nightgown folded neatly at the foot.

Beneath the bed were two carpet slippers, side by side, and a coat was hanging on a peg next to the door.

Of Mrs. Warren herself, there was no sign at all.

Hal felt her heart steady in her chest, relief flooding her momentarily, but then another kind of uneasiness took hold.

If Mrs. Warren was not asleep or in her sitting room, where *was* she?

"Mrs. Warren!" she shouted, making herself jump with the shock of the noise above the quiet hiss of the gas. "Mrs. Warren, where are you?"

And then, at the back of the bedroom, Hal saw another door, and it was standing ajar.

"Mrs. Warren?"

She stepped into the bedroom, her sense of intrusion growing at the feeling that, with every step, she was venturing farther and farther into Mrs. Warren's private sanctum. Part of her quaked at the thought of the woman's fury if she discovered Hal here, but part of her was driven on by a kind of fascination—taking in the cross on the wall above the austere bedstead, the photograph of Ezra on the nightstand, and the small, pathetically small, flannel nightgown folded across the foot of the bed.

She wanted to turn back—but it was impossible now. It was more than a sick curiosity to know what was behind Mrs. Warren's formidable façade. It was a desire—no, a *need* for answers. Answers only Mrs. Warren could give.

Her hand was outstretched. She was almost at the door—

"Hal?"

The voice came from behind her, making her jump convulsively and swing around, eyes wide in the darkness.

"Wh-who's there?"

No sign of anyone at first, and then something moved—a dark shape in the doorway, and he stepped forwards into the little room.

The snow had stopped, she realized with a sense of detached wonderment, and the moon had come out, sending a thin white light slanting across the bare boards between them.

"Hal, what are you doing?" There was no censure in his deep voice, just a kind of concerned curiosity.

"E-Ezra," she stammered. "I was—I was looking for—for Mrs. Warren."

It was true, after all.

"Why? Is something wrong"

"I'm fine," she managed. But it was not true. Her heart was beating so hard and fast it made a hissing in her ears, a roar she could barely silence enough to hear her own thoughts.

He stepped forwards into the moonlight, one hand stretched out as if to take hers, lead her back to safety.

"Hal, are you *sure* you're all right? You look very strange. And what's that you've got there—is it . . . is it a book?"

She looked down at her hands, in which she was still holding the yellow album, and then up at Ezra, at her *father*.

She met his eyes, and it was like falling into dark, leaf-strewn water, like falling into her own past.

Because suddenly, in a single, crystallizing instant, she understood.

Once, at school, Hal's teacher had had them conduct an experiment, where they cooled a bottle of water to below freezing, and then tapped it sharply on a table. When they did, the water froze all in an instant, the ice spreading with impossible swiftness, like some kind of magic spell.

As she stood there, gazing into Ezra's dark, liquid eyes, Hal felt as if the same process were taking place inside her—a painful chill spreading out from her core, turning the blood in her veins to ice, and her limbs stiff and frozen. Because she understood—finally—and without needing to know what had happened to Mrs. Warren.

She understood Mrs. Warren's odd expression that first day, Mrs. Westaway's will, and her strange, cryptic message to Harding.

She understood the wording of the bequest, and the "mistake" that had occurred—not Mr. Treswick's fault at all—how could she have ever thought that dry, careful little man would make such a catastrophic error?

She understood why Abel had denied Edward's presence at the lake that day, and why Ezra had refused to challenge the will or pursue the deed of variation, and that odd, throwaway line that had niggled and niggled and niggled at her subconscious.

And most of all she understood why her mother had cut herself off from her past, and Hal with her.

Get out—if you know what's good for you.

Not a threat, but a warning.

And she had understood it too late.

CHAPTER 47

Time seemed to slow as they stood, staring at each other. Hal's throat was dry, and her voice croaked when she finally spoke.

"It's an album. But—but maybe you knew that."

She tried to say the words lightly, but they sounded strange in her own mouth, and she realized she was hugging herself defensively, as though to protect herself from some unknown attacker. *Think about how you hold yourself, Hal, it's not just what we read in others—it's what they read in us.*

Her face was stiff, and she forced a smile, widening the corners of her mouth in what felt like a death-mask grimace.

"Well . . . I'm very tired . . ."

Ezra took the album from her hand, but he didn't move to leave. Instead he put his hand on the wall, leaning casually, blocking Hal's route to the exit, and he cocked his head and smiled at her as he leafed through the pages.

"Oh . . . this old thing. Gosh, I had no idea Mother had kept hold of so many pictures."

Hal said nothing, only watched as he turned the pages.

"How did you stumble across this old thing?"

"I—" Hal swallowed, hard. She forced her arms to drop to her sides, making her body language open, trying to look relaxed. "I couldn't sleep. I was looking for a book to read. I went to the study."

"I see. And . . . did you . . . look at the photographs, by the way?"

His voice was casual, careless even. But as he said the words, Hal knew—he knew.

She had seen something in him, some change in the way he held himself, some imperceptible difference in his stance. She had seen that flicker of recognition when she hit a nerve too often in her booth to be mistaken.

She saw it now.

"J-just the first ones," Hal said. She made her breathing slow, steady, listening detachedly to the tremor in her own voice, trying to quiet it, make her voice calm, soothing. "Why?"

"No reason," he said. But there was no pretense now. He was not smiling any longer, and Hal felt her heart quicken.

Get out—while you still can.

"Well . . . I think I'll go back to bed now, if you don't mind. . . ." She said the words slowly and carefully, keeping very calm, waiting for him to move aside. But he only shook his head.

"I don't think so. I think you did look at that album."

There was a long, long silence. Hal felt her heart beating inside her. And then it was as if something inside her broke open, and the words came tumbling out, full of bitterness.

"Why didn't you *tell* me? You knew. You *knew. You* were Ed. Why did you pretend it was poor Edward?"

"Hal—"

"And why did you let me go on thinking that my mother—that my *mother—*"

But she couldn't finish. She could only sink to the bed, her head in her hands, shaking with tears.

"My whole life has been a lie!"

Ezra said nothing, only looked down at her, motionless, and Hal felt the cold inside her harden into certainty.

"What did you do to her, Ezra?" She said the words softly, but they sounded like what they were: an accusation.

His face was neutral, but he was not able to hide his eyes, and in the stark, bright moonlight Hal saw the pupils, black against dark, dilate suddenly, wildly, with shock, and then contract. And she knew that she had hit the truth.

"You made a mistake," she said quietly. "Earlier tonight. It niggled at me all evening, something you'd said, I couldn't pin down what it was that was bothering me. I kept thinking it was something you'd said in the car, and running over our conversations, but it wasn't. It was something you said in the food court."

"Hal—" Ezra said. His throat was hoarse, and he cleared it, as if he were finding it hard to speak. He took his arm down from the wall, folded his arms. "Hal—"

"Mown down outside her own house, you said. You were talking about *Maud*, Ezra, not Maggie. And how did you know that, about the house?"

"I don't know what—"

"Oh, for God's sake." She stood up, facing him, her head barely to his chest, but suddenly she was no longer afraid, she was angry. *I am so angry,* she remembered him saying. *I am angry all the time.*

Well, this man was her father, and she could be angry too.

"Stop pretending," she said. Her voice was quiet, and the trembling had stopped. *This* was it. *This* was what she was good at—reading people, reading their body language. Reading between the lines to the truth they did not want to admit, even to themselves. "It wasn't reported in any of the papers that it was outside our house—in fact, the police deliberately kept it out of the public reports because I didn't want people doorstepping the flat. You weren't there. You've never been to my flat. Unless . . . you have."

"What are you talking about," he said, but the words were almost mechanical, as if he knew himself that she had seen through to the truth he had been hiding all this time.

For Hal had seen something. *Something* in Ezra's eyes, some flicker of consciousness that she had seen a hundred, a thousand times before. And it told her that she was right.

"You knew," she said, full of certainty. "You were there. *What did you do?"*

For a long, long moment he said nothing, he simply stood, his back to the door, his arms folded. His face was in shadow, the moonlight only showing Hal his brows, knit in an angry frown, but she was not frightened of him. She could read this man. And he was afraid. She had *him* cornered, not the other way around.

"Ezra, you're my—" The word stuck in her throat. "You are my *father*. Don't you think I have a right to know?"

"Oh, Hal," he said, and he shook his head, suddenly not angry anymore, but as if he were very sad, or very tired, Hal was not sure. "Hal, why the fuck couldn't you just leave it."

"Because I have to know. I have a right to know!"

"I'm sorry," he said softly. "I am so . . . so sorry."

And then she knew.

CHAPTER 48

"You killed my mother."

The truth hit her like a slap of icy water, knocking all the breath out of her.

She felt herself falling into a deep black certainty.

It was as if she had always known—and yet the shock of hearing it, in her own quiet, flat voice, was still absolute.

She found herself gasping for breath, a kind of slow drowning, and then she could not speak any longer, only shake her head—but not in disbelief. It was a kind of desperation for this *not* to be true.

But it was. And she had known it for longer than she had realized.

Perhaps she had known it since she had come to this house.

She just could not bear for it to be true.

"Maud was going to tell you everything," he said sadly. "She wrote and told Mother, she said you had a right to know, and that she was going to tell you when you turned eighteen. And I couldn't let her. I couldn't let her tell you the truth."

"You killed her. And you killed Maggie."

"I didn't mean to. God, I *loved* her, Hal, once, but she was—" He shook his head, as if trying, even now, to understand. "It was an accident, but she made me so, so *angry*, Hal, that's what you have to understand."

Keep them talking, Hal. Questions can make people clam up—make open statements, show them that whatever they are holding inside them, you know already.

"I understand," she said, though the words were painful in her throat, and hard to say. She swallowed. "You must have had a reason."

"Running away . . ." He said the words slowly, his head down, almost as if he were speaking to himself. "Leaving Trepassen, I could understand that. Mother made her life unbearable, and I was away at school, there wasn't much I could do. But then she came back, and God, she was so different, so *cold*, so hard. She came up to the house—it was July or August, I think, and I'd finished school. Mother was out and Maggie came to see me, and she said . . ." He gave a short, choking laugh. "She said, 'I'm not going to beat around the bush, Ed, you have an obligation to support this child.'

"I mean—can you believe it? The"—he seemed almost to choke with the memory of it—"the sheer *effrontery*. She ran away, left me wondering where the hell she was, what she'd *done*, and then she turns up out of the blue, without so much as an apology, demanding *money*. After all we'd been to each other, after all I'd—"

He sank to the bed, his head in his hands.

"Oh God." The words were out before she could stop herself, and as soon as they were spoken she heard her mother's voice in her head: *Never show them you're shocked, nothing makes people more defensive than censure. You're their priest, Hal. This is a confessional, of a sort. Be open—and they will give you the truth.*

She put her hands to her mouth, as if preventing herself from saying any more, and then simply stood there, looking down at the top of his head, cold with shock. A small, far-off, practical part of her mind was whispering: *If only you had your phone, you could have recorded this.* But it was too late. Her phone was far away, up in the attic, with no hope of her reaching it without alarming him. And besides, the truth was more important now. She *had* to know.

He spoke again, his voice harsh and cracked, his head still bowed as if with the weight of his confession.

"I asked her to go for a walk, I thought if we went out of the house, to somewhere with happy memories . . ." He trailed off, and then shook his head. "We went down to the lake. She always loved the boathouse, but when we got there it was so cold, there was ice on the water, and it was like everything had changed. When I tried to kiss her, she slapped me. She slapped *me*." He sounded incredulous. "And I was angry, Hal. I was *so* angry. I put my hands around her neck, and I kissed her—I kissed her, and when I let go . . ."

He stopped. Hal was cold with the horror of it.

She could imagine it so well, the icy *slap, slap* of the water against the jetty, and poor Maggie's desperate struggles, her feet kicking against the slippery planks. . . .

And then what? A body . . . slipped through the thin shards of ice into the cold black waters . . . a boat, deliberately holed, to pin it down and cover the bones.

And silence. Silence for more than twenty years.

"Oh my God," she whispered, her hands to her face. "Oh my God."

He looked up at her, and there were tears in his eyes.

"I'm sorry," was all he said.

And then he stood, and he reached out, and for a moment, a terrible moment, Hal thought that he was going to kiss her too.

But he did not. And then she realized what he was about to do.

CHAPTER 49

"Ezra, don't." Hal began to back away, but he was between her and the door, and the only place she could go was backwards, back towards the other door, the chink of darkness at the far side of the room. Was it an exit? Or a dead end? She had no way of knowing. "Please. You don't need to do this. You're my *father,* I won't tell anyone. . . ."

But he was coming closer, and closer.

"The others will realize—they'll know you came back—they'll see the tracks of the car. Mrs. Warren, she'll hear you—"

But even as she said the words, she knew they were futile. Even if Mrs. Warren *was* here somewhere, she had covered up one murder by her darling boy.

There was no point in screaming. No one would hear her. But while her brain told her that, her muscles knew that it was the only thing they could do, and she took a huge breath, filling her lungs, and screamed.

"Help me! Someone help me, I'm in ro—"

And then he was on her, like a cat on a mouse, his hand over her mouth, stifling the sounds.

Hal bit down, hard, tasting blood, and with one hand she scrabbled at the bedside table for something, anything to use as a weapon. A lamp. A cup. A photograph frame, even.

Her fingers were clutching, and she heard the crack of breaking glass, and then she had something in her grip, a lamp she thought, and she hit him over the back of the head with it as hard as she could, hearing the smash of the bulb and the crunch of the metal shade.

Ezra let go of her mouth to roar with pain and clutch at her hand, forcing her to drop the lamp, and she filled her lungs again—but this time, before she could scream, his hands were around her throat, crushing it.

She made one last reach for the bedside table—and then she gave up. She couldn't not. The pain in her throat was huge, a crushing pressure, and every instinct was forcing her to get her hands up, try to prize off his grip.

Fighting was no longer the most important thing. Breathing was.

Hal brought her hands up, digging her nails into his knuckles, trying to loosen his fingers enough to draw a single ragged breath, but his grip was immensely strong, and she could feel herself giving way, giving up, her vision disintegrating into fragments of black and red, and the roaring in her ears was like waves of darkness, and the pain in her throat was like a knife, and she had a brief flashing image of the blindfolded woman on the eight of swords, hemmed into her prison of blades, blind, bleeding, trapped, and as the room fractured into blackness she had time to think, *I am not that woman. She is not my fate.*

She thought of her mother, of how fast this had been. Seconds only, how strange that life could be extinguished so fast. . . .

Her legs were still kicking, more in instinct than by design, and through her fragmenting vision she could see Ezra's face, his mouth ugly and square with grief, tears running down his nose.

"I'm sorry," she heard through the roar in her ears. "I'm so sorry, I never wanted to do this—"

Her legs were barely moving now. She wanted to cry out, beg him, but she could not whisper, let alone speak. The pressure on her windpipe was too great, and she had no breath left in her.

Hold on.

She was not sure whose voice it was. Maggie's. Maud's. Or maybe it had always been her own—only her own.

Hold on.

But she could not. His fingers were crushing her, and everything was slipping further and further away.

There was no point fighting. He was too strong.

She let her fingers fall from his, stopped trying to pry his grip from her throat.

And as she did, her knuckles brushed something on the bed, something that had fallen from the nightstand in the struggle.

She closed her hand around it, and with almost the last of her strength, she picked it up, and smashed it into his face.

Hal heard the crack of the glass before she realized what it was—the broken photograph frame—and then she saw the spray of blood as a shard of glass dug deep into the bony ridge above his eye socket. He gave a scream of pain and took one hand away from her throat, feeling for the piece of glass sticking out of his brow, the pouring blood blinding him. For a moment Hal stared in horror. She had no idea what she had done—whether the glass had gone deep enough to penetrate something vital. But she could not stop to find out.

She let the picture frame drop, dug her fingers beneath his remaining hand, and then she swung her knee up and into his crotch with all the force she could muster.

And he let go.

Stumbling, gasping, her breath tearing in her raw throat, Hal made for the door at the far side of the room.

"Oh no you don't!" She heard his voice like a hoarse roar of pure fury, but it was too late to turn back even if she had wanted to.

As she flung herself against the door it gave way beneath her weight and she found herself falling, tumbling, down cold steps, until she stopped with a crunch at the bottom.

IT WAS EXTREMELY DARK. HAL'S head throbbed with the old bruise, where she had hit it before, and her throat screamed with pain from Ezra's near throttling.

The fall might have killed her, she thought, were it not for the fact that she had fallen against something soft and yielding.

It was only when she put her hand down to try to stand, and felt soft hair beneath her palm, that she realized what it was, and when she did she had to stifle the whimper that tried to escape her bruised throat.

It was Mrs. Warren. And, as Hal's fingers traced across her face, her glasses, her open mouth, Hal could tell—she was dead and completely cold.

But she had no time to find out more. Above her, she could hear Ezra moving with lumbering ferocity like a wounded animal, crashing into furniture as he staggered towards the open door. He would be down here in a moment, and then she would be dead—wounded or not, he was far, far stronger than her, and his blinded eye was not much disadvantage in this inky black.

She must be in some kind of cellar beneath the house. The only question was, was there another exit?

Hal put her hands out in front of her, and began to stumble cautiously through the penetrating darkness, feeling the shift and slither of things beneath her feet—the clank of bottles, the sharp pain where she hit her shin against some kind of box.

Back there in the darkness was Mrs. Warren's body, and as a shaft of gray moonlight pierced the blackness, and she heard a hoarse panting, she knew that Ezra too had found his way to the door, and was stumbling down the stone steps.

"Hal," he called, his voice echoing in a way that made her think this cellar must be large, much larger than she had at first thought. "Hal, don't run from me. I can explain."

Her throat was too hoarse and bruised to have answered, even if she wanted to—but there was no way she was going to give away her location down here. She stopped, pressing herself back against the wall, listening for his harsh breathing. It sounded as if he was facing the wrong way, and she edged quietly along the wall, holding her breath.

In the disorienting darkness she had completely lost all sense of direction, but the cellar seemed to stretch out in two directions, in front of Hal, and to her left. Mrs. Warren's body, and the steps upwards, lay to the right. Ezra seemed to be in front of her, venturing deeper beneath the house, so Hal continued her slow, painful edging along the wall, feeling the wetness of damp bricks at her back. There was hot blood on her hands, and she thought she must have cut herself when she hit Ezra with the photograph frame, though she had no memory of having done so.

"Hal!" His voice boomed, echoing back and forth beneath the vaults. Then there was a scratching rasp, and far away to her right Hal saw a flame ignite in the darkness, and the yellow glow of a lighter as Ezra held it above his head, surveying the darkness.

Two things happened in the instant before he extinguished the flame.

The first was that he saw her, she knew it from the way his face turned towards her, a hideous Pierrot mask that slashed his face into one half of white skin and another half painted in dark blood, black in the shadowy darkness.

But the other thing was that Hal saw the layout of the cellar—the clear path between the rows of dusty bottles and vaulted columns leading to the garden door at the far end.

For a moment she froze, each of them looking at the other, caught in the lighter's glow.

And then Ezra's face split into a terrifying grin, and he dropped the lighter, and ran.

Hal ran too.

She ran without seeing, barely knowing where she was going.

She ran, tripping over discarded bottles and mousetraps, hearing the crunch of small skeletons beneath her feet, and the splash of water. She fell, and she picked herself up, all the time hearing behind her Ezra's triumphant panting breath, for he knew this cellar, this was his house, his domain, and she remembered him saying how he and Maud had played hide-and-seek down here as small children.

This was his home.

But he was half-blind, and Hal was not, and she had a head start, and now she could see the faint glimmer of moonlight coming through the crack of the garden door ahead of her, and she put on a burst of speed and prayed—prayed to gods she did not believe in, and to the powers she had decried all her life, prayed for deliverance.

And then the cold metal knob of the door was beneath her hand and she was trying to turn it, with fingers that slipped with blood, and she could hear his pounding feet and his panting breath coming closer, and closer . . .

And then the door gave, and she was out in the moonlight, running, and running, and running in the blessed light of the waxing moon, almost as clear as day.

Her feet were taking her downhill, and she was halfway there before she realized, with a terrified lurch, where she was heading. She glanced behind her, but it was too late, he was out, he had seen her. If she doubled back to the house he would catch her. There was nowhere else to go, and maybe . . . maybe, a little still voice inside of her said, maybe it had always been meant to lead back here. Back to where it had started, and ended. Back to the boathouse.

Ezra was almost halfway across the lawn, his footsteps great slithering gashes in the white snow, when Hal broke into the cover of the little copse and began the slow fight through the brambles, tearing at her hands. She had no thought in her head apart from putting as much distance as possible between herself and Ezra—but perhaps, if she could somehow circumnavigate the lake and get to the other side, she could make it to the road, flag down a passing car. . . .

She crashed out of the brambles, her legs torn and bleeding, and found herself in a patch of moonlight at the shore of the lake. Behind her she could hear Ezra beginning to forge his own path through the undergrowth, and he was making better time of it than she was. She had already pushed aside the worst of it—all he had to do was follow in her path.

"Hal," he panted. "Hal, *please.*"

And there was something so desperate in his voice that a part of her almost wanted to say, *It's okay. I'll stop. I give in.* Oh God, she was so tired. . . .

In front of her the lake was a black slick, dotted here and there with patches of white. And as Ezra came plunging out of the undergrowth, Hal knew she had nowhere else to go.

"Hal," he gasped. He looked half-destroyed, his face dark with drying blood, the wound above his eye still wet and raw. His clothes had been slashed by the brambles, his arms and legs streaked with cuts, and looking down at herself Hal might almost have laughed, had she not been so terrified and exhausted.

"Stop," he said. He held out his arms. "Stop running. Please . . . please, just stop."

She wanted to answer him. She wanted to scream at him, to berate him for what he had done to Maud, to Maggie, to Mrs. Warren. She wanted to cry for the hopes she had had for her father, and for what she had found.

But her throat was too raw. As he came towards her, step after slow, careful step, his arms held out like the promise of a grim embrace, she could only shake her head, the tears running silently from her eyes, down her cheeks, and hold herself, as she would never let him hold her.

"Hal, please," he said again, and she stepped backwards, onto the frozen surface of the lake.

It cracked, but held, and she stepped again, seeing his face change in an instant, from cautious pleading to a kind of impotent, terrified rage.

"Please, don't," he managed. "It's not safe."

You *are the danger,* she wanted to say. *I'd be safer out here, beneath the ice, with my mother, than ever I would be with you.*

But she could only shake her head, and step backwards, and backwards, expecting each time she did to hear the snap of breaking ice, and feel the frigid waters of the lake envelop her.

Each time she did, the ice creaked and groaned, but it didn't break.

"Hal, come back," he cried. And then, almost laughing, "What are you going to do, for Christ's sake? Stay out there all night? You'll have to come back."

And again she stepped back. She was almost to the island now. And from there it was just another short crossing to the far shore, and the boundary of the property.

"Hal!" he bellowed, and above her she saw the flurry of wings as the startled magpies woke and took flight, cawing and wheeling in alarm, sending little patters of snow falling all around them in the quiet of the woods. "Hal, get over here *now*."

But she only shook her head for the third and final time—and then he stepped onto the ice.

It held. And Hal felt a wash of hot horror flood over her, and then a great coldness as he looked down at his feet, and then up at her, grinning at the realization of what this meant.

"Oh, you," he said as he began to walk towards her. "Oh, you little—"

But he never finished.

There was a tearing, rending crack, and the surface of the lake gave way. And Ezra plunged through, cracking his head on the ice at the edge of the hole as he went, and slid beneath the black surface.

"Ezra," Hal screamed, or tried to, but her torn throat would make only the smallest of sounds, a whimper, barely even recognizable as a name. "Ezra."

There was a languid flowering of bubbles on the surface of the water for a moment . . . and then no more. The lake was still and silent, and nothing moved. Ezra was gone.

CHAPTER 50

"Ooh, aren't we lucky," the nurse said, whipping aside Hal's curtains.

"Lucky?" Hal croaked. Her head ached and her throat was still almost too painful to talk.

"Visitors. And a lovely bunch of flowers. Do you want a hand putting on your dressing gown?"

Hal shook her head, wondering who the visitors might possibly be. It was probably the police again, although she felt as if she had run through the events at Trepassen more times than she could count, certainly more times than her aching throat had been able to take. Though would the police really be carrying flowers?

The nurse had gone, bustling away up the corridor to another patient, so Hal sat up in bed, pulled her T-shirt straight, raked her fingers through her hair, and tried to prepare herself for whoever might come through the curtains of her cubical.

Even so, she was not prepared for the two people who came nervously down the hallway. Abel and Mitzi, Abel carrying a bunch of flowers almost bigger than himself, and Mitzi bearing what looked like a homemade cake.

"Hello, Harriet," Abel said, rather tentatively, and Hal saw his throat move as he swallowed awkwardly. "I hope—I hope this is okay, I could understand . . ."

He trailed off, and Mitzi stepped forwards, her pink face even pinker than usual.

"Frankly, Harriet, we can both quite understand if you don't feel up to seeing anyone from Trepassen, so please don't hesitate to say if you'd rather we went away. This is pure selfishness on my part—I was so anxious when I heard the news. Harding is at home with the children, and Abel kindly agreed to give me a lift—oh, no, Harriet, please don't get up."

Hal was struggling out of bed, putting her shaky legs to the floor, and then she was in Mitzi's arms, enveloped in a hug so hard and close she felt breathless with the force of it.

"Oh, my darling," Mitzi was saying over and over. "Oh, my darling, what an ordeal, I can't tell you—that vile, horrible man—I can't even—"

She broke off and sat back, wiping fiercely at her eyes with a corner of her Hermès scarf, and Abel stepped forwards.

He did not embrace her, or not exactly; he simply put a hand on either side of her shoulders, holding her gently, almost as if he feared she would break, looking at her with such sadness in his gray eyes that Hal felt a lump rise in her own throat.

"Oh, Harriet," he said. "Can you forgive us?"

"Forgive you?" Hal tried to say, but the hoarseness in her throat broke up the words, and she had to swallow and try again before they understood her. "What should I forgive?"

"Everything," Abel said heavily. He sat opposite the head of Hal's bed on the hard little chair, and Mitzi perched on the foot of the bed. "For letting you sleepwalk into this. For turning a blind eye for twenty years. I knew in my heart of hearts that something was wrong, we all did. But he was so charming, so funny when he wanted to be."

"None of you knew the truth, though?" Hal managed. It was a question, not a statement, and Abel shook his head.

"Mother knew. And . . . and I think so did Mrs. Warren, almost certainly."

"Mrs. Warren?" Mitzi's face was horrified. "She knew, and she said nothing?"

"She loved him," Abel said simply. "And so did Mother, I think, in her own way. I suppose they felt . . ." He spread his hands. "What was done was done, after all. They couldn't bring Maggie back. And they thought, perhaps—forgive me, Hal." He took a breath. "I think perhaps they thought he had been . . . provoked. Beyond bearing. A crime of passion, in some way."

"Mrs. Warren knew," Hal said. Her throat hurt and she took a sip of the water beside her bed. "It's why he killed her. She tried to warn me. But I didn't understand. I thought it was a threat. I thought she tried to trip me up down the stairs and frighten me away, but it was—"

She stopped. What to say? It was Ezra? It was my father who did that, who set an opportunistic trap to stop me digging up my own past?

"And now she's gone," she finished. She felt numb with the futility of it. Maud, Maggie, even herself, she could understand. She could not forgive Ezra for what he had done, but she could understand it. He had killed out of rage and a kind of twisted love, and later to protect himself, to stop the truth from coming out. But Mrs. Warren . . . She thought of all the questions she still had—questions only Mrs. Warren could have answered—and she wanted to cry. Mrs. Warren's face, that first day, came back to her—the image she had had of a child watching a cat stalk towards a group of unsuspecting pigeons, watching with a kind of horrified glee for the carnage that was to come. At the time she had thought the cat was Hal herself. Now she understood—the cat was Ezra. And Mrs. Warren had perhaps not expected what was to come—if she had, surely even she would have said something. But she saw the danger, and did nothing to stop it. The only person she had tried to warn was Hal herself.

Get out—if you know what's good for you. While you still can . . .

"She was the only person left who knew the truth," Hal said slowly. "And he knew . . . he knew that she was going to warn me. . . ."

She thought back through the years, counting the bodies, falling like dominoes from that first moment of anger in the boathouse. And the last domino, Hal herself. Except . . . she hadn't fallen. He had.

"Abel . . . Mitzi . . . " She stopped, groping for what to say, and in the end the only phrase that came was the clichéd perennial response to the unbearable: "I'm so sorry for your loss."

"And I for yours," Mitzi said, and there was a kind of wisdom in her round, pink, horsey face that Hal would never have expected to find there, when they first met. An infinite compassion, beneath the self-satisfied façade. "He was your father."

It was not Hal who flinched at the word, but Abel, putting his face in his hands as though he could not bear it, so that Hal wanted to reach out, and tell him that it was okay, that it would all be okay. Whoever, *whatever* her father was—had been—she'd had not one but two remarkable mothers, women who had fought for her and protected her, and she was lucky in that.

But she could not find the words.

"When you're better"—Mitzi patted the sheet over her knees—"we'll have to get Mr. Treswick to come and see you again, Harriet."

"Mr. Treswick?"

"It seems . . . well, it seems as if Mrs. Westaway *did* know what she was doing when she drafted that will."

"Mr. Treswick has looked into it," Abel said. "In view of what we know now, the wording is quite clear and unambiguous. That legacy is meant for you, Hal. It always was. The house is yours."

"What?"

The shock was so unexpected that the word slipped out, like an accusation, and then Hal could not think of anything more to say.

Abel was nodding.

"Mother knew you were her granddaughter. I think that's very clear. And with the will . . . well, I think she wanted all of us to ask questions, start digging into the past. It's what she meant, I think, by that line to Harding in her letter."

"Après moi, le déluge," Hal said softly. And she finally understood what Mrs. Westaway had set in motion with her will. There had been malice, yes, but also cowardice. The truth had been a horror that she could not bear to face while she was alive. Instead her grandmother had waited until she herself was beyond pain—and unleashed this catastrophe on the living.

For a moment Hal imagined her lying there, bed-bound, waited on hand and foot by Mrs. Warren, and planning the cataclysm that was to come. Had she rubbed her hands as she signed that will, full of a bitter glee? Or had it been done with a weary resignation and pity for the living?

They would never know.

"What puzzles me," Abel was saying slowly, "is why the hell Ezra wouldn't agree to that deed of variation you suggested. It was the perfect get-out for him—an acceptance that you *weren't* Mother's granddaughter. I think Mother must have counted on you being as voracious and bloody-minded as the rest of us, and forcing the truth to come out in court. She never expected you to renounce your legacy without a fight. You were more noble than she could have imagined, Hal."

"I wasn't noble," Hal said. Her throat was sore, as if trying to stop her from saying the words, but she swallowed hard and forced them out, huskily. "I—I knew, when I got Mr. Treswick's letter, that there had been a mistake. I let you think that I was as confused as the rest of you, but the truth was, I wasn't. I came down here—" She stopped. Could she bear to do this? "I came down here to deceive you all. You don't know—you can't understand what it's like, any of you, to struggle so much, to never know where the next month's rent is coming from. You were rich, to me, and it felt like . . ." She stopped again, twisting the bedsheets with her fingers. "I felt like this was fate's way of righting the scales, and a few thousand here or there would mean nothing to you—and everything to me. I was on the run from a loan shark." How small and unimportant it seemed now, Mr. Smith and his small threats, in comparison with what she had survived. "And I only needed a few hundred pounds to make it all okay. I hoped—I hoped I could walk away with a little bit of money, and start again. It was only when I met you I realized I was wrong, and when I found out the legacy wasn't something small, but the whole estate, I knew I couldn't go through with it. But I think I know why Ezra wouldn't agree to the deed of variation."

"Why is that?" Abel asked, and there was a kind of wariness in his tone, as if he couldn't bear to be ambushed with more revelations. He looked, Hal thought, years older than when she had waved hello to him beneath the clock at Penzance station, but the pain and lines on his face somehow made the kindness in his eyes more apparent, and she felt ashamed of her suspicions, and that she could ever have thought poor Edward was behind all this.

"I think . . . I think he was worried that Harding would sell the house, and what they might find if he did. In the lake."

"What do you mean, Harriet?" Mitzi said. She leaned forwards, put her hand on Hal's. "Did Ezra tell you something, before he died?"

"I think my"—the word hurt, digging into her bruised throat—"my m-mother is still there, I think she's buried in the boathouse, in the lake. Can you ask—" She swallowed again, and coughed, her throat raw with too much speaking. "Can you ask the police to dredge inside the boathouse?"

"Oh God," Abel whispered. "Oh my God. And Mother lived with that for twenty years."

Silence fell on the little room, each of them bound up in their own thoughts, their own memories, their own horror.

Just then, there was the rattle of curtain rings, and a slanting ray of almost eye-hurtingly bright sunshine fell across the bed. In the opening of the curtains stood the brisk nurse from before.

"Visiting hours are over, I'm afraid, Mummy and Daddy," she said, rather archly. "Bye-bye until tomorrow, if you please. And our young lady needs to rest her voice."

"Just—just one minute," Abel said. There was a catch in his voice as he stood up, smoothing down his trousers, and Hal saw him blink as he smiled at her. "I'm sorry, Hal, it's unconscionable of us keeping you talking for so long, I know it must be painful for you. But there's one more thing I must give you before we go." A pained look passed over his face, and he rummaged in his pocket, and pulled out a photocopied piece of paper. "I was of two minds about whether to show this to you, Harriet, but . . ." He held out the photocopied sheet.

"I gave the original to the police, but we found this in Mrs. Warren's belongings. It's . . . it's a letter. There's no need to read it now, but . . . well . . ."

Hal took it, puzzled.

"Well, isn't that lovely," said the nurse. "But now it's time for our patient to rest."

"I'll come back tomorrow, darling," Mitzi said, and she bent and kissed Hal's cheek. "And in the meantime, I know what hospital food is like." She patted the tin she had set down on Hal's bedside table. "Homemade coffee and walnut, help fatten you up a bit."

"Well, Mummy," the nurse said. "Off we pop, for now. Oh, and if you could bring her day clothes when you come back tomorrow, Doctor has said she's ready to be discharged, so you can take her straight home."

"Oh," Hal said. She felt her heart sink, thinking of the long train journey back to Brighton, the cold little flat. . . . "I'm—Mitzi's not my mother. I can't, I mean, I don't—I live alone."

"Don't you have a friend who could come and stay?" the nurse said, looking a little shocked.

"I'm her aunt," Mitzi said, drawing herself up to her not-terribly-full height, "and we would be *delighted* to take Harriet home to ours until she's ready to return to her own flat. No!" She turned to Hal, silencing her openmouthed objections with a single look. "I don't want to hear another word about it, Harriet. Good-bye, darling, we'll come back with some clothes tomorrow. And in the meantime, I want every scrap of that cake eaten, or you will have *me* to deal with."

Hal watched them as they walked down the corridor, arm in arm, and she smiled at the companionable little wave Abel gave her as they turned the corner to the main ward; but in truth, when she lay back on her pillows, it was with relief, at being alone with her thoughts. She closed her eyes, feeling a great tiredness wash over her. The pain in her throat was a lot greater than she had let on to Mitzi and Abel, even without the horrifying range of possible outcomes the doctor had listed yesterday.

They ranged from the mild but worrying—like permanent harm to her vocal cords—through to the most serious of all: invisible damage to her brain from the lack of oxygen, or dislodged clots from broken blood vessels, which could cause strokes or even death weeks down the line. But that was very rare, the doctor had reassured her. Something to be aware of, but not to worry about, and in truth Hal was not worried—not anymore.

She was about to lie back on her pillow and close her eyes, when something crackled beneath her fingers, and she realized she was still holding the piece of paper Abel had passed to her. Slowly, she unfolded it.

It was a single page, covered in a long, looping handwriting so familiar that it made her breath catch in her throat. It was her mother's writing. Not the rounded, unformed characters of the diary—but the writing she had grown up seeing on Christmas and birthday cards, on shopping lists and letters. Seeing it now, she wondered how she could ever have thought that the same hand had written the diary entries. There were similarities, certain peculiarities, a kind of superficial resemblance, but there was an energy and a determination in the handwriting of the letter that made her heart clench in her chest, with a painful recognition.

Mum.

As she tried to focus on the page, Hal realized that her eyes were swimming with tears. It was like hearing her mother's voice unexpectedly—a shock in a way that the diary never had been.

She blinked furiously, and the letters swam into focus.

8th May, 2013

Dear Mother,

Thank you for your letter. And thank you too for the cheque you enclosed—I have put it towards a laptop for Harriet's birthday—she's hoping to go to university next year, so she badly needs one of her own.

However, this letter is not only to thank you. It's also to warn you of something.

I am writing to let you know that I have decided to tell Hal the truth. She turns eighteen next week, and she deserves to know her own story, and I cannot hide behind my own cowardice any longer.

The fact is, I have been frightened of him for too long—frightened of what he might do to Maggie when we were at Trepassen, frightened of how he might stop us from escaping, frightened of him tracking us down, and frightened of what he had done to her when she didn't return that last time. For I knew, Mother. I always knew. There is no way in the world Maggie would have left her newborn baby without a word. She went back there to face him, to fight for the future Hal deserved—and she didn't return.

I have blamed you bitterly for your silence—and yet I've committed the same crimes myself. I could have told the police my suspicions. I could have asked them to dig in the grounds, or dredge the lake, or search the cellars. But if I had done that, I would have lost custody of Hal to Ezra, if they found nothing. And I could not do that, Mother. I couldn't take the risk. I was too late to save Maggie with the truth—but I could save her child with my lies.

But Hal is about to become an adult now, and I can't hide behind excuses anymore. The only way I can lose her now is if SHE chooses to cut herself off from me. I would not blame her if she did—God knows, I've lied to her for so long, though I told myself my motives were good. I have deceived her unforgivably—I just hope that she can, in fact, forgive.

There is much that I will never forgive you for, Mother. But in spite of that, you have kept my secret faithfully these past few years, and I felt that you deserved to know the reasons for my decision. I don't know what Hal will do with the information—it's hers to decide. But it's possible she will come and seek you out. Be kind to her, if she does.

Yours,
Maud

Hal let the letter fall to the sheets, feeling her eyes well with tears, wishing that she could reach out and hug her mother, back through the years.

How had Mrs. Warren come by this letter? Had it ever reached Mrs. Westaway? Or had Mrs. Warren intercepted it? Either way, someone had told Ezra. And for the second time in his life, but not the last, her father had killed an innocent person to protect himself.

If only, if *only* her mother had not sent the letter. It seemed unbelievably naïve—to give up such hard-fought-for anonymity, to warn her mother of what she was about to do.

Had Maud underestimated Ezra? Or had she simply trusted Mrs. Westaway too much? They had been corresponding for a while, that much was plain from the letter. Perhaps she had slowly trusted more and more—thinking that if her mother had kept her secret safe thus far, she could trust her a little further, until at last she had entrusted Mrs. Westaway with a secret she could not keep.

But Hal wasn't sure. There had been something about Mrs. Warren's attempts to warn her . . . a kind of long-held guilt. She thought of that sitting room, the framed photographs of the cherubic little boy Mrs. Warren had loved for so long, and the man he had turned into.

Perhaps, for the sake of that little boy, she had written a letter—warning Ezra to be careful, to keep away.

And only afterwards realized what she had done.

Hal would never know the true chain of events. All she knew was that this letter was the first piece in a swift chain of betrayals that led to a hot summer's day, and the screech of a car's brakes, and her mother's crumpled body on the road outside her own house.

She closed her eyes, feeling the tears squeeze from between the lids and run down the sides of her nose, and she wished, more passionately than she had ever wished anything before, that she could go back and tell her mother, *It's okay. There is nothing to forgive. I trust you. I love you. There is nothing you could do to change that. Whatever angry things I might have said or thought or done, I would have come back to you, in the end.*

"Are you awake, my darling?" A Cornish accent broke into her thoughts, and Hal opened her eyes to see an orderly standing there beside a tea trolley, a white china cup in one hand and a metal pot in the other. "Tea?"

"Yes please," Hal said. She swiped surreptitiously at the trickle beside her nose, and blinked away the rest of the tears as the woman poured her a cup.

"Ooh, homemade cake. Aren't you the lucky one? I'll give you another saucer," the woman said, and she helped Hal to a generous chunk, and put it on her bedside tray.

After she had gone, moving on to the next person, Hal broke off a piece and put it between her lips, the buttercream melting on her tongue, soothing her sore throat, and taking away some of the bitterness of her thoughts.

She could not dwell in might-have-beens, she could only move forwards, to a different future.

The letter was still on her lap, and she folded it up carefully and laid it on the locker beside her bed. As she did, her hand knocked against the Golden Virginia tin, lying there, and on a sudden impulse she opened it up, closed her eyes, and shuffled the cards.

With her eyes closed, she might almost have been at home, in her little booth on the pier, feeling the soft frayed edges of the cards between her fingers, feeling their polished backs slide over each other, every movement changing the possibilities life dealt out, asking different questions, revealing different truths.

At last she stopped, holding the cards between her cupped palms, and then she cut the deck and opened her eyes.

A single card stared back at her, upright—and she found herself smiling, in spite of the tears that still clung to her lashes.

It was the World.

In Hal's deck the World was a woman of middle age with long dark hair, looking directly out at the querent. She was standing tall, her legs planted firmly apart, in the center of a garland of flowers. At the corners of the card were the four symbols from the Wheel of Fortune—showing that, like the wheel, the world was always turning, and the way that however much one might journey, in some sense one would always end up where one began.

The woman was smiling, though with a hint of sadness. And in her arms she held, almost as if cradling a child, a globe of the world.

Hal had had no question in her mind when she cut the deck, and yet here was her answer.

She knew what she would have said, had she turned up this card for someone in her booth.

She would have said: *This card shows that you have come to the end of a journey, that you have completed something important, that you have accomplished what you set out to do. The world has turned—the cycle is complete—your quest is at an end. You have endured hardship and suffering along the way, but these have made you stronger—they have shown you something, revealed a truth about yourself and your place in everything.*

Because the way that we see the world from above in this card, cradled in the arms of the woman, shows that at last you can see the full picture. Up until now you have been traveling, seeing only a part of what you wished to see—now you can see the whole system, the world, and its place in the universe, your part of the whole scheme.

Now you understand.

And it was true. It was all true. But it was not what Hal saw when she looked at the card—or not only what she saw. As a child, Hal had called that card by a different name. She had called it the Mother.

There was no mother card in tarot—the nearest thing was the Empress, her golden, abundant locks symbolizing femininity and fertility. But when Hal looked at this card, at the fearless dark-haired woman cradling the world in her arms, Hal saw her mother's face. She saw her dark eyes, full of wisdom and a little cynical; she saw her capable hands, and the sadness in her smile, as well as the compassion.

She had seen her mother in the World because her mother had *been* her world.

But the truth was, the world was stranger and more complicated than she had ever imagined as a child—and so was she.

She felt suddenly tired, immensely, unbelievably tired, and she pushed the cake away, packed the tarot cards back into their tin—all but the one she held in her hand—and then lay down on her side, her cheek against the cool white pillow, with Maggie's tarot card propped beside the locker, looking into Maud's face.

Her eyes drifted shut, and sleep began slowly to claim her.

As she lay there, she seemed to see patterns against her closed eyes—fiery shapes that changed from drifting sparks into spiraling leaves, and then into a flock of birds, bright against the red-black darkness, and she thought of the magpies at Trepassen House, wheeling and calling against the sky, and of the rhyme that Mr. Treswick had quoted that first day, as they drove up towards the house.

One for sorrow
Two for joy
Three for a girl
Four for a boy
Five for silver
Six for gold
Seven for a secret
Never to be told

And she thought of all the secrets down the years—of Maggie, tearing pages from a diary; of Maud, lying to protect her, in order to keep her safe from her own father. She thought of the secrets her father had kept, hugging his guilt to himself, until it had grown into a poison that had shaped his whole life.

She thought of Mrs. Westaway, and Mrs. Warren, living year after year with the terrible truth of what their darling boy had done, and the ugliness that lay in the leaf-strewn darkness of the boathouse.

And she heard the voice in her ear, her own voice now, firm, uncracked, unchanged by all that had happened. *No more. No more secrets, Hal.*

She had the truth. And that was all that mattered.

TURN THE PAGE FOR AN EXCLUSIVE SNEAK PEEK OF RUTH WARE'S HIGHLY ANTICIPATED FIFTH NOVEL, *THE TURN OF THE KEY*, COMING AUGUST 2019 FROM SCOUT PRESS

3rd September 2017

Dear Mr. Wrexham,

I know you don't know me but please, please, please you have to help me

3rd September 2017
HMP Charnworth

Dear Mr. Wrexham,

You don't know me, but you may have seen coverage of my case in the newspapers. The reason I am writing to you is to ask you please

4th September 2017
HMP Charnworth

Dear Mr. Wrexham,

I hope that's the right way to address you. I have never written to a barrister before.

The first thing I have to say is that I know this is unconventional. I know I should have gone via my solicitor, but he's

5th September 2017

Dear Mr. Wrexham,

Are you a father? An uncle? If so, let me appeal

Dear Mr. Wrexham,

Please help me. I *didn't* kill anyone.

7th September 2017
HMP Charnworth

Dear Mr. Wrexham,

You have no idea how many times I've started this letter and screwed up the resulting mess, but I've realized there is no magic formula here. There is no way I can *make* you listen to my case. So I'm just going to have to do my best to set things out. However long it takes, however much I mess this up, I'm just going to keep going and tell the truth.

My name is . . . And here I stop, wanting to tear up the page again.

Because if I tell you my name, you will know why I am writing to you. My case has been all over the papers, my name in every headline, my agonized face staring out of every front page—and every single article insinuating my guilt in a way that falls only just short of contempt of court. If I tell you my name, I have a horrible feeling you might write me off as a lost cause and throw my letter away. I wouldn't entirely blame you, but please—before you do that, hear me out.

I am a young woman, twenty-seven years old, and as you'll have seen from the return address above, I am currently at the Scottish women's prison HMP Charnworth. I've never received a letter from anyone in prison, so I don't know what they look like when they come through the door, but I imagine my current living arrangements were pretty obvious even before you opened the envelope.

What you probably don't know is that I'm on remand.

And what you cannot know is that I'm innocent.

I know, I know. They all say that. Every single person I've

met here is innocent—according to them, anyway. But in my case it's true.

You may have guessed what's coming next. I'm writing to ask you to represent me as my solicitor advocate at my trial.

I realize that this is unconventional and not how defendants are supposed to approach advocates. (I accidentally called you a barrister in an earlier draft of this letter—I know nothing about the law, and even less about the Scottish system. Everything I do know I have picked up from the women I'm in prison with, including your name.)

I have a solicitor already—Mr. Gates—and from what I understand, he is the person who should be appointing an advocate for the actual trial. But he is also the person who landed me here in the first place. I didn't choose him—the police picked him for me when I began to get scared and finally had the sense to shut up and refuse to answer questions until they found me a lawyer.

I thought that he would straighten everything out—help me to make my case. But when he arrived—I don't know, I can't explain it. He just made everything worse. He didn't let me *speak*. Everything I tried to say he was cutting in with "My client has no comment at this time," and it just made me look so much more guilty. I feel like if only I could have explained properly, it would never have got this far. But somehow the facts kept twisting in my mouth, and the police, they made everything sound so bad, so incriminating.

It's not that Mr. Gates hasn't heard my side of the story exactly. He has, of course—but somehow—Oh God, this is so hard to explain in writing. He's sat down and talked to me, but he doesn't *listen*. Or if he does, he doesn't believe me. Every time I try to tell him what happened, starting from the beginning, he cuts in with these questions that muddle me up and my story gets all tangled and I want to scream at him to just *shut the fuck up.*

And he keeps talking to me about what I said in the transcripts from that awful first night at the police station, when they grilled me and grilled me and I said—God, I don't know what I said. I'm sorry, I'm crying now. I'm sorry—I'm so sorry for the stains on the paper. I hope you can read my writing through the blotches.

What I said, what I said then, there's no undoing that. I know that. They have all that on tape. And it's bad—it's really bad. But it came out wrong; I feel like if only I could be given a chance to get my case across, to someone who would really listen . . . do you see what I'm saying?

Oh God, maybe you don't. You've never been here after all. You've never sat across a desk feeling so exhausted you want to drop and so scared you want to vomit, with the police asking and asking and asking until you don't know what you're saying anymore.

I guess it comes down to this in the end.

I am the nanny in the Elincourt case, Mr. Wrexham.

And I *didn't* kill that child.

I started writing to you last night, Mr. Wrexham, and when I woke up this morning and looked at the crumpled pages covered with my pleading scrawl, my first instinct was to rip them up and start again, just like I had a dozen times before. I had meant to be so cool, so calm and collected—I had meant to set everything out so clearly and *make* you see. And instead I ended up crying onto the page in a mess of recrimination.

But then I reread what I'd written and I thought, *No. I can't start again. I just have to keep going.*

All this time I have been telling myself that if only

someone would let me clear my head and get my side of the story straight, without interrupting, maybe this whole awful mess would get sorted out.

And here I am. This is my chance, right?

140 days, they can hold you in Scotland before a trial. Though there's a woman here who has been waiting almost ten months. Ten months! Do you know how long that is, Mr. Wrexham? You probably think you do, but let me tell you. In her case that's 297 days. She's missed Christmas with her kids. She's missed all their birthdays. She's missed Mother's Day and Easter and first days at school.

297 days. And they still keep pushing back the date of her trial.

Mr. Gates says he doesn't think mine will take that long because of all the publicity, but I don't see how he can be sure.

Either way, 100 days, 140 days, 297 days . . . that's a lot of writing time, Mr. Wrexham. A lot of time to think, and remember, and try to work out what really happened. Because there's so much I don't understand, but there's one thing I know. I did not kill that little girl. I *didn't*. However hard the police try to twist the facts and trip me up, they can't change that.

I didn't kill her. Which means someone else did. And they are out there.

While I am in here, rotting.

I will finish now, because I know I can't make this letter too long—you're a busy man; you'll just stop reading.

But please, you have to believe me. You're the only person who can help.

Please, come and see me, Mr. Wrexham. Let me explain the situation to you and how I got tangled into this nightmare. If anyone can make the jury understand, it's you.

I have put your name down for a visitor's pass—or you can write to me here if you have more questions. It's not like I'm going anywhere. Ha.

Sorry, I didn't mean to end on a joke. It's not a laughing matter, I know that. If I'm convicted, I'm facing—

But no. I can't think about that. Not right now. I won't be. I won't be convicted, because I'm innocent. I just have to make everyone understand that. Starting with you.

Please, Mr. Wrexham, please say you'll help. Please write back. I don't want to be melodramatic about this, but I feel like you're my only hope.

Mr. Gates doesn't believe me; I see it in his eyes.

But I think that you might.

12th September 2017
HMP Charnworth

Dear Mr. Wrexham,

It's been three days since I wrote to you, and I'm not going to lie, I've been waiting for a reply with my heart in my mouth. Every day the post comes round and I feel my pulse speed up, with a kind of painful hope, and every day (so far) you've let me down.

I'm sorry. That sounds like emotional blackmail. I don't mean it like that. I get it. You're a busy man, and it's been only three days since I sent my letter but . . . I guess I half hoped that if the publicity surrounding the case had done nothing else, it would have given me a certain twisted celebrity—made you pick out my letter from among all the others you presumably get from clients and would-be clients and nutters.

Don't you want to know what happened, Mr. Wrexham? I would.

Anyway, it's three days now (did I mention that already?) and . . . well, I'm beginning to worry. There's not much to do in here, and there's a lot of time to think and fret and start to build up catastrophes inside your head.

I've spent the last few days and nights doing that. Worrying that you didn't get the letter. Worrying that the prison authorities didn't pass it on (can they do that without telling me? I honestly don't know). Worrying that I didn't *explain* right.

It's the last one that has been keeping me awake. Because if it's that, then it's my fault.

I was trying to keep it short and snappy, but now I'm thinking, I shouldn't have stopped so quickly. I should have put in more of the facts, tried to show you *why* I'm innocent. Because you can't just take my word for it—I get that.

When I came here, the other women—I can be honest with you, Mr. Wrexham—they felt like another species. It's not that I think I'm better than them. But they all seemed . . . they all seemed to fit in here. Even the frightened ones, the self-harmers and the ones who screamed and banged their heads against their cell walls and cried at night, even the girls barely out of school. They looked . . . I don't know. They looked like they belonged here, with their pale, gaunt faces and their pulled-back hair and their blurred tattoos. They looked . . . well, they looked *guilty.*

But I was different.

I'm English, for a start, of course, which didn't help. I couldn't understand them when they got angry and started shouting and all up in my face. I had no idea what half the slang meant. And I was visibly middle-class, in a way that I can't put my finger on but which might as well have been written across my forehead as far as the other women were concerned.

But the main thing was, I had never been in prison. I don't think I'd ever even met someone who had, before I came here. There were secret codes I couldn't decipher, and currents I had no way of navigating. I didn't understand what was going on when one woman passed something to another in the corridor and all of a sudden the wardens came barreling out, shouting. I didn't see the fights coming; I didn't know who was off her meds, or who was coming down from a high and might lash out. I didn't know the ones to avoid or the ones with permanent PMS. I didn't know what to wear or what to do, or what would get you spat on or punched by the other inmates, or what would provoke the wardens to come down hard on you.

I sounded different. I looked different. I *felt* different.

And then one day I went into the bathroom and I caught a glimpse of a woman walking towards me from the far corner. She had her hair scraped back like all the others, her eyes were like chips of granite, and her face was set, hard and white. My first thought was, *Oh God, she looks pissed off; I wonder what she's in for.*

My second thought was, *Maybe I'd better use the other bathroom.*

And then I realized.

It was a mirror on the far wall. The woman was me.

It should have been a shock—the realization that I wasn't different at all but just another woman sucked into this soulless system. But in a strange way it helped.

I still don't fit in completely. I'm still the English girl—and they all know what I'm in for. In prison they don't like people who harm children; you probably know that. I've told them it's not true, of course—what I'm accused of. But they look at me and I know what they're thinking—*They all say that.*

And I know—I know that's what you'll be thinking too. That's what I wanted to say. I understand if you're skeptical. I didn't manage to convince the police, after all. I'm here. Without bail. I must be guilty.

But it's not true.

I have 140 days to convince you. All I have to do is tell the truth, right? I just have to start at the beginning and set it all out, clearly and calmly, until I get to the end.

And the beginning was the advert.

WANTED

Large family seeks experienced live-in nanny

ABOUT US: *We are a busy family of four children, living in a beautiful (but remote!) house in the Highlands. Mum and Dad co-run the family architecture practice.*

ABOUT YOU: *We are seeking an experienced nanny, used to working with children of all ages, from babyhood to teens. You must be practical, unflappable, and comfortable looking after children on your own. Excellent references, background check, first aid certificate, and clean driving license are a must.*

ABOUT THE POST: *Mum and Dad work mainly from home, and during those periods you will have a simple eight-to-five post, with one night a week babysitting and weekends off. As far as possible we arrange our schedule so that one parent is always around. However, there are times when we may both need to be away (very occasionally for up to a fortnight), and when this occurs, you will be in loco parentis.*

In return we can offer a highly competitive remuneration package totaling £55,000 per annum (gross, including bonus), use of a car, and eight weeks' holiday a year.

APPLICATIONS TO SANDRA AND BILL ELINCOURT, HEATHERBRAE HOUSE, CARN BRIDGE

I remember it nearly word for word. The funny thing was, I wasn't even looking for a job when it came up on my Google results—I was searching for . . . well, it doesn't really matter what I was looking for. But something completely different. And then there it was—like a gift thrown into my hands so unexpectedly I almost didn't catch it.

I read it through once, and then again, my heart beating faster the second time, because it was *perfect*. It was almost too perfect.

When I read it a third time I was scared to look at the closing date for applications—convinced I would have missed it.

But it was that very evening.

It was unbelievable. Not just the salary—though God knows, that was a pretty startling sum. Not just the post. But the luck of it. The whole package—just falling in my lap, right when I was in the perfect position to apply.

You see, my flatmate was away, traveling. We'd met at the Little Nippers nursery in Peckham, working side by side in the baby room, laughing about our terrible boss and the pushy, faddy parents, with their fucking fabric nappies and their homemade—

Sorry. I shouldn't have sworn. I've scribbled it out, but you can probably see the word through the paper and, God knows, maybe you've got kids, maybe you even put them in Little Plushy Bottoms or whatever the fashionable brand was at the time.

And I get it, I do. They're your babies. Nothing is too much trouble. I understand that. It's just that when you're the one having to stockpile a whole day's worth of pissy, shitty bits of cloth and hand them back to the parent at collection time with your eyes watering from the ammonia . . . it's not that I *mind* exactly, you know?

It's part of the job. I get that. But we all deserve a moan, don't we? We all need to let off steam, or we'd explode with frustration.

Sorry. I'm rambling. Maybe this is why Mr. Gates is always trying to shut me up. Because I dig myself a hole with my words and instead of knowing when to stop, I keep digging. You're probably adding two and two together right now. *Doesn't seem to like kids much. Freely admits to frustration with role. What would happen when she was cooped up with four kids and no adults to "let off steam" with?*

That's exactly what the police did. All those little throwaway remarks—all those unedifying facts. I could see the triumph on their faces every time I dropped one, and I watched them picking them up like bread crumbs, adding them to the weight of arguments against me.

But that's the thing, Mr. Wrexham. I could spin you a web of bullshit about what a perfect, caring, saintly person I am—but it would be just that. Bullshit. And I am not here to bullshit you. I want you to believe that—I want it more than anything in the world.

I am telling you the *truth*. The unvarnished, ugly truth. And it is all that. It *is* unpolished and unpleasant, and I don't pretend I acted like an angel. But *I didn't kill anyone*. I just fucking didn't.

I'm sorry. I didn't mean to swear again.

God, I am messing this up so badly. I have to keep a clear head—get this all straight in my head. It's like Mr. Gates says—I should stick to the facts.

Okay then. Fact. The advert. The advert is a fact, right?

The advert . . . with its amazing, dizzying, fabulous salary.

That should have been my first warning signal, you know. The salary. Because it was *stupidly* generous. I mean it would have been generous even for London, even for a live-out nanny. But for a nanny in someone's house, with free accommodation provided, and all bills paid, even down to the car, it was ridiculous.

It was so ridiculous, in fact, that I half wondered if there had been a typo. Or something that they weren't saying—a child with significant behavioral needs maybe? But wouldn't they have mentioned that in the ad?

Six months ago I probably would have paused, frowned a little, and then passed on without thinking too much more about it. But then, six months ago I wouldn't have been looking at that web page in the first place. Six months ago I had a flatmate and a job I liked, and even the prospect of promotion. Six months ago I was in a pretty good place. But now . . . well, things were a bit different now.

My friend, the girl I mentioned at Little Nippers, had left to go traveling a couple of months ago. It hadn't seemed like the end of the world when she told me—to be honest, I found her quite annoying, her habit of loading the dishwasher but never actually switching it on, her endless Euro-pop disco hits hissing through my bedroom wall when I was trying to sleep. I mean, I knew I'd miss her, but I didn't realize how much.

She had left her stuff in her room, and we'd agreed she'd pay half rent and I'd keep the room open for her. It seemed like a good compromise—I'd had a series of terrible flatmates before we found each other, and I wasn't keen to return to posting on Facebook Local and trying to weed out weirdos by text message and email, and it felt, in some small way, like an anchor—like a guarantee that she would come back.

But when the first flush of freedom wore off, and the novelty of having the whole place to myself and watching whatever I liked on the shared TV in the living room had started to fade a little, I found I was lonely. I missed the way she'd say "Wine o'clock, darling?" when we rolled in together from work. I missed sounding off to her about Val, the owner of Little Nippers, and sharing anecdotes about the worst of the parents. When I applied for a promotion and didn't get it, I went to the pub alone to drown my sorrows and ended up crying into my beer, thinking how different it would have been if she had still been here. We could have laughed about it together, she would have flipped Val the bird behind her back at work, and given her earthy belly laugh when Val turned around to almost catch her in the act.

I am not very good at failing, Mr. Wrexham, that's the thing. Exams. Dating. Jobs. Any kind of test, really. My instinct is always to aim low, save myself some pain. Or, in the case of dating, just don't aim at all, rather than risk being rejected. It's why I didn't go to university in the end. I had the grades, but I couldn't bear the idea of being turned down, the thought of them reading my applications with a scornful snigger. "Who does she think she is?"

Better to achieve perfect marks on an easy test than flunk a hard one, that was my motto. I've always known that about myself. But what I didn't know, until my flatmate left, was that I am also not very good at being alone. And I think it was that, more than anything, that pushed me out of my comfort zone and made me scroll down that advert, holding my breath, imagining what lay at the other end of it.

The police made a lot out of the salary when they first questioned me. But the truth is, the money wasn't the reason I applied for the post. It wasn't even really about my flatmate, though I can't deny, if she hadn't left, none of it would have happened. No, the real reason . . . well, you probably know what the real reason was. It was all over the papers, after all.

I called in sick to Little Nippers and spent the entire day working on a CV and getting together everything that I knew I would need to convince the Elincourts that I was the person they were looking for. Background check—check. First aid certificate—check. Spotless references—check, check, and check.

The only problem was the driving license. But I pushed the issue aside for the moment. I could cross that bridge when I came to it—if I got that far. Right now, I wasn't thinking past the interview.

I added a note to the cover letter, asking the Elincourts not to contact Little Nippers for a reference—I told them that I didn't want my current employers knowing that I was casting about for another job, which was true—and then I emailed it off to the address provided and held my breath and waited.

I had given myself the best possible chance of meeting them face-to-face. There was nothing else I could do now.

Those next few days were hard, Mr. Wrexham. Not as hard as the time I've spent in here, but hard enough. Because—God—I wanted that interview *so much*. I was only just beginning to realize how much. With every day that passed, my hopes ebbed a little more, and I had to fight off the urge to contact them again and beg for an answer. The only thing that stopped me was the knowledge that looking so desperate would certainly not help my case if they were still deciding.

But six days later it came, pinging into my email inbox.

To: supernanny1990@ymail.com
From: sandra.elincourt@elincourtandelincourt.com
Subject: Nanny position.

Elincourt. The surname alone was enough to make my stomach start churning like a washing machine. My fingers were shaking almost too much to open it, and my heart was hammering in my throat. Surely, surely they didn't often contact unsuccessful applicants. Surely an email must mean . . . ?

I clicked.

> Hi, Rowan! Thank you so much for your application, and apologies for taking so long to get back to you. I have to admit, we were slightly taken by surprise at the volume of applications. Your CV was very impressive, and we would like to invite you to interview. Our house is rather remote, so we are happy to pay your train fare and can offer you a room in our house overnight, as you will not be able to make the trip from London in one day.
>
> However, there is one thing I must make you aware of up front, in case it affects your enthusiasm for the post.
>
> Since we bought Heatherbrae we have become aware of various superstitions surrounding the house's history. It is an old building and has had no more than the usual number of deaths and tragedies in its past, but for some reason these have resulted in some local tales of hauntings, etc. Unfortunately, this fact has upset some of our recent nannies, to the extent that four have resigned in the past fourteen months.
>
> As you can imagine, this has been very disruptive

for the children, not to mention extremely awkward for myself and my husband professionally.

For that reason we wanted to be completely honest about our predicament, and we are offering a generous salary in the hopes of attracting someone who can really commit to staying with our family for the long term—at least a year.

If you do not feel that is you, or if you feel at all concerned about the history of the house, please say so now, as we are very keen to minimize further disruption to the children. With that in mind, the salary will be made up of a basic stipend, paid monthly, and then a generous year-end bonus on the anniversary of employment.

If you are still keen to attend the interview, please let me know your availability for the forthcoming week.

Best wishes, and I look forward to meeting you.

Sandra Elincourt

I closed down the email and for a moment just sat there staring at the screen. Then I got up and did a little silent scream, punching the air in jubilation.

I had done it. I had *done* it.

I should have known it was too good to be true.

WANT TO READ MORE?

AVAILABLE AUGUST 2019

BOOK CLUB FAVORITES — READER'S GUIDE

The Death
of
Mrs. Westaway

RUTH WARE

This readers group guide for **The Death of Mrs. Westaway** *includes an introduction, discussion questions, ideas for enhancing your book club, and a Q&A with author* **Ruth Ware***. The suggested questions are intended to help your reading group find new and interesting angles and topics for your discussion. We hope that these ideas will enrich your conversation and increase your enjoyment of the book.*

INTRODUCTION

Twenty-one-year-old Hal has been down on her luck since her mother's death two years ago. With a loan shark and his cronies beating on her door and physically threatening her, Hal is struggling to eke out a living at the tarot-reading booth she took over from her mother on Brighton's West Pier.

But on a day that begins like any other, Hal receives a glimmer of hope in the form of a mysterious letter bequeathing her a substantial inheritance. She realizes very quickly that the letter was sent to the wrong person—but that the cold-reading skills she's honed as a tarot reader might help her claim the money anyway.

Soon, Hal finds herself at the funeral of the deceased . . . where it dawns on her that there is something very, very wrong about this strange situation and the inheritance at the center of it.

TOPICS AND QUESTIONS FOR DISCUSSION

1. Hal learned tarot, her eventual trade as an adult, from her mother at a young age. What else did Hal inherit from her mother? How does Hal's understanding of her inheritance, physical and otherwise, change over the course of the novel?

2. How does the unknown identity of the writer of the diaries from Trepassen affect your understanding of the events? Did you guess at the identity before it was revealed?

3. How does the solicitor, Mr. Treswick, change the outcome for Hal and the Westaway family? Did he do his due diligence in finding and vetting Hal? Do you think Hal is glad to have been found in the end?

4. How did you react to Hal's ultimate decision to attend the funeral? What do you think her true motivation was? What would you have done in her shoes?

5. Hal is skilled at stepping into different roles—she plays Madame Margarida for her clients; she plays the regretful granddaughter for the funeral. What does this skill say about Hal's character?

6. The interplay of skepticism and superstition is as present throughout *The Death of Mrs. Westaway* as the swarms of magpies at Trepassen. How does this tug-of-war between skepticism and

superstition affect each of the characters? Would things have turned out differently if Hal believed in fortunes and fate?

7. "You should never have come back here," Mrs. Warren attempts to warn Hal (p. 219). Can Hal trust Mrs. Warren? Can she trust Mitzi, or any of the other Westaways? Why or why not?

8. Hal plays the mouse, but feels she is more the rat. Which is she really? How do the events at Trepassen change Hal's understanding of herself and her own identity?

9. Who is the real villain of *The Death of Mrs. Westaway*? Why? Does that change throughout the course of the book?

10. The house at Trepassen, cavernous and cold and rundown, almost takes on a life of its own. How much of that was due to the mark Mrs. Westaway left on the house? What sort of home environment did Mrs. Westaway create for her children? How does Mrs. Warren perpetuate that?

11. Abel, Harding, Ezra—and even Mrs. Warren—swear that Ezra was the favorite. How does that fact play out in the end? Was Mrs. Westaway protecting Ezra?

12. Were you surprised by the revelation between Ezra and Hal, or by the final revelation Hal discovers in the study and Mrs. Warren's wing? Why or why not?

13. Does Hal get what she deserves in the end? What does she gain? What does she learn? At what cost?

14. What do you think Mrs. Westaway's motive was in leaving her will as she did? How much do you think she knew about Hal before her death? Why or why not?

ENHANCE YOUR BOOK CLUB

1. Author A. J. Finn said, "*The Death of Mrs. Westaway,* [Ruth Ware's] latest, is also her best." If you haven't read Ware's other novels, go back and read *In a Dark, Dark Wood, The Woman in Cabin 10,* or *The Lying Game* and discuss with your book club. Which book is your favorite? How are they similar and different from one another?

2. Explore the world of tarot and fortune reading. Find a local tarot reader for a visit with your book club, or learn the basics online from Tarot.com or this article on Vogue.com: https://www.vogue.com/article/tarot-101-beginner-guide-how-to-small-spells. You might even find a book on tarot reading at your local library or bookstore.

3. The expansive and dilapidated house at Trepassen, the colorful cast of characters, and the page-turning suspense of *The Death of Mrs. Westaway* seem like a perfect fit for the big screen. Who would you cast as Hal in the film version? What about Ezra, Abel, Harding, and Mrs. Warren? Discuss with your book club.

4. Learn more about Ruth Ware by visiting her website at http://www.ruthware.com, or following her on Twitter @RuthWareWriter or at Facebook.com/RuthWareWriter.

A CONVERSATION WITH RUTH WARE

Q: *The Death of Mrs. Westaway* has it all: family secrets, an old Gothic manor, thrilling plot lines, page-turning pacing, flawed characters in a deeply human way. What was the genesis for this book? Did you start with a specific character, scene, or idea?
A: I think the core of this book was the fact that I had written three novels about people who were drawn into crimes or deceptions through no fault of their own—they were just in the wrong place at the wrong time, or witnessed something they shouldn't have. With *The Death of Mrs. Westaway,* I wanted to try something quite different and write a character who sets out to commit a crime. Because I knew that I wanted Hal to be a con artist, I decided to give her a career suited to deceiving people—so I made her a tarot reader, but a cynical one who doesn't believe in the power of the cards and instead uses her skills and intuition to claim a knowledge she doesn't have.

Q: The expansive estate and grand manor house at Trepassen, even in their disrepair, are quite impressive, and crucial to the story line. Is Trepassen based on a real place?
A: Not exactly—it's very loosely based on a real house in Sussex, near where I live, called Standen House, which is a very beautiful Arts and Crafts house. Standen House is in much better repair than Trepas-

sen, although largely unaltered since the 1930s, but it has a slightly haunted, melancholy air, as it was built for a large, loving family of seven children, who gradually all died or moved away, leaving the house in the custody of the youngest daughter, who had not married. She left it to the National Trust in her will and it's now open to the public, still furnished with the family's possessions, as if they had simply popped out for a country walk one day.

The long tiled corridors, the echoing rooms, and the orangery at Trepassen are all inspired by counterparts at Standen, and walking around the place, I couldn't help but imagine what it must have been like to be the one remaining sibling living there alone, growing older and frailer, with the house falling into disrepair around her.

But the Cornish setting owes a heavy debt to the novels of Daphne du Maurier—there is definitely a large pinch of Manderley in the mix.

Q: The sibling—and pseudo-sibling, in the case of Maud and Maggie—dynamics greatly affect the events of the novel. Were you inspired by any real-life siblings or relationships?

A: It's funny because out of all the siblings in the book, I think the closest sibling relationship is Maggie and Maud, who as you mentioned aren't really sisters at all. But I am very close to my sister and I definitely relate to the unconditional loyalty that Maggie and Maud develop for each other.

I have no idea where the brothers came from, though—they feel very real to me, and I love their complicated mix of affection and exasperation for one another, but I've no idea what inspired that. Sometimes my imagination is a mystery even to me.

Q: What kind of research did you do for this book? Did you already have experience with tarot, or is that something you researched specifically?

A: Believe it or not, I knew almost nothing about tarot and had never had a reading, though I have always loved the look of the cards and been a little fascinated by their imagery. It was really fun researching all that—I bought books about tarot reading and symbolism and had great fun picking and choosing how all the readings in the book would pan out. But of course, as I mentioned, Hal is a cynical tarot reader who doesn't actually believe the cards have any mystical power and uses her powers of observation for slightly-less-than-moral ends, so the other strand of research I did was into fake mediums and psychics, which was equally fascinating. I read about "cold reading" techniques, where the so-called psychic genuinely knows nothing beforehand about their mark but simply picks up information from their reactions and appearance, and "hot reading," where the person conducting the reading researches their mark beforehand to give the appearance of insight. I also went and had a tarot reading myself—I did this after conducting all my research, so it was fascinating to see some of the things I had researched play out in the reading. I also picked up some truly horrifying stories of people taken in by fake psychics. They were told to me in confidence, so I probably can't share them here—but suffice it to say, I would be very, *very* careful if anyone contacts you out of the blue.

Q: Mrs. Westaway herself is a bit of a shadowy figure. We only get to know her through the stories and recollections of others, and fleeting mentions in Maggie's diary. Why did you choose to keep her mostly off the page?

A: Partly it was practicality—the story is about Hal's journey of discovery, not Maggie's experiences at Trepassen, so I didn't want to include too much from the diary, and that meant limiting the scenes with Mrs. Westaway. Also many of the climactic scenes that I would have liked to feature were impossible to include in the diary. But partly I loved the idea of a character like Daphne du Maurier's Rebecca, who is a hugely looming, influential presence in the novel but who we only see through the recollection of others. I really enjoy books where a pivotal character exists mainly off the page, and we see different, disorted flickers through the lens of different observers.

Q: Like in *The Lying Game*, the narrative in *The Death of Mrs. Westaway* alternates Hal's story in the present day and the diary

entries from that fateful year—1994—at Trepassen. What draws you to weave the past into the present? What does this allow you to do with the narrative?

A: Hmm . . . I don't know, this is a good question! I guess one answer is that unlike some crime writers, I'm not actually very interested in the crime itself—the gun, the body, the poison, or whatever. What matters to me is not so much the pebble that is thrown into the pond but the ripples that emanate from that pebble and the effect they have on other people. I suppose by putting the crime in the past, it enables the effect of those ripples to be more pronounced and allows me to concentrate on that part of the narrative.

I also love writing about secrets—and the thing about secrets is that the longer you keep them, the bigger they become.

Q: How was writing *The Death of Mrs. Westaway* different from writing *In a Dark, Dark Wood, The Woman in Cabin 10,* and *The Lying Game*? How has your writing evolved with each book?

A: I'm not honestly sure, is the answer! This is probably something that the writer is worst-placed to comment on, because we are too close to the picture to see. I think *The Death of Mrs. Westaway* is probably darker and more Gothic than my earlier books, which are a bit more fast-paced and action-packed. But the theme of female friendship and loyalty is a constant.

Q: *The Death of Mrs. Westaway* is chock-full of plot twists and turns and red herrings that keep the reader guessing until the very end—do you outline your books to keep that all straight, or does it come to you as you go? How do you organize the plot for your novels?

A: I generally don't outline—or not very much. I have an idea of the structure in my head and sometimes if my editors ask me to I will jot that down, but it's not usually very extensive—a page or two at most. I also have a couple of paragraphs of notes at the end of the manuscript with jotted-down notes for things that I think should happen, or stuff that I need to go back and fix (or in the case of *Mrs. Westaway,* dates of birth and relative ages of all the characters, since that was important to the plot), but in general I hold 90 percent of the book in my head. I am always in awe of writers who have complicated charts with time lines and Post-it notes and index cards. I feel like I'm winging it most of the time!

Q: It must be exhausting to publish a new book every year! How do you stay balanced with your writing and touring schedule? Do you take any time off between books, or is it right back to the grindstone?

A: I usually jump right back in—as soon as I finish one book, I begin the next (often the very next day). Not so much out of a sense of duty, although I do have contracts and deadlines I need to meet, but more because I always get a sense of huge deflation when a book comes out, and I find the best way to combat that is having another one on the boil all ready to go. That said, this book is the first time I didn't do that. I was traveling and touring so much that it was all I could do to complete the edits on *Mrs. Westaway*; I just didn't have time to begin a new book. Mostly though, the two fit pretty well together—I get long stretches of time when I can hunker down in my writing cave (it's not a cave, I should probably make that clear) and then I get to break for fresh air and remember why I do it all.

Q: You've mentioned in past interviews that you are a fan of Agatha Christie novels. What else do you like to read? Do you read other novels while working on your own?

A: I love Christie, but actually the biggest influence on this book were two other writers: Daphne du Maurier (who I've already mentioned) and Josephine Tey—anyone who has read her novel *Brat Farrar* will probably see some common themes and elements with *The Death of Mrs. Westaway*. Plus Hal is no Tom Ripley, but I was definitely thinking about Patricia Highsmith's mesmerising con-man antihero when I was coming up with her character.

I love to read anything and everything, and I do read while working on my own books, but I find I can't read crime or psychological thrillers, at least not while I'm in the early stages of the idea. It's partly to do with finding the voice of my character—I have to learn to be silent for a little while, to listen to what my narrator is trying to say to me, and it's hard to do that while you're immersed in someone else's character. But it's also a practical issue—if I'm already committed to a story, I don't want to find out that someone else is writing on the same subject or has used the same twist. If I'm halfway through the book it's too late to turn back, so I would rather simply not know! For that reason, you'll often find me rereading old favorites that I know backward already, or wallowing in nonfiction or comedy or something completely unrelated. I just finished a volume of David Sedaris's essays, which is basically a perfect counterpart to writing crime.